Praise for Connie Briscoe and
A LONG WAY FROM HOME

"Connie Briscoe vividly evokes the joys of love and family, and the pain of separation. . . . *A Long Way from Home* is a wonderful celebration of strength and perseverance, and a brilliant song of hope."

E. Lynn Harris, *New York Times* bestselling author of *Abide with Me*

"Briscoe proves once again she is a great storyteller. . . . *A Long Way from Home* is worthy of Briscoe's earlier work, and shows that her talent as a writer extends beyond contemporary tales."

Fort Worth Star-Telegram

"Connie Briscoe joyfully honors her family, herself and all of us in this wonderful homage to the resilience and courage of the people who made her the woman and writer she is. *A Long Way from Home* is a book for *everyone* and especially anyone who knows that at the beginning and in the end, we are all joined by the same story."

Marita Golden, author of *The Edge of Heaven*

"Connie Briscoe provides her readers a fascinating peek inside the world of a proud family that refuses to let the turbulent times in which they live destroy their dreams for happiness and freedom. The strong women who leap from the pages of her book are unforgettable. As they fight to hold onto their pride and self-respect, readers will cheer for them and follow them into the vivid world that Connie has created. She accomplishes this with expressive grace and an easy style that makes it a wonderful read!"

Anita Richmond Bunkley,
coauthor of *Girlfriends*

"History books may tell in dry fashion about slave families. . . but the horror of it comes to life in Briscoe's compassionate prose. . . . *A Long Way from Home* has a sweetness and humanity that are appealing."

Providence Journal

"[Adds] to the rich historical record . . . bringing to life through rich detail the quotidian experience of Madison slaves."

Washington Times

"A rich, compelling story of family love, the enduring strength of black women, the social lives of slaves and ultimately triumph over adversity. . . . *A Long Way from Home* takes Connie Briscoe a long way from contemporary sister/girlfriend stories that she is known for to a fact-based journey through the lives of three generations of slave women."

State Journal-Register, Springfield (IL)

"Does a good job of showing some of the range of black experience in the pre- and post-Civil War era."

Seattle Times

"Imaginative."

Essence

"Able historical fiction. . . . Appealing . . . informative."

Publishers Weekly

"The ultimate family heirloom. . . . Briscoe is an accomplished writer."

Publishers Weekly

Other Books by Connie Briscoe

Big Girls Don't Cry

Sisters & Lovers

CONNIE BRISCOE

A Long Way From Home

AVON BOOKS
An *Imprint* of HarperCollins*Publishers*

This is a work of fiction. While names of actual historical figures have been included to frame the narrative, all other characters and events are the product of the author's imagination.

AVON BOOKS
An Imprint of HarperCollins*Publishers*
10 East 53rd Street
New York, New York 10022-5299

ISBN: 0-06-103021-X
www.avonbooks.com

First Avon Books paperback printing: October 2000
First HarperCollins hardcover printing: August 1999

Printed in the U.S.A.

❖/10 9 8 7 6 5 4 3 2 1

For Grandmas Corine and Irene,
and all loving grandmothers everywhere

Acknowledgments

I'm grateful to a number of people who helped me get this off the ground.

Tara Brazee, my researcher, often worked tirelessly and went beyond the call of duty. Her enthusiasm never wavered, even when it meant spending days in dusty old archives deciphering barely legible copies of handwriting that was sometimes more than a hundred and fifty years old.

Miles Reid spent a day showing me, my parents, and my grandmother around his hometown of West Point, Virginia. He pointed out sites and told us fascinating stories about my great-great-grandfather.

Clara Ellis Payne, a distant cousin who has done a lot of valuable research on the family, was generous enough to share some of it with me. Just sitting and talking to her gave me a better feel for our common ancestor, for whom Cousin Clara was named.

Some of the staff members at Montpelier, home of President James Madison, were especially helpful. Megan Haley, a research assistant, spent a day giving me and my parents a private tour of the mansion and grounds. She shared stories with us about the Madisons and some of their slaves. Jared Bryson, an archaeologist, spent an afternoon helping me and my assistant search some of the files. He also gave us a memorable tour of the slave graveyard at Montpelier. And Scott Parker, archaeologist, showed me the archaeological work being done to learn more about the slaves and their habitat at Montpelier.

Mario de Valdes y Cocom, a historian who does work for PBS, took time out of his own very active schedule to help me dig up information.

Reggie Washington at the National Archives spent time explaining how to use the vast resources of the archives.

I have to thank my folks, Leroy and Alyce Briscoe, who were always willing to venture out with me on tours throughout Virginia. I discovered that my mother is a great note-taker. And thanks also to my Grandma Corine, who has such a wonderfully unbelievable memory at ninety years of age and so cheerfully shared it with me. I was truly blessed when it comes to family.

I'm grateful to my editor, Carolyn Marino. Her enthusiasm and belief in this novel were very encouraging. I'm also grateful to two women who have been with me since the beginning of my days as an author. I now think of them as members of my team: Victoria Sanders, my agent, and Wanda Newman, my sign-language interpreter.

And finally, thanks to the countless others who spent a moment or an hour sharing a memory, an anecdote, or a thought with me.

You all helped make this a much richer story.

PART 1

1

Clara sat up on the edge of her pallet and rubbed her eyes with her fists. She could tell it was awfully late by the way the morning shadows fanned across the attic floor. Mama had been up long before the shadows, and by now she would be running around the mansion lighting fires, emptying chamber pots, and fetching fresh water from the well for Mass Jimmy and Miss Dolley and all the folks who always seemed to be visiting them. And if Mama knew her daughter's fanny was still lolling on a pallet way past dayclean, she would go into another one of her yelling fits. Clara just hated it when Mama got to fussing.

Still, it was awful hard to get moving. She had started having chores to do at dayclean when she turned ten almost a year ago, but she wasn't yet used to this getting up before the sun did. Sometimes she thought she'd never get used to it. She wiggled her bare toes and stretched her lips with a yawn until she thought her mouth would burst at the corners. She would just take a quick peek out the window before getting dressed, she thought. She stood and made her way across the plank floor, then pushed the shutters open and leaned out.

To the north, rows of pine trees lined a path leading to the small temple over the ice house. On the other end, a deer browsed near a weeping willow, and a few sheep grazed nearby as Ralph, a boy about Clara's age, appeared from around the side of the mansion. He was leading one of the horses to the gate, probably for a guest who wanted to take an early morning ride on the grounds of the estate. Suddenly, the deer raised its head and leaped away.

Clara took a deep breath and filled her lungs with the scent of roses and jasmine drifting up from the gardens. She loved this spot at the very top of the mansion, for she could see clear across the lawn and over the treetops to the peaks of the Blue Ridge mountains. The plantation stretched out before her was small compared to the grand estates along the James River, but it was still considered by many to be the finest in the Piedmont area of Virginia. After all, this was Montpelier, the home of James Madison, former president of the United States, and his wife Dolley. And for the lucky few like the Madisons, it was a time of pillared mansions, velvet ball gowns, and gilded carriages, of Southern ladies entertaining in Persian-carpeted drawing rooms and gentlemen galloping freely across their vast estates.

But seeds of change were sprouting throughout the Virginia countryside, and Clara often overheard white grownups talking about the glories of the old days. Good land was harder to come by now, fields were overcultivated, and there were simply too many slaves. Whites bitterly recalled the days, only a few years earlier, when a slave preacher named Nat Turner held the citizens of Virginia in terror as he led a band of angry men through the countryside killing every white in sight. By the time they caught Nat Turner and hanged him that November of 1831, more than fifty whites lay dead. It was one of the bloodiest insurrections in American history, and it had happened right there on Virginia's soil.

Colored folks talked about that time, too, but usually with more awe than anger. For them, these had been long days of retrenching freedoms, of women and men toiling from dayclean to daylean, and of dreams dying in the dark.

The horse neighed, and Clara snapped out of her reverie and looked down below. One of Miss Dolley's nieces walked down the gravel path in front of the mansion and mounted the horse as Ralph and now Ben and Abraham steadied the animal and handed the reins to her.

Clara closed the shutters, then ran back to her pallet and squeezed her feet into the hard leather and cardboard shoes lying on the floor. She looked down and tried hard to wiggle her toes. No such luck. They were her first pair of shoes, and Mama insisted she wear them, as all the other house slaves did. But the things were so dratted stiff, it felt like she was wearing rugs on her feet. How did Mama expect her to be able to run and skip and jump? Clara supposed she had the answer to that. If Mama had her way, her daughter's carefree days were over. Clara belonged in the big house now, Mama said, doing her chores. And for that, she had to look respectable; she had to wear shoes.

She sighed and pulled her dress over her head. She was extra gentle with the dress as she buttoned it at the collar. Mama had made it for her eleventh birthday, with new muslin fabric from Miss Dolley. Even though the special day was two months away, Mama let her wear it now, since most of her other dresses were getting too small. Mama said she was growing faster than a weed in a vegetable garden.

She smoothed the dress around her legs and looked down at the shoes once again. She wrinkled her caramel-colored nose with disgust, kicked the shoes off, and placed them side by side next to the pallet. There, she thought, stretching her toes on the plank floor. That felt more like it. Mama would get mad if she caught her walking around barefoot, so she would have to stay out of

Mama's sight. Probably a good idea, anyhow, since Mama was sure to make her do her chores if she caught her, and she had other fun things in mind.

Clara ran down the back stairs to the second floor of the mansion, then stopped and peeked around the corner. Even though she was supposed to use the back stairs all the way down, she was less likely to run into Mama if she used the main stairs. The problem was that the main stairs were all the way on the other side of the long hallway. But it was empty now, and if she was fast, she could probably make it across before anyone saw her.

She dashed down the hallway, skipped down the stairs two at a time, then jumped over the last three steps. Her feet hit the polished first-floor landing with a thud, and she promptly slipped and fell, landing hard on her butt.

"Drat!"

She struggled to her feet and rubbed her sore backside. That was when she noticed a strange lady standing just outside a parlor door, her eyes popped wide open as she stared. Clara froze.

"Goodness, child," the woman said, her cheeks flushed pink with agitation, "you nearly frightened me to death." She touched her silk fan to her heart as if to prove her point.

Clara licked her lips and backed away, planning to beat a hasty retreat. Too late, she realized, as Miss Dolley glided into the hallway from the other end. She wore one of her silk turbans piled high on her head, and her heels clicked with authority on the hardwood floor.

"There you are, Mrs. Campbell. I—" Miss Dolley stopped abruptly when she saw the expression on her guest's face and followed her gaze down the hall to Clara. The smile fell from her lips, and she turned back to her guest. "Is everything all right, dear?"

"Oh!" Mrs. Campbell exclaimed breathlessly. "I just need a minute to collect myself. Your girl nearly frightened me to death with all that running and jumping about on the stairs. Stealthy little creatures, aren't they?"

"I suppose," Miss Dolley said. She walked slowly toward Clara. "It's nearly nine o'clock, Clara. Where should you be this morning?"

Clara gulped. Dusting, sweeping. Anywhere but here, she supposed. But it seemed Miss Dolley didn't know that. Clara lifted a finger gingerly and gestured toward the stairway. "Um. I was fixing to walk down to Aunt Winney's cabin, Missus, and help her mind the children."

"Well, hurry along then," Miss Dolley said, shooing her off with a wave of her hand. "But use the back stairs, and stop frightening my guests."

"Yes, ma'am," Clara said. She darted down the hallway, all the while looking back at Miss Dolley and her friend. Miss Dolley chuckled as she gently took Mrs. Campbell's arm and steered her back into the parlor.

"Forgive my ignorance, being from the North, Mrs. Madison, but you permit your house servants to go barefoot here?"

"Only the children. With all the running about that they do, it's easier on the floors."

"I see. And at what age do they start to wear shoes?"

"At about ten. Clara is but eight or nine, I think."

"Ah. About the age when they stop being so cute . . ."

Clara paused at the top of the stairs. She wanted to remind Miss Dolley that she was about to turn eleven, but Mama said not to speak to white folks anymore unless they spoke to her first. Something about getting older and that was the way things were done. Clara didn't like the ways of these grownups all that much. But at least she had made it away from there without being sent to chore-land.

She rounded the corner and almost bumped into Aunt Nany coming up the stairs from the basement. Aunt Nany was carrying her shoes in her hands and tiptoeing. She dropped the shoes and let out a low shriek when she nearly collided with Clara, then caught herself and clamped one hand over her mouth. Aunt Nany had a musky smell about her, and it was all Clara could do to keep from wrinkling her nose and sniffing openly, but she didn't want to seem rude. Probably had something to do with that field hand from the Jones plantation that everyone said Aunt Nany was running off to meet most nights. Aunt Nany was Mama's younger sister, and Mama said she didn't approve one bit of all this rendezvousing with someone who worked the tobacco fields. Aunt Nany was probably sneaking back in now because she was as worried about running into Mama as she was Miss Dolley. Clara could understand that.

Clara reached down and grabbed the shoes. They were soft leather, and she loved touching the smooth surface. Aunt Nany was lucky enough to wear the same size as Miss Dolley, so she was one of only a few slaves who got to wear good shoes. Clara held them out, and Aunt Nany took them. Then Aunt Nany smiled and put her finger to her lips. "Shh," she whispered, then ran off. Clara watched as she disappeared down the hallway.

Clara descended the stairs, and the musky odor from Aunt Nany was replaced with one she knew well: freshly baked bread. She stopped at the bottom of the stairs and peeked around the corner. As expected, Aunt Matilda, lord and mistress of the household kitchen, was sweeping in a corner of the big room. Iron pots steamed in the brick fireplace, which ran almost the length of one wall, and the scent of Aunt Matilda's beloved hot wheat bread filled the air.

Clara tried to slip through the doorway and over to the pots without being noticed. Aunt Matilda was hefty, with powerfully built hands and arms—probably gained from lifting all the heavy pots—and wouldn't waste a minute before using those hands on the buttocks of some child she thought had stepped out of place. But it was Aunt

Matilda's eyes that scared Clara the most—they could burn plumb through flesh. And it was no secret that Aunt Matilda didn't approve of Clara's ways. All of the children were scared of Aunt Matilda, but Clara thought she got the worst of it. She supposed it was because she was the only one around the big house to pick on. The babies were taken by their mamas down to Aunt Winney's before Clara even got up out of bed, and the older ones had their chores. Clara dreaded having to face this scythe-eyed woman alone at breakfast every morning before going out to play.

She decided to try to get just some buttered bread and eat it on her way down to the cabins. She turned to the long table in the middle of the room and scooped up a couple of pieces of bread that had already been sliced but noticed they hadn't been buttered. Drat! She had to have butter on her bread, and sugar, too, when she could get it.

She looked up, ready to put on her prettiest smile for Aunt Matilda. But her heart skipped a beat when she realized that the woman had been watching her all along. Drat again. That Aunt Matilda was awful sneaky. No, what was that word Mrs. Campbell just used? Stealthy, that was it. Clara lowered her gaze to the floor. "Um, you got any butter, Aunt Matilda?"

Aunt Matilda squinted. "You done washed your hands yet?"

Clara could feel those eyes piercing her body. She had plumb forgotten to wash anything. Mama always left some water in their tin washbasin for her, but the shoes had occupied all her thoughts this morning. Still, she wouldn't give this woman the satisfaction of knowing she was about to stick grubby hands into the food so Aunt Matilda could have something to scold her about. Clara looked straight at her. "Yes," she said, lifting her head high.

"Unh-hunh. You better not be lyin' to me," Aunt Matilda said, shaking a big brown finger in Clara's direction. She leaned her broom against the wall, then went to the end of the table and found the butter in the midst of all the bowls and kitchen utensils. Clara reached out just as Aunt Matilda did—the woman was so dratted stingy with the butter—but Aunt Matilda snatched it away.

"Here, hand me that bread." Aunt Matilda stretched out her fingers, and Clara reluctantly handed the slices of bread over.

"And some sugar, too," Clara said. She tried to sound like it was the most ordinary request in the world, but the frown on Aunt Matilda's face told her it hadn't worked. Aunt Matilda stopped buttering and stared.

"Please?"

"That sugar for Massa and Missus and their guests. You know better."

Clara smiled meekly. "I suppose."

"Humph," Aunt Matilda said, shaking her head. "Lord knows where you get these high-falutin' ideas from."

Clara tightened her lips. "Please, Aunt Matilda? Just a little bit. They got so much, they won't even miss it."

"No, and don't ask me no more. You lucky you got butter."

Drat, Clara thought, sticking out her bottom lip. Seeing the pout on Clara's face, the cook added a smidgen more butter. As if that made up for the sugar, Clara thought wryly. She sighed loudly and pointedly, but Aunt Matilda just ignored her. Clara realized it was hopeless, so she decided to try to get something for the others down at Walnut Grove. "Can I get some bread to carry down to the cabins?"

Aunt Matilda handed her the bread, then wiped her hands on her crisply starched apron. She pointed across the table to a basket covered with a towel. "I done already set some aside. But you sit and eat some of that hominy 'fore you go running off down to the grove."

Clara shook her head. "I'm not all that hungry." She

grabbed the basket and made a beeline for the door.

"Don't matter if you not hungry," Aunt Matilda called after her. "You need something in your stomach. Don't you have chores to do around here, anyhow?"

Clara walked faster.

"You hear me talking to you, child? Lord have mercy, I swear, these young'uns today . . ."

Clara reached the door and sprinted across the back lawn, not stopping until she reached the top of the hillside leading down to Walnut Grove. Then she took her piece of bread from the basket and munched happily as she walked down the steep slope. Aunt Matilda's bread was manna from heaven, but you had to go through hell to get it.

The cook faded from Clara's mind as she neared Aunt Winney's cabin and heard the laughter of children. Aunt Winney's cabin had one of the biggest yards in the grove and at this hour, with all the grownups in the fields, it was always filled with children romping in the grass and dirt. Aunts Matilda and Winney were half-sisters, but you never would have guessed it. Both were stocky and as brown as the trunks of the walnut trees that surrounded the cabins in the grove, but Aunt Winney was as cheerful and funny as Aunt Matilda was grim and ornery.

Clara made her way past a circle of barefooted boys shouting and shooting marbles made from rocks. Jim, a head taller than Clara, jumped up when he spotted her. "Mornin', Queen Clara," he said. He removed a plaited straw hat from his head and bowed deeply from the waist. Then he laughed and pointed at her, and the other boys joined in.

Clara didn't even look in their direction, just kept walking. "Reckon you don't want none of this sweet-smelling wheat bread I got, then," she said coolly.

Jim and a couple other boys broke away from the circle and followed Clara. Jim reached for the basket, but Clara smacked his hand away. “Quit that. Aunt Winney gotta slice it first.”

“Aw, give us just one of ’em ’fore you give it to A’nt Winney.”

“No,” Clara protested. “That ain’t fair to the others.”

“That ain’t fair, that ain’t fair,” Jim said in a high tone of voice, mocking her. His big brown eyes danced with mischief.

She turned her nose up in a deliberately exaggerated manner and stepped around him. She entered the cabin while the boys huddled in the doorway.

“Lawdy,” Aunt Winney said. “Lookee what the cat done finally dragged outta bed.” She chuckled. She was sitting in a rocking chair with an infant in each arm. One was feeding and the other was crying but wouldn’t take his bottle. Several toddlers slept in crude homemade cribs scattered throughout the cabin. Jim’s younger sister Betty stood at a small table changing a diaper. She looked up at Clara and smiled. Betty and Jim had the same eyes—big, round, soulful.

Clara grinned sheepishly and placed the basket on Aunt Winney’s pine kitchen table.

“Kin we git some of that there bread now?” Jim asked from the doorway.

“I’s savin’ it for y’all’s dinner,” Aunt Winney said. “You done already had yo’ breakfast. Now git on away from that door.” She shooed the boys away, and they groaned and ran back to their marbles.

Aunt Winney looked at Clara. “Help ’em finish eatin’ their breakfast,” she said, nodding toward four toddlers sitting at the table. “Then I’ll comb that nappy head o’ yourn soon as I git done here.” She chuckled. “Lawdy, chile. Look like you got a beehive settin’ up there on top yo’ head.”

Betty snickered as Clara sat down at the table. She picked up a drinking gourd and put it to the lips of a small child, but as soon as Aunt Winney looked down at the babies in her arms, Clara turned to Betty and stuck out her tongue. They both giggled.

Clara loved the sweet smell of babies that always hung in the air of Aunt Winney's cabin, but she was getting out of here before anyone put a comb anywhere near her head. She tried to get the little kiddies to eat faster, since she knew that the sooner she finished her chores, the sooner she could run outside and play with the others. Even though Jim was always teasing her, Clara thought he was the handsomest boy around. And he was the best musician. Put a banjo in his hands or a flute between his lips, and you'd be tapping your feet and clapping your hands before you knew what had taken hold of you. Lord almighty!

As soon as all the children were fed and either resting or playing, Clara asked Betty if she wanted to jump rope. The girls found a rope out by the barn on the other side of the pond, then ran back to the front of Aunt Winney's cabin. Betty and another girl turned while Clara jumped. Several other girls gathered around and they chanted one of their favorite rhymes as the dust floated around Clara's bare feet.

My old missus promised me,
Before she died she would set me free,
Now she dead and gone to hell,
I hope the devil will burn her well.
My old missus . . .

Clara stopped jumping and singing when she heard the hooves of a horse thundering down the hillside. The other children stopped, too, and they all scurried off to hide. Some of them ran around the corner of Aunt Winney's cabin, others took off for the pond down at the bottom of the hill. Betty and Clara bumped into each other trying to get away, then scampered off and hid behind the cabin. Jim followed them.

They waited and listened, hoping to hear the horse gallop off. Instead the hooves slowed to a trot, then stopped. Clara thought it sounded as if they had stopped right in Aunt Winney's front yard.

"Who that?" Betty whispered from behind Clara.

Clara inched up to the corner of the cabin and was about to peek around when Jim came up from behind and shoved her. She jumped back and hit him. Betty pushed him. Jim thought this was so funny, he could hardly keep from laughing out loud.

"Go an' see who it is," he said, snickering.

"You go out there," Clara said.

"I ain't goin' out there an' git no whippin'. Y'all was the ones singin' that song."

"Chicken," Betty said.

"Come on out here, you little rascals."

The children stopped taunting each other when they heard the voice. Betty giggled and Jim shushed her.

"It just Mass Todd," Betty said.

Clara, too, was relieved that it was Miss Dolley's son and not some other grownup from the house. Mass Todd came down to the grove all the time, although it was usually in the evenings after the grownups got in from the fields. Sometimes he would bring along some of his pals from up North, where he was always going, mostly to drink and gamble, from what everybody always said. Mama said he was older than he looked, probably around forty, and Clara found it hard to believe he was so old since he was always kidding around with them. Still, he was a massa, and they had been singing a song about a mistress burning in hell. She wasn't taking any chances and neither were the others.

"I brought y'all some taffy from up North. But I can't

give it to you unless you come out."

They looked at each other. Mass Todd was known for playing tricks on colored folks. Still, candy was rare enough to take a chance on. Clara was the first to step out, but she kept what she thought was a safe distance from Mass Todd, sitting high up there on his big shiny horse. His wavy hair glistened in the sunlight, and thick lashes framed his eyes. To Clara it seemed there was always something mournful about those eyes, even when he smiled like he did now.

"Is that a new frock you're wearing, Clara?"

She nodded. "Yes, Massa. My mama made it for me."

"You're getting prettier every time I see you. How old are you now?"

"Ten, Massa. Be eleven in August."

"Well, now, ain't that something?"

Since it sounded like Massa was in a good mood, the others came out slowly and gathered around his horse.

"Where you done been to this time, Massa?" Jim asked.

"Oh, lots of places. New York, Philadelphia." He dangled several small bags of candy in the air. "Y'all been behaving yourselves while I was gone?"

"Yessuh!"

He dropped the bags down one by one and laughed as kids came running from all directions and pushed and scrambled to catch them in midair and scoop them up from the ground.

"No need to fight, now. There's plenty to go around." He watched until all the bags had been picked up, then shook the horse's reins and galloped off.

Aunt Winney came to her doorway, frowning, a baby perched on her hip. "Who that ridin' off out there?"

Clara hid her bag behind her back as soon as she heard Aunt Winney's voice. So did the others. Aunt Winney would make them give it to her until after their supper.

"It's just Mass Todd, A'nt Winney," Betty said.

Aunt Winney grunted. "What he want down here?"

"Nothin'," Clara said.

"Nothin'," the rest of them said.

The minute Aunt Winney turned her back, they all ran around the side of the cabin. Clara was right on the heels of Jim until she stumbled over a small rock. The bag flew out of her hand, and the taffy scattered all over the dusty ground. The kids running behind Clara stomped right over it. Clara grabbed her bare foot and hopped around to shake off the pain. Then she kicked the empty bag in frustration. "Drat!" She sat on the ground next to Jim and Betty and watched as the two of them stuffed their mouths with taffy.

"You gon' be nice to me from now on?" Jim asked as Clara eyed his bag hungrily.

Clara smiled innocently. "Ain't I always?"

" 'Bout as nice as a massa from hell be to a runaway slave," Jim replied sarcastically. Betty giggled. He held the bag in Clara's direction anyway, and she shoved her hand in.

"Mass Todd like you," Betty said.

"Do not," Clara said. Although she wasn't sure what was wrong with him liking her if he did, she didn't like the tone of Betty's voice.

"That 'cause she high yaller," Jim said.

"I ain't no high yaller," Clara said. "I'm light brown."

"You's high yaller an' yo' mammy, too," Jim said.

Clara jumped up. "Quit aggravatin' me."

"High yaller, high yaller."

Betty giggled.

Clara stamped her foot on the ground. "You take that back."

"Set yo' tail back down here," Jim said. "It's just the truth."

"I'm sick of everybody talkin' 'bout my color."

"They just be jealous," Betty said. " 'Cause high-yaller niggers is worth mo' money."

"Unh-unh," Clara said, sitting back down and holding her hand out for more candy. "My daddy black just like y'all, and Mama say he one of the most valuable niggers over on the plantation where he live."

"It be different for the mens," Jim said. "My daddy say the blacker and stronger the better. Come next year, I commence goin' out to the fields with him. He say I kin learn 'bout workin' the plow. Would a learnt this year since I's twelve, but Daddy say there ain't much work these days on account it been hard for Mass Jimmy to sell his crops."

"Clara! Clara! Where is that child?"

"Uh-oh," Clara said.

"That A'nt Susie?" Betty asked.

Clara nodded. That was Mama's voice and it didn't sound too happy. "I gotta go." She shoved as much taffy into her mouth as she could, then jumped up and ran around the cabin, nearly colliding with her mama.

"What's this I been hearing about you bothering Miss Dolley's guests and singing that song about her?" Mama still had on the starched white apron and cap she always wore when she did her chores around the house and she looked so out of place in this dusty yard.

"That song ain't 'bout no Miss Dolley, Mama." She could barely get the words out with all the candy sticking to her gums. "We . . . we don't really want her to burn in hell. We just sing it 'cause that the way it go."

Mama's mouth dropped open. "Jesus, child, you sound like a savage that just stepped out of the jungle. If I didn't tell you a hundred times not to use 'ain't,' it wasn't nary one. Decent folks don't use that word."

"But Mass Todd uses it all the time."

Mama's hands flew to her hips. "Don't you go getting sassy with me. Mass Todd can do whatever he wants. You're my child, and I don't want you using that kind of language. You hear me?"

Of course she heard her. The woman was practically breaking her eardrums. "Yes, Mama."

"I don't have time to be minding you every minute of the day. I got work to do." Mama grabbed Clara by the arm, twirled her around, and pushed her up the hill. "And look at those feet, black as the night. Didn't I tell you to wear your—"

"But I don't wanna go back up there," Clara said, stomping as she walked. She had her limits as to what she would do without protest.

"Did I ask you what you wanted to do?"

"No, but I . . ."

Mama started looking around on the ground, and Clara knew what that meant. Mama was looking for a switch. Drat. Mama was just a little bitty thing—Clara had already grown past her shoulders—and had the face of an angel when she smiled. But when it suited her purposes, Mama could aim those hazel-colored eyes in a way that made you feel like you were staring down the muzzle of a rifle. And if that didn't get your attention, she wasn't above using her hands. She found a fat switch all too soon for Clara's comfort. Clara wanted to run away but knew that would just get her in more trouble. So she bit her bottom lip and shut her eyes tightly.

"Ouch!"

Mama pointed the foot-long switch in the direction of the house. "Now get moving."

Clara walked up the hill with about as much eagerness as someone about to jump off a cliff. Mama was right behind her every step of the way. "And you didn't even fix your hair this morning. What's the matter with you?"

"My hair's not like yours," Clara said, sticking out her bottom lip. "It's too hard to comb."

"That's no excuse. You're a house slave and you need to start acting like one."

"But I don't like it up at the big house. Ain't no fun up there."

Clara felt the switch on the back of her leg and realized she'd messed up again. Her legs were really starting to hurt now. She whimpered and hurried up the hill.

"Better the switch now than the whip later," Mama said.

Not that old saying, again, Clara thought. She knew that she was risking another lash if she said so much as boo now, but she couldn't help it. Mama made her so mad sometimes. She was always jumping on her for this or that and everything else in between. But let one of the white folks around here say something and she'd bend over backwards to please. "They don't whip slaves around here," Clara protested.

They reached the top of the hill, both huffing and puffing, and Mama grabbed Clara's arm and swung her around. "Then you better hope you never leave. And Massa and Missus getting old. They won't live forever. No telling what will happen after they're gone."

"Mass Todd will be the new massa."

"Humph! You'll be sorry the day that man takes over this place. Mark my word."

"What's wrong with Mass Todd?"

"Never you mind. Just keep moving."

They reached the back of the house, and Mama shook the switch in Clara's face. "Now, I have to go in here and finish making the beds. Must be twenty guests in that house. You go on inside and see if Aunt Matilda needs help in the kitchen."

"Aunt Matilda doesn't . . ." Clara wanted to get out of helping Aunt Matilda—anything but that—but the look on Mama's face as she slowly lowered the stick and squared her shoulders told Clara that something was wrong. Clara had seen that look before, on Mama and many of the other grownup slaves. It was as if Mama had pulled a mask down over her face. Clara turned and followed Mama's gaze to see Miss Dolley lifting her skirt as she stepped down from the long portico that ran across the back of the mansion.

"Is that a switch I see in your hand, Susie?" Miss Dolley asked, as she rushed down the path toward them.

"Yes, Missus," Mama said calmly. "Just trying to keep my child in line. That's all."

"You know I don't approve of spanking the children." Miss Dolley draped an arm around Clara's shoulder. Boy, was Clara ever glad to see the old Missus. She loved the way her fancy skirts swished when she walked and the way she always smelled of tobacco and spices. The other slave women were always whispering about Miss Dolley's sniffing habit, and Clara had once heard a guest come right out and tell Miss Dolley that it wasn't ladylike. But Miss Dolley didn't seem to care what folks said. She just did as she pleased.

"What provoked this, Susie?" Miss Dolley asked. "Surely, not the matter of Clara startling one of my guests?"

So Miss Dolley did tell on her, Clara realized. Still, Missus didn't expect Mama to go beating on her with a big old stick. Then she remembered the song they were singing down at the grove and she shifted her feet and stared at the ground. She wondered if Mama would tell Miss Dolley about that.

"Uh, no, Missus," Mama said. "I was upset 'cause she didn't comb her hair and put her shoes on this morning. That's all."

Clara let out a deep breath of relief.

"That's hardly reason for such harsh treatment," Miss Dolley said. "She's just a child."

"Yes, ma'am," Mama said. She dropped the switch at her side.

"Clara, dear," Miss Dolley said as she turned to Clara

and smiled, "run down to the garden and pick some flowers for my chamber, while I speak to Susie."

Clara started then stopped when she remembered that Mama wanted her inside, not out. House . . . garden. Mama . . . Miss Dolley. She stammered in confusion. "Well, I . . ." She paused. No matter what she did, she'd get in more trouble.

"Run along, Clara," Miss Dolley said again, more firmly.

Clara glanced at Mama and saw a slight smile and a quick nod. She sighed with relief and ran off.

The slave graveyard was way out past the laundry, the smokehouse, and all the other outbuildings surrounding the big house. It was Clara's favorite place at Montpelier. Here, in a small wooded area, the grass seemed greener, the air fresher, and the only sound much of the time was the cooing of doves high up in the trees. Late in the evening, just before the sun went down, she would lie on her back and listen to the workers singing in the distance as they came home from the nearby tobacco and wheat fields.

She sat on the ground, leaned back against the stump of a tree, and closed her eyes. Those fun times were coming to an end. It seemed Mama gave her a licking just about every day now. It didn't used to be like this. She used to be able to run and skip and play all the time. Now Mama always wanted her working up in the big house.

She yanked blades of grass from the ground and threw them, one by one. She hated the idea of being cooped up there all day long. Everybody was always tiptoeing about, scared half to death to even open their mouths when Mass Jimmy and Miss Dolley were about. Especially Mama. And for the life of her, Clara couldn't see why. Miss Dolley was so nice to them most of the time. She gave Aunt Nany her old shoes, and Mama her old dresses. Mama had to take them in, but they were Mama's best clothes.

Of course, Clara knew she would have to start doing regular work someday, something besides watching the children at Aunt Winney's for a few minutes or running errands for Miss Dolley every now and then. But so soon? She didn't feel like a grownup, so why did she have to act like one?

She drew her knees up under her chin and wrapped her arms around her legs. When she was younger, she would stretch out on the grass and pretend to live in a big house of her own with tall white columns just like Montpelier. She wore long silk dresses and had five hundred slaves, only they lived in nice houses and didn't have to work all the time. She paid them lots of money so they could buy whatever they wanted, and they had shoes that fit their feet and real beds to sleep on at night. Mama lived in the big house with her, and so did Daddy, instead of on another plantation so far away.

She snickered at such thoughts now. Mama was always saying not to waste time dreaming about something that just can't be. To be content with what they had. That fancy stuff was for Miss Dolley and her kinfolk and friends, Mama said, not for them. And they would have to be happy with seeing Daddy on weekends.

For a long time, Clara had hoped, even prayed, that Mama was just plain wrong. They lived in the big house, didn't they? And she had played with Miss Dolley's nieces and nephews when she was little, hadn't she? So why shouldn't she wear velvet coats and ride in gilded carriages? Even though she now understood that the attic was a world away from Persian-carpeted drawing rooms, sometimes she still hoped Mama was wrong.

No matter what, though, Clara was determined to never, ever have to empty somebody else's slop jar. Mama was always saying it was the worst job on this here earth, but she still did it. Clara thought she'd rather be whipped ten times a day than do that.

She shook her head and stood up. She'd better go pick Miss Dolley's bouquet, then head on back to the house and do her chores. She'd done enough daydreaming for one morning.

2

Rainy fall days were starting to be her favorite. Mama had always said she liked rainy days, and Clara could never understand why before. Now she did. If she was going to be stuck in the big house, it might as well be gloomy outside. But that meant she had to be "presentable," as Mama constantly reminded her: hair combed and plaited, dress clean and starched, and first and foremost, shoes on her feet. Mama was always saying you can tell a lot about a person by the shoes on their feet, and especially if they didn't wear any at all. The only decent thing about all this was that Mama had made her a pretty white apron to wear over her dress.

Even worse, she had to get up at the crack of dawn with the others and get to her chores right after breakfast, mostly sweeping and dusting all the mirrors and paintings in the downstairs chambers and hallways. Then there was the old clock in the clock room. She had to be especially careful of that and of all the big old busts and statues. Mama said they were of famous people like George Washington and some Napoleon—whoever that was. Mama said one of the hangings on the wall was the Declaration of Independence, a real important paper that freed the white folks from the British. It hung in a hallway and Clara always found herself staring at it whenever she passed by. She wondered how one paper could free a whole mass of people.

It was all so dratted dreary she could hardly keep from dozing off most days, except when she got to dust in the massa's library up on the second floor. She loved to sneak peeks at the pictures in his books. But she was never to enter the massa's library or chamber without being told to do so. He was getting on in years and spent most days reclining on a couch. Mama said his body might be feeble but his mind was sharp as ever and he still had a lot of important company. So she was to stay away.

Things weren't all bad on rainy mornings, though. Most of the women would gather in groups in the big basement kitchen and work on different things. Today, some of them were putting up peach preserves while others cut up a chunk of hard soap they had made the day before by boiling meat fat in lye in a big iron kettle out in the yard. The best part was listening to them gossip about everything under the sun. Clara liked the soothing sound of their voices against the pitter-patter of the raindrops outside.

At this time of year, mornings were getting a bit nippy, so Mama usually worked near the fire with a group that included Aunt Matilda and Aunt Nany. Clara called just about all the grownup women "Aunt," but Nany was the only one who was a real flesh and blood aunt. She was a seamstress and sometime-chambermaid and could yak up a storm. Clara thought her aunt must love to hear the sound of her own voice from the way she was always running her mouth.

Aunt Sukey, Miss Dolley's personal maid, was in and out of the kitchen, depending on the whims of her mistress. This was one of the few times and places that the house slaves could chat freely without having to whisper. But even here they had to be on guard, and their ears were always tuned in to sounds on the stairs.

"Don't know why you so stuck on this Jacob fellow," Mama said. Clara watched with fascination as Mama stood beside the table and deftly peeled and sliced one peach after another. Mama moved so fast that Clara was sure she'd chop off a thumb any minute. All these women moved their hands fast, Clara thought, as she tightened the lid on a jar. How would she ever learn to keep up?

"Of all the decent fellas around here," Mama continued, never missing a beat with the knife, "you had to go pick him. What's wrong with Brother John or Brother Stu? Both of them always been sweet on you."

Here we go again, Clara thought. Mama didn't approve of anything.

"Can't help where love grows, I reckon," Aunt Nany said, giggling. She was slicing peaches, too, only much more slowly than Mama and with a big happy grin on her face.

"Who's Jacob?" Aunt Matilda asked, frowning as she skimmed the foam off the top of the mixture of peaches and sugar boiling over the fire.

Mama shook her head. "Jesus, Matilda. Don't you ever leave this house?"

Heck, no, Clara wanted to say. All that old woman ever did was cook and be mean to children like her.

Aunt Matilda grunted. "What I got to be running all around for? Everything I need's right here."

Mama and Aunt Nany exchanged looks of disbelief. Clara bent her head over the table to hide her smile from mean old Matilda.

"My Jacob works over at the Jones place," Aunt Nany said.

At the mention of the name Jones, Clara stopped smiling. Everybody knew that old man beat his slaves unmercifully. She'd heard awful things about the way he whipped them until blood oozed from their gashes, sometimes just for taking an extra morsel of food from the kitchen. And it seemed that one of them was always running—and getting caught. She'd never even seen the old man, but his imagined face—pale, wicked, pointed teeth bared in the dark—always crept into Clara's worst nightmares. She shuddered.

"He works in the tobacco fields," Mama said disapprovingly.

Aunt Matilda grunted. "Humph! Field hands and house slaves don't mix. Never did."

"Like I said, can't help where love grows," Aunt Nany said. "Jacob is the one I love, and Jacob is the one I'm going to be with. There's no use trying to stop it."

Mama let out an exasperated sigh. "You and I both know Mass Jones doesn't like 'broad wives. Everybody knows he hardly ever allows his people to marry off that plantation."

Aunt Nany twisted her lips as if she was tired of hearing all this. "It's a good chance he'll let Jacob do it. Jacob says Mass Jones told him he was one of his best workers."

"It's worth a try," Aunt Sukey said. Aunt Sukey was doing what Aunt Sukey did best, sitting and looking pretty in her secondhand French dress—one of many handed down to her from Miss Dolley—and fingering a small charm around her neck. She got away with such uppity behavior because she'd been with Miss Dolley for so long. She'd even lived with Massa and Missus in the White House up in Washington, D.C., and she probably knew her mistress better than anyone besides Mass Jimmy. Clara figured the other servants put up with Aunt Sukey's airs since she was so close to Miss Dolley and usually one of the first to hear all the juicy stuff they weren't supposed to know.

"Mind you, living apart has its good and bad sides, I have to admit," Mama said. "My Walker loves that feeling of freedom he gets when he leaves Albemarle County to come around here on weekends and see me and Clara.

And we don't have to bother none with one another's troubles during the week."

Clara gritted her teeth. Mama was always saying stuff like that, but she couldn't see one dratted good thing about Daddy living so far away. She wanted Mama to ask Massa to buy Daddy, so he could live with them. She had heard of that happening on other plantations. But Mama said Daddy was a driver and they don't come cheap. Besides, they didn't need another driver at Montpelier. Clara thought Mama was just too chicken to ask.

"Humph. Mass Jimmy his massa when he come here, that's all," Aunt Matilda said. "He just trading one massa for another."

"It's still a break from being on your own place all the time," Mama said. " 'Specially for Brother Jacob over there on the Jones plantation. I reckon he would love to get away from that miserable place to come here every weekend. But Mass Jones will never allow it."

"Reckon all Mass Jones can do is say no," Aunt Sukey said.

"He can do a heap more than that," Mama said.

"Jacob said if Mass Jones does say no, he'll just stop working so hard for him," Aunt Nany said.

"That's what I mean," Mama said. "That's when your troubles will really start. He'll probably sell him them. You can't trust a massa like that. He has his house slaves walking around looking like ragamuffins. Half of them don't even have shoes, and not just the children."

Not that again, Clara thought. "What's wrong with not wearing shoes, anyhow?" she asked. She knew she was stepping out of her proper place, as she was always being told these days, but she couldn't help it. Mama got on her nerves with this thing she had about shoes.

Mama stopped slicing and looked at Clara. "No decent house servant walks around not wearing shoes. Only field hands and white trash."

"But I saw one of Miss Dolley's nephews running around out in the garden with no shoes on," Clara said. Aunt Matilda smacked her lips with disapproval and Clara knew she should stop, but she pressed on. "And he's sure 'nough white."

"That's Miss Dolley's family and Miss Dolley's business," Mama said. "Some of those nieces and nephews of hers are nothing but nuisances, anyhow." The tone of Mama's voice was enough to finally silence Clara. She certainly didn't want to get switched in front of all these folks.

Aunt Matilda cleared her throat. "If I was you, I'd watch what you say around this here child. She got way too much mouth on her."

"She knows better than to repeat anything we say," Mama said. "Don't you, Clara?"

They heard footsteps on the stairs and hushed and picked up their paces. Aunt Sukey tucked her charm inside her dress and grabbed a spoon off the table just as Aunt Sarah poked her head into the kitchen. It was a good thing it was only Aunt Sarah, Clara thought, 'cause Aunt Sukey looked pretty silly sitting there holding a spoon up in midair.

Aunt Sarah was Mama's best friend. She was the head servant at Montpelier and one of only a few who could read and write. Aunt Sarah would join them in the kitchen whenever she could spare a minute, which was hardly ever. Clara had never thought much about Aunt Sarah being able to read until she started spending so much time dusting around the massa's books. As hard as she tried to figure out the words on those pages, she just couldn't make sense of them. She wanted to ask Aunt Sarah to teach her to read, but Mama said not to bother her. It took a long time to learn to read, and Aunt Sarah was too busy with her chores. Besides, Mama asked, what did she need to learn to read for anyhow? She didn't have any books and wouldn't be getting any in this lifetime. That was so like Mama, giving up without even trying. Clara didn't tell Mama she'd been sneaking into the massa's books when she was supposed to be dusting.

"Miss Dolley wants to see you, Sister Sukey," Aunt Sarah said.

Aunt Sukey sighed and tossed the spoon onto the table. It hit one of the jars with a clang, and Aunt Matilda put her hands on her hips and fired Aunt Sukey a look of disapproval.

"Sorry," Aunt Sukey said. "But I never get a minute's rest around here."

"You and me, neither," Aunt Sarah said. "But you better get your tail on up there. You, too, Susie, 'cause some folks just rode up to see Massa and Missus. And Lord knows what kind of shape they're in with all this rain we're having."

Mama frowned. "Shoot. I thought they weren't expecting anybody this weekend. Are they planning on staying?"

Aunt Sarah turned back toward the stairs. "Miss Dolley didn't say a word to me about it. Just asked for Sister Sukey here."

"Tell her I'm coming," Aunt Sukey said, standing up.

As soon as Aunt Sarah's footsteps faded on the stairs, Aunt Sukey planted her rump back in the chair. Clara and the others smiled knowingly. Aunt Sukey would take her sweet time going up. She was always stretching things right up to the breaking point, and Clara marveled at how Aunt Sukey seemed to know just how much she could get away with.

Mama sighed and set her knife down on the table, then wiped her hands on her apron. "I better go on up and see if Miss Dolley will be needing us."

That was so like Mama, Clara thought, as she twisted the lid on another jar. Mama was always saying that as the senior chambermaid, her job was to figure out what Miss

Dolley needed before Miss Dolley did. Mama always jumped, sometimes even before she was called.

Aunt Sukey waved her hand in Mama's direction. "Rest yourself. If she needs you, she'll let you know."

Mama paused, but frowned doubtfully.

"Let her come to you," Aunt Sukey said. She picked out one of the more ripe peaches on the table and took a hearty bite. "That's what I do."

"Don't you listen to that gal," Aunt Matilda said as she dipped her spoon into the syrupy mixture on the fire to test its thickness. "Just get yourself in a heap of trouble."

"Well, you and me two different gals, for sure," Mama said to Aunt Sukey. "But I reckon it won't hurt for once." She smiled and picked the knife back up. "I deserve a moment's peace."

Sounded to Clara like Mama was trying to convince herself more than anybody else.

"Reckon the rain makes me plain lazy," Mama said. "Everything seems to slow down and you can take your sweet time for a change. 'Sides, I don't get to work with Clara that much, since we're always in different parts of the house." She reached over and tightened the rubber top on the jar in Clara's hand. "You have to make them snug, baby."

"Sorry," Clara said, a little embarrassed. She had been so surprised that Mama didn't jump and run upstairs she wasn't paying attention.

"Humph," Aunt Matilda grunted. "Y'all just begging for trouble if you ask me."

Mama smiled and winked at Clara. Clara smiled back. Her mama had the prettiest smile on the whole plantation, and Clara always thought it was too bad Mama didn't smile more often. If anything, it seemed that Mama smiled less and less as the days went by.

"Thank the Lord this isn't anything like that wicked old man Jones' place," Aunt Nany said. "Massa never whips any of us. Only heard of that happening around here once or twice."

"That was the overseer's doing," Aunt Matilda said. "Not Mass Jimmy. Massa wouldn't allow it."

"Shoot. Where in tarnation you think he gets the idea it's all right to whip somebody if it's not from Mass Jimmy?" Mama asked, staring at Aunt Matilda as if she couldn't believe anyone could be so gullible.

Aunt Nany nodded in agreement.

Aunt Matilda grunted. "I don't believe Massa knew about that for a minute."

"I just hope he never gets to selling any of us," Mama said. "That's been happening at a lot of other plantations 'round here these days."

Not again, Clara thought. Mama was always thinking the worst.

Aunt Matilda shook her head. "I been here almost fifty years, longer than any of you, and never in all my born days has Mass Jimmy sold one of us that didn't want to go. Not a one."

See? Clara thought. Even old Matilda didn't think it would happen.

Aunt Sukey nodded. "I've been here almost as long. And up to now that's been the truth." That was another thing about Aunt Sukey, Clara thought. Nobody really knew how old she was. She looked about Mama's and Aunt Nany's age, around thirty, but folks whispered that she was probably closer to forty.

"'Course there's a first time for everything." The way Aunt Sukey said it made everyone stop and stare at her. "I wasn't going to say anything until I knew more, 'cause it's awful bad if it's true. And I don't want to start something around here." Aunt Sukey paused and pulled the charm out from beneath her dress. Clara noticed that the nail on Aunt Sukey's forefinger was turning pink from gripping the charm so tightly.

"But anyway, you remember a few days back, that man was up here from Louisiana to see Mass Jimmy? Man by the name of William Taylor?" She spoke in such a soft voice that they leaned in. "They stopped talking all of a sudden when Paul walked into the room."

They leaned even closer. Paul Jennings was Aunt Sukey's husband and Mass Jimmy's personal servant. He was always around Massa.

"Paul thought that was mighty strange, 'cause Massa and his guests usually don't pay him much mind. Well, just before they saw Paul, Massa was saying something about sending fifteen or sixteen of them down to Louisiana. Don't ask me what 'them' means, 'cause I don't know. Just telling you what Paul said he heard."

Clara looked at the others, trying to guess what they were thinking. She could feel her heart thumping as she waited for somebody to say that slaves would never be sold around here.

"That don't mean he was talking about us," Aunt Matilda said.

Clara nodded.

"Well, what else could it be?" Mama asked. "Massa doesn't have that many horses to send away. Or anything else for that matter, 'cept slaves."

Aunt Nany exhaled deeply. "I think you wrong about that, Susie."

"Wasn't me who said it. It was Sister Sukey."

"I'm not saying one thing or the other," Aunt Sukey said. "I'm just telling you what Paul heard."

Aunt Nany clasped her hands together and looked up to the ceiling. "Oh, my. Please, Lord, keep us here together with our families. . . ." Her voice trailed off in prayer.

Why did Mama always have to think the worst? Nobody else around here seemed to think Massa would ever sell any of them. Clara waited for somebody to speak up after Aunt Nany finished her prayer, but things got real quiet as they went back to work and slipped into their own worlds of thought. Maybe they were thinking that if they didn't talk about it, it wouldn't be true. Did that mean they really thought there might be something to it? Clara tried to keep quiet—she'd gotten in trouble once today already—but a hundred questions raced through her mind. "Do you really think they would sell us down there, Mama?"

Mama sighed and seemed to be thinking for a moment. "I don't know. But some of the massas around here are having trouble selling their tobacco and wheat, so they don't need so many of us anymore."

Clara thought about Jim down at the grove. He was way past the age when boys used to begin steady work in the fields. But as far as Clara knew, he hadn't worked a day yet. "Is Mass Jimmy having trouble?"

"Miss Dolley said Massa hasn't been getting nearly as much money for his crops as he used to," Aunt Sukey said. "And Paul said Massa has spent thousands of dollars to cover Mass Todd's gambling and drinking debts."

"And to bail him out of jail," Mama added, smacking her lips with disgust.

Mass Todd, jail? Clara knew he was wild and crazy, and Miss Dolley was always fretting about him because he spent so much time gallivanting around the country. But this was news.

Aunt Nany shook her head. "Oh, my. I got to tell you, I don't like the sound of all this."

"I bet Mass Jimmy regrets the day he had to take on that good-for-nothing boy as his stepson," Aunt Matilda said.

Aunt Sukey nodded. "They already had to sell some of their land to pay off the debts 'cause of him."

"I feel sorry for the poor old devil," Aunt Nany said.

"Humph!" Aunt Matilda said. "I don't feel sorry for him

one bit. Should have left him in that jail. Teach him a lesson."

"They have plenty of work down there on them cotton and sugar plantations in Louisiana, let me tell you," Aunt Nany said. "And Jacob said the massas here make more money selling their slaves down there than they do farming the land these days. And I heard the massas down there let them work the cotton till they drop dead with their hoes in their hands. Then they just buy some more slaves and—"

"Nany," Mama said, interrupting. "I think we've talked about this enough for now. Mind you, we don't even know if it's true that Massa was talking about selling some of us. And I don't want us scaring Clara anymore."

"I don't believe that nonsense, leastaways," Aunt Matilda said firmly. "Massa and Missus might be having some trouble, but it's plain as day there's still plenty to go around. Miss Dolley's always wearing a new dress and ordering something for the house. And Mass Jimmy said he'll never sell us. I heard him say it my own self once, with these two ears and—"

Aunt Matilda stopped when they heard footsteps on the stairs again. This time it was Miss Dolley, and they all jumped up, except Aunt Sukey. She took her time standing up. Clara had never been much scared of Miss Dolley before, but with all this talk about selling some of them down south, maybe she *should* be scared of her. Clara stood and cupped her hands in front of her, just like Mama and the rest.

"Sukey, I sent Sarah down here to fetch you," Miss Dolley said, pulling the shawl wrapped around her shoulders tighter against the basement chill.

"I was just on my way up, Miss Dolley," Aunt Sukey said.

"I can't seem to find my snuffbox, and Master Jimmy misplaced his copy of the *Morning Chronicle*. It just arrived from England, and we have guests who will want to read it."

"I'll go find it for you right now," Aunt Sukey said. "Don't you fret another minute, Miss Dolley." She lifted her skirt like a queen and turned toward the stairs.

Miss Dolley turned to Mama. "And, Susie, did Sarah tell you that we have company?"

Clara could feel Mama cringing without even looking straight at her.

"Yes, ma'am," Mama said. "I was just helping Matilda finish up here."

"Your first job is the chambers," Miss Dolley said. "Not here in the kitchen."

"Yes, ma'am."

Miss Dolley touched her fingertips to her forehead. "This was completely unexpected. Especially with this awful weather we're having. Nevertheless, we must carry on. Now I told them that on Saturday evening the servants are off, and they understand. But I'll be needing at least one of you to help out."

Clara smiled at the mention of tonight. On Saturdays, they all got off after half a day's work, and they would gather in the grove for a night of food, games, and dancing. Daddy would be there, too. But Clara stopped smiling when she saw the looks exchanged between Mama and Aunt Nany. Mama blinked and Aunt Nany's mouth seemed to drop a mile. Clara remembered that whenever they had guests on Saturday night, the chambermaids would take turns so none of them would always miss out on the fun. This must be Aunt Nany's turn to work, and that meant she wouldn't be able to sneak out to meet Jacob.

"This looks wonderful," Miss Dolley said as she walked around the table and inspected the preserves. She turned to Aunt Matilda with a big smile on her face. Clara couldn't imagine this woman would ever sell any of them. "Send for me when you're done, Matilda," Miss Dolley said. "And I'll take another look at it."

Aunt Matilda nodded. "Yes, ma'am. That's just what I was fixing to do."

Miss Dolley turned to Mama and smiled. "At some point, I need to talk to you about next week. We have more than three and twenty guests coming."

Mama stepped forward. "Yes, ma'am. I can come talk to you now if you wish."

"After you're done here should be fine," Miss Dolley said, waving Mama back. "How much longer will you be?"

"Um, well . . ." Mama looked at Aunt Matilda.

"About an hour," Aunt Matilda said.

"They would have been done by now, Miss Dolley," Clara said, " 'cept Mama said she gets to feeling lazy on rainy days and likes to take her sweet . . . time." Clara bit her bottom lip. She couldn't believe she'd just said that. Neither could the others, it seemed. Aunt Nany dropped the spoon in her hand and it clattered on the floor. Aunt Matilda gasped. Mama's mouth popped open, then clamped shut. She squared her shoulders and pulled the mask down over her face.

"I see," Miss Dolley said as she looked at Clara, a funny smile playing around the corner of her pursed lips. Then she looked at Mama, only she wasn't smiling anymore. "I'll see you in my chamber in an hour, Susie." With that, Miss Dolley lifted her skirt and disappeared up the stairs.

Mama smacked her cheek so fast, Clara never even saw the hand coming. She didn't feel it either at first, it was so unexpected. It was the only time Mama had ever hit her in the face. On her bottom, yes. On her legs, every day just about. But the face, never.

Then it hit her, and it felt like a bee had pierced her cheek. Tears stung her eyes.

"Jesus, child." Mama's voice trembled, barely above a whisper, but those steely hazel eyes screamed.

Clara covered her cheek with her hand and looked down at the floor. She couldn't believe what she'd said to Miss Dolley, but neither could she believe Mama just slapped her so hard in the face.

Aunt Matilda shook her head as she lifted a pot from the fireplace and set it on the floor for cooling. "I told you that child just got too much mouth for her own good. She's spoiled rotten 'cause you let her play with them young'uns down there in the grove way too long."

"Oh, shut up," Aunt Nany said. "She's just a child. She's supposed to play."

"Child my foot. She's eleven now, and around here that means—"

"Mind your own business," Mama snapped. "The both of you. The day you have children of your own is the day I'll listen to your advice."

They both tightened their lips as Mama grabbed Clara by the arm and marched her off to a far corner.

"If I didn't tell you a hundred times to watch your mouth around Massa and Missus, it wasn't nary one. Didn't I tell you that?"

Clara kept her eyes on the floor. The anger in Mama's face was still so raw, she could feel it without even looking up. It was a mistake saying that in front of Miss Dolley, she knew, and she didn't know why it slipped out. But she didn't deserve to be smacked in the face.

"Answer me when I speak to you," Mama said.

"Yes, Mama. It slipped out, I don't know why."

"Well, I'll be punished for your slip, as sure as the sun will rise."

"I'm sorry," Clara said, sniffling. "But Miss Dolley likes you. She won't do anything bad to you."

"Clara, you don't . . . you don't understand. She likes me as long as I do her bidding. But the minute I don't . . ." Mama paused and her eyes softened as Clara wiped tears from her cheeks. "It's my own fault," Mama said quietly, almost as if talking to herself. "Matilda's right in a way. I should have clamped down on you a long time ago, but I wanted you to . . ." Mama shook her head.

"You wanted, what, Mama?"

Mama sighed. "I guess I wanted to put things off for as long as I could. But no more. From here on, I'm putting my foot down. Especially with all this talk about Massa thinking about selling some of us. I'm going to see to it that you learn how to behave yourself if it's the last thing I do."

3

When Mama came into the drawing room with a basket of food, Clara found it hard to look her in the eye. Clara had been feeling pretty glum anyway as she dusted the busts on the mantelpiece. Mama filling a basket of food on Saturday afternoon wasn't unusual. She always did it for the parties down at the grove. What was different was that Mama set the basket on the floor next to Clara.

"Take this down to Sister Jane," Mama said. "I'll finish that."

"Yes, Mama." Clara put the feather duster on the mantelpiece and picked up the basket.

Mama patted her on the head. "I didn't mean to get so mad this morning," she whispered. "You know I wouldn't harm a hair on your head, don't you?"

Clara nodded.

"All the same, you have to learn not to run your mouth so much around these folks."

"Yes, Mama."

"Now you go on," Mama said, her voice a little louder but still low, out of habit. She and Mama were the only two people in the room, but that was how they always talked up here in the big house. "You haven't been down there during the day for a time now," Mama said. "And I know how much you miss it. 'Sides, Miss Dolley needs me here. She wants me to help with supper and hold the candles on the portico tonight."

"I can hold the candles for you, Mama. All you have to do is stand there while they talk. Then you can go to the party."

Mama shook her head and smiled. "You'd be fidgeting the whole time and driving the old woman crazy. Now go on."

Clara picked up the basket and left without saying another word. Although Mama didn't come right out and say it, Clara knew this meant that Miss Dolley was keeping Mama cooped up in the house the rest of the day as punishment. She had no idea Miss Dolley could be so mean. Miss Dolley must know how much Mama always looked forward to strolling down to the grove on Saturday afternoons to talk with Aunt Jane. It was a rare chance for her to get away and catch up on the latest gossip down there. It was already late September, and this might well be their last outdoor party until next spring, so tonight's festivities would be especially lively.

But the absolute worst was that Mama had to stand around holding a dratted candle all evening. That was one of the most demeaning chores around the house, since it didn't require anything in the way of know-how or skill, and all the house servants felt that way. Younger ones, in their teens and twenties, got stuck with it most of the time. The grownups had more important things to do, like cook and serve food and drink.

This was all her fault, Clara thought. She'd known good and well that comment would make Mama look bad in Miss Dolley's eyes. Yet, still she'd said it. Why? She had a nagging sense that somewhere in the back of her mind she wanted to get Mama in trouble, and the thought scared her. Yes, Mama got on her nerves when she acted like a weakling in front of Miss Dolley. Yes, she wished Mama would stick up for herself more. But Mama didn't deserve this.

She sighed and glanced up. Although it had stopped raining, the sun was still hiding behind a sky full of gray clouds. Water from the grass seeped through her shoes as she strolled down the hill, and she was tempted to kick the dratted things off her feet, but she'd already misbehaved enough for one day. The last thing she needed to do was return to the house, her feet caked with mud. The shoes stayed on.

It had been many weeks since Clara last visited the grove this early on a Saturday. As she approached the dusty yard near the cabin where Jim and Betty lived with their folks, Aunt Jane and Big Jim, she thought things seemed awfully still. Usually at this hour, just about everyone could be seen working to get ready for the party. Tables were set up and covered with brightly colored cloths. Pigs were roasting over wood fires, and dusty old bottles of brandy were wiped clean. Jim would be practicing on the banjo, and the scent of food and the sound of music and laughter would get even the gloomiest old soul in a party mood.

But all Clara saw this afternoon was a lone table sitting in the yard and a few chickens darting about. There were no goodies cooking, no bottles of liquor glistening in the daylight, no children running around chasing each other and annoying the older folks while they set things up. She frowned. She could see being late getting started because of all the rain this morning, but where was everybody now that the sun was coming out?

She finally spotted Aunt Winney, her crusty old brown face bowed to the ground, as she swept the lone step in front of her cabin. "Hi, Aunt Winney," Clara called out to her.

Aunt Winney stopped sweeping and looked up. She

squinted her eyes. "Oh, hi there, Clara."

Clara lifted the basket. "I brought something for the party."

"Party?" Aunt Winney said, frowning as if she'd forgotten. "Don't speck much o' nothin' be goin' on 'round here tonight."

Clara frowned. They always had a party on Saturday night, had for as long as Clara could remember. If it rained, they just moved it to one of the big barns on the other side of the pond. Aunt Winney must surely be getting absentminded in her old age. She was older than her sister Matilda, and Aunt Matilda must be going on fifty.

But Clara wasn't about to argue with Aunt Winney. She'd had enough disagreement in one day. She made her way to Jim and Betty's cabin and knocked. It took so long for anyone to answer that she stepped away to go around back and look for them. Suddenly, the door cracked open, and Jim peeked out. He didn't look at all like his usual cheerful self. His big brown eyes, always so full of merriment, kept darting down toward the ground. "What you doin' here?"

She held out the basket. "Got something from the kitchen for the party."

His expression didn't change one bit, but he opened the door wider, and she stepped inside. Big Jim sat at a wood table in the middle of the room smoking a pipe. Aunt Jane sat across from him, soaking her tired feet in a pail of water, while Betty lay on a pallet near the fire with her back toward the door. It had been so long since Clara was last here, and what she saw hit her like a twenty-pound sack of flour upside the head.

Pails full of water sat in muddy puddles in every corner of the room, catching drops of rain from the leaky ceiling. A bunch of holes in the cabin walls had been hastily patched with wooden planks. The shutter covering the lone window looked as if it would fall off its hinges with a touch. The worst part was the muggy smell that hung in the air.

Clara swatted a fly that flew smack dead into her face. She blinked and tried not to show her surprise as she stepped up to Aunt Jane and placed the basket on the table. "Mama sent this down."

"Thank you, baby," Aunt Jane said. She patted a chair next to where she was sitting. "Come an' set for a spell."

Clara didn't want to sit. The raggedy chair had splinters sticking out all over just waiting to snag her dress. And every time she took a breath of the fetid air, she wanted to cough. But she didn't want them to think she'd gotten all high and mighty now that she spent all her time up at the big house, so she sat down gingerly.

"How everything goin' up there?" Aunt Jane asked.

Clara shrugged. Somehow, the problems up at the big house didn't seem so important anymore. "All right, I reckon."

She was about to tell them she couldn't stay a minute longer, that her mama wanted her to come right back, when Betty moaned from her pallet. "What's wrong?" Clara asked.

"Ain't been feelin' so hot," Betty said. She rolled over and let out a deep breath of air.

"She been had a fever since yesterday," Aunt Jane said. " 'Spect it's some kinda cold."

Clara looked at Betty's bare feet and was sure that didn't help. Betty and Jim and all the other children who lived in the grove had never owned a pair of shoes, they weren't old enough yet. Even most of the grownups down here went barefoot except when they went to church. Clara suddenly felt ashamed of herself for acting all snooty. She was tempted to take her shoes off then and there and give them to Betty, but she had only the one pair she was wearing and Mama wouldn't like her giving them away one bit. "Want me to ask Miss Dolley for some medicine?"

Aunt Jane shook her head. "Got Sister Winney to mix up some roots 'n' herbs for her, and she been chewin' on some flagroot. We just keep a eye on it for a day or two."

Clara didn't say anything, but she thought Miss Dolley's medicines worked better than Aunt Winney's potions.

"Don't want Missus to know 'bout it, just in case we decide to go," Big Jim said. "They might not 'low us if'n they know Betty been feelin' poorly."

"Or they might make her stay behind," Aunt Jane said. "An' I ain't leavin' my babies behind."

Clara blinked. "Go? Go where?"

Jim stared at her as he sat next to his daddy. "You ain't heard nothin' yet?"

She turned to him. Something was different about the way Jim was behaving toward her, something she'd noticed from the moment he opened the door. "Heard what?" The way they all turned and looked at each other made her feel like some monster from the deep sea.

"Reckon you wouldn't up there," Jim said.

Why was he talking to her like that? If he was mad because she didn't come around as much anymore, didn't he understand that her mama made her stay up at the big house now that she was getting older?

"Massa gon' sell some o' us," Big Jim said.

What? Clara's mouth dropped open as she stared into Big Jim's face.

"Ask my daddy day 'fore yesterday if'n us want to go," Jim said calmly.

"Done already met the man want to buy us, too," Big Jim said.

Clara's whole body went numb. She looked from one of them to the other, trying to make some sense of what they were saying, trying to guess what they were really feeling, as the words sank in. But their stony faces told her nothing. That baffled her even more, and she swallowed hard trying to find her voice. "You . . . um, you mean that man from Louisiana that was visiting a short time back?"

Big Jim nodded. "Massa say he a good man and they's quality white folks."

Then what Aunt Sukey heard was true, Clara thought. Still, it was so hard to believe. "But . . . but did Massa say you had to go?"

"No, but . . ."

"Then why do you want to leave?"

"We don't *want* to go nowhere," Aunt Jane said. "But look 'round this here place, Clara. This ain't no paradise."

Clara felt her breath quicken as her gaze roamed the cabin. She couldn't imagine life without Jim and Betty around, but neither could she expect them or anybody else to live this way. "When did it get like this?"

"Been like this for a time now," Jim said. "You ain't knowed nothin' 'bout it 'cause you ain't been comin' 'round here much these days."

"I know," Clara said, looking down at her fingers. "I work up at the . . . the big house now." Why did she have such a hard time getting those words out? She had nothing to be ashamed of.

"I 'member a time you said you was gon' work down here when the time come," Jim said.

That was so long ago, Clara thought, it was a wonder he remembered it. She looked at Jim, and the raw bitterness that glared back felt like a kick in the gut. She glanced away. Jim was starting to get on her nerves with his nastiness. It wasn't her fault things had changed around here.

"Some cabins worser than this one," Betty said in a weak voice, breaking the silence.

"These hard times for Massa," Big Jim said. "He say he ain't got the money to buy material to fix up the cabins."

They didn't seem so hard up at the big house, Clara thought. Miss Dolley still wore pretty new dresses. They still entertained in grand style. And there were no leaky roofs. Clara shook her head to clear it. She couldn't believe Massa would allow this. "Maybe if you wait, they'll get better. Mass Jimmy—"

"Pft! What the hell we be waitin' for?" Big Jim asked, shaking his head.

Clara paused and bit her lip.

"The roof to cave in?" he continued. "Massa got mo' slaves than he got work. Some days I just sits 'round here doin' nothin' all day long. Drivin' me plumb crazy. An' my boy ain't never worked a day yet. That ain't nachal."

"An' it ain't gettin' no better, neither," Aunt Jane said. "Fact is, it gettin' worser every day."

The room got quiet except for the sound of water dripping into a tin pail. Clara didn't know what to say or do. It felt like she was treading on eggshells here. Jim wouldn't even look at her, but leaving now would seem so cold.

"Massa say this here man Taylor got hisself a big ole place that's growin'," Big Jim said. "Might even make me a overseer with all the field experience I got. Maybe get us a decent place to live in. Hard to pass up on all that with the way things been 'round here."

"We still got 'nough to eat, but less an' less meat an' mo' hominy 'n' grits," Jim said. "I's sick of hominy."

Clara swallowed hard, feeling guilty about the bacon she'd had for breakfast that morning.

"Ain't decided one way or 'nother yet," Big Jim said. "Massa say, take till next week to study on it."

"I don't wanna go," Betty said, pouting. "Everybody we know is here."

"Me neither," Jim said. "But I understand why Daddy might make us. He ain't got much choice."

Clara shook her head sadly and shifted in her seat. She couldn't imagine anything more dreadful than being sold away. Mama was probably looking for her by now, but . . .

It struck her like a bolt of lightning. Would Massa sell . . . ? No, no, never. Mama was way too important to them. They needed Mama. Why, she worked from sunup to sundown, day in and day out. Had all her life. And they would never sell her without Mama. Would they? Clara leaped up off the chair and clutched her throat.

"I . . . I . . ." She stopped, barely able to catch her breath.

"What's a matter, chile?" Aunt Jane asked.

"Nothing . . . I . . ." She paused and tried to slow her breathing but it didn't seem to do much good. She had to get out of here before she went crazy. "It's just that I . . . Mama wanted me to come right back. I . . . I have to go. Sorry."

She dashed out of the cabin and up the hill as if a mountain lion was at her feet. She ran past the house and kept running—across fields, through trees—until finally, she reached the slave graveyard. She stopped and leaned against a tree, her chest pumping wildly with each breath she took.

She hated them—all of them—with their ugly-assed white faces. Old Mass Jimmy, with his puny self, always walking around like he was so dratted important. Man was so old now, he could hardly even leave the house. Well, she hoped he would shrivel up and die tonight. And that tobacco-breathed Miss Dolley, always saying how her servants were like family. Yeah, her white family and her nigger family. They could find thousands of dollars to keep that no-good bum Mass Todd out of jail, but not a cent to keep Betty and Jim. They couldn't even help them keep their cabin decent.

And what if they sold Mama and her? Worse, what if they sold one of them without the other? She had heard of children or their mamas being sent away, never to see each other again. Even house slaves. She shook her head. The thought was so scary she didn't want to think it, but she couldn't help it. They might live half tolerable with enough food to eat, clothes on their backs, a dry roof over their heads. She could have ten pairs of shoes and a hundred dresses, but in the end she would still be nothing but a slave, a piece of property no better than a horse. And just like a horse, she could be bought and she could be sold at the whim of Massa.

She slumped down to the ground. Always before, when she heard about some house slaves poisoning their massa, especially so-called privileged slaves of so-called kind massas, she could never understand how the slaves could be so hateful. And when everybody was talking about Nat Turner butchering all those white folks down in Southampton a few years back, she'd thought the devil must have made him do it. Now she knew who really had the devil in them.

The breeze picked up, and a wet chill ran through the thin fabric of her dress. She realized the ground underneath her was still damp. She shivered, but she was too drained to move. Besides, she was never going back to that evil house, not as long as she lived.

It was the sound of leaves crunching under heavy hooves that startled her awake. She opened her eyes, and her still groggy mind caught a fleeting glimpse of something thundering toward her on four legs, something with sharp claws, bared teeth—and a white face. Such a creature could only live in her imagination, she knew. Still she jumped up and ran around to the other side of the tree.

"Clara, that you?"

Her heart leaped with joy at the sound of Daddy's voice. It had been a week—much too long—since she'd last heard it. She ran and jumped into his arms just as he alighted from his horse. He laughed, holding the reins in one hand and catching her with the other. He planted a big wet kiss on her forehead, then dropped her down on her feet. She looked up and smiled into his brown face.

He looked so handsome in his riding coat and leather boots. He was many years older than Mama, but in good shape. Clara thought his gray hair and the tiny lines that formed around his eyes when he smiled made him look trusty and wise.

"How my best gal doing?" he asked, not really expecting an answer. "Your mama sent me out here to fetch you. Said you been gone near two hours." He patted the horse's saddle. "Jump on up, and I'll give you a ride back up to the house. Done caught us a possum for tonight."

He reached out to help her onto the horse, but Clara took a step back. Daddy frowned. Prince was Daddy's pride and joy, and he knew that she always jumped at the chance to ride him. But she was in no mood to ride a horse now. She found herself wondering, as she looked at Prince holding his head high with pride, how he felt about folks always riding on his back, making him go this way and that. Wouldn't he rather be free?

"What's the matter with you?" Daddy asked. "You still like roasted possum, don't you? The way your mama fixes it up with potatoes and butter. Mmm-umph!"

"I'm never going back. I hate it up there."

"Oh? And just where you fixing to go if not back up there, might I ask?"

Clara hadn't thought that far ahead. She just knew where she was *not* going. Daddy stood there and looked at her, waiting patiently for her to explain herself.

"Daddy, can me and Mama come live with you? Please?" Since they couldn't be free, living with Daddy would be the next best thing.

Daddy sighed. "We done explained that to you a hundred different times. Mass Bell don't need no more help around the house. He gives me a good horse and a pass to ride over here most weekends, and I'm thankful for that."

"But I want us to live together all the time."

Daddy shook his head. "Even if you lived with me,

sugar, I'm gone so much during the week, driving them white folks all around. We wouldn't see each other much more than we do now anyhow. I'm just getting back from Baltimore, and I'm setting out for Richmond next week. What's gotten into you?"

"They fixing to sell some of us!" she shouted, waving her arm toward the big house. "They're going . . ."

Daddy blinked. "What?"

"Mass Jimmy and Miss Dolley gonna sell some of us and . . . and . . ." She stamped the ground. She was so flustered she couldn't talk straight.

Daddy held out a hand. "Whoa. Calm down, sugar. Where on earth did you hear that?"

Clara swallowed and tried to calm herself. "Down at the grove."

"Who told you?"

"Big Jim and Aunt Jane. Massa asked them if they wanted to go and they're thinking on it." She swallowed again to flush the tears welling up in her throat.

Daddy clenched his jaw, then put his arm around Clara's shoulder. "Come and walk with me a bit."

"I'm not going back. We ain't no better than the farm animals to them. It's evil up there."

"Set out in that direction with me, then."

"But I want to go with you, Daddy. I . . ."

"You can't do that, Clara. And there's no use in you trying to change that 'cause there's not much me or your mama can do about it." He said it so firmly that Clara knew he meant it. She shut her mouth. "Now you either walk or get up on this here horse."

She wiped her wet nose with the back of her hand and walked alongside Daddy. Prince trailed, with Daddy holding the reins.

"Your mama said she heard the same thing this afternoon. Truth is, nobody knows just what's going on yet. First time I ever heard of Mass Jimmy selling anybody."

Daddy shook his head, as if he was having trouble believing it, too.

"Then why is he doing it?"

Daddy knitted his brows. "Must need the money, that's the only reason I can think of. Like a lot of white folks 'round here that down on their luck, his crops not doing so good."

"But they got plenty of everything, and Massa's always saying we're like his family. Guess that was a lie."

Daddy exhaled with exasperation. "Look, Clara, 'cause you old enough to hear this now. You family to them folks only so long as they need you and it don't hurt 'em none to keep you. Mass Jimmy better than most, but he going to think about his white family first. In hard times, us colored folks always the first ones to suffer 'cause the truth is, Mass Jimmy and all the rest of 'em can do whatever they want to you, me, your mama, and all the rest of us. Now I don't reckon you and your mama got much to worry about. So many guests up at that house all the time, since Mass Jimmy used to be president. And they need your mama to help out."

"But what about me?"

Daddy paused. "Mass Jimmy don't believe in splitting up families."

"How do you know?"

Daddy grunted. "I just know. It ain't never happened around here before and it's not going to happen now."

Slaves had never been sold around here before, either, Clara thought, and that was happening now. But she didn't want to push her daddy on it, since it was clearly making him touchy. Besides, she didn't want to think about being sold away herself, if she could help it. It was driving her plumb crazy. "What about Jim and Betty?"

"What about them?"

"Big Jim said Mass Jimmy asked him if they wanted to go. Said the man that wants to buy them might make him a overseer."

"Then maybe they'll go, but as a family."

Clara looked down at the ground, and Daddy squeezed her shoulders. "At least they'll be together. And your mama and me will still be here."

In other words, thought Clara, be thankful it's not worse.

4

Sunday was church day, and all were dressed in their finest: the women in brightly colored calico or muslin dresses with petticoats that had been abundantly starched to imitate the fullness of the hoop skirts that their mistresses wore, the men in suits and shoes shined with grease. Some of them, mainly the elderly and small children, rode along in wagons. Others walked, flinging their shoes over their shoulders. Their feet belonged to Massa, they reasoned, but their shoes were theirs and they wanted to protect them.

Sometimes, if Daddy's massa was sick and not going to church, Daddy would bring the horse and buggy over and drive Clara and Mama to church. But most of the time they walked along with the others. Only difference was they wore their shoes, at Mama's insistence.

This was the most gratifying time for the slaves at Montpelier, for this was the one day of the week that they belonged to the good Lord instead of to those lording over their chattel. Or so it had always seemed to Clara. She almost grunted aloud at the thought as she sat in the pew next to her mama. Now she knew that all the prayer on earth wouldn't save them from being sold if that was Massa's wish. The old man was more powerful than God—at least here on earth.

She glanced up at the bead necklace that Mama wore only on Sundays and special occasions. Always before, Clara had admired the necklace for its beauty. Its dark blue color reminded her of the sky on a clear winter evening. But on this day, she found herself wishing it had magical powers. Then she could put a voodoo hex on Massa and Missus. She had heard that mixing up some frog bones, snakeskin, and ashes and putting them under the steps would do the trick, and she briefly considered where she might hide such a bag until she was ready to make her move. She had visions of Massa wilting up in his bed like a dead worm and Missus coughing up tobacco juice until her guts spilled out.

She sighed and looked down at her fingertips, trying to force the evil thoughts from her head. Shame on herself for letting her mind wander so far astray in the middle of Sunday service. Lately, she'd been having some awful mean thoughts. Sometimes, she didn't want to open her mouth for fear of what might come out of it.

After the services, Mama, Daddy, and Aunt Nany strolled down to the grove together for the picnic that was held after church. It was usually a lively affair, sometimes lasting through supper and into the night. But Clara had a feeling that on this day there would be no fiddle, no "settin' de flo" and no cakewalks.

Something else was different, too. The house and field slaves usually planted themselves in separate groups on the benches and blankets while they ate, although they would cross back and forth to chat. Today, they all mingled, shaking their heads and talking about how they couldn't believe the goings-on at Montpelier. Clara had never seen so many black folks in one place looking so numb, she thought, as she sat on a wooden bench between Mama and Daddy in front of Aunt Winney's cabin. Walnut Grove looked like it had just been struck by a cyclone.

"Anythin' better'n that goin' back to Africa stuff Massa be talkin' 'bout," Big Jim said as he leaned against the side of the cabin, a long blade of grass dangling from his lips.

Aunt Winney nodded as she rocked back and forth in her old rocking chair, smoking a pipe that looked as if it had endured a million puffs and would endure a million more. "A-men!"

Uncle Paul chuckled and nodded. Not that long ago, he almost never came down to the grove unless it was to run an errand for Mass Jimmy. But Massa was getting older and rarely left his room, so Uncle Paul would sometimes come down on weekends and late in the evening to sit and talk to Aunt Winney or one of the other old-timers. Clara thought he looked so out of place, sitting there on a hard-backed chair with his hat resting on one knee. His velvet waistcoat was finer than anything the slaves who lived in the grove ever wore. But if there was one thing all coloreds at Montpelier, house and field alike, agreed on, it was that they didn't want to hear any talk about going back to Africa.

"Massa's always talking about that to just about anybody who'll listen," Uncle Paul said.

"Back to Africa." Daddy scoffed. "What in tarnation that s'posed to mean? Ain't never been there. How am I gonna go back?"

Aunt Winney chuckled and grunted in agreement.

"Reckon Massa thinks that's the only way to free us," Uncle Paul said. "Since we'd never be accepted here if he freed us."

Big Jim spit the blade of grass from his mouth and shook his head. "I done tole Massa, I don' want nothin' to do with no Africa. Walk all the way down to New Orleans an' pick that cotton every blessed day o' my life 'fore I go to some Africa."

Aunt Jane nodded emphatically.

"Don't blame you one bit," Aunt Nany said. "I hardly

get to see my Jacob as it is, even though he lives right over at the Jones' place. Lord knows that Jones is the meanest man that ever walked on God's green earth. Still, why would we want to go to some strange land and leave our families behind? Would they do that? Heck, no."

"I keep hoping he'll free us in his will and let us stay here, like President Washington did with his slaves," Uncle Paul said.

"Humph. Doubt he'll ever do that," Mama said, as she twisted the blue beads around her neck with her forefinger. "What's going to happen to Miss Dolley if we all leave here?"

"Who cares!" Jim shouted. He sat next to his sister and mama on a blanket, yanking blades of grass from the ground. "They don' care nothin' 'bout none o' us. I hopes they all burn in hell."

Amen, Clara thought. Her sentiments exactly.

"Hush yo' mouth, chile," Aunt Jane said, giving Jim a reproachful look. "That ain't no way to talk. You knows better."

Jim folded his arms defiantly across his chest. Clara wanted to speak out, to tell Jim she'd like to see them rot in hell, too, but she knew Mama wouldn't approve any more than Aunt Jane did. She had always thought it was different out here so far away from the big house, more free. But they couldn't say what they really felt even out here amongst their own. The colored grownups were afraid to breathe without permission from the white folks, and it didn't matter whether they worked in the big house or in the fields.

"Some folks over at Monticello thought Mass Jefferson was gonna free 'em when he died," Daddy said.

"Pft!" Aunt Nany said. "Only ones that went free was that gal Sally Hemings and her children, 'cause he favored them. The rest of them were auctioned off."

Big Jim snickered. "Mass Jefferson was just freein' his own chillen, that's all."

"Go on away from here with that talk," Aunt Matilda said. "You really believe that?"

Big Jim nodded. " 'Course I do."

Aunt Nany nodded, too. " 'Member now, they look more white than black, since Sally was half white to begin with. And she had her first child right after she came back from France with Mass Jefferson. Doesn't take a genius to figure this stuff out."

"You believe it, Mama?" Clara asked.

Mama nodded. "Why shouldn't I? But I wouldn't wish that fate on anybody. Slave or free."

"Why?" Clara asked.

"'Cause mulattos and quadroons so mixed up. They're not one thing or the other."

"They don' never really fit in nowhere," Aunt Jane said. "Somethin' ain't right about 'em waitin' hand an' foot on folks what look just like them."

Mama nodded. "Sometimes they pass for white if they get free, and live better than the rest of us," Mama said. "But that's rare."

"And if they do get their freedom, they have to keep looking over their shoulders all the time," Uncle Paul said. "Always worrying somebody will catch them."

"Or getting a tan in the summer," Mama said. She clapped her hands and chuckled. "If you got to be a slave you're better off looking the part. That way—"

The way Mama froze all of a sudden made Clara and the others turn to look. Emerging from the walnut trees on the hillside was Miss Dolley, wearing one of her high silk turbans. With her was Mass Todd, her niece Miss Mary, and a few of their Sunday guests, all dressed gaily in their silks and satins and smiling as if they'd just won prizes.

Aunt Sukey followed close behind. She held a parasol over Miss Dolley and was looking just about as fine as the rest of the bunch save the look on her face. There was the usual boredom in Aunt Sukey's gaze but lately Clara had begun to see something else—a kind of bitterness or maybe even hatred—especially in the way Aunt Sukey would sometimes twist her bottom lip ever so slightly. Clara had never sensed that before, and she wondered if it was Aunt Sukey's expression that had changed or her own perception of it.

Clara turned back toward the group. Just seeing those white faces made evil thoughts pop into her head again. She looked up at Mama and Daddy, then the others. All of them had just pulled those invisible masks down over their faces. Clara lowered her eyes and bit her bottom lip.

"Why, Winney," Mass Todd said, grinning broadly as he and a man about his age with a beard and a fancy ivory-handled cane sauntered up. "Have you got any of your famous sweet potatoes today for me and my friend here from New York?"

Aunt Winney pulled the pipe from her lips. "Not today, Massa," she said, as she struggled up from her rocking chair. "If'n you wants, I kin—"

"Never mind," Mass Todd said, waving her back into her seat.

Aunt Winney sat down and stuck the pipe back into her mouth as Mass Todd turned to his companion. "Winney grows the biggest potatoes in that little patch of garden of hers."

"Indeed?" said the man. "They look like such a contented bunch."

Contented? Contented? Clara thought she'd never seen a more gloomy looking bunch of folks. Not only did the man talk funny, he must be half blind, too.

"They ought to be," Mass Todd said as he turned to walk off. His companion followed, twirling his cane at his side. "They've hardly a care in the world," Mass Todd continued. "They never work on Sundays or Saturday afternoons. They don't have to worry about money or where their next meal is coming from. Especially the house niggers and the little pickaninnies. They . . ."

Clara looked up. Daddy was clenching his jaw, and Mama rolled her eyes to the high heavens.

"Damn fool," Aunt Winney said just loud enough for those around her cabin to hear.

She and Mama and Aunt Nany exchanged knowing looks as the party from the big house made its way back up the hillside. Clara wanted more from them, at least a little more cussing, but that was all that was said on the matter.

"Come on," Mama said, nudging Clara as she sighed and stood up. "Best be getting on back to use some of our so-called free time to look after their guests."

Aunt Nany stood up, too, but Clara had the hardest time getting her legs to lift her body. She felt like yelling at everybody—at the white folks 'cause they were so dratted evil, at the black folks 'cause they couldn't save themselves from the evil whites. But most of all at herself, because she was every bit as helpless as the rest of them.

Clara bolted straight up. She opened her eyes wide, but couldn't make out a thing in the dark. Then she heard it again—a scream that pierced the still morning air like an arrow. A chill crept up her spine.

It had come from far away, in the direction of the grove. She blinked, forcing her eyes to adjust to the darkness. Mama and the others were already sitting up on their pallets, and the looks on their faces told her that it was finally happening: the slaves who had been sold were being roused to leave.

Clara had never been so terrified in all her life. It felt like claws were gripping her chest, squeezing the very breath out of her body. She folded her legs and wrapped her arms around them tightly, then buried her face between her knees to muffle her sobs.

"Clara," Mama said softly from behind her. "It'll be all right."

Clara gritted her teeth. How could Mama say that? It was bad enough hearing the others outside screaming their heads off. What if those evil white folks suddenly came up here and took some of them from this attic? What was to stop them? Mama couldn't prevent what was happening, no, but she didn't have to be so dratted calm about it, either. All of the grownups were acting just like Mama: they just sat and stared as if they had been frozen to their pallets.

She crawled across the cold plank floor, intending to give Mama a piece of her mind. But when she reached Mama's pallet and saw those red-rimmed eyes, she sat back on her heels. Mama looked as if she had been crying most all night. Clara buried her head in Mama's neck.

"The ones going all agreed to go," Mama reminded her as she rubbed Clara's back. "I expect it's just the shock of it really happening that's getting to them now." She sighed. "Pull yourself together. We have to get up, 'cause we still got work to do." Mama was saying the words even though Clara could tell by her voice that her heart wasn't in it. It was like Mama and the others were some kind of machine akin to a spinning wheel. They knew how to act only one way or not at all, no matter what anybody did to them.

Clara dragged herself off the pallet and stood in her nightshirt and bare feet. She rubbed her eyes. How in tarnation was she going to get any work done that day? she wondered as she walked to the washbasin. There were no more screams as she dressed, but she could hear horses neighing, wagons circling, and voices shouting. Just as she slipped her feet into her shoes, she heard hoofbeats on the dirt pathway. Everyone stood stock-still and held their breath until the sound disappeared into the distance.

Aunt Nany broke down sobbing, and Mama went to comfort her. Clara ran to the window at the front of the attic and looked down. On the pathway outside the gate, where the horses had just stirred up a cloud of dust, a frail old man dressed in black walked away slowly. He was leaning heavily on a cane, and Uncle Paul walked a few paces behind him. It was Mass Jimmy, Clara realized at once, and her shoulders shook with anguish as her eyes filled with tears. She wondered what the old man was thinking, what he was feeling. Was he happy to see them go? No. She couldn't imagine that such tragedy could make anyone happy. Still, he must not grieve the way they did, or he would never have let this happen.

She heard Mama calling her and she wiped her eyes and turned away from the window. Aunt Nany was standing behind Mama, her cheeks still flushed from crying. In her hands, she carried her prized pair of leather shoes, and both arms were filled with small bundles. Clara's stomach turned. "Mama, where's Aunt Nany going?"

Mama's lips quivered and she seemed unable to speak. Clara swallowed hard as Aunt Nany set the bundles on the floor and walked up to Clara. "You're not leaving, too?" Clara asked. She could feel her voice cracking.

"No," Aunt Nany said. She put an arm around Clara's shoulders and tried to smile. "I'm just moving down to the grove."

Clara felt relief and dread all at the same time. "The grove?"

Aunt Nany nodded, and the smile fell from her face as her eyes filled with fresh tears.

"But why?"

Aunt Nany took a deep breath. "They want me to work in the fields now."

Clara looked from Aunt Nany to Mama. Aunt Nany didn't know anything about field work, and Mama needed Aunt Nany to help out here. They could barely get all the work done now.

"They told her late last night," Mama said.

"They can't do that!"

"They can and they did." Aunt Nany held the shoes out. "Here. I want you to have these, Clara. You'll be wearing this size in no time at all, and I won't have any use for them where I'm going."

Clara put her hands behind her back. "You can still wear them to church on Sunday."

Aunt Nany reached out and placed the shoes in Clara's hands. "The others will think I'm acting uppity if I wear 'em. Expect they think it anyhow, but I got to live with them now."

Clara took the shoes and watched in silence as Aunt Nany bent over to pick up the bundles. Her heart jumped with each step her aunt took across the attic and down the stairs. First Jim and Betty, now Aunt Nany. It didn't matter who you were or how hard you worked, to them you were still just a nigger. She looked down at the shoes in her hand. She wanted to cry, but that never did any good anymore. She could cry a river of tears and all these evil white folks would do was sell her downstream to the highest bidder.

She threw the shoes on the floor.

"Jesus, child." Mama looked at her, her red-rimmed eyes wide with surprise. "Don't you want them? They're leather."

Clara scoffed. "What difference does it make what shoes I wear? My feet will still be black."

Mama tightened her lips. "Stop that talk this minute. What's wrong with you?"

Everything. "Mama?"

"What?"

"Let's run."

"What?"

"Let's run. Up North. You and me and Daddy before—"

"Stop it, Clara. I don't want to hear another word out of you. Running is not the answer. Most of the folks that run get caught and then things get worse than they were before."

"Then what is the answer, Mama? I'm scared they might sell us or send us down to the grove. The way they live down there now is awful."

"Miss Dolley can be a difficult woman at times, but I don't think she would ever sell—"

"I wish you would open your eyes, Mama, and stop always taking up for her all the time. You think she gives a fig about us?"

"I believe she does, in her own way." Mama paused and sighed. "Any way you look at it, running is not the answer to our troubles. We have to make sure she knows she needs us around here. With Aunt Nany gone now, I want you to help out more. And you have to be nice around Miss Dolley, no matter how mad you get at her."

But that was crazy, Clara thought. What she wanted to do was throw these dratted shoes in that evil old woman's face.

"You don't want to give her any reason to move you down to the fields," Mama continued, as if reading her mind. "I can't prove it, but I suspect all that sneaking off with a field hand from another plantation didn't help Nany any."

"But all she did was fall in love."

"I know." Mama sighed. "Look, I don't like it any more than you do. Mind you, Massa and Missus can be a pain at times. But my way of handling things has gotten us this far, and it's the only way I know."

5

Clara nearly dropped the pot out of her hands. Some mess that would have made—top falling off, pee splashing all over the yard, all over her. Too disgusting to even think about. But Aunt Sukey had rattled her with the news: Mass Jimmy was dying.

Aunt Sukey lifted her skirt high off the ground and slid away from Clara and her pot. Clara was several steps away but she didn't blame Aunt Sukey one bit. This was a chore she hated, and would never get used to if she lived to a hundred. She had to hold her breath and take tiny steps all the way from the top floor of the big house to the yard. The first time she did it, not long after Aunt Nany moved down to the grove, she dropped the pot on the stairs. Old Miss Dolley stood over her and watched as she got down on all fours with a rag and mopped up every stinking drop. That was nearly two years ago, and Clara hadn't come anywhere near to dropping a pot since.

"Miss Dolley sent for the doctor, and he said it won't be long," Aunt Sukey said, keeping one eye aimed at the pot as Clara steadied it.

Clara looked at her mama, standing several yards away. Mama lowered a big stick she had been using to pound the dirt and dust out of a Persian carpet strung up on the clothesline. Mama's mouth fell open as she lifted her free hand to wipe the sweat off her brow, then bowed her head and said a quick prayer under her breath.

Clara walked carefully to a nearby pit, dumped the pot, and set it on the ground near some bushes. She wiped her hands on her apron and walked quickly back toward the clothesline. She wanted to hear every word of this.

By the time she got back, Aunt Sukey had dropped her skirt and was standing next to Mama, her arms flying in the air as she talked. It was the most animated Clara had ever seen Aunt Sukey. ". . . talking about giving Massa something so he can hang on for a few more days and make it to the fourth of July, same as they did with Mass Jefferson. But Massa said no, he would go when the time comes."

Clara and her mama exchanged looks, and Clara saw the same thing in Mama's hazel eyes that she felt herself: fear. Aunt Sukey's words scared her more than anything had since the news two years back that some of them were about to be sold had spread across the estate like wild fire. No surprise, no sorrow. Just plain old fear was what she was feeling. And not for Mass Jimmy, either—for themselves. No shame in that, she told herself. All of her life he'd been an old man, steadily getting older. Why, he must have been in his seventies when she was born. She saw him often enough, but it was usually at a distance—across the lawn or through an open door. Massa had more than a hundred slaves, and he probably knew her only as Susie's child.

The news didn't surprise her much, either, since for the past six months Mass Jimmy had hardly been able to stand without help, much less walk, and Uncle Paul had said that lately he was even having trouble talking and writing. His mind was still good, and together with Miss Dolley, he was still very much in charge. So life at Montpelier had carried on pretty much as usual.

Clara was now a full-fledged chambermaid, emptying slop jars and changing soiled linen alongside her mama, just as she swore she'd never do. Things were a lot different from what she'd dreamed of only a couple of years ago, when thoughts of wearing pretty dresses and learning to read danced through her head. But at least she still parked her rump on a pallet at Montpelier every night. Now with Massa deathly ill, there was no telling what would happen to them if he died. No, the only thing she felt was fear. Her body was cold all over despite the summer heat.

"Anyhow," Aunt Sukey said. "Paul wants us all to meet down at Sister Winney's cabin tonight if you can get away."

"What for?" Mama asked.

"To talk about what to do when it happens."

"Humph," Mama said. "Nothing we can do 'cept wait and take it, whatever it is."

It was so like Mama to grin and bear it, Clara thought. Just like when some of them were sold away to Louisiana and Aunt Nany was kicked down to the grove. As far as Mama was concerned, that kind of stuff was the story of their lives and would be until the day they died, no matter how much meeting and talking they did.

Clara never did learn what happened to Jim and Betty and their family. News drifted back that Betty got sicker along the journey but that was all they'd heard in the two years since. For all she knew, the whole family could be dead and buried somewhere.

"Jesus," Mama said, her eyes growing weary. "Whole world's coming to an end. What's to become of us with Massa gone? I suspect we'll be hearing a lot more from that Mass Todd."

Aunt Sukey twisted her lips and clutched the charm around her neck. "Then we're all doomed. That's for sure. But Paul said Massa said he was going to put it in his will that none of us can be sold without our permission, unless we misbehave."

"Misbehave?" Clara asked. "What's that supposed to mean?"

"Whatever Miss Dolley and Mass Todd want it to mean," Mama said.

Aunt Sukey nodded and turned toward the mansion.

"Let us know the minute anything happens, Sister Sukey," Mama said.

"'Spect it won't be long," Aunt Sukey called back over her shoulder.

Suddenly an idea hit Clara. She had long come to the conclusion that the only road out of this particular hell led North, to freedom. You either grinned and suffered it, like Mama, or you took your chances and ran. She usually kept her contrary thoughts to herself, since Mama hated it when she talked about freedom, but there was a limit to how much she would bite her tongue, even for Mama. She called after Aunt Sukey. "Aunt Sukey. Massa ever say anything about freeing us in his will?"

"Heavens," Mama said, frowning. "Don't bother Sister Sukey with that crazy talk, now, child. I reckon she got other things on her mind."

"Why is that crazy, Mama? Mass Washington did it after he died. And Mass Jefferson freed some of his."

Mama smacked her lips with annoyance and picked up the stick.

"All I can tell you," Aunt Sukey said, "is that Paul did say something way back. Something about Massa worrying that would make things too hard on Miss Dolley after he's gone, so he would leave it up to her."

"See?" Mama said. "What did I tell you?"

Clara heard something different in Aunt Sukey's words than what Mama seemed to hear. But then Mama always thought the cup was half empty. "Sounds to me like he told Miss Dolley she could free us after he's gone, if she has a notion to?"

Aunt Sukey twisted her lips. "Knowing Miss Dolley

like I do, I wouldn't go getting any ideas."

Clara looked at Mama as Aunt Sukey lifted her skirt and walked back toward the house. "Why would she need to keep all of us after Massa is gone?"

"To do the same things we been doing around here all along. You better stop that crazy talk about some freedom."

In Clara's opinion, it was keeping all of them after the Massa was gone that was crazy. "But Mass Todd's not even here half the time."

"Hush," Mama said, her breath coming fast and heavy between strokes as she hit the carpet harder. "You talk like Mass Jimmy's already in his grave. And when he does go, you better pray Miss Dolley finds something for all of us to do. Where you think you're going anyhow?"

"I would go far away from here, that's for sure. As far as I can get. I don't want to spend the rest of my life worrying if somebody or another is going to up and decide to sell us away one day. What if something happens to Miss Dolley and Mass Todd starts running this place? I don't like the way that man been looking at me lately."

Mama's arm froze in midair. "What you talkin' 'bout?"

Clara shrugged. "He just looks at me funny sometimes, that's all."

Mama's hazel eyes flashed. She threw the stick on the ground and pointed her finger in Clara's face. "You stay away from that man, you hear?"

Clara backed up, surprised at the venom in Mama's voice. She knew Mama had never liked Mass Todd much but she'd never expected this outburst. And why yell at her? "It's him that's looking at me, Mama."

"If he so much as touches a hair on your head, you come to me."

Clara nodded.

"Did you hear me?"

"Yes, Mama, I heard you."

"No-good bastard," Mama said. She picked up the stick again and pounded the quilt with both hands. Clara picked up her own stick and they beat in silence for a moment. If Mass Todd's behavior was bad enough to get Mama to cursing, she was never going to let that man get anywhere near her. Lord almighty, if only she could get away from this place.

"Mama?"

"What?"

"You wouldn't want to go away, even if she freed us?"

Mama shook her head vigorously. "Heavens, no. Mind you, things are bound to get worse around here after Massa goes, but where would I go? What would I do? Starve to death, that's what. Or freeze out in the cold."

"We could go up North and find work."

"Humph. Doing what? And what about your daddy? He would still be here."

Clara sighed. That was the only bad thing she could think of about the whole idea of being free. "Maybe we could work and buy Daddy's freedom."

Mama stopped and looked at Clara. "Jesus, child. Where you get these crazy ideas from? You don't know a thing about freedom, 'cause I don't know anything about it. It takes money and know-how to live free. You don't just up and do it. Now get back to emptying those pots. I got to finish up here. We have too much work to do to stand around talking this nonsense."

Clara dropped her stick and turned toward the house. "Freedom can't be as bad as this," she muttered under her breath.

Mama seemed to think she had gone plumb crazy, talking so much foolishness about them getting their freedom. Just the night before, as they lay side by side on their pallets, Mama told her to hush her mouth, said she didn't want to hear another word about it. But in the two days since Massa took sick, it was all Clara could think of. The way she saw things, it was crazy not to think about freedom if there was even a glimmer of hope. Maybe it was mean to think about Massa dying, but as far as she knew, in all his eighty-some years of living, the old man had never set one of his slaves free. Not one. It wasn't her fault that his death seemed to be their only hope.

Clara turned onto her back and looked up at the ceiling. It was so dark she could hardly see her hand, still it was awful hard to doze off. She would have better luck trying to sleep in the middle of a Saturday night jubilee. Thank goodness Mama was off in a corner somewhere with Daddy. That meant she wasn't nearby to tell Clara to lie still and go to sleep. Aunt Sarah and the other women who had mates were over there, too.

Since it was a Saturday night, sleeping arrangements in the attic had been changed to provide a bit of privacy for the couples. Sheets were pinned to the ceiling to block the views but that didn't do a blessed thing to quiet the huffing and puffing and groaning. Clara grew up thinking grownups did an awful lot of moaning in their sleep on Saturday nights. She was almost thirteen now and still didn't know what all the ruckus was about. But over the years since, she'd caught a glimpse or two behind the sheets and now had a better idea. One thing she knew was never to go anywhere near that corner of the room on Saturday nights.

She turned again, this time onto her stomach, and rested her chin on clenched fists. She'd always known that some colored folks lived free, mostly up North but also in some of the big Southern cities like Richmond and Washington, D.C. Still, the idea that she could live free had always seemed too far-fetched to even hope for. And until a couple of years back, she'd been happy enough not to think much on it, probably because she was too dratted stupid to know any better. She'd thought she would always be happy right here at Montpelier, even though most of the grownups around here didn't seem all that happy. Contented, yes. Happy, no. For some dumb reason, she thought she'd be different. She knew better now.

She wasn't the only one around here hoping for a better tomorrow. There was a buzz circling the plantation—a freedom buzz. Seemed folks were split three ways. Some claimed they would be gone before the rooster crowed if they were set free one night. Others wouldn't hear of leaving. Most came down somewhere in between. Aunt Sarah wanted freedom only if her husband and grown children were also freed. They all lived at Montpelier, so Aunt Sarah was cautiously hopeful. Aunt Nany's husband Jacob lived on another plantation like Daddy, but since she'd been shoved out to the fields Aunt Nany said she would go in the blink of an eye. Most of the old-timers, like Aunts Matilda and Winney, said they weren't going anywhere. This was where they were born and this was where they would die.

The surprise was Paul Jennings. Clara and most everyone else thought he would never, ever leave Montpelier. He'd been Mass Jimmy's valet for the last twenty-five years. He shaved him every morning and had even lived with him up there in the White House. Everyone knew Uncle Paul was as loyal as they came. But Uncle Paul said he'd take his freedom at the drop of a hat if offered once Mass Jimmy was gone. He'd seen and learned so much while traveling around with Massa and Missus that he was certain he could make it on his own. At first, Aunt Sukey was adamant about not leaving Miss Dolley, but the more Uncle Paul and the others talked about freedom the more she began to warm to the idea.

Uncle Paul thought that it would be best if Miss Dolley gave them all a choice. He thought about half would take their freedom and leave and that about half would probably stay. A lot of possibilities were talked and dreamed about over those heady few days as they all waited to see what would happen to Massa. Even most of those who said they would never leave seemed eager to talk about what freedom might mean. They put on solemn faces as they went about their chores, but whispered about freedom behind closed doors—in the attic, the cellar, and the faraway corners of the mansion. Aunt Matilda said she could hardly turn around in the kitchen before somebody from down at the grove stuck their head in the kitchen door to ask about Massa's health.

Clara knew her mama would never leave Montpelier, but just having the choice would feel like a present from heaven. Imagine knowing they could leave if they wanted. She closed her eyes and tried to imagine all the good things that freedom would mean. They could go see Daddy whenever they wanted. Maybe she could move up North alone when she got a little older and earn the money to buy Daddy's freedom. Maybe she could even go to school and study reading and writing someday.

Best of all, she would never have to worry about being sold away, no matter how she acted or what kind of luck the massa was having. She wouldn't have to live in fear of being snatched away from Mama and Daddy or her own children and grandchildren. She got so giddy just thinking about all this that she found herself laughing out loud when she should have been sleeping.

Before she knew it, a wisp of daylight streaked across the plank floor and up onto her pallet. She opened her eyes and squinted. She wasn't sure how much sleep she'd gotten but it didn't feel like much. She smiled and stretched leisurely, as thoughts of freedom danced in her head. Any other day, the folks in the attic would all have been up and moving about by now, but it was Sunday and they were just beginning to stir when Aunt Sukey came up. It was unusual to see Aunt Sukey up there at that hour, and everyone stopped what they were doing and watched as she beckoned Mama and Aunt Sarah. Miss Dolley needed them right away, Aunt Sukey said.

Daddy put his arm around Clara's shoulders as Mama and Aunt Sarah followed Aunt Sukey down the stairs. Daddy didn't say anything, but Clara could tell by the way the corner of his eyes wrinkled up that he was worried. She buried her face in Daddy's chest. Now that it seemed about to happen for real, she was getting scared. She searched her memory, trying to remember the last time she'd seen the old man. It had been several days ago as she dusted in a hallway and Uncle Paul opened the door to Massa's room. She caught a glimpse of his small body, draped in black and reclining on a French sofa. So tiny, so frail. Yet, in that being lay her fate and that of so many others from the day they were born. For a moment, she'd wondered why fate had put him there, with the whole world at his feet, and her here.

Daddy told her to finish dressing for church, and she shook her head to clear it. She would have to trust in the Lord to do what was right for everybody.

She heard footsteps on the stairs again, and everybody stood stock-still. It seemed to take a lifetime, but Mama finally appeared on the landing, her eyes all puffy and red. She couldn't stay, Mama said. She had to get back down to Miss Dolley and the others. She just wanted to let them all know that Mass Jimmy was dead.

Clara scanned the crowd gathered on the lawn in front of the big house to hear Miss Dolley speak after the old man was put to rest. They came from the kitchen and the grove, the parlors and the fields. Some were so young they hadn't yet learned to walk, others so old they couldn't. Why, there must be a hundred, she thought, as her eyes looked around. She'd always known that, of course, but knowing and seeing were two different things. If they were freed, they would need money, papers, transportation. It dawned on her at that moment that Miss Dolley would never free them all at once. She wouldn't do it in good times, much less now, when her husband had just died and she was on her own.

Clara still hoped, perhaps irrationally she knew, that Miss Dolley would offer freedom to some of them—Uncle Paul and Aunt Sukey, Aunt Sarah, Mama. They had worked closely with Massa and Missus for so long, right there in the big house, through good times and bad. Surely the old woman felt something special for them, Clara thought, as she looked up at the portico that ran along the front of the mansion.

Miss Dolley, dressed in black from head to toe, stepped out the front door, flanked by her niece, Miss Mary, and her son. To everyone's surprise Miss Dolley stayed in the background with Miss Mary as Mass Todd walked to the top of the stairs—or stumbled would be more like it. He had a wine goblet in his hand and had clearly been drinking.

"I wanted all y'all gathered here so I'd only have to say this once," he said. His speech slurred more than a little, and he leaned heavily on one of the white columns. "All sorts of rumors been floating 'round here, and I wanted to set things straight. Despite the recent departure of my dearly beloved stepfather, y'all will continue 'round here just the same as always. Mother has put me in charge. . . ."

A gasp ran through the crowd on the lawn. "Lord! Jesus! Heavens!" Clara's heart thumped in her ears and she glanced at Mama, standing next to her. There was no mask over those hazel eyes now. Mama had a look of pure disgust on her face and she didn't seem to care who saw it.

"Lord have mercy," Mama whispered.

Clara shut her eyes and shook her head. This couldn't be happening, she thought.

"Nobody is going anywhere, so you can just get back to your sho . . . your chores same as before. Things are unner . . . under control as I . . ."

Clara squeezed her eyes. The man was so drunk he could hardly talk straight.

"Yeah," somebody said, snickering. "If'n he kin stay on his feet an' outta jail, we be just fine."

Some of the others chuckled with scorn. By now, so much chatter filled the yard that Clara could barely hear Mass Todd. She didn't know whether to cry or scream. She opened her eyes and looked at the new massa of Montpelier. Then she turned her gaze to Miss Dolley and clenched her fists. Clara was more upset with her than with Mass Todd. They belonged to her, but instead of freeing them, the old woman was handing them over to a drunken scoundrel who had spent more nights in jail and brothels than he had at home. Mass Todd might be Miss Dolley's son but he was still a fool who could barely look after himself, much less all of them.

Clara had long ago stopped thinking of herself as "family" to the Madisons, even though Miss Dolley still preached that nonsense. But never in a hundred years did Clara really think the old woman would do this to them.

6

At first Clara thought a spider was crawling on her cheek. Lord knew enough of them lived in the crooks and crannies of this dusty old attic. But just as she reached up to smack it away, the smell of liquor hit her nose, and she knew this was a two-legged creature on her. Besides, she remembered, it was winter, too cold for spiders. Ralph, one of the young men who worked the stables, must have gotten drunk out in a field somewhere and now he was stumbling all over her trying to find his pallet. Damn it. Was she ever going to give that idiot a piece of her mind. She worked her tail off all day around the house. She didn't need this nonsense at night. Ralph would never have dared try something like this when Mass Jimmy was alive.

When she turned onto her back and opened her eyes, the face she saw was white. Mass Todd. She thought she would puke right there on the spot. She tried to swing her arms, but his strong hands pinned them on her breasts. He leaned over her, and before she could catch her breath, his slimy lips were all over her face. She kicked with every ounce of energy she could muster to get away from him, to free herself from his grasp. But the drunken old fool had grown so bloated the past few years, it was like trying to get out from under a hog.

She was starting to run out of steam when she felt something land on top of them both. Mass Todd cussed at the top of his lungs and sprang up. That was when Clara saw Mama clinging to his back like a tick on a hairy dog. She was beating him about the head and shoulders with a stick.

"Shit," he screamed, trying to dislodge Mama. "Get the hell off me, you stupid little cunt." He finally managed to shake Mama off his back, but she charged and knocked his drunken figure to the floor. Then she commenced pounding his head with the stick. By this time, Clara had recovered enough to realize she'd better put a stop to this before somebody got hurt. It had already gone too far. Others were waking, sitting up, and staring.

Clara sprang to her feet and pulled Mama away. She tried to calm Mama while Massa struggled to get his flabby figure up from the floor. His curly hair was tousled in the back, where Mama had landed the most blows, and he tried to straighten it with his fingers.

"Crazy good-for-nothin' nigger bitch!" he screamed at Mama. "I ought to take your ass out and string it up to a goddamn whipping post."

"You touch my girl again, I'll show you crazy. I'll whip your ass backwards till you won't know which way to shit."

Mama lunged, but Clara held her back. It wasn't easy. She had to hold Mama with both arms and use all her strength. Even though she was taller than Mama now, the woman seemed to possess the strength of a bull seeing red. Clara had never seen her mama like this—hazel eyes blazing, hair sticking up all over her head. Clara was glad to see Aunt Matilda and Aunt Sarah join them, both wielding sticks of their own. The four of them stood in a semicircle facing Mass Todd. Otherwise, no telling what that pig would do to Mama.

All the women in the house had taken to carrying big

sticks to bed in the six years since Mass Jimmy's death. Miss Dolley spent most of her time at the house on Lafayette Square in Washington, D.C., these days, and Mass Todd was supposedly running things now. The truth was that he was usually off somewhere, often for weeks or months at a time. He would leave one or the other of them in charge, usually Aunt Sarah in the house, and then take off without telling them where or when he would be back. Almost all the fields had gone to waste, and the slave quarters and many of the outbuildings were in desperate need of repair. Some of the cabins had simply been abandoned they were in such sorry shape, while two or three families crowded into the rest.

And yet, any of them would probably say that the biggest problems came when Massa was home. They could always hunt for possum and borrow a few seeds from the neighbors. And fruit trees were plentiful around the estate. But when Mass Todd came home, he usually brought along other lowlife—gamblers and drunks—like himself. In the old days, colored women and girls in the big house would move to a cool spot on a lower floor of the mansion to sleep when they wanted to escape the heat in the attic. Not anymore. These days, no one wearing a skirt at Montpelier ever slept alone when Mass Todd and his buddies were around. The place was like a wild frontier.

Still, this attack on Clara was a first. There were rumors of Massa making late-night calls on one or the other women down at the grove. And he was always giving Clara lewd looks that made her want to slap him or run as far away from him as possible, but he'd never so much as touched her until now.

"Woman, you must be crazy, is all I can say," he said, glaring at Mama. "All of you must be crazy." He backed away and tripped over an empty pallet. It took him a few seconds to right himself. "You seem to forget, I own every one of your black asses and I'll do as I damn well please."

"Massa," Mama said, her voice calmer. "She's just a child, barely sixteen. What you want with a child, Massa?"

Mama was lying, since Clara was now nineteen. But that fat old pig wouldn't know the difference. Clara also suspected it wouldn't have mattered to him one way or the other, either. She was nothing more than a piece of property to him anyhow.

"You been drinking, Massa," Aunt Matilda said. "Don't do something you just be sorry for later."

"I got a right to do what I damn well please. I—"

"You ought to be ashamed of yourself, Massa," Aunt Sarah said. "Suppose Miss Dolley hears about this when she comes home? You know she wouldn't like this, not one bit."

At the mention of his mama's name, Mass Todd blinked and straightened his shoulders. Clara had always felt pity for the man. He seemed such a lost soul, with eyes that looked sad even when he smiled. Not anymore. Old fool could die drunk in a ditch for all she cared.

He walked to the top of the stairs and stopped and leaned one hand on the wall for support. Then he turned his head to face them. He raised an arm and pointed a wobbly finger at Mama.

"I want you and that ornery daughter of yours to move to the basement first thing in the morning. You can just sleep down there from now on."

Mama's eyes popped open. So did Clara's. "But, Massa, it's mostly men that sleep down there," Mama said. "You can't—"

"Shut up, bitch." He glared at Mama. "I've made up my mind. Matter of fact, y'all can move on down there tonight for daring to talk back to me."

"Massa, please, we've slept up here long as I can remember," Clara said. "We—"

"Do it. Now. Or I'll sell both of your high-yaller asses

down to New Orleans, and you can fuck a different whoremonger every night. Betcha you'd like that, wouldn't you?" He sneered.

Mama gasped and took a step away from him.

"Hunh? Hunh?" Massa's sneer turned into a smirk. "That shut that black trap of yours right up, didn't it?"

Clara couldn't believe her ears. She wanted to cry but was damned if she'd give this man the satisfaction of seeing her in tears. She took Mama's hand and patted the back of it to calm herself as much as her mama.

"Now, I've had enough of you uppity black bitches for one night. I'm going down to the grove where the real niggers are." With that, he stumbled on down the stairs.

Mama threw her stick down, then grabbed Clara's chin. "Are you all right?"

Clara nodded.

"Answer me when I'm talking to you."

The truth was that Clara was so stunned by it all, she felt numb. But this wasn't the time to tell Mama that. Mama was squeezing her chin so tight it hurt. "Yes, Mama."

"Where did that man touch you?"

Clara frowned. Why was Mama snapping at her? She hadn't done anything wrong. "Just . . . just his mouth was all over my face."

"Are you sure that's all? His hands didn't . . . didn't . . ."

Clara pulled her chin from her mama's grasp. "No, Mama. They were just holding me."

Mama frowned. "Holding you? Where?"

"My hands, Mama, holding my hands down." Mama was so fired up about the whole thing that Clara had put aside her own anguish. Now the moment of the attack came flooding to the surface—his flabby body, his slimy lips, his foul breath. She shuddered as a tear ran down her cheek.

"What are you crying for, if he didn't touch you?" Mama asked.

" 'Cause you . . . *I* didn't do anything wrong, Mama."

"I know that."

"But you act like I did."

"I . . . I . . ." Mama paused, then pulled Clara close and hugged her. "I'm sorry," she said, patting Clara's back. "The thought of that disgusting man touching you makes me so mad."

"Me too, just as much as you. But I'm all right, really."

Mama let out a deep breath. "If he ever tries anything again, you bite, scream, kick, whatever you have to for as long and hard as you can."

Aunt Matilda shook her head. "If Miss Dolley knew about this . . ."

"She wouldn't believe it," Aunt Sarah finished for her. "She's blind and deaf when it comes to that boy. 'Sides, who here would have the nerve to tell her that her son attacked Clara?"

Mama shook her head vigorously. "I don't want anybody saying a word of this to Miss Dolley. Even if she believes it, she might sell us to keep us away from him."

"Sometimes I think being sold would be a better hell than this," Aunt Sarah said.

Mama shook her head firmly. "If we could be sold with our families, maybe. 'Cause it feels like the world is coming to an end around here. But that Mass Todd would split us up just to be spiteful."

"Will he really sell us down to New Orleans if we don't move down to the cellar, Mama?" But Clara knew the answer before she even finished the question. So many of them had been sold since Mass Jimmy's death, she'd lost count. This was way different from when Massa and Missus sold a group of them. Back then, they were asked if they wanted to leave and sold with their families. Not this time. One by one they were being kicked out—from the field, the house—often screaming and begging not to be sold away from their loved ones. And this time it was mostly women.

Clara remembered the day Aunt Nany and her two girls left with a trader from Richmond. The worst part was seeing Mama suffer as her sister was dragged away in a wagon, crying and clinging to her girls, one still a baby in diapers. Their daddy ran all the way over from the Joneses' place, even knowing he'd get flogged good for doing it. Jacob had chased that wagon until he could no longer keep up. There was no telling where Aunt Nany and her girls ended up, or even if they were still together. That had been less than a year ago, and Mama's eyes still got red whenever Aunt Nany's name was mentioned.

They could never agree on how much of a hand Miss Dolley had in all of this. Clara was pretty sure it was as much Miss Dolley's doing as it was Mass Todd's. But Mama said maybe Miss Dolley was just not strong enough to resist her wayward son. Clara thought that deep down inside, Mama really knew that Miss Dolley was a stronger woman than that. Mama just couldn't bring herself to believe Miss Dolley had a hand in all of the wickedness going on around here these days. But Clara wouldn't put it past Miss Dolley for a minute, or any white person for that matter.

Regardless of whose doing it was, the end was the same. Folks who had lived on this land all their lives, whose mamas and daddies had been born here, raised here, and died here, were being expelled right and left. Now Mass Todd was spit-raving mad at her and Mama and had banished them to the basement. Did that mean they would be next to go? Mass Todd almost never had company even when he was home—unless you counted the no-account gamblers who always clung to him like leeches. He was known around the country as a rogue, and respectable white folks would have nothing to do with him if they could help it, even if he was the stepson of a former president and the flesh and blood son of a former first lady. So Mass Todd didn't really have much need for household servants, not the way Mass Jimmy and Miss Dolley had.

Mama saw the look of fear on Clara's face. "Maybe he'll change his mind and let us move back up here once he sobers up," Mama said.

Clara nodded. No point letting Mama know how much she doubted that or how scared she was. It did no good to show her fear, since there wasn't much Mama or anybody else around here could do about it, except worry. And Mama already had enough troubling her these days. They might be hanging on, but it was only by a thread.

It didn't take them long to gather their few belongings. They'd dwindled down to a couple of pallets, a few dresses, and a pair of shoes each. Mama carried her blue bead necklace in an old wooden box and a few other odds and ends. With help from Aunt Sarah, they moved it all in one trip.

They huddled together on one pallet on the cold, damp floor. Clara didn't think she would ever get any sleep down here. If she thought the attic was bad with a few spiders, it was far worse down here with fat water bugs darting about. And she'd heard stories of folks down here being bitten by rats in their sleep. She squeezed her eyes and told herself that if she couldn't see it, it wasn't there.

"Clara," Mama whispered as they hugged each other under the blanket.

Clara opened her eyes. "Yes, Mama?"

"Don't you ever say anything about what happened tonight to your daddy. No good can come of it. It'll just get him mad, and then there's no telling what he'll do."

"I understand, Mama." But she didn't really, didn't even try to. She shut her eyes, again. All she wanted was to hold onto some sanity.

* * *

Miss Dolley would be riding up any minute now. Mass Todd, with his fat and wobbly self, actually looked sober, probably for the first time in months, although Clara wasn't so sure that was a good thing. He had let the place go to pot, not to mention himself. Since the old lady was coming for a visit, he was all in a dither, running about barking orders at them. He'd had them working around the clock for two days to get the house and grounds in shape. He was fussing at Clara now, trying to get her to move faster as she polished the drawing room floor.

"Where's that mama of yours at?" he asked, standing over her.

Clara was bent on all fours in front of the fireplace, rubbing wax onto the hardwood floor. "Upstairs, Massa." She didn't dare look up. She couldn't stand the sight of his pasty old face. Every time he came anywhere near her, he brought memories of that dreadful winter night a few months back. A chill ran up her arms as she scrubbed.

"What the devil is she doing up there?"

"She hasn't been feeling good lately, Massa."

"Always something ailing that woman lately. What's it this time?"

"Stomach problems, Massa."

"Simple nigger."

Fat pig.

He turned on his heels, waddled toward the front entrance, and peered out the windows. Then he waddled back and stood over her. "Can't you move any faster than that, damn it? Mother will be here any minute. We'll never get this place cleaned up in time."

"Yes, Massa," she said and picked up her pace. Fat, ugly, ungrateful old coot. No better than common white trash. If he would stop all that pacing and give the damn polish a chance to set, she'd have been finished a long time ago. Her gaze followed his heels as they scraped across the floor—again. She wanted to grab those big feet and make them stand still. This was his own doing. He had sold half of them away, now he had to work the rest of them like mules. That was why Mama had been feeling so poorly lately. Man worked her too damn hard. Didn't he understand Mama needed rest to get better? Mama was tired. They all were.

She felt a wave of dizziness and sat back on her heels. She had been working too fast and too long, since before sunup. She wiped the sweat from her brow with her arm. The red kerchief wrapped around her head was soaking wet.

Massa stopped in front of her again. "Taking a break, are we? Maybe I ought to go and get that mother of yours to fill in for you?"

Clara bent back over and scrubbed.

"And where's Sarah?"

"Upstairs, Massa," Clara said, barely able to catch her breath between strokes. Scrub, scrub, scrub. Slop jars and stinky sheets. Stained floors and dusty carpets. She was so blessed tired. Every muscle in her body ached. Would she ever live to see a time when these things didn't fill her days from dayclean to daylean?

"Don't tell me she's taken ill, too. Lazy bunch of niggers."

"No, Massa. She's getting Miss Dolley's room ready."

"Oh. Then I'd better go check to make sure she . . ." His heels hurried off in that direction, and Clara mopped behind them. Good-bye, she thought. Good riddance. Now maybe she could get some work done.

They both heard the horses at the same time. Mass Todd stopped in his tracks and turned to the front window. "It's Mother's carriage. Go on." He shooed Clara away with a wave of his hand. "That will have to do for now, pitiful job that it is. Go see if Sarah needs help."

Clara stood and slowly made her way up the back

stairs. But instead of checking on Aunt Sarah, she kept straight on up to the attic. The best thing about Miss Dolley coming home was that Mass Todd had ordered them back up there. He knew as well as they did that Miss Dolley wouldn't approve of them sleeping in that basement. Clara hoped that whatever had been ailing Mama the past couple of months would have a better chance of clearing up now that they were back in a dry space.

She was so tired and so sore that by the time she reached the top floor she had to pause and lean against the wall to catch her breath. Mama was standing and looking out the window. "That Miss Dolley riding up?" she asked as Clara approached her.

"Uh-huh. What are you doing up, Mama? You should be resting."

"Missus will start making her rounds as soon as she gets in, and I don't want her to see me sitting on my fanny doing nothing. Where's that little rug I was mending this morning? I can't seem to remember anything these days."

"It's right over here in the corner, Mama," Clara said as she set the rags and wax on the floor near other cleaning supplies. "But you don't have to do that now. Rest."

"Hush, child, and fetch me the rug." Mama winced and held her stomach as she settled into an old rocking chair near the window.

Clara gave Mama a doubtful look. "Look at you. Can't even move without moaning."

"I'll be fine," Mama said, holding her hands out for the rug. Clara knew better than to argue with the woman once her mind was set. She lifted the small rug and handed it to her along with her needles.

"Place falling apart," Mama muttered under her breath as she stitched. "Some of the rugs worn so thin, your heel scrapes the floor when you walk on them."

Not to mention our clothes, Clara thought as she eyed Mama's worn dress and her own. And our pallets, our shoes, everything. As she draped a tattered blanket over Mama's lap, she noticed that Mama's hands were shaking. They did that a lot these days. Mama could still sew straight but she had to stitch slowly, sometimes ripping the stitches out and starting over.

"That's 'cause Miss Dolley took most of the good things to Washington with her," Clara said.

"Reckon she needs her things up there. Last time Brother Paul came back here with her, he said things not much better up there in Washington. Missus is barely hanging on. If you ask me, the problem is that Mass Todd. He never does anything around here 'cept cause trouble."

"Yes, Mama." Even after all these years and all that had happened around here, Mama could never find much fault with Miss Dolley for anything.

"Why, Missus just sold a piece of land around here trying to make ends meet, to some man named Henry Moncure. Lives over there in Richmond."

Clara frowned and placed her hands on her hips. Sold a piece of Montpelier? The estate was huge. She wasn't sure just how big, but Miss Dolley could sell hundreds of acres and they might never notice it. Still, Mass Jimmy must be turning in his grave. "Now, how do you know that, Mama?"

"Sister Sarah told me. She and Miss Dolley still write letters back and forth."

Clara would never get used to the idea that Aunt Sarah could read and write that good. Aunt Sarah had taught Clara how to write her name and a few other words years ago, but that was about all either of them ever had time for, especially after Mass Jimmy died. So, here she could barely write her name, and Aunt Sarah was writing letters to a white lady. Clara shook her head and smiled. That was better than having magical powers as far as she was concerned.

A wisp of thin gray hair fell in Mama's eyes, and Clara

reached over and brushed it back. Mama smacked her lips. "It's all 'cause of that no-account Todd," Mama said. "Fool man has ruined everything. Brother Paul said he spends Miss Dolley's money faster than she can send it to him. Mind you now, she hasn't got much, and he already spent all the money Congress gave her for Mass Jimmy's papers. Thirty thousand dollars, gone, just like that." Mama fanned her hand in the air for emphasis. "Heaven help us all."

They both quieted down at the sound of the stairs creaking under footsteps. Just as they expected, it was Miss Dolley, wearing a black silk dress. She carried an armful of blue damask fabric that looked like curtains. She might be going through rough times but her clothes were holding up well, Clara thought as she smoothed her tattered apron and stepped forward. Mama stood and leaned on the back of the chair for support.

"Susie, Clara," Miss Dolley said with a smile. "So good to see you both." She was wearing one of the turbans she was famous for, although the color was a bit faded and they had long since gone out of style. Clara noticed that it had a small veil attached to the end of it and she remembered Uncle Paul saying that Miss Dolley's eyesight was failing her.

"Good to see you, too, ma'am," Clara said as she took the fabric from Miss Dolley's hands.

The smile fell from Miss Dolley's face when she took a good look at Mama. "Why, you've lost weight, Susie. Are you eating properly?"

"It's just a little stomach trouble, ma'am."

"I don't like the looks of it," Miss Dolley said. She reached up and touched Mama's forehead with the back of her hand. "What are you taking?"

"Sister Winney fixed me some roots. That helped some."

"We don't have much real medicine around here since you left, Miss Dolley," Clara said.

"I see," Miss Dolley said. "Well, I'm going to ask my doctor to send some calomel over. And if you don't feel better after taking it, promise me you'll have Master Todd send for the doctor if I'm no longer here."

Right, Clara thought. If he does it, that'll be the day.

"Yes, ma'am," Mama said. "I appreciate it, sure do."

"Please, sit back down," Miss Dolley said to Mama. She held the blanket as Mama seated herself, then she tucked it in around Mama's legs. "Now, how are you both doing otherwise?"

"We're doing just fine," Mama said, giving Clara a warning glance. "You don't need to trouble yourself about us, ma'am."

Clara knew exactly what that was all about. Mama didn't want her telling Miss Dolley about Mass Todd attacking her in the middle of the night and then banishing them down to the basement for defending themselves. Or about them not getting much in the way of new clothing and blankets for years now. Or about them getting just enough food to keep from starving. Oh, yeah, Clara thought. She could give Miss Dolley an earful. Their lives had never been worse, and it was so tempting to try to get Miss Dolley to understand their plight.

But Mama was right. Miss Dolley might tuck Mama into her rocking chair and offer to fetch medicine, but she'd never side with them. No matter what her son did, Miss Dolley would always see them as the problem, never her family.

Miss Dolley was looking at Clara and smiling, waiting for her answer. Clara looked at the floor. "We're fine, Missus."

Mama exhaled deeply and patted the blanket in her lap. Miss Dolley's smile broadened. "Good. I know things are probably a bit difficult for you now. But these are trying times everywhere, and Master Todd is doing the best he can under some terrible circumstances. We're really quite fortunate to have him to look out for us now that

Master Jimmy is gone. It's good to hear that you're doing well. I'm so pleased. Sarah said the very same thing just a minute ago and I . . ."

Blah, blah, blah. Clara wanted to laugh and cry at the same time. It was impossible to keep a straight face, so she gritted her teeth and focused on the floor. Trying times, her foot—which was what she'd like to plant in Mass Todd's rear end. The problem was him, not the times. But Miss Dolley couldn't see that, or maybe she didn't want to.

"Now, I have a bit of news," Miss Dolley said. "Despite my son's tireless efforts, we are still struggling and coming up short. So I've decided to sell more land to Mr. Moncure and allow him to rent part of the house. . . ."

Mama gasped and put her needles down in her lap.

"Yes, Susie, I shudder to think of anyone other than Madisons living under the roof here at Montpelier. But it's the only way to hold on to the rest of the land. Mr. Moncure will stay in the old part of the house, where Master Jimmy's mother lived before she passed away."

"Will he be bringing family with him, ma'am?" Clara asked.

"I think his family will stay in Richmond and New Orleans, for the time being anyway. He shouldn't be much of a burden to any of you, as he'll have servants of his own with him. In fact, he's decided to purchase a few from me. But the rest of you will remain here just as you are, under Master Todd's care."

Clara sighed. The devil you know is better than the one you don't, she supposed.

Miss Dolley pointed to the drapes in Clara's arms. "Now, for more mundane matters. My drawing room curtains in Washington need mending, and my eyesight has failed me miserably. I can't tolerate much light at all, and I can't possibly sew without light." She laughed gaily.

Mama smiled and Clara tried her best to do the same. "I'm real sorry to hear that, ma'am," Mama said.

"So, where is Nany?" Miss Dolley asked. "I haven't seen her and I want to get her started on them right away, as I'll be here for only a few weeks."

Clara and Mama exchanged looks. No one was ever sure just how much Miss Dolley knew about the goings-on at Montpelier. Mama said it was hard to believe she would allow them to be sold away from their families and life-long friends. But Clara thought it just as hard to think that Mass Todd would sell them without telling his mama. After all, they belonged to Miss Dolley.

"Nany's gone, Missus," Mama said softly.

Miss Dolley frowned. "Gone where?"

"Mass Todd sold her, Missus," Clara said, watching Miss Dolley closely. "Her and her girls, and some of the others."

Miss Dolley's mouth dropped open.

"You didn't know, did you, ma'am?" Mama asked.

"Not . . . not about Nany, no. Oh, dear." She blinked. "Who did he sell them to?"

"We don't even know, Miss Dolley," Mama said. She sounded hopeful that Miss Dolley would try to find them, maybe even bring them home. Clara didn't want Mama getting her hopes up only to have them dashed, but she could understand. She couldn't help feeling a little hopeful herself.

"I must see him about this right away," Miss Dolley said. She walked toward the stairs, then stopped like she'd just remembered something else. "Susie, with Nany gone I'll need you to mend the curtains for me. There are more downstairs. You can get them from Sarah."

Now Clara's mouth dropped open. Miss Dolley knew Mama was dreadful sick. The last thing Mama needed was to be bending over some heavy old drapes morning and night. "But, Miss Dolley, Mama—"

"How soon will you be needing them, ma'am?" Mama asked, interrupting Clara.

"Oh, in a few weeks. And I brought several gowns that need mending, too. The balls are endless in Washington, and I can't afford new ones, unfortunately."

"Fine, Miss Dolley," Mama said.

Clara watched in stunned silence as Miss Dolley walked to the top of the stairs, her face the picture of complete content. In no time at all, Miss Dolley's expression had changed from one of distress at Aunt Nany's predicament to one of delight at the thought of dresses and dances. It didn't take much for her to cast aside poor Aunt Nany's fate for something she no doubt found much more pleasant. Miss Dolley was as bad as Mass Todd in her own way. She might talk sweet when it served her purpose, but she was blind to anything she didn't want to see. She didn't care anything about any of them. She was just another selfish mistress.

"Are you losing your mind?" Clara said as soon as Miss Dolley's footsteps died on the stairs. Mama stood and took the curtains from Clara's arms, then walked to a long wood table backed against the wall. Clara followed her. "You can't do all that work. You're sick. And I can't help. With her here, Massa will be working me day and night."

"We don't have much choice," Mama said, sorting through the curtains. "She wants these mended, and Nany's not here. Everybody else has got a heap of work to do already or else they don't know anything about sewing curtains. That leaves me."

Clara clenched her fists. It was all so frustrating. Mama should be resting in a feather bed like Miss Dolley would if she got sick. Instead, Mama had to work her tail off and grab whatever time she could on a hard pallet. Sometimes she seemed to be fading right before Clara's eyes, getting weaker and thinner by the week. And Mass Todd and Missus couldn't care less.

Clara suddenly understood the Nat Turners and the Gabriel Prossers of the world. She understood why the slaves who were closest to their massas were often the ones to strike out the most viciously. It was like dangling a bag of candy in front of a child and telling her she could only have pot-licker, day after day. Sooner or later, that child was going to snatch that candy any way she could.

"Do you think she'll try to get Nany back?" Mama asked.

Hell, no, Clara thought. She'll talk to Massa, might even scold him a bit, but that will be about it. Then she'll pack her bags and head on back to Washington, D.C. A couple of fancy society balls and her poor servants back at the plantation will be long forgotten. It was all Clara could do to keep from bursting out in tears right there on the spot. But she didn't want Mama giving up all hope, even if she had none left herself. Mama needed her strength to get well. She shrugged. "Maybe, Mama. We'll . . ."

Suddenly Mama grabbed her stomach and leaned over the table and winced. Clara took a step toward her. "Sit down, Mama. See? You can't be—"

Mama waved her away. "Hush, child. I'll be fine soon as I catch my breath." She inhaled deeply and forced herself to stand up straight. "I know what I'm doing," Mama said. "Or do you want to end up like your Aunt Nany?"

Clara sighed. What the hell difference did it make? Would working hard and trying to be angels for white folks really save them in the end? And save them for what? More of this? If this was what they were saving themselves for, then maybe they were better off somewhere else or even dead.

"Why do you always do this, Mama? No matter what she does, you take up for her or at least go along with her. You never stand up to her. You just . . ."

"I'm not taking up for her. I just think I understand her 'cause she's a woman. Most of the things that go on around here are not her doing. It's that Mass Todd, and before that it was Mass Jimmy. They the ones that make all the decisions. It's like that at all these places around here."

Clara shook her head. "She may be a woman, but she's white first when it comes to us. She's got more say in what goes on around here than you know, especially now. She just hides her evil ways behind Massa's britches."

7

They should have known better than to try to fool Daddy. Right after Miss Dolley returned to the Federal City, somebody, somewhere, told Daddy that Mass Todd attacked his daughter. The news that Daddy was fit to be tied reached Clara and Mama long before he did, and Mama was worried sick about what he might do. But Clara was relieved that Daddy finally knew. It was hard keeping something like that from him. Whenever he mentioned Mass Todd's name around her, she would have to look away. But Daddy wasn't stupid; he knew something was troubling her.

She began to wonder if it was good that Daddy knew, though, the day he came charging down the path on Prince. Clara and Mama were in the yard near the kitchen doing the laundry along with other women. In the old days, Massa and Missus had had several women who did nothing but laundry, but Mass Todd sold them all and ordered those remaining to take care of the laundry from now on. Since Mama still had stomach pains from time to time, Clara lugged the baskets full of dirty linen and clothing up the stairs from the basement and out to the yard, while Mama stirred the linen in a big copper cauldron sitting over an open fire. She used a big wood stick, and Aunt Sarah used another stick to move them to a separate pot to cool off.

The minute Clara saw Daddy galloping up on Prince, she knew something was dreadfully wrong. She stopped dead in her tracks, with a laundry basket resting on her hip. It was Thursday, and Daddy hardly ever came to Montpelier during the middle of the week and never rode hard like that around the big house. If he brought Prince up to the house at all it was always in a trot or leading him by the reins. Usually he tied Prince out by the gate.

As soon as Daddy reached the side of the mansion, he jumped down and ran toward them, stirring up a cloud of dirt with his riding boots. He practically knocked Aunt Sarah off her feet as he brushed past her.

"Why you didn't tell me what that fool done to Clara?" he shouted as he stomped up to Mama. "Everybody in the whole damn county knew but me. And I'm her daddy!"

He was shouting so loud that the other women working in the yard stopped and stared. Clara had never heard Daddy screaming at Mama like that, and her heart dived to her stomach. But Daddy didn't even seem to know anybody else was there. Mama lowered her stick and wiped the sweat off her brow, then she looked up at him. "I didn't tell you 'cause I knew you would get to acting crazy, just like you're doing now. And there was no use in—"

"What the hell you 'spect?" Daddy shouted as he paced back and forth in front of the steaming laundry pot. "Ugly-assed white bastard all over my daughter. What the hell do you 'spect me to do? Roll over and play dead?"

"No, Walker," Mama said. "But there's not a heap more you can do 'sides get mad. I was trying to spare you."

"Don't spare me nothing, woman. What the hell did that bastard do to her?"

Clara dropped the basket on the grass and ran up to him. She reached out to touch his arm, but he yanked it away, never taking his eyes off Mama. "Tell me what he did to her."

"I don't think you need to know all that, Walker," Mama

said, shaking her head. "There's nothing you can—"

Daddy grabbed Mama's arm. "Tell me, damn it. I heard he was all up on top her. Jumped on her while she was sleeping. That true?"

Mama swallowed. She seemed to be trying to buy some time. "Who told you that?"

"What difference does that make who told me? All I want to know is, is it true?" He looked at Clara. " 'Cause if it is . . ." He pounded a fist in the palm of his hand. "Is it?"

Clara looked at Mama, not sure what to say, but Mama looked just as helpless. Clara looked at Daddy. "Yes, Daddy, but . . ."

Daddy grabbed the wooden stick from Mama's hand and slammed it against the copper pot. The stick broke in two like a piece of straw, and hot water splashed all over the sides of the pot. Mama and Clara had to jump back to keep from being scalded.

"Where is that sick bastard?" Daddy yelled. He threw the broken end of the stick down and punched his palm with his fist again. "I'll choke him teetotally dead with my bare hands."

"Daddy, Mama and them put a stop to it before anything really bad happened. I'm all right."

"Ain't no grown man got no business messing 'round with a kid like that. Where is he?"

"Jesus, Walker," Mama said. "You got to calm yourself. What the devil do you think you're going to do to Mass Todd anyhow? Not a blessed thing, and you know it."

"I ain't going to touch him, bad as I want to knock that pale-assed drunken head off his shoulders. But I'm gonna talk to him, you can bet your bottom dollar on that. If he thinks he can get away with this, what's to stop him from doing it again? Huh?"

Mama took a deep breath but kept her mouth shut.

"Now you going to tell me where he is, or do I have to run through every damn room of that house up there?"

"He's not here," Mama said. "And even if he was, I'm not fool enough to tell you where."

"You lying. But that's all right. I'll find him myself." Daddy whirled around in the direction of the house.

"Daddy, don't. Mama's not lying. He's not here." It was true. Mass Todd had taken off on a long trip that weekend, right after Miss Dolley left. Thank the Lord, Clara thought. She didn't even want to think what might have happened if Massa was in the house and Daddy confronted him. A part of her wished Daddy could give that old fart a good licking, but she knew that would only be asking for more trouble in the end. Mass Todd was the stupidest, dumbest, craziest fool in Virginia, and everybody around here, black and white, knew it. But he was still a white man, a massa. He had banished them to the cellar for protecting themselves, and he made them go right back down there the day Miss Dolley left. Her carriage hadn't even gotten to the end of the path before he came after them. Clara shuddered just thinking what he would do to Daddy if Daddy said one word to him in anger. With luck, by the time Massa returned, they would have gotten Daddy to come to his senses.

Something was always happening that made Clara think it had to be the worst thing that would ever happen. Was there no end?

The day Daddy came to them with the news that he was running had to top everything else. Running—as in up North, slave catchers, and bloodhounds. Mass Todd was still halfway around the world for all she knew, yet even from there he was putting a hex on their lives.

In no time at all, word had gotten around that Daddy came charging over to Montpelier looking for Mass Todd. A few days later, Daddy's massa called him into his office and asked if it was true. Daddy didn't deny it, said he was waiting for Mass Todd to return from his trip and then planned to warn the man to stay away from his daughter. Mass Bell took Daddy's horse right there on the spot, and the next day he took Daddy's job as the family driver and ordered him out to the tobacco fields. Mass Bell said he couldn't have one of his niggers running around threatening white folks without being punished. A couple of days later, a slave in the Bell household warned Daddy that Mass Bell was talking about selling him.

"Only reason I never ran before was 'cause of you and your mama," Daddy said, touching Clara's cheek as the three of them huddled together in the moonlight near the door leading to the cellar. He had stopped there to say good-bye.

"They done took away my horse and put me in the fields and I put up with that. But if they fixing to sell me away from you and your mama . . ." He paused and shook his head. "There ain't no use in me staying."

Clara was crying so hard as she clung to Daddy that she could hardly catch her breath. Lord, have mercy. Rip her guts out. Chain her to a post and beat her to a pulp. But please, not this. She might never see her daddy again.

"I tried to get you to calm down that day," Mama said, her sobs muffled by Daddy's chest. "Wouldn't listen to me, with your stubborn self." They were both trying not to cry too loudly. Mass Todd was still away, and since it was almost midnight everybody was asleep. But running demanded the utmost secrecy, even from other coloreds. "Don't do this, Walker," Mama said. "What if they catch you?"

"I'll be all right. I know these woods better than most. I'll head over to the docks down at Norfolk. Heard some of them Yankee captains will stow us away. If I can just get up to New York, I should be set."

"That's a long walk," Mama protested. "What about the pattyrollers?"

"And alligators and snakes?" Clara said. If anything scared her more than not seeing him again or that the bloodhounds would catch him, it was that some wild swamp animal would eat him alive.

"Ain't no alligators up this far north, sugar," Daddy said. "I been around these parts enough to know that. Maybe a few snakes, and them bloodhounds on my trail, but I got me this." He pulled a sack full of grave-dirt potion from his pants pocket and said Aunt Winney made it for him. She'd told him to rub it on his feet to throw the dogs off scent. "And I got me this." He reached into the pocket of his overcoat and pulled out a big knife. Mama had just stolen that from Aunt Matilda's cupboard.

"Run with me," Daddy said as he tucked the knife back into his overcoat.

Clara's heart leaped at those words. She had heard of other families running together before. And unlike a lot of runaways who didn't know what they were doing, Daddy knew these parts well from all his years driving the Bells around. But Mama shook her head. "I can't. I'm too sick to do all that walking."

"I know these parts like the back of my hand," Daddy said. "And I got people that will help us along the way."

"Mama, maybe if Daddy and me help you."

"And if we stop a lot . . ."

Mama shook her head firmly. "It's dangerous enough without somebody slowing you down like I would."

They got real quiet, because they knew that Mama spoke the truth.

"Clara," Mama said, finally breaking the silence. "If you want to go . . ." Mama paused and took a deep breath. "You're big enough now. And this may be the only real chance you ever have to get away from here. You always did talk about it."

Clara stared at Mama. She was so stunned she couldn't speak. She couldn't believe Mama was even thinking about letting her go. For a fleeting moment, her heart leaped with joy. But she soon realized that she could never leave Mama here alone, especially now that she was sick. Yes, she thought about freedom every blessed day of her life, so much sometimes that it felt like she could taste it or smell it or reach out and hug it. But Mama was more precious to her than anything, even freedom. Maybe she would get another chance someday. Maybe not. But running without Mama was out of the question. She shook her head. "I'm not leaving you, Mama."

"Clara, you—"

Clara tightened her lips and shook her head. "No. That's final and there's no use talking about it anymore."

Mama quieted down and clasped Clara's hand.

Daddy smiled understandingly at them, even though it was a sad smile. Then he gave Mama a long kiss good-bye. He turned to Clara and took her head into both hands and kissed her on the forehead. "If I make it . . ." He paused and set his jaw firmly. "After I get up there and get settled, I'll come back for you. I promise you that."

Clara nodded. As Daddy rubbed her arms, she studied his face hungrily in the moonlight. She wanted to remember every wrinkle, every contour, and its exact shade of brown.

"Look at my baby," he said. "All grown now. You look after your mama, hear, sugar?" He was smiling but his voice cracked at the end, and Clara knew she dare not try to speak.

They stood arm in arm as he ran off and watched until he disappeared among the trees. That was when Mama broke down. She'd been sobbing softly all along but now she bawled like a baby. Clara realized Mama had been holding it in, so Daddy wouldn't feel so bad about leaving them behind.

"All he did was what any daddy would do," Mama said between sobs. "Tried to defend his daughter's honor. But they don't think we have any of that anyhow."

Clara sniffed. A part of her wanted to cry out, too, but

mostly she felt numb. She stared at the path Daddy had just taken. She couldn't believe her daddy had just run off and might never come back.

"He doesn't deserve this," Mama said.

Clara looked at Mama. She'd never seen Mama's hazel eyes looking so sad.

"Times have changed around here so much," Mama said, shaking her head as she looked at the ground. Her voice was soft, almost as if she was talking to herself. "Whole world is coming to an end. I don't know how to act half the time. Sometimes I feel so sick and tired of it all, I'm not even sure I want to go on."

Clara frowned. "What are you talking about, Mama?"

Mama sighed long and deep. "Oh, child, I'm not about to do anything foolish. Still, you wait hand and foot on these people all your life but they don't give a damn about you. Why the hell do we do it?"

Clara swallowed hard. It was a question she asked herself every day of her life, but she was surprised to hear Mama talking this way. Mama, whose faith never seemed to let up no matter what these white folks did. They had finally gotten to Mama.

Mama took Clara's hand and led her back into the house and down to the cellar. She walked straight to the box where she kept her blue beads. "Here," Mama said as she draped them around Clara's neck. "I want you to have these. For all I know, they'll take you away from me one of these days, and that's all I got for you to remember me by."

Clara touched the beads and shook her head at the same time. "Never. I'm never going to let them do that."

Mama squeezed her hand and tried to smile. "You just remember. No matter what happens, even if one of us ends up down there in Louisiana or Georgia somewhere, they can never separate our spirits. They can't touch that. You hear?"

Clara nodded. "Yes, Mama."

8

They had two massas now, Clara thought wryly as she stripped the sheets from Mass Henry's bed, and twice as much work to do. Mass Henry had moved into the wing of the house where Mass Jimmy's mama stayed before she passed away. Mass Todd didn't care much what the big house looked like until Miss Dolley was set to visit, but Mass Henry liked his things neat and clean all the time. So now they had the whole mansion to look after with half as many slaves to do it. She was so damn tired all the damn time, Clara thought as she paused to wipe the sweat from her forehead. She balled up the dirty sheets and dropped them in a heap on the floor.

And if that wasn't bad enough, the massas hated each other and hardly ever stayed at Montpelier at the same time. Mass Henry was some kind of merchant in Richmond and his business took him back there often. But the main reason was simply that they couldn't stand the sight of each other. No surprise in that, since they were about as different as night and day. Mass Henry was a family man, with a wife and several children living in Richmond. Mass Todd was, well, there was no word in the English language to adequately describe such vermin, Clara thought.

Mass Todd detested the idea of another man renting a part of "his" house, and he did whatever he could to make life miserable for Mass Henry. He got especially piqued whenever he found any of the house servants tidying Mass Henry's wing. But Mass Henry treated them a lot better, so they were always slipping over to his wing to help out. Mass Henry had been shocked to learn that Clara and Mama slept in the cellar, and whenever he was there he insisted that they move back up to the attic. Then Mass Todd would pitch a fit as soon as he came home and send them back down to the dungeon.

Still, Mass Henry was a massa, and Clara trusted him only so far. Anyone who believed they could let their guard down because they thought they had a kind massa was a damn fool as far as she was concerned. She had once thought Miss Dolley and Mass Jimmy were "kind." Ha! Look how they turned out. It was like saying the devil was kind because he grinned while you burned in hell.

She opened a clean sheet and shook it across the bed. Mass Todd was always finding something to pick a fight about with Mass Henry, especially when he got drunk, which was about as often as a pig squeals. Clara suspected that was why Mass Henry didn't bring his family around more often. If Mass Todd was in a particularly foul mood, Mass Henry would cut his visits short, just as he had last night when Mass Todd came back from one of his long trips. Clara once overheard one of Mass Henry's guests call Mass Todd a "serpent in the Garden of Eden."

As if to remind Clara of that truth, the fat pig burst through the bedroom doorway. Clara jumped back a foot. He had never tried anything since that dreadful night two years ago, but he still scared the bejesus out of her.

He grabbed Clara by the wrist and yanked her right up to his face. She could smell the liquor on his breath and it wasn't even noon yet. Her heart took a dive as she realized in a flash that this part of the house was isolated, and no one would hear her screams. But he shoved her toward the door.

"Go downstairs to the front lawn and wait with the others."

Clara frowned. "What?"

"You gone deaf now?"

"No, Massa. It's just that the bed is—"

He threw his hands in the air. "Then get the hell on out of here. Where's Susie?"

"Mama's upstairs, Massa. But she's too sick to—"

Before Clara could finish, he waddled past her and down the hall toward the attic stairs. Clara followed close on his heels. "Massa, what you want with Mama. She's—"

He whirled around and shoved her so hard she fell flat on her tail. "Didn't I tell you to get the hell on outside and wait until I get there?" He turned and took the stairs two at a time, huffing and puffing with each step. She froze, not knowing what to do. Massa was always having these outbursts, especially when he'd had too much to drink, but this was strange even for him. She wanted to follow him up the stairs and try to protect Mama. Lord knew Mama was sicker than ever. Mass Henry had sent for the doctor when he was here, and he bled Mama and told her to rest. But Clara knew that if she disobeyed Massa Todd's orders to go outside, he would get even madder at the both of them.

She stood up and slipped quietly to the bottom of the stairs and strained to hear. She hated it when this man was home. The only reason she didn't run away was because of Mama. And the day Mama passed on was the day she was leaving. Mass Todd was a serpent all right, but this was no Garden of Eden. This was hell.

Suddenly she heard two sets of footsteps at the top of the stairs. She turned and flew down the hallway and across the front parlor. She ran out the door, across the portico, and down the stairs. She was startled to see Uncle Paul, probably here to pick up some things and carry them back to Washington for Miss Dolley, and Aunts Sarah, Matilda, Winney, and the other Montpelier slaves all huddled together at the bottom of the stairs. She was also struck by how few there were compared to the last gathering on the lawn, shortly after Mass Jimmy died. Why, there must be fewer than half as many, maybe fifty at the most. They were all squinting against the hot afternoon sunlight as they stared up at the mansion.

"What does he want now?" Clara asked no one in particular.

Aunt Sarah shook her head. "We don't know any more than you do."

"Lord have mercy," Aunt Matilda said. "Man is losing his mind." She was still holding a wooden spoon from the kitchen.

"He done lost it a long time ago," Aunt Winney said. She was leaning so hard on her stick cane, that Clara wondered how she managed to walk all the way up the hill from Walnut Grove.

They hushed and looked up as Mass Todd strode out and flopped down the steps. Mama lagged behind him, struggling to keep up. Clara ran up to help her just as the sound of a horse and wagon floated down the driveway. They all turned in that direction.

"I want you all to back up here," Mass Todd said. "Go on, back up there now." He held his arms out, palms up, and backed them under a weeping willow.

Clara watched anxiously, her heart beating faster as the wagon drew nearer. Thoughts of slave traders popped into her head, but she quickly forced them out. It didn't make sense for Massa to sell all of them at once. Even he wasn't that crazy, was he?

The wagon stopped just outside the gate, and Mass Jimmy's brother William Madison and a strange white man jumped down. Clara was relieved to see Mass William. At least he wasn't what she and the others dreaded seeing most. But as Mass William and the other man entered the gate, Clara grew uneasy. There was something about Mass William's face. He never looked happy around Mass Todd—not many sober folks did—but on this morning Mass William looked mad enough to spit in somebody's face. He stopped inside the gate and folded his arms across his chest, while the other white man walked right up to them and stood beside Mass Todd.

Clara looked from Mass William to Mass Todd, trying to get a fix on what this was all about. The two men avoided looking at each other, and Clara thought that if all the other folks weren't around, the two would have struck blows by now.

Mass Todd gestured in the direction of the other white man. "This here is the sheriff. He's come to look you all over, except for Paul."

A buzz flew through the crowd. "What for?" someone hollered from behind Clara. "Look at what, Massa?"

Mass Todd raised his hand to quiet them. "I want all of you to know that this is none of my doing. Mr. Madison here . . ." He paused and gestured toward Mass William, still standing over by the gate. "He's taking my mother and me to court, trying to get hold of some of our land. And as a result of these unfortunate actions, you've been seized by the sheriff. . . ."

The buzz grew louder. "What that mean, Massa?"

"Does that mean us gon' be sold?" someone shouted above the noise.

The crowd grew so quiet as they waited for an answer that Clara was sure they could all hear her heart thumping. She clutched Mama's hand as the sheriff stepped forward.

"What that means is this," the sheriff said. "You've been taken by the court. Now you won't have to do anything for the time being. Carry on around here just like you always have. But if these two here can't settle their differences before the next court date, then, well, I'll have to auction you off."

The screams were loud enough to be heard on the other side of the Blue Ridge mountains. Clara gasped. "Lord have mercy."

Aunt Sarah screamed. Aunt Matilda began to sob.

"Lawdy, Massa, you ain't gon' let 'em take us, is you?" Aunt Winney shouted, waving her cane in the air.

Clara realized her mouth was hanging open and she covered it with her hand. Bad as things were around here these days, she had prayed it would never come to this. She didn't give a rat's ass about leaving this place. What scared her was being separated from Mama, Aunt Sarah, and the others.

She turned and looked at Mama, so thin and frail. They had never heard anything from Daddy in all the months since he'd run, and Mama's eyes had long since lost their sparkle. Even now she just stood there, staring straight ahead, her face devoid of expression. It was as if she had given up completely, totally, finally. "Lord almighty," Clara said under her breath. She squeezed Mama's hand. These were some dark days, but somebody had to keep fighting.

"What about our families, Massa?" Clara shouted to be heard above the others. "Can't you at least sell us together?"

Massa ignored the question as he did all the others being thrown at him. The sheriff raised both hands, trying to calm them. "Now I need to take a head count here, so I want—"

All hell broke loose. Aunt Matilda hollered and threw the spoon in her hand on the ground. Then she broke away from the crowd and ran around the side of the mansion toward the kitchen. A couple of other women ran down toward the grove. Mass Todd shouted for them to come back but they ignored him. He fumed and stomped and was about to chase after them when Aunt Sarah grabbed hold of his arm. "Massa, please. Don't do this. This is our home. We all—"

He snatched his arm away. "Get off me. This ain't my doing. Didn't I just tell you that?" He pushed her hard, and she fell on the ground. Clara let go of Mama's hand and went to help Aunt Sarah up, but she refused to budge.

"I can't believe you would allow this, Massa," Aunt Sarah said, her tears falling on the grass. "Please. I beg you, don't do this. We've waited on your family hand and foot all our lives. Massa, please don't do this."

Clara dropped down on her knees and clasped her hands together. "If you have to sell us, Massa, sell us with our families. Please. Can you just do that?"

"I can't promise you anything. It's out of my hands and—"

"Whose hands is it in, Massa?" Clara asked.

Mass Todd grunted and he and the sheriff walked back to where Mass William stood in silence. Clara stood and helped Aunt Sarah up as the slaves who hadn't run off watched and waited in silence. Clara stood between Aunt Sarah and Mama, shaking like a leaf. Uncle Paul stood close behind them. After a few minutes, the sheriff came back and stood before them. Mass Todd and Mass William stayed at the gate, standing several feet apart. "Nothing is going to happen now," the sheriff said. "So you can all just go on back to work until further notice."

Work? How the hell did he expect them to get any work done now? Clara thought, as she watched the sheriff and Mass William climb into their wagon. If she had a gun she'd shoot them right then and there. All three of them. She didn't care what they did to her. The only thing that stopped her from lashing out now was knowing that Mama . . . Something told her to turn and look just as Mama swayed. Clara and Uncle Paul caught her together. Uncle Paul lifted her limp body and carried it around the house toward the door leading to the cellar.

My *mistress,*

I don't like to send you bad news, but the condition of all of us, your servants, is very bad, and we do not know whether you are acquainted with it. The sheriff has taken all of us and says he will sell us at next court unless something is done before to prevent it. We are afraid we shall be bought by what are called Negro buyers and sent away from our husbands and wives. If we are obliged to be sold perhaps you could get neighbors to buy us that have husbands and wives, so as to save us from misery which will in a greater or less degree be sure to fall on us at being separated from you as well as from one another. We are very sure you are sorry for this state of things and we do not like to trouble you with it but think, my dear mistress, what our sorrow will be. The sale is only a fortnight from next Monday but perhaps you could make some bargain with somebody by which we could be kept together.

Sarah,

July 5, 1844

They huddled together in the yellow glow of a lone candle as Aunt Sarah read the letter aloud for the third time. At the end, she paused and looked around the kitchen table at each of them—Clara, Mama, Uncle Paul, Aunt Matilda—as they nodded in consent. She gently lifted the paper and blew on it to dry the ink. Then she handed it across the table to Uncle Paul.

"If this doesn't get Miss Dolley to do something, then . . ." Aunt Sarah's voice trailed off as Uncle Paul read the letter to himself once more. Aunt Sarah couldn't bring herself to finish the sentence, but she didn't need to. Uncle Paul looked up, nodded, and handed the letter back to Aunt Sarah. He rubbed his eyes as she folded it and placed it in an envelope. Then she sealed it with wax and handed it back to him.

"I'll make sure she gets it," Uncle Paul said.

Clara reached over and touched Mama's hand. Mama had insisted on staying up for this, as late as it was. "Are you all right, Mama?"

Mama grunted. "Don't trouble yourself about me. Didn't think I'd ever get over it when they took your daddy away from me, but I'm still here." She sighed. "I could survive that, I reckon I can survive anything."

Clara nodded, and they all joined hands and bowed their heads as Aunt Matilda led them in prayer.

9

Clara hoisted the laundry basket high up on her hips and stepped down the rickety stairs leading out of the wash house. She had spent the morning scrubbing Mass Henry's clothes and rinsing them in a pot of steaming hot water. Now they were ready to be hung to dry. As she crossed the yard on her way to the clothesline, she could hear little girls laughing and singing down at the grove, and she remembered a rhyme she used to sing many years ago.

My old mistress promised me,
Before she died she would set me free . . .

She shook her head. The rest of the rhyme slipped her mind but it was just as well. Life at Montpelier had changed so dramatically since those bygone days. Mass Jimmy was long gone and Miss Dolley, although still living, had sold all of Montpelier and most of the slaves to Mass Henry not long after getting Aunt Sarah's letter. She kept Aunt Sukey and Paul Jennings and a few others for herself.

Mama always said they had a lot to be thankful for.

Miss Dolley had cared at least enough to sell what was left of them to a decent massa. And Clara was thankful. She just thought the old woman's motives were a little less kindly. Indeed, Miss Dolley was probably damn glad to be rid of them. Since Mass Jimmy died, it was no doubt that this place had become a drain on her time and her money, especially the way Mass Todd had run it. She'd probably only held on as long as she did because she knew how dear this place had been to Mass Jimmy and his family. Clara would have been willing to bet her last cent that a good part of Miss Dolley was relieved to have finally washed her hands of it, and of them.

The biggest changes, though, had come from within herself. She was a long way from the naive little girl who didn't really know what it meant to be a slave, and when she finally realized it, was stupid enough to wish for freedom. She shook her head. Some days it took every ounce of willpower she could summon to keep going. But she had to be strong for Mama and the others. Those little girls singing that song would come to realize all that in due time. And then they would have precious little to sing about.

Clara was just about to set the basket on the ground when she heard a horse galloping toward her. She whirled around to see Mass Todd as he rode up dangerously close to her. The horse reared its front legs, and she dropped the basket and jumped back. Lord almighty. Fool man. She covered her breasts with her hands. Mass Todd, looking fatter and drunker than ever, laughed and pulled his horse back. For a minute, she thought he was going to fall off, he was so drunk. "Nice dress you're wearing there, Clara."

Drunken fool wasn't worth a fart in a whirlwind. He shouldn't even be here. He didn't own this place anymore. Because of his shoddy management of Montpelier, their lives were ruined. For the first time in years, she had on a halfway decent dress, no thanks to him. She backed farther away and, in the folds of her skirt, made a fist with her hand. He couldn't see it, but if he dared to get down off that horse and come anywhere near her, he would damn sure feel it.

He made a move to do just that—get down from his horse—but was so drunk and fat, he had trouble lifting his rump. She turned to flee and bumped smack into Squire May, the driver who had replaced Daddy on the Bell plantation, as he rounded the corner of the laundry house. He was whistling, but the tune fell quickly from his lips. Judging from the look on his chocolate-colored face, Clara imagined he probably had a pretty good idea that something fishy was going on here. He glanced down at the basket and laundry strewn over the yard and rubbed his dark beard. For a fleeting moment, Clara worried about what he might do. Everybody in these parts knew that Mass Todd had attacked her. They also knew that her daddy had to run after going up against the white folks in trying to defend his daughter. She hoped Squire wasn't about to do anything foolish.

"Mornin', Massa," Squire said, nodding in his direction.

Mass Todd squared himself in the saddle and grunted. Squire turned to face Clara. "Morning, Sister Clara. Everything all right here?"

"Things just fine," Clara said.

Squire bent over to pick up the laundry basket and handed it to her, then he scooped up some of the laundry. "You need help with this, I reckon."

"Thank you, Brother Squire," Clara said. She kept an eye on Mass Todd as she gathered the rest of the laundry, but he was so busy draining a bottle of liquor, he seemed to have forgotten all about her.

Mass Todd grunted some more, put the bottle back in his pocket, and galloped off. Clara exhaled deeply.

"What's that fool doing hanging around here anyhow?" Squire said, finally letting the agitation show on his face.

"I reckon he came to bother Mass Henry about something. They still fighting over this land, even though the law says it's Mass Henry's now."

Squire shook his head. "You shouldn't be walking around here by yourself as long as he still comes about. Send for me, I'll come look out for you."

"I got to move around to get my work done, and I can't send for you every time I leave the house. But don't you worry about me. I can take care of myself."

Over the past several weeks, she had come to know this man—tall, proud, handsome, and dark as the night. And he made no secret of the fact that he was sweet on her. But she wasn't having any of it. No amount of pride in a black man would help her fight off these white beasts. She had to do that herself. She had learned that when her daddy tried it.

"You just be careful then," he said. "You fixing to come to the fish fry down at the grove tonight?"

"I don't have time for that nonsense, Brother Squire. And you know better than to ask."

"Pretty gal like you ought to get out and have some fun sometimes," he said stubbornly.

Clara shook her head. "You wasting your time if you trying to get me to change my mind. It's made up."

Squire smiled. "Now, Sister Clara, you knows I been trying for the longest time to court you. How am I gon' do that if you ain't never around?"

Clara couldn't help but smile in return. If there was one thing this Squire was not, it was bashful. But he didn't understand. With everything going on around here she couldn't even think about falling in love with someone from another plantation, or anyone for that matter. Look what it had done to her daddy and her mama. Look what happened to Aunt Nany and Jacob. No thanks. She would concentrate on taking care of her mama and herself. Lord knew that was hard enough to do anyhow.

"I know no such thing," she said. "Don't want to know it, neither." She lifted the basket onto her hips and turned toward the clothesline.

"Guess I'm going to have to mosey on down there and get Sister Winney to gimme one of her love potions then."

Clara chuckled and shook her head as she walked away. "You're wasting your time, foolish man. Don't say I didn't warn you."

"You let me be the judge of that," Squire called after her.

If he knew the whole truth, he wouldn't waste so much time on her, Clara thought, as she pinned the clothes on the line. She wasn't about to let herself fall into that trap called love. She would manage just fine without all that nonsense.

She picked up the empty basket and went inside the big house. It was getting harder and harder to climb all these stairs, she thought as she made the trip from the basement to the attic for what must have been the tenth time that day. She wasn't so sure of her age anymore—twenty-one; twenty-two—but she knew she was too young to always be so damn tired.

She reached the attic and headed for the window overlooking the front lawn, where she knew Mama was watching the comings and goings at Montpelier. Mama smiled when she saw Clara. "How you feeling today, Clara?"

"Fine, Mama," Clara said as she fussed with the blanket in Mama's lap. As soon as she finished looking in on Mama, she would head back down and finish her chores. She had floors to polish and furniture to dust, but she tried to check in on Mama several times a day. Mama was barely bigger than a broomstick now, but her mind was as sharp as ever. Best of all, her spirits had gotten better since Mass Henry had taken over and they'd moved back to the attic permanently, and for that Clara was thankful to him. Since there weren't as many slaves around these days and those who were still here had to work double duty, Mama had the attic all to herself during the day. Clara exhaled deeply. "Just a little tired is all."

"That's natural," Mama said.

Clara frowned.

"In your condition, it's normal to be tired."

Clara blinked. She hadn't even thought of that. "But it's only been a few months."

"So. Your body is changing now, with the baby and all."

Clara wasn't going to argue with Mama on this, since it was her first time being with child. She sighed again. Whatever the reason, she had no time to be tired. None at all. She had two people to look after these days as it was, Mama and herself. She wasn't yet ready to think about the one on the way. Besides, whenever she did think about it, it was with regret. She found no joy in bringing a child into this world, only to wait hand and foot on some ornery white folks all its life.

"I saw Brother Squire walking over there by the willow tree not long ago," Mama said, pointing out the window. She paused and squinted at Clara as if waiting for her to speak. But Clara said nothing. She knew where this was leading and she was having no part of it.

"You say he's not that child's daddy, right?"

"Mama, we've talked about this a hundred times. No, he's not."

Mama sighed with resignation. "You picked out a name yet?"

"No, indeed. No time to even think on that."

"I hope you plan on telling me who the daddy is before I leave this here earth."

"You not going anywhere anytime soon, Mama."

"Let's hope not, at least not before your time."

Clara said nothing. Maybe if she didn't talk, Mama would drop it.

"Why is it such a big old secret, anyhow?" Mama asked.

Clara exhaled with exasperation. If Mama knew who the daddy was she would know the answer to that question. But Clara wasn't telling a soul, not even the baby's daddy. She didn't know if she'd ever get up the nerve to tell anybody in this lifetime—because the daddy was white.

Lord almighty, she thought. Bad enough she was bringing another human being into this life of misery. But for this one, it could be even worse. She'd heard about it time and time again. Not black, not white. Folks always gossiped about them behind their backs. And they would talk about the mama, too, something terrible. What would she do with such a child?

She sighed. If she had any luck, something bad would happen to this baby, for both their sakes. She had heard of some mamas suffocating their newborn babies, rather than bring them up in this world. Clara knew she could never do something like that with her own hands, as miserable as the little creature might grow up to be. Shame on her for even thinking that way, but the world could be a mean old place. The hereafter couldn't help but be better.

If this baby was coming, Lord, please don't let it look too white. A little yellow would do just fine. A lot of brown would be even better. Let them think the daddy was a light-skinned Negro. Then folks wouldn't be so curious about who the daddy was. A slave child with no daddy around was about as common as a weed in an overgrown garden. But if the child looked white, people would always wonder. If you were going to be a slave in this world, you were better off looking like one.

10

"Push," Aunt Winney said.

She said it so calm-like, standing down there between Clara's thighs, that Clara wanted to scream at the top of her lungs. Aunt Winney might have birthed a hundred babies, but this was Clara's first time having one, and it was damn near killing her. Didn't anybody understand that? She wanted to scream at Mama, too, for standing there and looking at her with that sickening smile on her face. And at the baby for taking so blasted long to come out.

But she knew that if this was ever going to get done, she had to do as she was told, no matter how bad it hurt. So she pushed. When she stopped, Mama wiped her forehead with a wet towel.

"Get the hell away from me," Clara shouted, pushing Mama for probably the tenth time. Mama smiled knowingly, and Clara immediately regretted lashing out. She didn't know why she was shouting at Mama. This certainly wasn't Mama's fault. Still, she couldn't help it. Every time someone came near, she thought she would suffocate. She didn't need consoling, she needed to get this baby out.

"Just stay back," Clara said. She breathed deeply and tried to calm down.

"All right," Mama said, stepping back a few feet. "But you're doing fine."

"Oh, please," Clara said. "This is hell."

Aunt Winney chuckled, and Clara fixed her with a fierce stare. It was a good thing the woman was down there at her feet, Clara thought. Or she would have jumped up off these raggedy old sacks spread underneath her and slapped her on the spot. She didn't care if this was Aunt Winney's cabin. She didn't care if it was Aunt Winney's table. How dare that old woman laugh when her body was being ripped apart.

Aunt Winney smiled. "Push."

If that woman said that word one more time, she was going to jump right up off this table and . . .

"Push."

Clara pushed.

Clara leaned up, her body drenched in sweat, and anxiously watched Aunt Winney's back as the old woman bathed the tiny baby girl with water that Mama had just heated over the fire. Clara had gotten only a glimpse of the baby right after the birth. All she had seen was a pair of little white feet, but that didn't mean much, since all babies had white feet. Or so she hoped.

Aunt Winney wrapped the baby in a towel and handed her to Mama. Mama held the baby close to her breasts as she crossed the cabin to Clara. Mama hesitated, then held the baby up for Clara to see. She was as white as a sheet, and Clara's heart sank. She tried to hide her true feelings, but something must have shown on her face.

"Some babies is pale like that when they first born," Aunt Winney said as Mama laid the baby down next to Clara. "'Specially if the daddy be light like you. She gon' darken up real soon. Mark my word."

Mama stepped back and clasped her hands near her

waist. "I'll wager that Brother Squire isn't the daddy."

"Squire?" Aunt Winney chuckled. "Lawdy, no. He way too black to be that chile's—" She stopped when she sensed that something in the air wasn't right between Clara and her mama.

Clara said not a word, even though she could tell Mama was waiting, hoping she'd finally say who the daddy was. But Clara wasn't ready to do that. Maybe she would never be ready. She looked down at the baby lying next to her as Mama lowered her head in prayer.

Yes, Mama, Clara thought. Pray for my little one, 'cause she'll be needing all the blessings she can get looking like this in our world. And while you're at it, Mama, pray that Aunt Winney is right, and that this baby will darken up, even just a little. That way she can avoid the shame that comes with this particular curse. Me, too.

She wrapped the baby in her arms. The child looked so tiny, so pretty, and so utterly helpless. None of this was her doing. All the little thing wanted was a chance. And it would be up to her mama to try and give it to her.

Clara knew she was going to have to change her ways. Instead of always seeing the bad side of things and thinking about running the first chance she got, she was going to have to make the most of what was here. It wasn't going to be easy. She wanted to get away from this place someday so bad. But she had to stop thinking about what she wanted and start thinking about what this child needed. Running was dangerous enough as it was and would be even more so with a child. And if she got caught, they might take her baby away to be spiteful. She couldn't risk that.

"What will you call her?" Mama asked, touching the baby's pink cheek.

Clara smiled for the first time that morning. "Maybe I'll name her Susie or Susan, after you."

Mama smiled but shook her head. "Wait till after I'm gone for that."

Clara nodded. Some colored folks named new babies after someone dear who had just departed. Thank goodness that hadn't happened with Mama yet. She thought of Daddy, and wished he were here to see his grandbaby. But some things just weren't meant to be. Maybe she could think of a girl's name that sounded like Walker. Then she remembered the baby's color and thought that maybe Daddy wouldn't be so proud to have such a white-looking granddaughter named after him.

She sighed. Barely out of the womb and already her color was starting to shape her life. "I think this baby needs a nice, fresh start," Clara said. "Maybe I'll call her Ellen. Always did like that name, and it will be nobody's but hers."

"Ellen," Mama repeated. "That's a pretty one."

PART 2

11

Susan lifted the white crinoline. She wanted to see the new shoes on her feet, with their square toes and dainty spool heels. But the hoop skirt was so voluminous, she had to kick her foot out just to glimpse the toe, and she nearly fell. She covered her mouth with her hand and giggled as she steadied herself.

"This one is just perfect for you," Miss Rebecca said, as she half dragged her mama's green brocade gown out of the Victorian wardrobe. Miss Rebecca's white face looked even paler than usual with the glow of too much rouge weighing down her delicate cheekbones. She held the gown out toward Susan. "Here. Try this one on."

Susan took the gown from her mistress and held it at arm's length. *"Mon Dieu! La belle robe!"*

"What?" Miss Rebecca asked, blinking at Susan with wide eyes.

"Um, it's beautiful, Missus."

"Honestly, Susan. You know my papa doesn't like you talking that French."

"Yes, Missus. I just forget sometimes."

"I won't say anything, but you must be careful not to talk like that around him."

"Oh, I am, Missus." Susan held the dress close to her

breasts and watched as Miss Rebecca slipped into a fine blue silk gown that she'd chosen for herself. Susan held the gown in her own hands out again and admired the richness of its colors. It was so *verte*, er, green, she thought, and reminded her of the trees in the woods surrounding Montpelier. She was dying to try it on.

But what if Mass Stephen came in and saw them? She glanced toward the bedroom doorway, her mind skipping back to how upset Massa had gotten when he caught Miss Rebecca reading *Jane Eyre* to her and pointing to the words. Massa went straight to his wife and told her he better not ever catch Susan anywhere near a book again or he would send her out to the fields for a week as punishment. Miss Marie went straight to Mama.

"I expect you to keep better tabs on this kind of thing, Clara," Miss Marie told Mama. "You're the head housekeeper here."

Missus was a plain-looking, petite woman, and she always wore dresses with a lot of frills and ruffles. Her Southern drawl was so deep that it still startled Susan whenever she heard it. Mama said it was because she was from Alabama and that's how they talked down there.

"Yes, ma'am," Clara said.

"I don't mind it so much," Miss Marie said. "She's a bright girl, and it seems such a pity not to give her some learning. Ellen, too. And what harm can possibly come from it? But your master is adamantly opposed to it, and we don't want her to end up in the fields picking up the habits of the nigras out there. Not even for a week. Why, it will ruin her for house work."

"I agree, Miss Marie," Mama had said. "And I intend to put a stop to it." Mama gave Susan a warning glance. "She knows better. Miss Rebecca is so kind to her that I think Susan sometimes forgets her place."

"I'll speak to Miss Rebecca," Miss Marie said. "But that child is so spoiled, I'll warrant it won't do a bit of good.

That's why I'm counting on you, Clara, to see that it doesn't happen again. We certainly cannot allow Susan to dust in the library anymore."

"You're right, Missus."

"Now, tell me, Clara," Miss Marie said. "Just how well does she read?"

"Not so good at all, ma'am. I reckon she learned a few words from Mass Benjamin and his wife and their girls when they lived here, Missus. But that's all, and that was near five years ago, when she was around seven or eight."

"Ah, yes," Miss Marie said. "The Thorntons were from England and no doubt knew no better. Well, what about the French? I've heard her using some French words, too."

Mama shot Susan another warning glance. Susan looked down at the floor.

"From Mass Henry, Missus," Mama said.

"Henry?"

"Mr. Moncure, ma'am. That was before the Thorntons."

Miss Marie sighed with exasperation. "I do declare, these foreigners will ruin our darkies. Well, we're from Alabama and that sort of thing just isn't tolerated down there. See that it stops."

"Yes, Miss Marie," Mama said. "It won't happen again." Mama nudged Susan. "Right?"

"Yes, ma'am."

Susan looked at the green dress in her arms. No telling how Massa would feel about her dressing in the missus's Sunday go-to-meeting clothes. She shook her head. "I don't know, Miss Rebecca. What if somebody comes in and sees us?"

"So what?" Miss Rebecca said, a look of puzzlement crossing her brow.

"But 'member what Massa said when he caught you reading me that book? He said he would send me out to the fields for a whole week if he caught me doing it again."

"Honestly, Susan." Miss Marie puffed her breath and

stamped a foot. "You're always so scared about these things. Papa didn't really mean that. Why, he would never send you out to the fields. And your mama won't mind. Clara thinks anything is fine as long as you're with me."

Susan frowned doubtfully. It wasn't her mama that she was worried about.

"It'll be fine," Miss Rebecca said with a toss of her shoulder-length sausage curls. "Papa loses his temper sometimes, but his bark is bigger than his bite. And it's only a dress, after all, not a book."

Susan smiled and looked at the dress. It was awfully pretty. Every time she saw Miss Marie parading around the mansion in one of her fancy dresses, she wondered what it would be like to wear a dress with a real crinoline, instead of having to use starch to make a dress fuller, like Mama did. Still . . .

Seeing the doubt stuck on Susan's face, Miss Rebecca extended her arm and pointed her finger with mock authority.

"Susan, slave girl of Montpelier, home of Mr. and Mrs. Stephen N. Shaw, their daughter Rebecca, and her ornery brothers, I command you to put on that dress. Immediately." She then burst into a fit of giggles, just as she always did when pretending to order Susan around.

Susan laughed, too, though not quite as merrily. She supposed that trying on a dress wasn't nearly as dangerous as reading. She took one more quick glance at the doorway, then did as she was told.

They buttoned each other up in the back, and Miss Rebecca went to her mama's dresser drawer and removed a green satin ribbon. She tied it into a bow around the chignon at the back of Susan's head, then spun Susan around and stepped back and smiled approvingly. "That dress goes just perfectly with your hazel eyes."

Susan smiled. "Honest?" She looked at Miss Rebecca's scarlet cheeks. "Can I have some rouge, too?"

"You don't need any. Your complexion has a natural glow. Mama says you look Italian on account of your hair being so long and dark."

Susan shook her hips. The crinoline was fussy, but she loved the way it made her dress sway. She felt so elegant. She tried to curtsy, the way she'd seen the missus do at her fancy balls, but somehow it didn't feel quite right.

Miss Rebecca laughed. "No, silly, it's like this. Keep your back straight at all times."

Susan watched Miss Rebecca execute a perfect curtsy. She tried again, holding her head high.

"Chin down, then out," Miss Rebecca said. "Ever so slightly."

Just as Susan tilted her head, a sound came from the doorway. *Mon Dieu!* She nearly tripped in her heels as she jumped up, so sure was she that her worst fears were about to materialize right before her very eyes. She breathed a sigh of relief when she saw that it was Miss Marie and not Massa. Still, it was too soon to relax completely. Why had she let herself be talked into this foolishness? She folded her hands and stepped back near the wall.

Miss Marie entered and stopped in the middle of the room. "Heavens. What are the two of you up to now?"

Miss Rebecca stepped forward excitedly. "We're playing dress-up, Mama. What do you think? It almost fits me, too." She lifted the dress off the carpeted floor to show that it was only a few inches too long, then held her arms out and twirled around.

Miss Marie smiled at her daughter. "Why, you look just lovely, dear."

"And look at Susan," Miss Rebecca said. "Doesn't she look pretty?"

Susan looked up at Miss Marie and tried to smile.

Miss Marie straightened her shoulders and blinked. "Why, yes, dear, she does. Where is your sister, Susan?"

"Ellen is helping Mama light the fires, Missus." It had turned unseasonably chilly for a late summer evening, and Miss Marie had ordered fires made in all the chambers after supper.

"I asked Clara if Susan could play with me after supper," Miss Rebecca said, as if sensing that all was not right in her mama's eyes.

"Those are two of my best dresses, you know, Rebecca."

"We'll be real careful, Mama."

Miss Marie smiled and waved her hand with resignation. "Oh, I suppose it's all right. But run along. I have letters to write." She moved to her writing table and sat down.

"Let's go to my room," Miss Rebecca said, and Susan was all too happy to beat a retreat. She followed her young mistress out the door.

"Be careful in my dresses," Miss Marie called after them.

They both laughed as Miss Rebecca tried to sit on her feather stuffed bed. The hem of her skirt popped straight up in the air. "I suppose I'll have to get used to these things when I go away to boarding school next year," Miss Rebecca said as she stood back up. "They're very fashionable now."

"I suppose," Susan said. Boarding school, fancy balls, and silk gowns—Susan wondered what it must all be like.

"Oh, I wish you could come with me, Susan, but Papa said it will be better to take Sally along, since she's older and darker. Folks might think you're white, and Papa worries you'll try to run away."

What a crazy notion, Susan thought, as she shook her head with alarm. "I would never do that, Miss Rebecca."

"I know, and I tried to tell Papa you would never desert me."

Susan blinked. The truth was that it was Mama and Ellen she would never desert. But she wouldn't dare tell

Miss Rebecca that. Let Missus think it was loyalty to her that would keep her slave girl from running. "Aren't you afraid to leave your mama and papa when you go to school?"

"A little. Mama says I'll get used to it, though. All well-bred ladies do it, you know. But Papa says that since we've only been living at Montpelier a little over a year, we don't know you well enough to be sure you wouldn't try to escape. And Sally's been with us since before I was born." Miss Rebecca leaned close and whispered. "But she's so dern old and no fun at all."

They both giggled.

Miss Rebecca stared into Susan's face. "How did you and Ellen get so white? Do you know? The two of you look so much alike, only you're ever so much prettier."

Susan shrugged. She knew, of course, that their daddy was white, but she also knew her mama didn't want her talking about that around white folks. Heck, her mama didn't even like her talking about it around colored folks.

"Well," Miss Rebecca said. "You're both still colored, even if you are white, so that makes you slaves. Even the Bible says so."

Susan frowned. This was the first she'd heard that. "The Bible says that?"

Miss Rebecca nodded. "My papa said so." She looked around the room. "Now, where did I put my Bible?" They both spotted the black book sitting atop the mantelpiece. Miss Rebecca lifted her skirt and walked over to the fireplace, then tipped up on her toes and reached for it. Susan stayed put. She wasn't about to go anywhere near any books.

As soon as Miss Rebecca landed on her heels, she screamed. She dropped the book on the hearth rug and turned around, a look of pure terror on her face. Susan glanced down and saw that the hem of her mistress's gown was ablaze.

"Mon Dieu," Susan yelled. She ran forward but stopped short when she realized that if she got any closer her own skirt would catch fire. "Get back," she shouted, flinging her arms in the air. Miss Rebecca, now screaming nonstop at the very top of her lungs, stumbled off the hearth rug, and Susan yanked the small rug up and beat at the fire. By now, it had spread up the side of the skirt, and Miss Rebecca fell to the floor. Smoke was getting in Susan's lungs and she coughed but she kept right on beating.

Miss Marie ran into the doorway, then ran right back out and yelled for her husband. In a matter of seconds, Mass Stephen came tearing into the room. Miss Marie stood just inside the door, waving her arms frantically, as Massa snatched the rug from Susan's hands. He beat at the dress, but by this time the blaze had been extinguished and there was only smoke.

Susan backed against the bedpost, coughing and blinking back the tears forming in her eyes as Massa picked his daughter up off the floor. Miss Rebecca's shoulders shook as she sobbed. Rouge and lipstick were smeared all over her face. Massa lifted her skirt, and they could see that the fire hadn't burned through the fabric of the crinoline. Still, he ripped the dress and hoop skirt off and flung them on the floor. Miss Marie ran into the room, brushed past Susan, and took her sobbing daughter into her arms.

Massa began to pace up and down the floor, anger showing plainly on his flushed cheeks and tight lips. He was about the same age as his wife, and his accent was just as deep. "What the devil happened here?" he asked his daughter, but Miss Rebecca just sobbed. She was too upset to speak.

Miss Marie patted her daughter's hair. "There, there, dear. It's all right now. You weren't burned. Thank goodness your father got here in time."

"How did this happen, Rebecca?" Mass Stephen repeated, still pacing up and down the floor.

"I . . . I was reaching for the Bible to show . . . to read to Susan the part where it says colored people were meant to be slaves. And my skirt must have brushed the fire."

At that moment, Massa and Missus seemed to remember that Susan was in the room. Massa stopped pacing, and they both turned and stared at her. From the looks on their faces, you would have thought a snake had suddenly slithered through the door.

Massa strode toward her, and she tried to blend into the bedpost.

"What happened here? She could have been killed, or badly injured."

Susan choked back her coughs and blinked. Why were they accusing her? She hadn't done anything wrong. When was Miss Rebecca going to tell them that she had saved her?

"You should be helping Clara," Missus said.

"What the devil is she doing in those clothes?" Massa asked, pointing at Susan and looking at his wife.

Miss Marie cupped the bun at the back of her head, then looked at Miss Rebecca. "Go to my room, Rebecca. I'll be there shortly."

"But, Mama—"

"Do as your mother says."

Miss Rebecca left without another word, and Miss Marie wheeled around to face Susan. "You have no business wearing my things." She sighed and looked at her husband. "No doubt Rebecca put her up to this." She turned back to Susan. "But you should know better. You're what? Fourteen now?"

Twelve, Susan thought. Same age as Miss Rebecca. And it was all right for them to play in her dresses only a moment ago. "No, Missus, I'm—"

"Take that dress off immediately," Miss Marie interrupted.

"Yes, ma'am." Susan was only too glad to be excused

from this room. She turned to leave, but her mistress's voice halted her. "Take it off here and give it to me. Now."

Susan gasped. Right in front of Massa? She knew better than to delay when Massa and Missus were so upset about the fire. She reached back and fumbled with the buttons, but her hands were shaking so badly, she couldn't seem to undo them.

"Hurry up, child," Miss Marie said, tapping her foot.

Susan finally got the last button undone and slipped the dress down over her feet and gave it to Miss Marie. The crinoline followed. Her nipples were obvious under her thin petticoat, and she tried to cover them with her hands.

"You may as well burn that with the other one," Massa said. "You can't wear it now." He turned to Susan. "Go on. Get out of here."

Just as she turned to leave, Miss Marie reached up and snatched the ribbon from Susan's head. It felt like half the hair on her head was being ripped out as it fell and dangled across her back. Susan winced.

"This is inexcusable, Marie," she heard Massa say as she entered the hallway. "Rebecca could have been seriously injured, or worse."

"I know, dear," Miss Marie said. "It makes me shudder just thinking about it. Thank goodness you were here to put that fire out. Rebecca likes the girl, but I can see she's getting much too attached."

"You've got to get control around here. This kind of thing would never happen back in Alabama with our nigras. They knew their place."

"I agree, dear. But these Madison nigras are impossible. They're so insolent, especially the ones around the house. I'll speak to Clara immediately."

"Humph. A lot of good that will do. That woman is the worst of the whole lot. I tell you . . ."

* * *

Mama's eyes got wider by the minute as Susan sobbed out her story. Susan knew from listening to her own voice that she hardly made any sense, but she couldn't think straight. She stopped and sniffed and waited to hear what Mama would say. But Mama didn't say a word to her. She fixed her jaw firmly, told Ellen to finish lighting the fire in the parlor, and beckoned Susan to come with her.

Susan followed Mama down the long hallway to a door and watched as Mama removed a key from around her neck and inserted it into the lock. They stepped into a storeroom filled with mops, brooms, boxes of soap, and bottles of oil. Mama closed the door behind them, and the smell of cleaning products filled the tiny room.

"You have no business putting on Miss Marie's clothes. You know that." Mama's tone was firm but gentle.

"I know, but Miss Rebecca begged me to. She kept pushing me. And Miss Marie said it was all right until the dress caught fire. Then she—"

"Lord almighty, child. How many times do I have to tell you to be careful around these folks? We don't know them all that good. You can't let a few smiles go to your head."

Susan sniffed and looked at her feet.

"Stop that sniffing. Won't do you a bit of good." Mama removed the shawl from her shoulders and draped it around Susan. "Here. Before you catch cold."

"Do you think they're going to make me work out in the fields, Mama? I don't know anything about field work. My hands will get all—"

Mama held up her hand. "Hush. They won't do that as long as I got a breath left in me. Although it might be just what you need to learn yourself a lesson."

Susan's eyes got wide. She couldn't believe Mama would even think like that.

Mama smiled. "Don't worry. Did Massa say anything else just now about sending you out there?"

Susan shook her head. "No. But he was awful mad."

"All right. I'll go talk to Miss Marie." Mama shook her head. "Lordy. Always something, I swear. I should have made you come with me and Ellen instead of giving in to that Miss Rebecca. Lord knows she's spoiled enough as it is." Mama picked up some rags from a shelf and shoved them into Susan's hands. "Now, I want you to put on some clothes and then go dust the shelves in the library . . . no, not there. Dust in the drawing room, the dining room, anywhere but the library. And stay away from Miss Rebecca. She's nothing but trouble if I ever saw it."

Susan nodded as Mama put her hand on the doorknob. "Mama? How did we get to be slaves?"

"What?"

"Did God make us slaves?"

Mama frowned. "No, indeed. God didn't make us no slaves. God made us colored and the white man made us slaves."

"But I'm not colored. So why am I a slave?"

Mama narrowed her eyes. "You might not look colored, child, but your mama is, and that's close enough for them." She frowned. "Who told you that stuff about God, anyhow?"

"Miss Rebecca said it was in the Bible."

"Humph. Well, I don't know about that. They always saying something or other is in the Bible, and they make sure we can't read it to tell otherwise." She put her hand on the doorknob again.

"Mama?"

"Now what?"

"Did you ever wish you were free, like white folks?"

Mama let go of the knob and stared at the door. It was whenever Mama got that faraway look on her face that Susan most noticed the gray hair that was starting to show around Mama's temples.

"You don't have to be white to be free," Mama said softly. "But you sure as heck have to be white to enjoy being free." She looked at Susan. "Is that what you wishing for?"

Susan wasn't sure. She didn't ever want to leave Mama and Ellen, but she couldn't help thinking about freedom, being around Miss Rebecca and other white folks all the time. "No . . . yes, I mean . . . I don't know. Sometimes, I guess. Miss Rebecca gets to do so much that I can't do."

"That's Miss Rebecca. Being free isn't the same for us, even if you look white. Way back, before I knew any better, I thought I wanted to be free. But when my daddy left and I had the chance, I didn't take it."

"Why?"

" 'Cause I didn't want to leave your Grandma Susie behind. God rest her soul. Mama was sick at the time and couldn't go with us. And I reckon she just didn't want to leave here. Then Ellen and you came along."

Susan had never known this grandma whose name she now carried. Grandma Susie died not long after Ellen was born. But she could understand Mama not wanting to leave her own mother behind. It was exactly how Susan felt about Mama and Ellen whenever she thought about freedom. It would have to be all of them or none of them. She sighed deeply. "So you got stuck here?"

"We have a decent life here. At least we know pretty much what to expect from one day to the next. You don't know how lucky you are, child. It was real bad around here for a while. But me and my mama, we hung in there as best we could. Did some things I wouldn't brag about, but we made it. And lots of folks still have it bad, even some white ones. There's no point being free if you're starving."

"At least they don't have to worry about being sold. Or sent to the fields to work."

"And neither do you, if you behave yourself."

Susan bowed her head. She certainly tried to stay out of trouble, but sometimes it seemed impossible.

"Besides, running is too dangerous," Mama said. "To this day, I don't know if your granddaddy made it. " 'Spect he didn't, since we never heard from him."

Susan always thought about her own daddy whenever Mama mentioned Granddaddy Walker. Who was he? About the only thing Mama had told them about their daddy was that he was an important white man and used to be the massa of Montpelier. Mama said they were better off not knowing, at least until they were old enough to handle it. "Did you miss Granddaddy after he left?"

" 'Course I did. I loved that man dearly. But we managed just fine without him, since we didn't have much choice."

Still, Susan thought, it must be nice to at least know who your daddy is even if he wasn't around to help take care of you.

"And you will, too," Mama continued. "Don't I take good enough care of you?"

Sometimes it seemed like Mama could read her mind. She nodded. "Yes, but—"

"You have a roof over your head, don't you? And plenty to eat. You even have nice clothes to wear."

Susan nodded again. "I know, Mama."

"Then let's get going. You go put on some clothes, while I think of what I'm going to say to Miss Marie. She's probably looking for me right now. I swear. This wasn't all your fault, but I know she's going to make it seem that way. These white folks don't ever think they're wrong. It's always us. But don't trouble yourself about this. I'll take care of it, just like I always do."

Mama had moved them from the mansion into a cabin several years earlier, when she married Squire May from over at the Bell plantation. Mama said that made him their stepdaddy but they didn't get to see nearly as much of him as they did their half-brothers and half-sister, since Squire still lived at the Bell plantation.

In the evening, when Mama was still up at the big house turning down beds and fetching warm milk for the white folks, Susan and Ellen would mind their half-siblings. Alex and Polly were both toddlers, only a year apart, and starting to get into everything, and Beverly was a boy now going on seven. Sometimes Ellen would have to stay and work at the big house in the evenings, too, since she was already fourteen and taking on more work. On those days, Susan would watch the children by herself. She would play with them after supper, then get them ready for bed and sometimes tell them a story or two to get them to sleep. Alex and Polly would drift right off, but Beverly was another matter altogether. He would often make her repeat the same story over and over until he finally drifted off to sleep.

The cabin was drafty in winter and hot to the point of suffocation in summer, but Mama liked it because it gave them a place to get away from the prying eyes and ears of white folks. It was the only place where she and Ellen could talk freely. And talk they did, some nights for hours. Since the little ones were asleep and Mama was up at the big house, their talks almost always drifted to the subject of their daddy. Who was he? Where was he? What did he look like?

"You were too young," Ellen said that night after they had put the little ones to bed. "But I can remember a man coming to our room at the big house every night. He would always bring us both a penny." Ellen sat cross-legged on the uneven little bed while Susan brushed her hair. Ellen's hair was long and straight like Susan's but was a reddish brown. People always did a double take when they first saw Ellen, since not many colored folks had reddish hair.

Papa Squire was a carpenter in addition to being a driver, and he had made them two beds out of logs he cut from the trees himself, with straw for the mattresses. The beds took up just about the whole room, with barely enough space left for a table and chairs in a corner. The little ones slept in one bed with Mama, and Susan and Ellen shared the other.

"You remember all that?" Susan asked.

"I sure enough do."

"I kind of remember an old man, with white hair."

"You probably just got that from me talking about him, 'cause you were hardly walking then."

Susan giggled. She had to admit that was probably true, since every time she imagined his face it was a little different.

"Anyhow, I'm not even sure he was our daddy," Ellen said. "Mama never said he was. I'm just guessing."

"Mama said our daddy was a real important white man from Richmond," Susan said.

"That's about all she ever said, though."

"I know. I wonder why she won't talk about him."

"Reckon she doesn't want us to slip up and say the wrong thing to the wrong people, and get ourselves in trouble."

Susan raised her eyebrows. "Maybe it was President Madison."

Ellen giggled. "Don't be silly. Mama said he was dead long before I was even born, let alone you."

"You never know. Maybe she just said that to throw us off the scent. Maybe we really are the daughters of a president of the United States."

"You best get that foolishness out of your head. I think Mama won't talk about it 'cause it has something to do with Granddaddy Walker leaving. 'Cause if he made it up North and never came back for them . . . well, that's sure enough about as hurtful as him not making it."

"But what's that got to do with our daddy?"

Ellen shrugged. "I don't know, 'cept Mama hardly ever talks about the time after Granddaddy ran off, and she always talks about the days before that. And Mama said Grandma Susie was never the same after that and that she had to grow up in a hurry, doing whatever she could to look after both of them. So I reckon it's all tied in."

"Maybe. We probably won't ever know."

"Mama said she might tell us when we get older."

"Well, I'm never going to run away. It's too dangerous. 'Sides, it's not so bad here."

"It can get dangerous here, too, if you don't learn to stay out of trouble. That's why you better watch yourself with that Miss Rebecca. Those folks from Alabama don't mess around."

Susan squirmed. Mama said Massa was mad enough to spit about the fire, almost as mad as he was when he caught her reading. But Mama said she had calmed him down for now. Mama had pointed out that Susan tried to help by picking up the rug and beating the fire before Massa arrived and saved everybody. Susan shook her head. That wasn't how it really happened, and Mama knew it, but she was so relieved that Mama got her out of trouble, she didn't even care who got credit for putting out the fire. Nor did she care if she never saw a book or a pretty dress again.

12

"Happy birthday, Susan."

Susan stopped humming and looked up from the crate she was packing in the dining room. Aunt Sarah stood in the doorway holding an armful of bed linen and smiling at Susan and Ellen.

"I remember the day you were born. You, too, Ellen. I just can't ever remember the dates, I'm getting so old now." Aunt Sarah chuckled. "But happy birthday."

Susan smiled. Aunt Sarah had been here at Montpelier longer than anybody but somehow managed to keep going. Mama was the head housekeeper now, and Aunt Sarah did what she could to help out. "Thank you, Aunt Sarah."

Aunt Sarah walked off and Susan went back to humming. She didn't know what she was humming. She sort of just made tunes up as she went along. It made her work more pleasant.

The Shaws were moving back to Alabama in a few days, so everything had to be packed and shipped. Then the house would have to be cleaned from top to bottom for the new owner. Mama said it was a man from Baltimore.

Susan looked down the square mahogany table at Ellen. It would take them the better part of the morning to finish packing the china and silverware in here, then it was on to the parlor. But she didn't mind, really. It gave her a chance to handle all the beautiful crystal and silver and fine linen. She just had to remember to be careful, since Miss Marie didn't take kindly to anything being damaged.

She had mixed feelings about the Shaws leaving. Miss Rebecca was away at school these days, so she didn't see her much anymore anyway. And ever since she could remember, owners had come and gone almost as fast as the seasons. First was Mass Henry. The main thing she remembered about him was that he sometimes spoke French to them. She'd picked up a few phrases and he always got a kick out of hearing her use them. It was hard to remember not to use French around other white folks.

The Thorntons from England stayed the longest. They talked funny, too. Even though it was English, at first she could hardly understand a word they said. But they were nice and patient. The Missus had two baby girls while living here, and she let Susan help her watch over them, even though Susan was only about seven at the time. Missus would read to them all at night, and after her babies fell asleep she would keep right on reading to Susan. Sometimes she even helped Susan read a few words. She used to say that it was a shame for such a smart young girl not to learn to read. That was why Susan had been surprised when Mass Stephen got so mad at her for listening to Miss Rebecca read.

A Mass Willard owned Montpelier at one time, too. Mama said Mass Willard had been visiting Montpelier since the Madisons' time, but he didn't live here all that long and never brought any family with him, so Susan didn't much remember him. Now they were getting yet another massa. These white folks came and went faster than you could change a sheet. And they were all so different that before you could get used to the strange ways of one family, they were packing their bags and a new one was moving in. In a way, it felt like the colored folks were the real owners. They had been here the longest, knew every crook and cranny, and all the history.

Mama said it was now nothing like it was when the Madisons were here. Mama and Aunt Sarah always talked about those days, and Susan loved hearing the stories about Grandma Susie and Aunts Nany, Sukey, and Winney, about Mass Jimmy, Miss Dolley, and Mass Todd—all dead now. Paul Jennings was free and lived in Washington, D.C. Even when Mama and Aunt Sarah complained about those days, especially about Mass Todd, Susan could tell they really missed them. Mama was always saying it used to mean something to be a Madison Negro.

Susan brushed a wisp of hair from her eyes and was trying to think of another tune to hum when Mama came tearing into the room and grabbed Ellen by the arm. The look of terror on Mama's face was one Susan had never seen on anyone before, let alone Mama. Susan frowned. Did somebody die? She was about to ask, but Mama put a finger to her lips and signaled for Susan to put down the silver teapot and follow her.

They followed Mama down the back stairs, through the old basement kitchen, and out the side door. The hot sun scorched their backs as they dashed across the lawn. Mama didn't say a word the whole time, didn't even look back at them, as her skirt fluttered in the breeze with her brisk steps.

As soon as they entered the cabin, Mama shut the door and turned to face them. She was huffing and puffing like she'd just run all the way from Walnut Grove instead of only from the big house. Her cheeks were flushed and her kerchief, usually tied so neatly on her head, was hanging loose. Something was awfully wrong.

"When Massa and Missus move to Alabama . . ." Mama paused, and her chest heaved up and down so violently that Susan thought it would burst. Mama looked at Ellen. "I heard they fixing to take you with them."

Ellen turned bleach white.

Susan's jaw dropped.

"What?" Ellen said. Her voice was so soft that Susan could barely hear her. Ellen shook her head slowly. "But . . . but why me? They have Sally for Miss Rebecca."

Mama threw her hands in the air and paced up and down the floor like a caged animal. "They tell me that Sally is with child, so I reckon they think she won't be well enough to go back to school with Miss Rebecca when the time comes."

Ellen sank down in a chair.

"It doesn't make sense," Susan said. "I'm the one that's with Miss Rebecca when she's home."

"I know, but Ellen's older."

And less trouble, Susan thought, feeling guilty. They wanted Ellen because she never caused them a moment's worry or got into trouble.

"I don't really know why they're doing this," Mama said. "All I know is they're fixing to take Ellen with them when they go, and I have to stop it. I have slaved in this place every day of my life, and I'm not going to stand for this."

Susan was so glad to hear Mama was going to put up a fight. They had no right to take Ellen away from her family. Montpelier was her home.

She looked at Ellen. Her sister seemed to be in shock. She just sat in the chair and stared in front of her. Susan looked back toward Mama. "What can we do, Mama? Maybe . . . maybe if you talk to Miss Marie."

Mama shook her head. "I'm afraid it's past that. I'm—" There was a knock and Mama ran to the door and threw it open. Susan was stunned to see Papa Squire rush in carrying an old burlap sack over his shoulder. He almost never came to Montpelier during the week since he had his own work to do over at the Bell plantation. From the look on his face, though, he already knew all about Ellen. He placed the sack on the table, then put his hands on Mama's arms.

"If you still got your mind set on this, I done found a place to take her."

Susan loved the sound of Papa Squire's voice—deep and soothing—and the way he always whistled when he walked. Lately, his beard was turning gray, just like Mama's hair.

"Where?" Mama asked.

"There's a old shack, 'bout a half day's walk from here. Used to be used as a way station by the Underground Railroad, but they abandoned it. They tell me it's darn near falling apart now, but it should keep us dry till we can get this mess sorted out."

Susan looked at her sister, and she knew Ellen was wondering the same thing. Were he and Ellen going to run?

Mama frowned. "Won't they come looking for her there?"

"Sooner or later, yes. But I ain't fixing to stay more than a day or two, then we move on someplace else. The thing to do now is get her out of here quick, 'fore they come looking for her. 'Cause once they do that . . . That is if you're sure this is what you want to do."

My God, Susan thought. It was true. He was planning to run with Ellen. This couldn't be happening. "Mama, what's going on?" Susan asked.

"They have to hide out in the woods until this thing clears up. It shouldn't be—"

Ellen jumped up and rocked nervously on her feet. "Mama, I don't want to run. Why can't you just talk to them? Tell them I'm a good worker. They'll listen to you. You're the head . . ."

Mama put her arm around Ellen. "Listen, baby. From

what I been hearing, this has gone too far to do any talking. Aunt Sarah heard them making plans to come and tell us like they already made up their minds. We don't have a choice, unless you want to go with them."

Ellen shook her head and clung to Mama. "No, no, no. But . . . oh, God." She buried her head in Mama's neck.

Susan started crying herself then. "How long will she have to stay out there?"

Mama looked to Papa Squire for the answer to that question. He shook his head and rubbed his beard. "I'm hoping just until after the Shaws leave. You said a few days?"

Mama nodded. "Day after tomorrow. Been packing for weeks now, but there was never even a hint of this. That woman stood right there by me in that dining room and never said a word. Not a word. Well, I'll be damned if I let her do this without putting up a fight." Mama stopped and gritted her teeth.

"You tell them you don't know where she's at when they ask you," Papa Squire said. "Act like you just as shocked as anybody. I'm hoping if they can't find her when the time comes for them to leave, they'll go on without her. Then we'll come back here and take it from there. I know we can't stay out there but so long and—" He stopped and shook his head, not knowing what else to say.

"What about you?" Mama asked him. "I hate to even think what might happen to you for doing this."

"Oh, I know what will happen to me." He clenched his jaw. "Massa will skin my hide till it's raw. But that's the price I'll have to pay. Won't be the first time, or the last."

Susan knew that to be true. He had the scars on his back to prove it.

"You don't reckon Mass Bell will sell you?" Mama asked.

"He'll make some threatening noises. But I been with

Massa and his daddy before him long enough to . . . Well, can't never be sure, but I seriously doubt it. Anyways, it's a chance we just have to take. She can't go out there by herself. And she can't stay here, neither."

Mama lifted Ellen's chin. "He'll look after you, baby." Mama tried to smile. "He might be getting on in years, like your mama, but he's strong and he knows these parts real good from driving the Bells around. I wish there was another way out of this, Lord knows I do. But this is the best we can do for now."

Ellen nodded, but Susan noticed her eyes were twitching something awful.

"Well, we best get moving," Papa Squire said, picking up the sack from the table. "'Fore they come for her."

"Wait," Mama said. "Let me give you some things to take."

Papa Squire went to the lone window, a mere hole in the wall with wooden shutters, and peered out anxiously as Mama moved around the cabin quickly, picking up bread, preserves, and a spare calico shift for Ellen. Susan was almost afraid to look at Ellen for fear of breaking down and upsetting her even more. Lord knew Ellen had enough to face. Susan still couldn't believe this was happening. She and Ellen had been together every day for fourteen years, all of her life. The thought of losing her big sister, even for a few days, made Susan sick to her stomach, especially when she thought about them living out there in the woods. What if Massa hunted them down with dogs and guns? Worse yet, what if this didn't work and Ellen had to go with Massa?

She couldn't let Ellen go without at least a hug. She moved closer and put her arm around Ellen's shoulder. Ellen tried a smile, but it turned into a grimace and more tears.

"Mama will fix this," Susan said. "She always does."

Ellen sniffed and nodded. Susan wished she could say

something to convince her sister, but the truth was that she needed convincing herself. They stood silently arm-in-arm, while Mama wrapped the food and clothes in a piece of cloth and tied the ends with a string. Mama handed the sack to Ellen and hugged her again. Before Susan knew what was happening, Papa Squire was kissing Mama good-bye and leading Ellen out the door. It all felt like a dream to Susan. She turned to Mama, and they stared at each other in silence for a moment. She couldn't stand this. She ran to the door and threw it open. She had to say good-bye to Ellen one more time, she had to thank Papa Squire for putting himself in danger. She . . .

Mama grabbed her from behind, pulled her back inside the cabin, and slammed the door shut. "When we go out there, we have to act natural," she said, facing Susan. "We have to go back up to that house and finish our work, acting like nothing is wrong. Do you understand me?"

"I can't, Mama." Susan shook her head. "I can't work, I can't even stop crying." She blinked, trying to hold back the tears.

"Damn it." Mama grabbed her shoulders and shook her so hard her eyes went cross. "Don't tell me that, 'cause I don't want to hear it. Now you march right on up there, and I don't want to hear a peep out of you, not one. We got to give them more time to get away."

Susan sniffed and wiped her eyes, but the tears kept coming. Mama tilted Susan's head up. "Look, I won't let you put your sister in more danger than she's already in. As hard as this is on us, think what she's going through. And Papa Squire. You just think about them."

Susan gritted her teeth. Of course Mama was right. Mama shook out a clean rag and reached for Susan's nose, but Susan took the rag from her and wiped her own face dry. She cleared her throat and squared her shoulders. Then she took a deep breath, walked out the cabin door, and headed up the path to the big house.

13

Mama had always said word traveled like lightning on a springtime evening when a slave was noticed missing in these parts. In less than twenty-four hours, every soul on every plantation within a day's walk would be talking about who had run the night before. Sometimes they ran up North, other times they just hid out in the woods to protest bad treatment or to avoid being sold. Either way, it was the same. Mama knew. She had seen it happen with her daddy.

They had to give Ellen and Papa Squire as much time as possible, so they went back into the dining room and packed up the china. Susan tried her best to act natural as she stood at the table and wrapped silver candlesticks, one by one. But her hands trembled so badly, she had to rewrap most of the pieces several times to get it right. Mama stood at the mahogany sideboard and carefully packed china plates, saucers, and teacups. They both worked so quietly—lost in their private worlds of worry—that you could have heard a pin drop.

When Mass Stephen entered the room a couple of hours later, Susan nearly dropped the candlestick in her hands. *Mon Dieu!* She prayed that Massa was only needing some chore performed, although it would be most unusual for him to make the request himself, rather than through his wife. Susan dared not stop working or even look up, so afraid was she that he would see on her face the fear she felt fluttering in her breast.

Out the corner of her eye, she watched his long legs stride purposefully across the room. He was most certainly looking for something, or someone. Crates and boxes were piled high everywhere, so it was difficult to see straight through to every corner. Susan glanced at Mama, hoping to catch a sign from her that all was right. But Mama was focusing on the china teacup in her hands as if wrapping it was the most important task she'd ever performed in her entire life.

As Massa peered around the boxes, Missus came to the doorway, cooling her thin cheeks with a silk Chinese fan. Massa stopped suddenly and stood in front of the fireplace.

"Where's Ellen?" he asked, his voice thundering across the room.

It was impossible to ignore the glass as it shattered on the floor and split into dozens of little pieces, and Susan looked up. Mama's hands were frozen in midair. The broken teacup lay at her feet.

"Oh, my Lord!" Missus said. She ran into the room and pointed with her closed fan. "That cup belonged to a set from my mama, and now you've ruined it. I want you to pick up every single—"

Massa held up his hand to silence his wife. "Not now, Marie," he said sternly.

Missus tightened her lips and resumed her fanning.

"Where is Ellen, Clara?" Massa repeated, enunciating each word carefully.

Mama blinked and stared at the table. "Last I saw her, she was in the drawing room, Massa."

"Well, she's not there now," Massa said. "I've searched all over this house and she's nowhere to be found."

"Then I don't know where she is, Massa."

Mass Stephen narrowed his eyes. "You'd better not be lying to me, Clara. Heaven help you if you are."

"No, Massa, I swear I don't know where she could be, unless she went down to the cabin for something."

"Do you think she would run?" he asked.

Susan almost dropped the candlestick in her hand. She placed it gently down on the table.

Mama shook her head emphatically. "Run? Lord almighty no, Massa. She's got no reason to run. She's loyal to you and Missus."

Susan almost smiled. She had never heard Mama lie so boldly. She sure was good at it.

"Mr. Bell just sent one of his overseers here. Seems Squire is missing, and one of his field hands claims that Squire and Ellen ran off this morning."

Susan was stunned. What colored person would do such a thing?

"I didn't want to believe it, but now I can't find her." Massa turned toward Susan, and she cringed, dreading what might be coming. But he paused as John, Montpelier's head overseer, strode into the room. Susan breathed a momentary sigh of relief, even as her heart picked up a beat. John, a beefy, greasy haired sort, had come from Alabama with the Shaws. Susan despised him more than any other human being on the face of the earth because of the ease with which he would pick up a whip and use it without warning. The only good thing about him was that he never had anything to do with the household help. Until now.

" 'Scuse me, suh," John said. "Ah done searched high an' low fo' her. The cabins, the fields. Nothin', suh."

Massa grimaced. "Just as I feared." He turned back to Susan. "Do you know where she is?"

Susan shook her head quickly, maybe too quickly. She was scared to death and she was sure it was written all over her face. She lowered her eyes to the floor.

"You want me to take care o' this fo' you, suh?" John asked. "Ah can get it outta these two, right quick."

"No. I can't have any welts on the younger one. I want you to round up the other overseers and go search for Ellen."

Mama blinked and glanced at Susan, and Susan frowned. What in tarnation did that mean? *No welts on the younger one.* But Susan didn't have time to think about it now, she was too worried about Ellen. The thought of this vile excuse for a human being catching Ellen was horrid. They had to stall as much as they could. She stepped forward. "Massa, did they check Aunt Louise's cabin down at the grove? She watches the children in the daytime, and Ellen sometimes goes down there to see them if she gets a free minute or two."

Massa narrowed his eyes at her, then turned to his wife. "When did you say you last saw her, Marie?"

"Why, just this morning she was in here, right after breakfast."

"Then they can't have gotten all that far if'n they on foot," John said. "Ah'll get right on it, suh."

"And check Louise's cabin if you haven't already," Massa said. "If you don't find them by tonight, we're going to have to get a bounty hunter in here first thing in the morning."

"We'll find 'em, suh. Got me a coupla hounds ah can use to catch the scent but Ah'll need somethin' belongin' to her, a piece o' clothin' or somethin' that ain't been washed out."

"Take her to the cabin with you to find something," Massa said, waving in Susan's direction.

John approached Susan, but she stepped back and avoided his eyes. The last thing she wanted was this no-account white trash touching her.

"Take me," Mama said and walked to the door as if the matter was settled.

Massa eyed Mama suspiciously, then seemed to change his mind. "All right. You cooperate, Clara, and we'll go easier on Ellen when we find her. But make no mistake about it, we'll find her. We'll find them both."

"I'll cooperate, Massa. I'm sure it's all perfectly innocent, and she's around here somewhere. But tell him to keep his hands off of me." Mama jerked her head in John's direction.

"Now, what would Ah want to touch the likes of you fer, nigga," John said, sneering at Mama.

Massa waved his arm. "Just go on, both of you. I don't want any nonsense out of either of you, and I want Clara back here the minute you're done."

Any relief Susan felt at not having to go with John was quickly overshadowed by the thought of Mama being alone with that man. She stepped forward. "I'll come with you, Mama."

"You'll stay right here," Massa said, pointing a finger at Susan. "I'm keeping you in the house to make sure your mama cooperates." He turned to his wife. "Marie, take her up to that guest chamber and lock the door."

"But, Stephen," Miss Marie said. "I have precious things in that room—most of the valuables from my mama. And after the way Clara just dropped my mama's . . ."

"Marie, please," Massa said, exhaling deeply. "I don't have time for this now. One of my slaves has gone missing."

"Yes, dear."

"Massa, I'm going to cooperate," Mama said. "You don't have to lock her up on account of me."

Massa ignored Mama. "Take her up, Marie. Go on," he said, shooing them all from the room. "I want that wench found, and fast. And I don't want to have to spend a damn fortune and a lot of time looking for her, either, or I swear there'll be hell to pay."

Miss Marie beckoned Susan and lifted her voluminous

skirt. "Come, child," she said and walked through the doorway.

Susan followed Miss Marie out the room, all the while looking back at Mama and John as they walked down the hallway in the opposite direction. She especially kept an eye on John. He was staying a safe distance behind Mama now, while Massa watched from the dining room doorway, but Susan just knew he'd be hitting and shoving Mama with his filthy callused hands all the way to the cabin as soon as they were out of sight.

Susan stood in the middle of the room and listened as Miss Marie locked the door from the outside. Then she let out a deep breath of air. How could they lock her away like she was some savage animal? And poor Mama, out there with that vile white trash. The door swung back open, and Susan turned to see Miss Marie stick her head inside.

"Stay off that bed," Miss Marie said. "And don't dare touch anything in here. You nigras are so clumsy, always breaking something or other." She slammed the door shut and locked it again.

Susan stared at the door. It took every ounce of willpower she could muster to keep from pounding on it and telling Missus exactly what she thought. She was nothing but an old country bumpkin, anyhow. Her gaze roamed around the room. Mahogany bed and wardrobe, stuffed sofa and side chair, glass vases and wooden baskets filled with fresh flowers, lace curtains on the windows, thick down quilt on the bed. So what? Susan had lived around nice things all her life, and not once had she ever been told to keep off it. She knew her place and didn't need to be reminded like some common field hand. These country bumpkins didn't know a thing.

She shut her eyes. Everything was changing so fast. She was confused and could hardly think straight. This morning started out like any other. They were a family going about their business, packing and cleaning. She was even thinking how she would miss the Shaws. And it was her birthday. Now look what had happened. Ellen was hiding in the woods with Papa Squire, Mama was being knocked about, and she was locked up in a room all by herself with a bunch of things she'd been warned not to touch.

She didn't know what seized her. All she knew was that a dark fury rose up inside her like a tidal wave. When she opened her eyes, she was standing at the edge of the very bed she'd been ordered to stay away from, staring down at the thick, soft fabric covering it.

She spit. She watched as it dissolved into the fabric, then spit again.

Susan was sitting on the carpet with her back against the wall when Mama stumbled into the room. Miss Marie glanced around, then shut the door and locked it behind her.

"Ugly bitch," Mama said to the door as she brushed off her skirt.

Susan jumped up and ran to Mama and hugged her. "Did he hurt you, Mama?"

"No, indeed, child. I'm fine."

"What did you give him of Ellen's?"

Mama smiled slyly. "Gave them one of her old dresses," Mama said. "That red one she done already outgrew."

Susan frowned. "But . . . they'll catch her."

"Not by that dress, they won't, since I washed it and put it away a long time ago. Only place that might lead them to is the laundry house." Mama chuckled.

Susan smiled, until she thought what that might mean. "What if they get mad and come back for you?"

Mama shook her head. "I don't even care anymore,

child. I'm past caring what they do to me. It's you and Ellen I worry about. And Squire. I'll do whatever I can think of to give them more time to get away."

"Mama, what are we going to do?"

"Not much we can do now, child, 'cept wait."

They sat on the floor with their backs against the wall. Miss Marie came in a few hours later and they both jumped up, fearing the worst. But Miss Marie said not a word. She simply looked around at her precious belongings, then shut the door and locked it. Susan and Mama figured no news was good news.

Mama shook her head. "I thought the Shaws were high-class folks, but high-class folks don't break up families unless they cause trouble. Reckon I was wrong about them."

"But didn't you say Mass Jimmy sold some colored folks one time?"

Mama frowned as if just remembering. "He did. But he was in trouble. He needed the money bad." Mama shook her head and looked down at her fingers. "Truth is, I don't know why any of them do this to us." She narrowed her eyes. "All of 'em will turn on a dime. Smile at you one minute, stab you in the back the next."

Mama closed her eyes, and Susan thought she was just weary from all the worry. Then she saw a tear slide down Mama's cheek. Susan had never seen Mama cry before.

"Should have run," Mama said.

"Huh?"

"Should have run when I had the chance. As soon as you both were old enough to walk."

"You couldn't know this would happen."

Mama wiped her eyes and sighed. "I should have figured that with all these different massas coming and going, sooner or later one of them would do something like this."

"You can't blame yourself." Susan put an arm around

Mama's shoulder. "It will be all right. They'll come back in a few days, after the Shaws are gone."

"I hope to God you're right."

Miss Marie came back at dusk, holding a candle, and Mama asked if they could have a bite to eat. Miss Marie said she would see about it and shut the door. She never came back again that night.

14

The sound of the key turning in the lock woke Susan. She knew from the color of the darkness that it was a good hour before she usually started her day. She was surprised that she had been able to sleep, since the floor was so hard and she was worried sick about Ellen. Ellen. She struggled up from the floor. Did this mean they'd caught her? Susan couldn't think of any other earthly reason for them to come get Mama and her at this hour.

The door opened, and she blinked against the glow of two oil lamps flickering in the hallway. One was held by Massa, the other by someone standing farther back whose face she couldn't see. As near as she could tell by the height of the lamp, it was a man, and her heart began to beat faster. God forbid it was that vile overseer.

Mama stood up as Massa stepped in and looked them up and down. He signaled to the figure behind him, and a strange man, tall and thin with gaunt cheeks, stepped into the room. He had a thick, dark mustache and wore a cheap suit of clothing. He was definitely not the sort that usually came calling on the Shaws.

"This one here," Massa said. To Susan's horror, he was pointing at *her*. She giggled nervously. Surely Massa was making a mistake, whatever this was about. Anything else was too horrible to think. The man took a step forward, but Massa held up a hand to stop him. "Just a minute," Massa said and he looked at Mama.

"Clara, this here is Mr. Taylor. He's come from Richmond to fetch Susan."

Susan blinked, thinking she hadn't heard right. Or else she was still asleep. That was it. She was still asleep on the hard floor. She was worried about Ellen, and she was having a nightmare. She giggled again.

"Fetch her?"

That was Mama's voice. Mama was in the dream, too, and she sounded so worried.

"Fetch her where, Massa?"

"To Richmond."

"What for?" The tone of Mama's voice was rising, almost to a shriek. Susan wanted to tell Mama not to worry. It was only a dream.

"She's going to Mr. Montgomery, the gentleman who used to own Montpelier. He—"

"I know who he is, Massa. Mass Willard owned Montpelier before you came. But what's he want with my baby?"

"He needs a nursemaid."

"A what?"

"His daughter was just married and—"

"But, Massa—"

"And he needs a nurse for her children. We were going to send Ellen, but she must have gotten word of it 'cause we can't find her anywhere. I've sent word to Mr. Montgomery that Susan will take her place."

Susan blinked. *Hard.* It was time to wake up from this dream. It was starting to feel too real.

"Lord almighty, Massa! Tell him to get somebody else." Mama was screaming now. "She's just a baby herself."

"She's old enough for this. And if she comes along peacefully, I may be able to arrange for her to come back here to visit from time to time. . . ."

Mama shook her head. "No, Massa. I know about these things. I've seen it time and time again. You take her, I won't ever see her again."

Massa sighed impatiently. "I promised Mr. Montgomery a nursemaid and a gentleman always keeps his word. Now—"

"But a gentleman doesn't go 'round splitting up families, Massa. You can't . . . Where is Mass Willard? 'Cause I don't believe he would do a thing like this. Where is he, Massa? I want to talk to him."

Mass Stephen ignored the question and signaled to the mustached man. Mr. Taylor took a step forward, and Susan knew then that she was never going to wake up from this nightmare. She jumped and flew around to the other side of the bed. "Stay away from me!" she screamed, flailing her arms out in every direction. "Mama, don't let them take me."

Mr. Taylor hesitated and glanced back at Mass Stephen. Mr. Taylor looked stunned.

"Massa," Mama said, her breath coming fast and heavy. "I don't understand this. I've been good to you and all the other massas before you. I looked out for you when you first got here. Your daughter played with Susan. And now you . . ."

Mass Stephen ignored her and signaled to Mr. Taylor, then he turned and left the room.

"Massa, you going to burn in hell, you do this to my baby! Massa!" Mama started to run after him until she saw Mr. Taylor walking toward Susan. She turned and grabbed him from behind.

"You stay away from that child," Mama said sternly. "Don't you touch—"

He shoved Mama away, and she hit the wall with a thud.

"Mama!" Susan yelled. She hoped Mama wasn't hurt,

but she was too scared to come from around the bed and check. The man came closer until she was backed into a corner. He grabbed her by the arm, and she swung wildly to free herself from his grasp. She yelled, kicked, and punched him with her fists. He let go, took a step back, and slapped her hard across the cheek with the back of his hand. It knocked her against the wall, and her hand flew to her face. He didn't say a word, just stood in the same spot and glared at her.

She was no match for this and was about to give in, but Mama had recovered, and she pounced on his back. Susan's cheek was still hot and sore, but there wasn't a minute to lose. She jumped up on the bed and crawled across to the other side, then she hopped down and prepared to flee. She had no idea where she was going. All she knew was that she had to get out of there. She had to save herself. They didn't want Mama, they didn't want Ellen. They wanted her.

She ran smack into the overseer's chest.

"*Mon Dieu!*" She backed away.

He laughed at the expression on her face, then grabbed her and threw her over his shoulder. She pounded his fleshy back. "Put me down!" she screamed as he carried her out into the hallway. She couldn't see Mama, but she could hear her yelling at the top of her lungs at both John and Mr. Taylor.

John dumped her on the floor and grabbed her hair, which by now had fallen down over her shoulders. He yanked her up to her knees and pointed a callused finger in her face.

"Listen heah, you nigga bitch. Quit carryin' on like this an' do as you're told, or Ah'll carry yo' uppity French-talkin' ass out to mah whippin' post and beat you down to yo' last breath."

Susan whimpered and tried to crawl away, but he grabbed her dress at the shoulder and jerked her to her feet. She heard the fabric as it ripped at the seams.

"Now get on down them stairs 'for Ah throw you down there, gal." She tried to look back to see Mama, but he shoved her and she stumbled down the top step. She hesitated, and he shoved her again and again until they reached the last three steps. He pushed harder, and she stumbled to the bottom, landing on her hands and knees with a thud. As bad as it hurt, she didn't want to get up. She didn't want to move. Not ever. Getting up meant walking, and walking meant leaving Montpelier.

"Must you be so damn rough?" she heard Massa ask. Susan's gaze roamed up the hallway floor until she saw his shiny black boots in the doorway of the drawing room. "Montgomery isn't going to want to see his nursemaid all roughed up."

"Ain't much else you can do when niggas act like this, suh," John said. "It's the only thing that gets through to 'em. Ah didn't bring mah pistol, didn't think Ah'd be needin' it with a coupla wenches, but I might have to go and fetch it."

John stood over her with his hands on his waist and his dingy boots in her face, as she listened to the sound of Mama stumbling down the stairs, no doubt being helped along by Mr. Taylor. When Mama saw her there on the floor, she ran down the remaining stairs two at a time and stopped in front of Mass Stephen.

"Massa," Mama said, her voice cracking. "Please don't do this. My family's been here for generations. She's never been away from Montpelier. This her home. How's my baby going to manage without her mama?"

"You tell me where Ellen is, Clara, and I won't need to sell your baby."

Don't do it, Mama, Susan wanted to yell. It's a trick.

"I don't know where Ellen is, Massa," Mama said, shaking her head. "I swear I don't."

"Very well," Massa said. He waved his hand nonchalantly. "Take her." He spun on his heels.

"Massa, wait, please," Mama said. She paused to catch her breath. "If I can find Ellen, you won't sell both of them to Mass Willard, will you?"

Be careful, Mama. Don't let him trick you.

Massa turned back to face Mama. "One of them is going to Richmond. I've given my word. Money has exchanged hands. But I'll let you decide which one."

Susan couldn't believe she was hearing right. How could he do this?

Mama shook her head. "Massa, please. Don't do this. Haven't we done right by you? What you want to . . ."

Massa turned his back.

"Massa, I'll try to find Ellen. I'll . . ."

Susan jumped up and grabbed her mama from behind. "No, Mama." It was a trick, and a low-down dirty one at that. If Mama produced Ellen, he would sell them both now.

"But, baby, I . . . I don't know what else to do. She's seventeen now and you still a child."

"It's all right, Mama."

Mama began to sob, and her shoulders shook violently. Susan looked up to see Mass Stephen standing in the doorway watching them. He was playing this dirty trick to get Ellen back. Well, it wasn't going to work. She fixed him with a hateful stare. "We don't know where Ellen went, so I reckon it's going to be me."

Massa glared at her, then walked off. Mr. Taylor came up from behind and reached for Susan's arm. She jerked it away. "I'm coming. You don't need to shove."

She took Mama's hand, and they walked down the hallway with Mr. Taylor and John close behind. They walked past the parlor, past the front door, the dining room, and the library. Their earlier screams had alerted the others in the house, and they had come running from their pallets and morning chores to see what was happening. Black and brown and yellow faces stood in doorways and up against walls, watching silently as they passed by. Aunt Sarah stood in a corner, her old face looking broken as tears streamed down her cheeks.

They rounded the corner and walked down the back stairs, then through the old basement kitchen and out the door. The sun was coming up now, and Susan could see their cabin not a stone's throw away. Beyond that was the smoke house and the well. The flower garden lay off in the distance, framed by the majestic peaks of the Blue Ridge mountains. For some reason, all the courage she'd felt in the hallway vanished in the thick August air. She didn't want to leave her home.

The screech that erupted from her throat, she barely recognized as her own. She dropped Mama's hand and tried to run back into the house, but Mr. Taylor caught her and threw her back on the ground. John held Mama back as Mr. Taylor tried to drag her by the hair across the yard to a wagon. When that didn't work, he wrapped his arm around her waist and half carried, half dragged her to the lane. Her kicking feet stirred up a cloud of dust.

Susan stopped screaming when she saw Mama break away from John and run off in the direction of their cabin. She wanted to tell Mama to come back and help her, but it was taking all her energy just to fight off this man as he lifted and tossed her into the back of the wagon. She lay still for a moment, trying to catch her breath and plan her next move. Then she saw the chain in Mr. Taylor's hands, and she knew it was over. She and Mama had been foolish enough to think they could fight this, that they had a chance, when they had none. Nothing and no one could save her.

She sank down in the wagon and lay on her back while Mr. Taylor wrapped the chain around her waist. She could tell he was surprised that she had stopped resisting. She closed her eyes, determined not to let him see her pain as he bolted the chain to the wagon. Then she heard her mama's voice calling her name. She had lost all hope that Mama or anyone else could save her now, but she lifted herself up on one elbow and peered over the side of the wagon as Mr. Taylor jumped into the seat and took the reins. Mama was running toward her, holding something in her outstretched hands, but Susan couldn't make out what it was. She wiped her eyes and blinked. Then she saw it—Grandma Susie's strand of blue beads.

Susan struggled to sit up. She wanted to be able to take the beads and hug Mama one last time. Mama begged the driver to wait as she ran. "Please! Wait! This belongs to her." But he ignored her and lashed the horse.

The wagon lurched forward, and Susan fell back. She struggled up again just in time to see Mama stumble and fall to the ground. The beads flew out of her hands and scattered across the lawn. Mama struggled back up empty-handed and ran after the wagon as it picked up speed. Susan's shoulders shook with each sob as they pulled farther and farther away. She knew this was an image of Mama that she would not ever forget.

15

Susan lay on her back in the wagon as it bobbed along the rocks and ruts lining the road. The wagon was hard and dusty, the ride bumpy, but she was numb to any pain.

Her mind tried to make sense of what was happening. She had been plucked away from her family as casually as you would pluck the feathers from a chicken. Now she was chained to a wagon and being hauled down a long road by a stranger. There had to be a law against this. Everyone in the county knew she belonged at Montpelier, that her family had lived there for generations. Surely someone would put a stop to this if only they knew.

She leaned up and peered over the side of the wagon. They passed by open fields of corn and hay. They passed over hills and meadows, then entered a grove of trees, but she didn't see a soul about. The only sound was the horse's hooves clopping on the dirt road and the wagon rocking from side to side. Then they moved deeper into the woods, and all hope of anyone seeing her grew thinner as the trees grew thicker. Even if she screamed at the top of her lungs, no one would hear her. She fell back into the wagon.

They left the woods and turned onto a well-traveled

road. Mr. Taylor lashed the horse, and they picked up speed. They were a long way from home now, but she still hoped to see someone familiar. The wagon began to slow its pace, and she heard the sound of another horse's hooves in the distance. She struggled to sit up and stretched her neck, trying to see around Mr. Taylor. The wagon halted at an intersection in the road, and she squinted in the late morning light as the other horse drew nearer. A stocky white man with a face that was red from too much sun sat in the saddle. She was trying to think whether she recognized him when she saw a rope in his hand, and her eyes followed it to what was trailing behind him—a gang of eight colored boys tied two-by-two by their wrists.

Her mind spun as she stared, searching for something to tell her that her eyes were playing a dirty trick. Susan thought they were some of the sorriest-looking beings to walk on two legs that she'd ever seen in her life. Their brown clothes were tattered and dirty and they were dripping with sweat.

The red-faced driver pulled back on the reins of his horse. "Mornin'," he said, tipping a well-worn hat to Mr. Taylor. Mr. Taylor nodded in return. Some of the boys looked up from the ground and stared at her. That was when the man on the horse seemed to notice her, too.

"Now that's a likely gal you got there. Wouldn't happen to be fer sale, would she? I pay top dollah, 'specially for high-yaller wenches."

Susan gasped and looked down at her dress. It was dirty, rumpled, and ripped at the shoulder, and she realized that her hair clung to her sweat-glistened face and neck. She slid down into the wagon. *"Mon Dieu!"* she whispered. Was there no escape from this living hell she'd entered?

"This one's just been sold," Mr. Taylor said. "On her way to Richmond."

"A shame," the other man said, smacking his lips. "Fine wench like that would fetch a considerable sum in the French Mahket down in New Orleans."

She heard the horse's hooves and the shuffling of tired bare feet as the boys passed by. Mr. Taylor yanked the reins, and she crouched in a corner and tried as much as possible to make herself invisible outside the wagon. Now she knew that even if she screamed, no one would care. All the whites were in this together.

The wagon slowed again, and she saw the tops of strange-looking buildings in the distance. She thought they must be approaching another plantation, but as they drew nearer, she realized that the buildings didn't look like any houses or barns she'd ever seen. She was tempted to sit up, but dared not.

The wagon stopped, and Mr. Taylor jumped down from his seat. He walked back and yanked on the chain to make sure it was still secure. Satisfied that it was, he pointed a finger in her face. "Now, you just stay put till I get back, ya hear? Won't be more'n a minute or two."

Susan said nothing. Where in tarnation did he expect her to go when she was chained like an animal? Where did he expect her to go when she didn't have a whiff of an idea where she was to start with. That's what she'd like to know. Dratted fool. She listened as his footsteps faded away and wondered what was going to happen to her next. She decided to at least take a quick peek at her surroundings, and she sat up and stared at the odd buildings. Most of them were brick, with funny-looking doors and windows. They were smaller than the big house at Montpelier but much bigger than a cabin, and sturdier looking. And white folks walked up and down the way, going in and out of them.

If it wasn't a plantation, then where were they? All her life, she'd heard folks talk about a town nearby called Orange. Miss Marie and Miss Rebecca used to talk about going there to buy cloth and other goods at the store. That must be what all these white folks were doing. She glimpsed Mr. Taylor coming out of a building and ducked down. She expected him to get back up and ride off, but instead he jerked on the chain until she sat up. "Now you listen to me good, gal."

She hated the way he talked to her—slow and loud, like she was some kind of imbecile. And his tobacco breath was some of the foulest she'd ever had the misfortune to get a whiff of. Worse than a dog's breath. She had a mind to tell him so, but she just turned her head slightly to avoid the stench as he dangled the key in front of her.

"I'm going to unlock this here chain now," he said. "But if I get so much as a peep outta you, it goes right back on, ya hear? And I'll shackle your wrists and feet, too, if I have to."

She was reluctant to get out in this raggedy dress. One shoulder was bare after the sleeve had been ripped by that vile overseer, and the dress was so soiled from riding in this dingy old wagon that she was embarrassed to be seen in it. But she certainly couldn't trouble herself about some old clothes now.

She jumped down from the wagon, and a man came out of a building and took the horse by the reins. Mr. Taylor paid him some money, and then he looked at her and pointed to the horse trough. She wrinkled her brow, not understanding.

"You better get a drink now. Be a while 'fore you get another chance."

"But that there's for horses."

He sneered. "It's water, ain't it?"

She righted her shoulders and lifted her head high. She wasn't drinking from that thing, she didn't care how thirsty she got.

Mr. Taylor shrugged. "Suit yourself."

He walked off without another word, and for a

moment she thought of fleeing in the other direction. But she quickly realized that someone would see her, even if Mr. Taylor's back was turned. Besides that, she had no idea where she was and wouldn't know which way to run. He glanced back at her. Of course, he knew that. She lifted her skirt and followed.

They walked in silence with her tagging along behind, almost having to run to keep up. They passed most of the buildings and then walked down a long, narrow, tree-lined road. He finally stopped next to an awning sitting out in the middle of nowhere. Several feet away lay some kind of contraption made of metal and wood. It looked like a ladder, except it was lying flat on the ground and ran in both directions as far as she could see. She looked about, trying to figure out why they had stopped here.

Mr. Taylor spat on the ground, took a watch out of his coat pocket, looked at it, then put it back. He stretched his neck and looked in the direction of the ladderlike contraption. A bearded white man approached and stood on the other side of the awning, and he and Mr. Taylor exchanged nods. The bearded man looked at Susan, and his eyes roamed from her face down to her bare shoulder. He rubbed his hand over his beard in a way that made Susan feel queasy, so she looked in the other direction.

She heard a loud whistle and rumbling sound off in the distance, and all eyes turned in that direction. At first, she couldn't see anything, but the rumble grew louder and soon she saw something moving toward them. She saw no horses or mules pulling it, only a big puff of black smoke swirling in the air, the biggest she'd ever laid eyes on. It was much bigger than anything that ever came out of the smokehouse back at Montpelier.

Susan had heard white folks talk about a big machine that moved without any animals pulling it. They called them boxcars or trains, but she had always imagined a kind of giant carriage or maybe several carriages chained together. As this thing drew closer, she could see that it was nothing like any carriage she'd ever seen. It was monstrous, with a big metal rail in front that swept the track as it moved forward. And it was coming so fast.

She jumped back as it roared up in front of them with a big gust of wind. Her skirt flapped around her legs as she turned. All the noise scared her, and she wanted to get away. But Mr. Taylor caught her and held her back.

"It's only a blasted train," he said with exasperation. "Won't bite ya."

Susan didn't believe a word this man said. It wouldn't bite her, that much was plain. But what was to stop it from crushing her to death?

"Listen, you idiot," he said, as the bearded man stared at them strangely. "If you don't settle down, I'll march your ass right back to town and you can just spend the night in jail for all I care. Didn't bargain for all this trouble. Mr. Montgomery said you'd come peaceable-like. He even told me to put you in the car with me, but I 'spect not, not the way you been carrying on."

Susan didn't know what the heck that meant, but she thought she'd rather spend a night in jail than go anywhere near that big thing. But as it sat there in front of them and quieted down a bit, it seemed less threatening. She also noticed a man leaning out a door and faces in the windows.

Mr. Taylor grabbed her by the arm and pulled her along the walkway in front of the train. Finally, he stopped and turned to face her. "Now, you going to get on one of the cars back here," he said, talking more loudly than usual to be heard over the train. "Got that?"

She shook her head. No, she didn't get it. She wasn't getting on any car or train and that was final.

He spat on the ground, then pointed his finger at her. "Listen here, gal. You do what I say, unless you want to spend the night in jail. Then I'm going to put your uppity ass on the auction block tomorrow, ya hear me?"

She lowered her head. She didn't know which scared her more—this big old thing, or the auction block. She wanted to cry but was determined not to let this man see her do that. He'd probably just laugh in her face.

Some folks got off at the front of the train, and a colored man came by and opened the door to the car near them. He shoved two leather suitcases inside, then walked off. Two copper-complexioned girls not much older than Susan got off and were immediately tied together at the wrists by the bearded man who had been waiting for them. Mr. Taylor signaled for Susan to get inside, and she took a deep breath. It was this or the auction block.

As she was about to step into the car, several brown hands reached out to help her, and she let them pull her inside. She turned around, expecting Mr. Taylor to climb up behind her, but he backed away and walked off just as the colored man shut the door in her face. What kind of horrible trick was Mr. Taylor playing on her now? Putting her on this train and then deserting her? As much as she hated the man, his was the only face she knew.

She turned to face the others in the car. Colored men, women, and children of all ages and all complexions stared back. Although she saw none as light as she was, a couple came close. Some of them wore chains on their feet, others were unshackled. One of them, a woman of medium complexion, stood up. "He be standin' there waitin' for you when we gets to Richmond."

The woman's dress was so threadbare you could see straight through it, and she didn't seem to care. Susan backed away. She wanted no part of this. It was obvious that most of these folk were field hands, and badly kept ones at that. She didn't belong here, even if her clothes were a bit tattered. And the stench! There was one tiny window, and the air was suffocating. She wasn't smelling like a rose, she knew, after fighting and being hauled away in a dirty wagon for miles with the hot sun beating on her back. But this was unbearable. These were exactly the kind of coloreds Mama had kept her away from all her life. She wanted so badly to go back home to Mama and Ellen and their cabin near the big house.

"Well, lookee here," the threadbare woman said, shaking her hips and turning up her nose. "I's just tryin' to help out, is all."

The train jerked, and Susan stumbled over one of the suitcases and fell back on her rump onto the hay-covered floor. The woman thought this was hilarious. She slapped her thighs and laughed. A few of the others snickered. Let them laugh all they want, Susan thought. She didn't care. She slid across the hay into a corner.

"Ain't got to act all uppity," the woman said.

She wasn't acting uppity.

"Leave her be," a man said. "She just a chile. Probably scared outta her wits."

She wasn't scared of these folks, at least not as scared as she was of the white ones. She just wanted to go home.

"That ain't no 'scuse for actin' all uppity," the woman said. "They prally gon' ship her fancy tail down there to that New Orleans soon as we gets to Richmond, and it serves her right."

"I heard they ships mo' niggers down to the deep Souf outta Richmond then just about anywheres."

Someone on the other side of the train wailed at hearing this.

"Lawd, I hopes some quality folks from Richmond buy me," a man said. "I don't want to go down South."

"I heard that in Richmond, niggers live almost free-like, comin' an' goin' much as they please."

"That ain't what I heard," another man said. "Heard they'll slap yo' behind in jail for just 'bout anything, even just walkin' down the street, if'n they don't like how you looks. Reckon I'd rather see a whip than rot away in one o' them jails they got special for colored folks. Least with a whip it be over and done with."

"Stop that talk," a woman said. "Y'all is scarin' the chillen in here."

Susan knew they all hated her. So what. She wasn't going to trouble herself about them. She had more pressing matters to worry about.

"It mostly them free niggers what end up in jail. They whip us slaves in Richmond just like they do anywheres else."

Someone said Richmond was a dangerous place with all sorts of bad folks, black and white, and vices like gambling, drinking, and prostitution. Someone else said most areas of the city weren't fit for a lady to walk the streets alone, especially at night. And it wasn't unheard of for a colored girl or woman to be snatched off the streets and sold off down South.

Susan wished they'd all just shut up. She was so tired. She wiped the sweat from her forehead and closed her eyes.

The train roared on and things quieted down as some of the folks dozed off. Others sat and stared into space. Susan's eyes kept closing, but she fought with all her might to keep them open. Every time she closed them, she saw Mama running with the blue beads.

She was getting cramps sitting in the corner, so she shifted her weight from one side to the other. Mama was always saying how lucky they were to be working in the house at a place like Montpelier, since they always got high-class massas and misses even after the Madisons left. And Mama always said if you worked hard and did as you were told, those kinds of white folks would treat you decent most of the time. Well, it was high-class white folks who had sold her without so much as a moment's regret.

Those same high-class white folks had dumped her on this train, and they didn't give a hoot one way or the other if she never came back. And it was someone colored at the Bell plantation who squealed on Papa Squire and Ellen. High-class, low-class, white, colored. How could she ever trust another soul?

Ellen. She had been so wrapped up in her own nightmare that she'd forgotten that Ellen was hiding out in the woods somewhere with Papa Squire. Or worse yet, maybe they had been found by the hounds and that sorry excuse for a human named John. She shook her head to clear it. She couldn't trouble herself about Ellen now. She had enough troubles of her own. She had to get back to Montpelier, somehow, someway, even if she died trying. If Ellen could run, why couldn't she? Never mind that she didn't have someone like Papa Squire to help her. She was going to have to figure out how to do it on her own.

She thought back and tried to remember the route they had taken in the wagon. She remembered open fields and rolling hills. She remembered the woods. But it was the first time she'd ever set foot off the grounds of Montpelier, and it had all seemed an ever-changing blur. She wished she'd paid more attention. From now on, she was going to have to watch and listen closely to everything and everyone around. She was going to study as much as she could about this Richmond and its strange people. Then she was going to steal away home the first chance she got.

16

Susan blinked in the glare of the evening light streaking through the window of the car. The others were climbing out, so she stood and walked to the door. She looked up and down the platform, trying to spot Mr. Taylor among all the people scurrying about. A part of her wanted to jump and run, but that would be stupid. She hadn't the slightest idea where to go.

She finally spotted Mr. Taylor approaching the car. He signaled for her to get out, so she stepped down onto the platform. Dust was flying everywhere from all the folks moving about, and she coughed and fanned her face. She wasn't going to try to resist anymore. Judging from how long they'd been riding on the train, she was an awfully long way from home. If she wanted a halfway decent chance of finding her way back, she was going to have to bite her tongue and wait for the right moment. She had no doubt it would come. It might take a week, it might take months, but the time would come. For now, she would stay alert and learn as much as she could. She would outsmart these double-dealing white folks if it was the last thing she ever did.

Mr. Taylor took her by the elbow as the train pulled out of the station. As he led her across the platform, she studied the scene around her. Never had her eyes taken in so much at once. Colored men, all wearing similar suits of clothing with lots of shiny buttons, rushed about. Their arms were filled with baggage or pushing carts and whites followed along closely behind. A stout blond man brushed by her, yelling "porter" at the top of his lungs and signaling in the direction of one of the strangely suited men. A pretty colored woman in a crisp calico dress and brightly patterned head wrap walked up and down the platform carrying a tray of food. Everyone seemed to be going in a different direction.

They left the platform and walked onto a road where more colored men were transporting more baggage for more white folks. Carriages and buggies were lined up and down the road, and there was one building after another in both directions for as far as she could see. She followed Mr. Taylor as he dodged in and out and walked briskly up to a colored man standing in front of a buggy. Mr. Taylor said some numbers and the words "Grace Street," then he climbed up and beckoned for her to follow. She hesitated, not sure whether she was to get in with him or sit up front with the driver. Mr. Taylor beckoned again, and it was clear she was to sit with him.

She lifted her skirt and struggled up onto the seat opposite him, as he leaned back on the cushion and lit a cigar. She sat upright and looked out the side as the buggy lurched forward. Almost immediately, her senses were saturated by the sights whirling by. She had heard stories all her life, some good, most bad, about the people, sounds, and smells of the city. But she had never expected this. Why, nearly half the folks she saw in the street were colored men, women, and children of all ages and complexions. Her eye caught one woman, about the color of baked bread, strolling along as casually as you please in a dress Miss Marie would have been perfectly happy to wear. She carried a parasol and walked just as straight and proud as any white mistress. Susan had never seen such a sight and never thought she would. She glanced at Mr. Taylor out the corner of her eye, expecting some kind of reaction, but he acted as if it was nothing unusual. So did all the other white folks in the street. As the buggy bounced down the road, Susan stretched her neck and kept her eye on the colored woman with the parasol for as long as she could.

The colored men were no slouches, either, in their waistcoats and patent leather shoes. Wherever did they get such finery? And so many of them. To be sure, some of them were dressed no better than she was, in the familiar cotton or calico. Others looked far worse. But they only served to make the finely dressed folks stand out all the more. Back home, these colored belles and dandies would be arrested on the spot.

Buildings taller than any she'd ever laid eyes on lined the street, one right after the other. Some were made of stone with little windows, others seemed to have a wall of glass so that anyone passing by could see everything inside. She wondered what went on in such buildings. Must be an awful lot, she reasoned, judging from all the folks going in and out of them.

The buggy slowed and turned onto a narrow bumpy road. The driver pulled off to the side and waited as Mr. Taylor jumped down and signaled for her to follow him. She frowned and looked around. All she could see was a few small buildings, most with big glass windows on both sides of a door. Only a few people were out and about here, and none of the buildings appeared to be the kind of dwelling where respectable white folks would live. She didn't like the looks of this.

"You done gone deaf now or somethin'?" Mr. Taylor asked. He spat on the ground impatiently. She stepped down from the buggy, and Mr. Taylor pointed to a trough filled with water in front of one of the buildings. A small red flag hung on the door, flapping in the hot breeze.

"You need to get cleaned up some. Mr. Montgomery's house ain't that far from here and your face and neck are smeared with dirt. Go on over there and rinse off."

She started to protest. The thought of washing in something made for animals was disgusting. She was used to bathing in porcelain basins or ponds and streams. And she was certainly not used to washing in front of vile white men. But if she was going to get a chance to run, she had to be cooperative. Otherwise, they'd always watch her like a hawk and she'd never get half a chance. Besides, it had been a long, hot journey, and she needed to rinse off. It wouldn't take long to dry in this hot sun.

She lifted her dingy skirt and walked to the trough. Mr. Taylor strolled in the opposite direction, and for that she was thankful. She picked up the drinking gourd hanging on a wooden rail above the trough and dipped it in. She scooped some water into the gourd and eyed it closely. She picked out a few specks of grass and flicked them on the ground, then sprinkled the water over her chest and neck. It had warmed from sitting out in the hot sun, but it still felt pretty good. She poured the rest of it down her back, then she scooped and cleaned out some more and poured it over her arms. She sprinkled a few drops on her tongue, then spit them out. She hadn't had food or water since this morning, but she had her limits.

As she hung the gourd back up, she noticed that a piece of paper was pinned to the red flag hanging in front of the building. She looked up the road and saw that Mr. Taylor's back was still turned. She crept up to the window and peered in. The room was dark and narrow and mostly bare, with benches lined up along the walls. At one end stood an old weathered desk, and at the other, a platform raised a few feet off the floor. The grit and grime on the floor was so thick, she could see it clearly through the window. What an odd little room, she thought.

She glanced up the street again to make sure Mr. Taylor

wasn't watching. She also looked at the driver, still sitting in the buggy. If anything bothered him about what she was doing, he didn't let on. She stepped closer to the flag, glanced at Mr. Taylor once more, then moved closer. She couldn't read all the words on the piece of paper but understood enough to catch the meaning. "Sold tomorrow morning . . . a boy, a girl . . ."

She backed away so fast, she tripped over her own two feet. She caught herself just before falling and walked quickly toward the buggy and climbed in. Mr. Taylor returned and sat next to her, and she realized she was out of breath. She tried to look calm as a hundred thoughts ran through her mind. Had she just seen one of those places where colored folks were bought and sold like cattle and horses? An auction house?

She was so lost in thought, she didn't see the neighborhood change. All she knew was that they were suddenly on a smooth road lined with trees. There were no more buildings with glass windows. These looked like houses, some like small versions of Montpelier, except they had precious little land between them. Many of them had pretty flower gardens in front and smaller outhouses in the back. She wondered where these folks kept their slaves and farm animals.

The driver pulled up in front of the biggest house on the street and stopped. It sat high up on a hill and was almost as grand as Montpelier. It had white columns and a front portico, just like Montpelier, and a sprawling front lawn. Mr. Taylor jumped out of the wagon, extinguished his cigar with his fingertips, and placed it in a pocket. Susan climbed down, then followed him up the stairs and around to the side of the house.

She was not going to get upset now, she told herself as they waited for someone to answer the door. She had made it this far in one piece, hadn't she? She chewed the inside of her mouth and smoothed her skirt, now stiff and dirty after the long journey. She tried to put the torn shoulder of her dress in place and the loose strands of her hair into the bun at the back of her head. Not that she really cared what she looked like to these folks. She just hated the idea of looking no better than a field hand. Mama would have had a fit if she saw her.

The side door opened, and a light brown face with gentle eyes greeted them with a smile. It was obvious the woman was expecting them, for she immediately stepped back and opened the door wide. Mr. Taylor walked in and he and Susan both followed the woman down a hallway and into a small parlor.

"Sit and rest a spell," the woman said to Mr. Taylor. "I'll get the missus." The woman backed out of the room and shut the double doors behind her.

Susan stayed in the middle of the floor while Mr. Taylor paced up and down the carpet. Then he sat in one of two matching wing chairs in front of the fireplace. He crossed his legs, then uncrossed them. He tapped his foot on the carpet. Susan couldn't imagine what he had to be so jumpy about. She was the one about to meet a new mistress. He would simply go his own way—after being paid a tidy sum, she supposed—probably to snatch some other helpless girl away from her home and family. She clenched her fists. She had to calm down. She wanted to put these people at ease so they'd give her the freedom to move about. If she acted difficult, hoping that they would get mad and send her back to Montpelier, it would be just her luck to end up being sent farther south instead.

She took a deep breath and looked around. Anything to keep her mind off what was about to happen. The room was smaller than the parlors at Montpelier but the furnishings and carpets were every bit as nice. The room had high ceilings and big old paintings on the walls and dark, heavy draperies. In fact, some of the bric-a-brac seemed oddly familiar. Then she remembered that Mass

Willard had owned Montpelier at one time. She barely remembered the name and had completely forgotten his face, since it had been so long ago.

The doors swung open, and Mr. Taylor jumped up. He stood with his hands behind his back as an older white woman entered the room. Her gray hair was pulled back sharply from her high forehead, with a perfectly straight part down the middle. She carried her slim figure with a dignified carriage as she brushed past Mr. Taylor, ignoring his bowed head. She walked up to Susan and looked into her face, and her thin lips tightened. Susan felt panic stir in her gut.

The woman reached out and lifted Susan's chin with a stiff forefinger. As she turned Susan's face this way and that, Susan noticed a plump, dark-complexioned woman enter the room and stand near the doorway. She wore a light-colored scarf tied neatly around her head and a starched white apron. Susan wanted to turn and get a better look but dared not. She knew the missus would think it rude.

"How old are you?" the woman asked. "That is, if you know." Her voice was sarcastic as she dropped Susan's chin and stepped back.

"Fourteen, ma'am."

"Hmm," the woman said, just as a man entered the room. Susan couldn't see much of him, except to note that he was tall and had white hair. He wore a linen suit and carried gloves and a tall hat in his hand. He gave the gloves and hat to the woman standing near the doorway and walked toward Mr. Taylor. They spoke softly. That must be Mass Willard, Susan thought. She hoped he was nicer than this old lady seemed to be.

"Well, I had certainly expected her to be in better shape than this," the woman said, eyeing the torn shoulder of Susan's dress.

Susan studied her fingers. Then send me back, she

thought, as the missus turned to the white-haired man.

"I thought you said she was a house servant, Willard," the missus said. "She looks no better than a field hand."

Susan bit her tongue. Anyone would look bad after what she'd been through. The man came and stood next to his wife. She glanced up and it felt like someone had socked her in the jaw. He was older and a bit more stout, his hair was thinner and whiter, but this was the man who used to bring a penny to her and Ellen every night. Could this be her daddy?

17

Mon *Dieu!* It seemed that time stood still, as if everything that had ever happened to her—big and small, long ago, this very day—was leading to this moment.

Susan tried to keep a straight face, even though her cheeks burned and her mouth felt like a sandpit. But if her shock was obvious, Mass Willard didn't let on that he noticed. He walked up and stood in front of her. He looked a bit annoyed as he told her to turn around.

"What the devil happened here?" he asked before she could get completely around. He faced Mr. Taylor. "She's got bruises and scratches on her face and arms."

"Couldn't be helped, Mr. Montgomery," Mr. Taylor said. "She and the mother put up a heck of a fight. She had to be chained to the—"

Mass Willard grimaced. "Chains? I specifically said no roughness and no restraints."

Mr. Taylor shifted his weight. "I know you did, sir, but she was difficult the whole way, fighting and carrying on."

Mass Willard grunted. "She doesn't look so difficult to me. She's such a tiny thing, looks a lot like her grandmother."

This man knew Grandma Susie? Susan blinked as he bent down slightly and looked at her, a smile playing around the corners of his lips. "Are you difficult?" he asked.

Susan swallowed hard and shook her head. "No, Massa."

"This is just what I didn't want," Mass Willard said, turning back to Mr. Taylor. "You should have sent for word as to what to do, if you couldn't figure out how to handle a seventy-pound girl without using force."

Mr. Taylor let out an exasperated gust of air.

Mass Willard looked back at her. "How do you feel?"

"Fine, Massa."

"Was the trip rough on you?"

"No, Massa. Not especially."

His eyes narrowed. "Where did you ride on the train?"

"In the back, with all the other coloreds, Massa."

"Sir," Mr. Taylor said, clearing his throat. "She was too unruly to place in the front cars, so I—"

"I'm talking to her," Massa said, interrupting impatiently. He turned his attention back to Susan. "How are you feeling? Been sick?"

Susan shook her head. "No, Massa."

He looked at his wife. "Think we can get her fixed up before Elizabeth gets back from her honeymoon?"

Missus stood with thin lips puckered and both hands cupped firmly in front of her lap. She looked doubtful. "They're due back only a week from now."

"Besides a few scratches, it looks to me like she's just dirty," Massa said. "It's nothing that a little attention won't fix. A bath, a few new dresses to give her more of a city-house look."

"Not the bruises," Missus said, shaking her head. "The bruises are going to take some time. And a city-house look takes much more than a few dresses, dear. If she's to be a gift to Elizabeth—"

Mass Willard waved his hand nonchalantly. "The bruises are minor. They'll heal eventually. Call the doctor in if you have to."

Missus twisted her lips. "If you think so, dear. I'll see what we can do."

"Damn it, Taylor," Massa said. "I don't like this one bit. She's supposed to be a wedding gift to my daughter and now she's all banged up."

"Sir, I—"

Massa held up a hand to silence him. "Come into my study. We'll talk there."

Susan's eyes followed Massa as he walked to the door with Mr. Taylor in tow. She watched his every step until they disappeared from the room. So much was swimming through her head, it was a muddled mess. Was this man her daddy? Did the missus know? Why bring her here if the missus didn't want her?

"Aunt Martha," Missus called.

Susan tumbled out of her reverie as Missus signaled the plump colored woman who had been standing near the doorway. "Aunt Martha," Missus said, her hands still cupped in front of her. "How will we go about this? We haven't much time, and she's a mess. I expected her to be much more refined than this. For the life of me, I can't understand why Master Willard is so set on this. Miss Elizabeth isn't even with child yet. Goodness knows, there must be a thousand other things we could give her, with them just starting out. Master Richard is only a doctor."

The colored woman stepped forward and stood beside her mistress. She was the color of the tree trunks at Walnut Grove, and her face looked every bit as rigid. Her hair was gray, but Susan could tell that her wrinkled brown eyes didn't miss a thing. She walked around Susan and looked her up and down like she was a new piece of furniture that had just been delivered.

"You know how Mass Willard is once his mind is set, Miss Nancy," Aunt Martha said.

Missus turned down her lips and squared her shoulders. "This girl looks like she just left the tobacco fields."

This was too much. "I worked in the big house all my life, ma'am. My mama did, too."

Aunt Martha's jaw dropped open. "Land sakes. Don't you talk to Miss Nancy like that, gal. I don't know where you're from, but 'round here we wait till we told to speak."

Susan looked down at the floor. She knew she'd stepped out of her proper place but she was tired of them talking about her as if she were some field hand.

"First thing she needs is a good hot bath with some lye soap," Aunt Martha said. "Then we have to find her some decent clothes." She narrowed her eyes at Susan. "Where you coming from?"

"Montpelier."

Aunt Martha wrinkled her nose. "Mont . . . pee . . . who?"

What was the matter with this old woman? Had she been living in a swamp all her life? Everyone knew about Montpelier. It was almost as famous as Monticello, home of President Jefferson. Susan looked Aunt Martha in the eye. "It's a plantation," she said.

Disapproval crossed Aunt Martha's face. "Oh, I see. So you been living on one of them plantations?"

Not just any plantation. The Madison plantation. There was a big difference, although Susan suspected she'd have a time of it trying to make this woman understand that. It was all Susan could do to keep from smacking her lips with frustration. If Missus wasn't still standing in the room, she would have done just that.

"It was once the home of President Madison," Susan said calmly. She made sure she enunciated each word properly.

"Yes," Miss Nancy said. "Master Willard owned it for a short while, although we never lived there. I was finally able to convince him that we belong here in the city. Though I wonder what's been going on there lately, considering how you look."

Susan bit her lip and looked back at the floor.

"Humph," Aunt Martha said. "Well, nobody told me she was coming from a plantation, Missus. She's going to need more work than I thought. I broke in a country gal once before and it was a time, I tell you. They have some of the strangest ways you ever did see." She squared her shoulders. "But it can be done. I'll have to stay on her day and night, but it can be done. Sooner or later, I'll knock those country ways out of her."

How dare this woman talk about her this way. She was a Madison Negro. Why, she'd wager she was more . . . what was the word Missus used? Refined? She had more of that in her baby finger than this Martha did in her whole body.

Missus shook her head. "I'd rather not have you tied up like that, Aunt Martha, if it's going to take so much. I knew she was from Montpelier, but we were led to believe that she would be in much better condition. Now that it seems she will need a good deal of training, you'll need to get someone else to help you."

"Right, Missus," Aunt Martha said. "Let me think on it. Sister Fanny might be good for now. With Miss Lizbeth away, she hasn't got as much to do."

Miss Nancy shook her head disapprovingly. "I don't know why Miss Elizabeth didn't take Fanny. A young woman traveling to a foreign land for nearly three months without her personal maid, why, I can't imagine how she's getting along."

"Me neither, ma'am," Aunt Martha said. "It's not right. But Miss Lizbeth said she didn't want to take too much help on account of those Europeans. They look down on slavery over there."

"That shouldn't have mattered to me," Miss Nancy said. "I would have taken all the help I needed. But these young people today."

Aunt Martha shook her head. "They something, Missus, I tell you."

"Very well," Missus said. "Fanny should do nicely, since

she's familiar with Miss Elizabeth's habits." She waved a hand in Susan's direction. "Now let's try to get her cleaned up. A hot bath, change of clothes."

"Right, Missus. Sister Fanny is drawing the bath water now." Aunt Martha looked at Susan and gestured toward the door. "Follow me. And no dilly-dallying about. We got a lot of precious things in the mansion, and I can't have you bumping into 'em."

Susan had a mind to tell this old woman to shut up as she followed her down the hallway. She had seen enough Persian carpets and marble busts and oil paintings to last a lifetime. Just because she lived in the country, didn't mean she wasn't used to nice things. Just because her clothes were a bit tattered, didn't mean she wasn't refined.

They walked up the stairs and down another hallway. Aunt Martha led her into a small room where she saw the biggest indoor washbasin she'd ever laid eyes on. Susan had seen tubs, but they were wood and always outdoors. And they were only big enough to sit up in. This one was big enough to stretch out in. And it seemed to be made of porcelain.

Aunt Martha instructed her to strip down completely, then step into the tub. The old woman dumped a washrag and a bar of soap into the water. "Now you scrub yourself good and clean from head to toe. And don't get to dilly-dallying around. The second thing you're going to have to learn, after you learn to talk to the missus respectable-like, 'cause that comes first, is that we takes care of ourselves here. It's not like on them plantations. We takes a bath every week with hot water and soap."

"I bathe in the stream every Friday evening in the summer. Sometimes more than that."

Aunt Martha grunted. "There's a world of difference between a stream and a tub of warm water. And bathing more than once a week is wicked. Miss Nancy will tell you that herself."

Mama used to tell her that white folks thought bathing more than once a week wasn't natural, but Susan didn't care. She loved the feel of the water streaming down her back, and she had to admit to herself that this warm water felt awfully good against her skin. She decided to ignore Aunt Martha and just enjoy the bath.

"Now you soak a while. I'll be back with some towels for you in a minute."

Aunt Martha shut the door behind her, and Susan realized that for the first time in a long while she was all alone, with no one she had to fight or argue with. She slipped down and let the water cover her shoulders. She wanted to put her head back and close her eyes, she was so tired. But she was afraid she might doze off, and she wasn't comfortable doing that in a tub full of water in a strange house.

So much had happened that day that it was hard to sort through it all. If being separated from her mama and sister wasn't gut-wrenching enough, now she was faced with the thought that the massa of this mansion might be her daddy. It was too much. She could remember an old man with white hair bringing Ellen and her a penny every night when they lived in the big house. She couldn't remember exactly how long ago that was or exactly what he looked like. They'd had so many massas at Montpelier, and all of them looked old to her.

She sighed. She longed to ask him, yet knew she never could. If she was wrong, even if she was right, it would be thought blasphemous. If he was her daddy and wanted to admit it, she would have to wait for him to make the first move. And if he took his time about it, she might not be around for him to do it. Whether he was her daddy or not didn't change a thing. She was still running the first chance she got. Richmond was a dangerous place, and this was such a strange household. It was obvious the missus didn't want her here, and they were all a bunch of stuck-ups, especially that Martha. The old woman seemed to think anybody not from the city was some kind of hick.

Oh, how she longed to be back home at Montpelier. She missed the flowers and the trees and the wide-open spaces. She missed all the familiar faces and the places where she could run and hide when she had things on her mind. But more than anything, she missed Mama and Ellen. She was dying to know what had become of her sister and Papa Squire. Did they get caught or were they still out hiding? Did they know what had happened to her?

She knew this had to be tearing Mama apart. Mama had lost both her daughters in less than a day's time. And Susan knew she would never, ever forget the sight of Mama running after the wagon with those blue beads. She was going to make it right, for Mama's sake as well as her own. No matter how they treated her here, she was going to slip away one of these days. And she was going to go back to Montpelier.

Someone was shaking her shoulder. Had she overslept again? Mama would be furious. Susan jumped, expecting to see Ellen standing over her in their little cabin, trying to rouse her. But something was wrong. The room was dark, with a lone lamp burning on a table, and she was in a tub full of water, not in the bed in her cabin. And the hand on her bare shoulder wasn't Ellen's. She started to cry.

"There, there," a woman said, patting her head. Susan wiped her eyes with her wet fingers and looked up into a smiling face that reminded her of Mama. The woman had a soft butternut complexion and wide brown eyes that glowed in the candlelight. She was even about the same age as Mama, maybe a few years younger. And her expression was the first one of genuine warmth that Susan had seen since leaving Montpelier that morning.

"You're just tired," the woman said. "It's no wonder, with the journey and all and being separated from your family. But you need to get out of that there tub, child, before your skin shrivels right off of your back."

This was the first person to say anything about her missing her family. Everyone else seemed to think she didn't have one, or else they didn't care. For some reason, that made Susan feel a little better. In another time and place, she would have liked this woman right away. But she worked for the family that had stolen her from her mama. No matter how nice anybody here was to her, she wasn't going to bend.

She sat up. She couldn't believe she'd fallen fast asleep in the tub. This woman was right about one thing. She must be awful tired. She looked at her fingers. They were all wrinkled up and felt rough to the touch. The woman held several clean towels in her arm and handed a small one to Susan. "Here, wrap that around your head," she said. Then she gave Susan another towel for her body. It was big and fluffy, not like the worn ones the coloreds had to make do with at home.

"Thanks, er . . ."

"Fanny," the woman said as Susan stepped out of the tub. "Here, sit down, and I'll help you dry your hair off." Fanny pulled a hardbacked chair away from the wall, but Susan hesitated for a minute. Why was this woman being so nice? For all she knew, this woman would snip her hair off down to its roots. Then she realized that she really didn't even care. They had cut her away from the very thing that mattered most to her. What did she care about some hair?

She wrapped the big towel tightly around her body, then sat in the chair. Fanny rubbed her hair with the towel, and her fingers were firm, yet gentle. It was obvious she'd done this many times before. Then Susan remembered that Fanny was Miss Elizabeth's personal maid. Before Susan knew it, she had closed her eyes. She was tired, and Fanny's hands were so soothing.

"You got the prettiest hair," Fanny said as she picked up a brush and ran it down Susan's head. "Just like my mistress's except hers is more red than brown."

Susan's eyes popped open. Ellen had red hair. In fact, this moment reminded her of when she and Ellen would brush each other's hair before bed. She swallowed hard and closed her eyes. It was all she could do to keep from crying. "Thank you."

"Aunt Martha said you came from the Madison place?" Fanny asked.

Susan nodded.

"That the President Madison place?"

"Uh-huh."

"Who did you live there with? Your mama?"

Susan nodded. "And my sister."

"Older, younger?"

"Older."

"Uh-huh. What was it like there?"

Susan opened her eyes. Just thinking about how lovely Montpelier was lifted her spirits. "Oh, it's beautiful. Lots of trees and flowers, and mountains everywhere you look. I worked in the big house with Mama and my sister, but we had a cabin of our own right close by. It's my home, and I miss it so much already."

"It sounds real nice. But this here is your home now."

Susan shut her eyes. Wrong, she thought. Montpelier would always be her home, even if she never made it back, and she didn't want to hear otherwise. But she wasn't going to argue. She would just run away when the right time came.

"Massa and Missus good folks. They'll be good to you, 'specially since you going to be taking care of Miss Lizbeth's children. That's their oldest daughter, and Mass Willard dotes on her. Ever watched after children before?"

"No, never." That wasn't exactly true. She'd helped care

for her half brother and half sister and the Thornton babies, even though she wasn't much more than a baby herself at the time. But if they thought she was inexperienced, maybe they'd send her back home.

"Never?" Fanny said. "Sounds like I got my work cut out for me then. Never mind, we can practice on a doll baby. We have plenty of time, since she's not even with child yet."

"What's she like?" Susan wanted as much information about these people as she could get.

"Miss Lizbeth? Why, she's the kindest, sweetest woman you ever want to meet. All of them are. Miss Nancy can be kind of testy at times, but she's all right. You're lucky, you'll see. I don't know how they treated you where you just came from and I know you miss your family and all, but here they'll treat you good long as you don't cause problems."

"What if . . . what if I'm not so good with the children?"

"Ain't much to it 'sides holding 'em and feeding 'em when she don't want to do it. You'll get the hang of it in no time at all."

Maybe not, Susan thought slyly. Maybe not on purpose. Fanny touched her back and she opened her eyes. "Your hair is so long, it's going to take a while to finish drying on the ends. But least it's not dripping wet anymore."

Susan stood up. "I didn't bring any clothes with me."

"You can wear one of my night dresses for tonight," Fanny said, shaking out something short and tan-colored. She handed it to Susan and helped her slip it over her head. "Now let me show you where you'll sleep."

Fanny picked up a lamp from a nearby table, and Susan followed her out of the room and down the hallway to the attic stairs.

"It ain't much, but it's comfortable," Fanny said as she

led the way up the steep steps. "Naturally, after the babies start coming, you'll be sleeping with them. But for now, this will be it." She opened the door to a small room. It had a slanted ceiling and was sparsely furnished, with two small beds under a window and a small table between them. A chest of drawers sat on the wall opposite the window.

"You can take that one over there," Fanny said, pointing to the bed on the far side of the room. "Missy used to sleep up here with me, but she got married and moved out." She set the lamp on the table and turned to face Susan. "Now, she just comes here during the daytime to work."

Susan frowned as she stood beside the bed. Moved out? Was Missy a slave, and if so, where did she move to? But Susan was too tired to ask any questions tonight. Everything on her and in her was drained, and all she wanted to do now was sleep. Besides, she'd already talked too much to this Fanny. She didn't want to get into the habit of doing much of that. What she wanted more than anything right this minute was to be left alone so she could stretch her tired body on this bed.

Fanny removed a coarse woolen blanket from the chest of drawers and laid it across the bed. "Now, you rest. You look so tired. Are you hungry?"

That was when Susan realized she was starving. She hadn't eaten since yesterday and it was dark out now. She nodded.

"I'll bring you something from our supper. Tomorrow, I'll show you around the mansion and the yard, and maybe we can go into town and get you something to wear. I'll see what Aunt Martha thinks."

Aunt Martha. She could do without hearing about that woman. Susan's thoughts must have showed on her face, because Fanny chuckled.

"Aunt Martha's not as hard as she seems sometimes,

'specially once you get her away from Massa and Missus. A lot of that is just show for them."

If that was the case, Susan thought, Aunt Martha was a darn good actress. And Massa? What about him? Susan wanted to ask but she was so tired, she didn't think she'd hear the answer. She was sure she'd learn more than enough about him soon. Fanny backed out of the room and closed the door, and she fell across the bed.

18

Susan sat up and rubbed her eyes. She knew it must be awful late. Fanny's little bed had been neatly made and across it lay the ugliest dress Susan had ever had the misfortune to lay her eyes on. This was her first time waking up anywhere besides Montpelier, away from her own bed and her own clothes, and she didn't like it one bit.

She stared at the coarse fabric of the dress spread across the bed. Fanny had said last night, when she brought Susan some boiled ham and cornbread, that she would leave a dress for her in the morning. Only Fanny didn't say anything about the dress being blue. Susan knew she should get up and wash and dress and start the day. But she couldn't take her eyes off that blue dress. It was the exact same shade of blue as Mama's beads, and it reminded her of Mama running, Mama falling, Mama dropping the blue beads. She wished she had the beads now so she could hold them in her hands. That might at least make all this more bearable.

A tear slid down her cheek. She wanted to jump up and run away from this mansion this very minute. But even if she could find her way back home, she didn't have a penny to her name. She quickly wiped the tears on her cheeks. She didn't want anyone feeling sorry for her, not that anyone here ever would. She could bawl until candlelight, probably, and nobody here would care.

She got up and walked to the chest of drawers. Fanny had left a pitcher full of fresh water standing beside the basin. She wondered where they got their water, since she'd seen no well or streams nearby. Fanny seemed nice, unlike that old coot Aunt Martha. But she didn't care how nice Fanny or anybody else around here was to her. She wanted to smell the roses that were in full bloom this time of year at Montpelier. She wanted to wake up in her own cabin and run to the kitchen with Ellen, where Aunt Mamie baked fresh biscuits every morning.

And she wanted her own clothes. She pulled the blue dress over her head. The fabric was so stiff, she wouldn't even need to scratch her back to get rid of an itch. And the dratted thing drooped all over her body like a sack. Look at this, she thought, pulling the dress up over her shoulders. Old rag didn't fit anywhere near right. She yanked open the top drawer of the chest and threw things around looking for something to pin the dress up with.

The door to the room opened and her head jerked up. Aunt Martha walked in, looking like she'd been up and about for hours on end, followed by Fanny, who was smiling. Aunt Martha was scowling.

"What you doing in there?" Aunt Martha asked, eyeing her suspiciously.

"I was looking for some pins," Susan said, backing away from the drawer.

Aunt Martha glared at her. "That dress is way too big for you."

Susan wanted to say something sassy so bad, her tongue itched. But she bit it instead. "That's why I wanted the pins."

Aunt Martha looked at Fanny. "That the best you could come up with?"

"It's the smallest one I have," Fanny said as she walked

to the chest. She rummaged through the drawers, while Aunt Martha stood with her hands cupped at her lap just like Susan had seen Miss Nancy do the day before. The way Aunt Martha watched over them, you'd think she was guarding the White House. Fanny found a couple of pins and tightened the dress around Susan's shoulders.

"You take her 'round yesterday?" Aunt Martha asked.

Fanny shook her head. "No, indeedy. She was too tired from the trip and all, so I let her rest up."

"Humph. I should think she done rested up plenty now, late as she slept. You can do that this morning right after she eats."

"That's just what I was fixing to do," Fanny said. "Then I was going to take her into town to get some things to wear."

" 'Fore you set out, I have to see Missus about that. She may have some things 'round here."

"Suit yourself," Fanny said.

"Do you knit?" Aunt Martha asked, looking at Susan.

"No."

Aunt Martha grunted. "If you going to be a nanny to Miss Lizbeth's babies you gonna have to knit. Babies will need booties and such, and nice ones. Sister Fanny will show you how."

Fanny tapped Susan's shoulder. "We'll start on that after I show you around."

"And as for your name," Aunt Martha said, "Miss Nancy said we to call you Susanne from now on."

Susan frowned. She hadn't heard that right. "What?"

"We already got one Susan here. Miss Nancy's two other daughters go by Susan and Ellen."

Susan's jaw dropped. Susan and Ellen? How was that possible?

"And Miss Nancy says it will be too confusing with two Susans 'round here. So you'll go by Susanne."

Susan shook her head to clear it. Aunt Martha said all

this as if she was telling Susan to dust the parlor. "But . . . but my name is Susan. Everyone always calls me Susan."

Aunt Martha set her jaw firmly. "Not 'round here they won't. If Miss Nancy say you to be called Susanne, that's what we're going to call you." She walked to the door. "Now come on here. It's already late enough."

Susan glanced at Fanny. But if she expected help from her, she wasn't getting it. Fanny avoided her eyes and followed Aunt Martha to the door, then they both turned and looked at her. Susan snatched her skirt up and followed them. Wasn't it enough that they'd stolen her from her family? Now they were taking her name, too? She was going to get away from this place one way or another, even if she had to rob a bank to do it.

Fanny showed her around the mansion after breakfast. First, they went to all the bedchambers and upstairs sitting rooms, then they walked downstairs and into the drawing room, a huge place with walls papered with landscapes and furniture that Fanny announced was Victorian. Susan barely paid attention, even when they reached the library. She was still reeling about her name change. But when they reached a small room off the kitchen that Fanny called the water closet, she listened closely as Fanny proudly explained how water was pumped indoors for bathing and cooking. It was amazing, even though Susan didn't understand most of what Fanny was saying.

They walked to the back of the mansion and out a small door to the yard. In the center was a square paved area, and two women were doing the laundry in an iron pot sitting on an open fire. Steam rose from the pot into the air and filled the tiny space. Five or six children ran and skipped around the narrow grassy edges of the yard. To the left was a small garden, where two men worked with hoes and shovels. At the back of the yard were three brick two-story buildings.

The first housed a kitchen, where two older women were cooking, the second a storage room, and the last a stable. Narrow balconies ran across the top floors of each building. Fanny said the top floors were sleeping quarters for the slaves who didn't sleep in the mansion. Surrounding it all was a high brick wall, and the only way out of the enclosure was through the big house.

The whole setup made Susan feel like she would gag if she stayed too long. The view was blocked on three sides by brick walls. On the other side stood the mansion. The air was stuffy, and children ran around in every direction. How could they stand it?

She wiped the perspiration from her forehead as Fanny quickly introduced "Susanne" to the women doing the laundry. They were both dripping with sweat and hardly seemed friendly. One looked up from her work stirring the pot, nodded, then looked back down. The other one never even glanced up.

"They're always squabbling back there," Fanny said as she led Susan back into the mansion. "With each other or with us." She fanned her face with her hand. "Whew! Hotter than a brick oven out there."

"Why do they fight so much?" Susan asked, although she hardly thought she needed to. She'd catch an attitude, too, if she had to stay cooped up back there all the time.

Fanny shrugged. "They always finding something to argue about. Who gets which room, who does what chores. Just about everything. I try to stay out of it myself."

"Do they ever get to leave the yard?"

Fanny nodded. "Mass Willard gives all of us time off on Saturday and Sunday, and if you got somewhere to go, he might give you a pass. Naturally, they all got somewhere to go come Saturday night. And some of the menfolk work in the city and leave every morning. But Monday to Friday, this is it for most of 'em."

They entered the kitchen at the back of the mansion. Miss Nancy stood at the head of the table holding a saucer and cup of coffee in her hands as she watched three women slice potatoes and other vegetables from the garden and thread them on strings. Susan knew from seeing the same work at home that the vegetables would be hung outdoors to dry until ready to be cooked, then stored in the cellar for winter. A clabber-colored girl of about eight and dripping with sweat stood behind Missus and cooled her with a big fan.

Miss Nancy wore her gray hair in the same style as the day before, parted perfectly straight down the middle with a large knot at the nape of her neck. Except this morning it was held back with a silk net. She bent down to put her cup and saucer on the table, and a large ring of keys dangled from her neck. "How are you coming along, Fanny?"

"Just fine, Miss Nancy. I was showing Susan, er . . . Susanne around. Aunt Martha said to get her started knitting some booties."

Hearing herself being called Susanne made Susan mad enough to spit. It sounded as if they were talking about somebody else, not her.

"Good," Miss Nancy said. She went back to her preserves without ever once looking directly at Susan.

"Ma'am?" Fanny asked.

"What is it?" Miss Nancy looked up, her expression slightly annoyed.

"Susanne could really use some new clothes. All she had was the dress that was on her back, and that's worn to pieces."

Miss Nancy looked at Susan for the first time that morning, although it felt more like the woman was looking straight through her. Susan looked down at her fingers.

"Yes, I remember that rag from yesterday," Miss Nancy

said. "And the one she's wearing now isn't much better. There's nothing in storage?"

"No, Missus. Everything's way too big or too small."

"Very well. Go into town tomorrow and get a few things at Mr. Levy's. Have him put it on our account."

Fanny smiled. "Yes, ma'am."

"Now, don't go spending all our money. All she needs is a couple of dresses for daytime and one for church, and one pair of shoes for work and one for church. And some undergarments. That's plenty for now. We'll get her winter things when we order for the rest of the household."

"Yes, ma'am, just what I was thinking."

Miss Nancy picked her cup up from the table and turned her attention back to the preserves.

"Er, ma'am?"

Miss Nancy looked at Fanny. "Yes?"

"Sorry to keep troubling you but, um, should we walk or take the carriage?"

"Oh, yes," Miss Nancy said. She fingered the keys around her neck. "I'll be needing the carriage myself tomorrow morning. Let's see. How far is it on foot?"

"About an hour, ma'am."

"That's rather far to walk back with packages, isn't it? Especially in this heat." She looked at the girl fanning her, and the little girl picked up the pace.

"Yes, ma'am," Fanny said, nodding vigorously.

"You could have Mr. Levy deliver the things but that could take a couple of days. He can be so slow at times. And I can see that she needs the things now. I guess you'll have to hire a carriage then. I'll write a note and give you the money to pay the driver. Remind me tonight."

"Thank you, ma'am," Fanny said, and they left the room.

"What does 'hire a carriage' mean?" Susan asked as they climbed the stairs.

Fanny stared back at her, eyes wide with surprise. "Just

what it says. We get one of them cabs on the street and tell the driver to take us into town. We just have to walk over to Main Street, since not too many come down Grace."

Seemed these folks rode around in carriages all the time. Before yesterday, she had rode in a carriage only once, with Miss Rebecca. "Who's coming with us?"

"Nobody," Fanny said, looking even more puzzled.

Susan couldn't believe her ears. "You mean nobody white will go to town with us?"

Fanny smiled and shook her head as she opened the door to a small parlor on the top floor. "Heck. I don't know what you're used to, but around here we do that all the time. Nobody cares beans long as you get a note from your massa. Some drivers don't even care about that as long as you got cash." She chuckled. "But don't ride in one unless you got a note, 'cause if the police catch you, it's stripes down your back, thirty-nine of 'em. All the driver gets is a ten dollar fine." She paused. "How do you get around out there on them plantations?"

Susan shrugged as they entered the room. "We don't. We hardly ever have to go anywhere. Everything we need is right there."

"Mmm-umph," Fanny said, shaking her head as she removed balls of white yarn and knitting needles from a drawer. "I was born in the city. So I don't know much about country life. But everybody I know that comes from a plantation said they would never go back if they could help it. Every last one of 'em."

"Pft. What's so special about riding around in a carriage? I'd rather have wide-open spaces and lots of trees and flowers. Only thing around here is brick and stone."

Fanny chuckled. "They say there's other things about living in the city that's different from out there."

"Like what?"

Fanny nodded toward a chair at a small round table. "Sit down. I want to get you started."

Susan sat at the table.

"Some of Mass Willard's men live out on their own," Fanny said, as she sat across from Susan. "They hire their own time, and Massa lets them keep some of the money to pay room and board in the city and buy food. Raif, that's my husband, he hires his own time over at Tredgar."

"Tredgar?"

"The ironworks. They make cast iron for chain cable and weapons and such. Raif is a puddler. He rents a room over at Shockoe Creek during the week."

"What's Shockoe Creek?"

"A colored area."

"Oh." Susan watched as Fanny spread the yarn and needles out on the table. She had to admit that sounded very different from living on a plantation. Still, she thought she would be afraid to live on her own. She'd wager that the men who did that hardly got enough to eat or a decent place to sleep. And a woman just wouldn't be safe living out in a city like Richmond, from what she'd heard about the place.

"At least on a plantation we don't have to worry about being snatched off the streets and sold away. I heard they'll snatch just about anybody, here, especially girls and young women, and sell them down to New Orleans."

Fanny chuckled again. "Where in tarnation did you hear that nonsense? That doesn't happen here any more than it does out there on them plantations. Only time I ever heard of that happening was with runaways. They get caught and their old massas don't want 'em anymore so they sell 'em. Now pay attention to what I'm showing you."

Susan watched as Fanny showed her how to hold the needles and knit. Then Fanny excused herself, saying she had to prepare for Miss Lizbeth's return. Susan had to admit that she liked this knitting. She felt more relaxed than she had since the day she left home. But Susan missed chatting with Ellen, especially the way they used to talk and brush each other's hair late at night. And she had no idea what Miss Lizbeth would be like. If she was anything like her mama, Susan knew she was in for a hard time.

She sighed and dropped the needles in her lap. Then she put her head down on the table and closed her eyes.

19

Miss Nancy wrote them a pass before she headed out with her daughters the next morning but forgot to write the note so they could hire a carriage. Fanny decided that she and Susan would just have to walk and have Mr. Levy deliver the packages after all. Fanny was pretty upset about this, but Susan didn't mind. She was just glad to get out of the house. She had been cooped up for two days and welcomed the chance to get some exercise and fresh air. At Montpelier, they couldn't just walk off, but all they had to do for a refreshing break was step out the door. Here, stepping into the yard was more miserable than staying in. Besides, walking would make it easier to study the route.

Fanny did get permission from Miss Nancy to allow Susan to borrow an old dress for the trip into town from the youngest daughter, Miss Ellen, who was about the same age as Susan. Fanny had pointed out to Miss Nancy that she wouldn't want the folks in town to see Miss Lizbeth's new nurse looking shabby, would she?

As they dressed for the trip into town, Fanny tried to fill Susan in on what to expect. It was clear that this trip was exciting for Fanny. She said she loved getting out to shop. Even though she wasn't buying anything for herself, she loved the hustle and bustle of the city and looking at pretty things in the shop windows. The only sour note was when Fanny warned Susan that if they approached a white person on the sidewalk that she was to move aside, even if it meant stepping off the curb.

They walked along the street and Susan felt herself getting caught up in all of Fanny's excitement as her eyes darted from one sight to the next. She saw all the sights she had seen during the ride from the train station on the day of her arrival and more. And this time she was free to ask questions. What stunned her more than anything was the sight of a pretty honey-complexioned colored woman on the arm of a dashing white man. The two came out of a building and strolled down the street looking like they thought they owned the world. The woman wore a stylish two-piece dress with puffed sleeves. She had on a fancy bonnet and even carried a beautiful handbag. Susan had never seen a colored woman carrying a handbag like that. Most of them tied their things up in handkerchiefs or slipped them in pockets.

"That's one of them grog shops," Fanny said, turning her nose up with disapproval as they passed by the door that the stylish couple had just exited. Susan slowed her pace and tried to get a look inside as a colored man opened the door to go in. But Fanny reached back and grabbed her by the arm. "You come away from there. There's all sorts of frolicking going on in them places, drinking and gambling and such."

"And colored women can go in them?" Susan stretched her neck, trying to find the mixed couple up ahead.

Fanny poked her bottom lip out. "Colored women, colored men, white men. The owners are white but they don't care beans about the color of the hand that feeds 'em. Sometimes they get busted and have to close down, but they just pay the fine and set up shop somewhere else. I think it's disgusting to see our kind waste what little money we make that way."

As they got closer to town, Susan could smell the river, and she saw huge wagons in the street being pulled by horses and mules. Fanny said they were probably headed for the docks down at Rockett's Landing and she warned Susan to stay away from there, too. "The ironworks and the armory down there, and the grog shops down that way are even worse than they are around here. No decent colored woman would set foot anywhere near that place. They're some of the meanest streets in town."

"How far is the train station from here?"

"Not far. Just north of here."

"Do the trains come by every day?"

"Every day, all day. They go to different places."

Susan nodded. She wanted to ask more, like when and how much. But she'd have to be patient. She didn't want Fanny to get suspicious.

Soon they were surrounded by people and stores of all kinds. Gentlemen and ladies shared the sidewalk with rowdies and women of the night wearing too much makeup. Negro men and boys stood on the corners peddling newspapers. They even passed a barbershop with a glass front where she saw colored men inside cutting white men's hair. As she slowed her pace and stared in the window, out the corner of her eye she saw Fanny step hurriedly down off the sidewalk. Susan looked up just before bumping smack into a finely dressed white woman on the arm of a white man carrying a walking stick. Their eyes met, and Susan stood stock-still, fully expecting to be scolded on the spot or worse. Instead, the man calmly took off his hat and tipped it in her direction. The woman smiled and nodded and they both walked around her.

Susan stood there with her feet glued to the pavement. Suddenly Fanny was by her side, touching her elbow and pulling her along.

"I thought we were supposed to move for them," Susan whispered.

Fanny giggled. "We are. I've seen many a colored person scolded and even hit for not doing it."

"Then why were they so nice about it?"

" 'Cause, child, they obviously thought you were white."

Susan blinked. She didn't know what to say to that.

"If that woman had known you were colored, she probably would have bopped you upside the head with her parasol or something. Or he would have hit you with his cane."

Susan stared at Fanny, who was still grinning from ear to ear. "But . . . but I'm with you, so . . ."

"They probably thought I was your servant or something, child."

Fanny giggled again, and Susan couldn't help but smile. It was astonishing. No one ever mistook her for white at Montpelier. That much was certain. It was such a strange feeling.

She was still thinking about it when Fanny pulled her inside a doorway. They entered a small room with a long counter running down one end. Shelves lined the other walls, and they were filled with bolts of fabric in many colors and patterns and all kinds of accessories, including handbags, fans, hats and bonnets, and gloves. Lifelike figures dressed in fancy ladies' outfits were dispersed throughout the room.

"Those are mannequins," Fanny said, upon seeing Susan staring.

Susan nodded and watched as Fanny walked to a shelf and sifted through the linens and laces. So, they were allowed to touch all these pretty things, Susan realized. She lifted her eyes and looked around the room until she noticed a rack on which several black dresses were hanging. She walked over. She'd never seen so many dresses of one color in one place. They had different patterns and textures and shapes and were all so pretty. A velvety one with lace at the collar caught her eye, and she reached out and ran her hand along the smooth fabric.

"Morning, Fanny," Susan heard a man mumble behind her. She swung her hands behind her back and looked to see a short white man wearing glasses coming from behind a mannequin. He had his shirtsleeves rolled up to the elbows, a tape measure around his neck, and pins in his mouth. Susan backed away from the rack. She hadn't realized someone else was in the room with them.

"Good morning, Mr. Levy," Fanny said.

The man noticed Susan then and removed the pins from his mouth. He stepped forward. "Good morning, ma'am," he said, smiling.

Susan smiled and nodded as he moved toward the rack of dresses she had just been admiring. "Those are new arrivals. Perfect for the house servants of a fine lady." He pulled one from the rack and held it out for her. "I can have one or more delivered if you like."

Susan frowned. She was not sure what she was supposed to say. She looked over at Fanny.

"This here is Sister Susanne, Mr. Levy," Fanny said. She walked over and stood beside Susan, an amused smile playing around the corners of her lips. "She's going to be the nurse for Miss Lizbeth's children. She's a wedding gift from Mass Willard."

Mr. Levy blinked and cleared his throat. "Oh . . . oh. How nice." His face changed as he looked Susan up and down. Then he turned his back and placed the dress back on the rack. "And how is your mistress, Fanny?"

Now Susan understood. This man had thought she was white, too. What a strange place this city was. Fanny winked at her, and Susan smiled and shifted her gaze to the floor. Darn that Fanny for making her want to laugh in front of a white man.

"She's still away on her honeymoon," Fanny said as Mr. Levy turned back to face them. "Sister Susanne here has come all the way from Montpelier and we'll be needing some things for her."

"Montpelier? The old Madison estate?"

"Yes," Susan said.

"How nice."

"We'll be needing a couple of things for her to wear around the house and something for church."

"Well," he said, picking the velvety dress up again. "In that case, what do you think of this one?"

They spent an hour picking out dresses and shoes, and Mr. Levy said he would have them sent over the next morning. It was all so new to Susan. Being able to pick and choose what she wanted at a shop especially for Negroes was astounding. And to have a white man wait on them! At home, her nice things were all hand-me-downs from a mistress, or Mama had made them.

As they were about to leave, her eye caught a small round handbag. She picked it up and turned it over. It was made of light blue velvet with a satin drawstring. She opened it and ran her fingers across the satin lining. It was the prettiest thing she'd ever laid eyes on. She looked at Fanny hopefully.

Fanny smiled but shook her head. "That's real nice, but I don't know how that would sit with Miss Nancy. She might think it's a bit too fancy."

Susan let her fingers linger on the smooth surface, then carefully placed it back on the counter.

"I know," Fanny said. "I'll ask Miss Lizbeth when she comes back. She ain't so strict as Miss Nancy is and might allow it."

As soon as they stepped out the shop, they both burst into a fit of giggles over Mr. Levy's faux pas. Fanny especially got a kick out of it. Susan thought it was funny and scary at the same time.

They took a different route home, this one closer to the river. If she thought what had happened so far was odd, nothing prepared her for what Fanny told her as they strolled past a park toward a little shop on a corner. Fanny said it was owned by a free black man named Oliver Armistead. Susan had never met a free black man or woman, much less one who owned his own store.

"White folks let coloreds have stores here?" Susan asked.

Fanny nodded. "Most of 'em just little rinky-dink cookshops for other colored folks. Whites don't know about 'em. And every now and then, they go around and shut 'em all down. At least the ones they can find. But this store is different. Brother Oliver sells food and such, and the white folks allow it."

Susan frowned. "But why?"

"You ever heard of James Armistead, changed his name to James Lafayette?"

Susan shook her head. She'd heard of a Lafayette who had something to do with the revolution, but not James Lafayette.

"He was a colored man that spied on the British for General Lafayette during the war."

"A colored spy?"

Fanny nodded. "He was a slave from around here back then, and after the war they freed him. They say Brother Oliver is somehow related to him. Anyways, around here it's enough for a colored man just to have the name Armistead. I think that's why they pretty much leave Brother Oliver alone."

Susan nodded. Now that she thought about it, she remembered Aunt Sarah talking about a colored man who was freed as a reward for spying on British troops during the Revolutionary War. "Is that how this Brother Oliver got free?"

"No, he bought his freedom."

"My mama always said life is hard for free coloreds."

"Your mama's dead right," Fanny said. She shook her

head. "A lot of free colored folks live here in Richmond, but most of 'em are struggling just to make ends meet. They can't find jobs and they live in shacks in the meanest part of town. A lot of times they got it worse than we do, 'cause white folks don't want 'em around. Most of 'em would just as soon send 'em out of the state."

"Then why are so many of them here?"

"There's a place for them. They work for a lot less than any white will. They'll do just about anything. Heck, they'll do stuff slaves won't do if they can help it."

Fanny opened the door to the shop on the corner. It was small, with a sawdust floor and a short counter along one end. Behind that stood shelves lined with bottles of spices. Sacks of cornmeal, flour, and coal, and bushel baskets filled with dried legumes were piled on the floor. A colored boy about Susan's age, wearing a big smile and a white apron, stood behind the counter. He stared at Susan with open curiosity. "Afternoon, Aunt Fanny."

"Good afternoon, Brother Lucas. This here is Sister Susanne. She's going to be watching Miss Lizbeth's young ones."

Lucas smiled at Susan and nodded. "Afternoon."

"Good afternoon," Susan said.

"Is Brother Oliver around?" Fanny asked.

Lucas shook his head. "No, ma'am. Mr. Armistead over at the docks pickin' up some things."

Susan was stunned. *Mr. Armistead*? She had never heard anybody call a colored person, free or slave, "Mister." Back at Montpelier, such talk would get a child smacked upside the head and a grownup far worse if a white person heard it.

Fanny snapped her fingers. "Oh, too bad. I wanted him to meet Sister Susanne. When will he be back?"

"Don' know 'zactly. Coupl'a hours or so, I reckon."

"Oh, we can't wait that long. Got to walk back. You got any of that store tea and gumdrops?"

Lucas nodded and reached up on the shelf as Fanny pulled a silver coin from her pocket. She handed it to Lucas, and Susan stared at every move. It was the first time she'd seen that much money change hands between two colored people.

They left the store and started the long walk back to Grace Street, munching on gumdrops along the way. Fanny chatted excitedly about the day. "I figure if I'm going to spend my money, might as well be in a colored store. That's what Raif always tell me when he gives me spending money."

Susan mostly just nodded and sucked on the candy as they walked. It was all so strange. Why, the very notion of a colored man owning a store was unheard-of back home. And here Fanny was telling her lots of coloreds lived free and owned their own stores and houses right here in Richmond. Fanny said the stores might not be much, selling only a few odds and ends, much of it just some junk, and many of the free coloreds who owned them lived far worse than most city slaves. Still, Susan would never have believed any of it if she hadn't just seen it with her very own eyes.

She needed some quiet time to herself to absorb all they had seen and done that morning. She would give anything to have Mama and Ellen see all of this. Mama probably wouldn't approve of much of it, but Ellen would have loved the freedom to move about, to pick out what she would wear, and seeing colored folks running their own stores.

Susan sighed. The excitement had even taken her mind off running, but only temporarily. She knew that it would always be like that here, so far away from home. No matter what she did and learned and saw in Richmond, Mama and Ellen would always be at the back of her mind. No matter how much fun Fanny was or how many dresses Missus let her buy, it would always come back to missing them. She supposed she would never again be able to have fun without having a dark cloud looming overhead.

Susan spent the next few days quietly knitting booties in an upstairs parlor. During breaks she walked around the mansion and grounds on the pretense of familiarizing herself with the place. The real intent was to plan her escape. She could pretty much retrace her steps from the mansion back to town now, but if she'd learned anything the past few days it was that she would need a lot more than that to get away. After their trip into town, she was convinced she could pass for white and make it into town without being noticed. But she would need money, lots of it, and a way to sneak out of the mansion without being seen.

For a while, she toyed with the idea of telling Fanny what she was going to do and flat out asking her for the money. But she dropped that idea. They had become close, but not that close. And she didn't see how she could ask Fanny for that much money without telling her why she wanted it. Still, she was determined to find a way. If not now, later.

She sometimes ran into Mass Willard—always dressed neatly in a suit, gloves, and hat—as he left in the morning and she made her way from the kitchen to the upstairs parlor. Fanny said he was on his way to the bank where he was president. He was also involved in a lot of affairs in and around Richmond and was always on the go. He was very active in the church and had helped start the one he and the missus were members of. He always greeted Susan, and she answered politely. That was pretty much all that went on between them until the day before his daughter was due back from Paris.

"Good morning," he said in the hallway near the front entrance. He had his hat and gloves in his hands.

"Morning, Massa." She smiled, then continued toward the stairs.

"How are things coming along, Susanne?" he asked, his voice halting her.

Terrible, she wanted to say. She wanted to go home, back to Montpelier. And she would never get used to being called Susanne, even if she lived to be a hundred.

"Fine, Massa," she said. "I'm learning to knit and sew real good."

"Excellent. We're counting on you doing a good job with Miss Elizabeth's children. She's our eldest and naturally Mrs. Montgomery and I are anxious for some additions to the family."

"Yes, Massa. I understand. They'll be your grandbabies and I plan to take good care of them for you."

"Good," he said. "You'll be spending a lot of time with them so that makes you a very important part of this household. I trust everyone is treating you well?"

She tried not to think of the irony of this man preaching to her about family when he had just snatched her away from her home. She smiled thinly. "Yes, Massa. Everyone is very nice, and I thank you."

With the exception of Fanny, that was a lie. Most of the time, Miss Nancy seemed to look straight through her, although just yesterday Susan had caught the woman staring at her strangely when she'd suddenly turned in Miss Nancy's direction. They had both looked away quickly. Later that evening as she sat alone in the upstairs parlor knitting, Miss Nancy had swept into the room. She was dressed in black from head to toe, giving her pale face a tired look. Susan placed the needles on the table and stood up.

"How is the knitting coming, Susanne?" Miss Nancy had asked.

"Fine, Missus. I finished one booty yesterday and just started on the other." She picked up the little white booty and held it up. Miss Nancy simply glanced at it, then looked into Susan's face. Susan cast her eyes to the floor.

"Do you happen to know when you were born?"

"August."

"I mean the year. What year?"

Susan lowered the booty. "No, ma'am. I just know I'm fourteen."

Miss Nancy blinked and her eyes got a faraway look. She dabbed beads of sweat on her nose with a lace handkerchief, then looked back at Susan. "Who was your master when you were born?" she said with tight lips.

Susan suddenly felt hot, too. Where was all this leading? "Uh, Mass Henry. He left when I was only about two or three. Mass Todd, Miss Dolley's son, was still—"

"And who was your master after that?" Missus said impatiently.

"Mass Benjamin, ma'am."

"And then it was my husband?"

Susan nodded.

"And after that the Shaws?"

Susan wiped the perspiration from her forehead with her hand. "Yes, Missus."

"I see. And your mother . . ." Missus frowned. "What's she like?"

"Ma'am?"

"What does she do at Montpelier?" Missus said, spitting the words out. "Does she work in the mansion or the fields?"

"The mansion, ma'am."

"What does she look like? Is she a mulatto, like you?"

Susan shook her head. "More brown, Missus."

"Do you have any brothers or sisters?"

"One sister, Missus. Her name is Ellen." Susan sneaked a look at Miss Nancy's face. She wanted to see how the woman would take that news. But the minute she saw, she regretted her words. Miss Nancy looked as if she was about to take ill.

"What? Your sister's name is Ellen?"

Susan nodded and quickly looked back down.

"How old is she?"

Susan swallowed. "Seventeen."

"What do you know about your father?"

Susan almost dropped the booty in her hands. "I . . . I don't really know."

Missus had been doing a decent job of controlling the tone of her voice. But suddenly she lost it. "You don't know what, you silly girl? You don't know who he is, or you don't know where he is. Or what?"

"I don't know who he is or anything about him."

Without another word, the woman turned on her heels and left the room. Susan stared after her for a long minute, then sank down in the chair. The Missus was as much in the dark as she was about her daddy and none too happy about it. Susan once thought she wanted to know if Mass Willard was her daddy, but she had just changed her mind. If he was and Miss Nancy ever found out, Susan had a feeling that the missus would become her worst enemy. Mama was right. Sometimes it was better not knowing.

20

"Oh, she's just perfect," Miss Lizbeth exclaimed upon meeting Susan. Aunt Martha had instructed Susan to be sure to bathe that morning and put on her good dress and tie her hair back with a net. She should look her best when meeting Miss Lizbeth.

Susan stared as Miss Lizbeth jumped up from the sofa in the drawing room, where she had been sitting between Massa and Miss Nancy, and walked toward her. *Mon Dieu!* she thought as Miss Lizbeth came closer. She could hardly believe her eyes. That red hair and round face. So much like Ellen! Was this ever a nasty surprise.

Miss Lizbeth clasped her hands together and turned back toward the sofa. She blew her daddy a kiss. "Just perfect." Miss Lizbeth turned back to face her, and Susan prayed that she would be able to keep a straight face. Miss Lizbeth wore her hair in a chignon like her mama, but managed a softer look with coils falling around the neck and ears. And she wore a frilly beige dress with pink flowers and leg-of-mutton sleeves—something Susan was sure Miss Nancy, with her dark no-nonsense dresses, would never be caught dead wearing.

Mass Richard, Miss Lizbeth's new husband, was tall and thin with long sideburns that nearly reached the top of his high collar. He stood near the fireplace with his elbow resting on the mantelpiece. Miss Lizbeth's two younger sisters, Misses Susan and Ellen, sat at the round marble-topped table in the center of the room. They looked nothing like Ellen or herself, Susan thought. And the more she looked, the less she thought Miss Lizbeth was anything like her sister, either. Although attractive, Miss Lizbeth was not nearly as pretty as Ellen. And it was already clear that Miss Lizbeth was the bubbly type, maybe even a bit silly. Ellen was far more reserved. The only real similarity was the hair. Thank goodness. The thought of having to look into her mistress's face day after day and seeing her sister was too much to bear.

"Where are you from?" Miss Lizbeth asked.

"Montpelier."

"Montpelier? Really? The James Madison estate?"

Susan nodded. At least the woman knew about Montpelier.

"Father, you are so clever. However did you manage to get her?" Miss Lizbeth looked at her daddy, who was standing in front of the fireplace now with his chest all puffed out and his face beaming with pride. Both he and Mass Richard puffed on fat cigars in celebration of the newlyweds' safe return to Richmond. Miss Nancy sat with her hands clasped as usual in her lap.

"Never mind that," Mass Willard said. "I've got my ways." He took a big puff of his cigar and blew the smoke into the air. Miss Nancy fanned it away from her face.

"Her mother actually worked in the mansion when President Madison was living," Miss Nancy said.

"Oh, really?" Miss Lizbeth said.

"Yes," Susan said. "And Miss Dolley."

"Oh, my," Miss Lizbeth exclaimed. "What was she like? Did your mother say?"

"Mama always said that she was a very kind mistress, ma'am. And that Mass Jimmy was the nicest massa around."

"What about Miss Dolley's son, that John Payne Todd?" Miss Susan asked. "I've heard some wild tales about him."

Susan looked down. She wasn't sure what to say. Mass Todd was a beast from what Mama told her, but it wasn't her place to say something like that about a white man, any white man. "Mama said he was a handful."

Mass Willard chuckled, and the girls giggled.

"Is he still living?" Miss Ellen asked.

"He died five or six years ago," Mass Willard said before Susan could answer.

"He was a regular scoundrel from what I've heard about him," Mass Richard said. "I read that someone once referred to his presence at Montpelier as a 'serpent in the Garden of Eden.'"

"All right," Miss Nancy said sternly. "I think that's enough on that topic. It's no way to talk about the son of a former first lady."

Mass Richard cleared his throat. Miss Lizbeth smiled broadly as she took Susan's hands and swung them from side to side. "We're going to get along fine. I just know it."

"With any luck," Mass Willard said. "She'll be watching one of my grandchildren in about nine months time."

"Father!" Miss Lizbeth dropped Susan's hands and turned toward her daddy. Her tone chided but her eyes laughed.

Miss Nancy blinked and tightened her lips. "Really, dear. Must you be so indiscreet?" Miss Nancy patted the seat cushion next to her. "Come and finish telling us all about Paris, dear."

"Yes, please do," Miss Ellen said.

For once, Susan thought, she liked what Miss Nancy was saying. She wanted to hear about Paris, too. She stayed back near the doorway, her hands clasped in front of her, as Miss Lizbeth walked toward the sofa. Miss Lizbeth clasped her hands together, then sat beside her mama. "Oh, it was simply divine, the whole trip. Wasn't it,

Richard? Everyone dresses so fashionably. And the people are so different. Especially in the way they treat the coloreds there. You'd be amazed. They don't have slaves."

No slaves? Susan thought. Of all the things she'd heard about France, she never heard that. It sounded like the North here in America. She wasn't to hear very much more about Paris, though. Miss Nancy raised her hand to silence her daughter.

"Oh," Miss Lizbeth said and stopped abruptly.

Miss Nancy turned a stony eye toward Susan. "That will be all, Susanne."

Susan nodded and backed toward the doorway.

"We'll talk later, Susanne," Miss Lizbeth said. "Perhaps tomorrow afternoon, after I've had some time to get myself unpacked and settled in. I think it's important that we get to know each other, don't you?"

Susan smiled and nodded.

"Susanne," Miss Nancy said, not even bothering to look in Susan's direction, "help Fanny unpack Miss Elizabeth's trunks."

It seemed as if Miss Nancy had two voices—one especially for her and another for everybody else. She and her daughter were like night and day. "Yes, Missus."

Any other time and place, Miss Lizbeth would be easy enough to like. But Susan wasn't even going to think about that. No matter how nice her new mistress was to her, this wasn't Montpelier. It never was and never would be.

She found Fanny in Miss Lizbeth's chamber pulling a gown out of a trunk. "Miss Lizbeth has got this Saratoga trunk filled to the brim with fancy new things from Paris—shoes, handbags, dresses, you name it. Lookee here." Fanny held up a flat hat, decorated with flowers. Another hefty-sized trunk sat against the wall, and still another at the foot of the bed, its lid popped open to reveal still more belongings.

Susan had never seen such an odd looking hat until she first arrived in Richmond. "What is that?" she asked. "I saw ladies wearing them in town."

"A beret," Fanny said. She sniffed and took a handkerchief from her dress pocket and blew her nose. "Got a cold coming," she said. "Something going around." She put the handkerchief back and held the beret up over her thick head of hair, which she always wore pinned up in braids or tied with a scarf. She cocked the hat rakishly to one side.

Susan laughed. "You'd better stop that before she comes up here and catches you."

"She'd probably laugh herself. Did you meet her yet?"

Susan nodded. "I just came from meeting her."

"Didn't I tell you my mistress was nice? If it wasn't for Miss Nancy, I swear, she'd let me do just about anything I want. I was hoping she'd move out and take me with her when she got married, but Mass Richard just got out of medical school and they're going to live here till he gets his practice going."

Susan started helping her unpack. "I'm surprised Mass and Missus took kindly to Miss Lizbeth marrying a doctor."

"They didn't at first, and I think Miss Nancy still favors another one of Miss Lizbeth's suitors whose daddy owns a flour mill and a lot of land in another county. Lord knows, enough of 'em came a-courting my mistress, but Mass Richard is the one she favored."

"How old is Miss Lizbeth?"

"Twenty-six. And that's another reason why they came 'round to it. She's their firstborn, so they were getting kind of anxious to see her married off. 'Sides, he's a good man when you get down to it. I think Mass Willard likes it just fine that she has to stay home." Fanny leaned close to Susan and whispered. "But that Nancy still thinks Miss Lizbeth could have done a lot better than a doctor. I heard her say that to one of her friends just the other day." Fanny shook her head with disbelief.

"I don't think she likes me much, either," Susan said.

"What makes you say that?"

Susan didn't want to reveal too much. Some things were better left unsaid. She shrugged. "Oh, nothing in particular. She's just not as nice as the rest of them."

Fanny sniffed and nodded understandingly. "That's just her way. She's Mass Willard's second wife, you know? His first wife died way back. I was her personal servant. Then Mass Willard married Miss Nancy, and she came up from South Carolina and brought Aunt Martha with her. So I was given to Miss Lizbeth when she was born. I wasn't much older than you at the time, maybe fifteen or sixteen."

Fanny paused and coughed. "Anyway, his first wife, she came from a real important family around here, and it took Miss Nancy a time to fit in. I think that might have something to do with her attitude. You got to walk a careful line with her much of the time, but you'll be fine as long as you don't step over it."

Amen to that, Susan thought. And that probably went double for her, since Miss Nancy seemed awful suspicious about who her daddy was. They were still working and chatting when Miss Lizbeth came to the room a couple of hours later looking for a handkerchief.

"You got it coming, too?" Fanny asked as she went to the dresser and removed a handkerchief for her mistress.

"I've had it for two days now. Master Richard has been giving me everything under the sun to cure it but nothing seems to work." She waved her hand around the room. "Did you see all the pretty new things I got in Paris, Fanny? I nearly drove Master Richard mad with all the shopping trips." She laughed with delight as Fanny gave her the handkerchief.

Fanny chuckled. "Yes, ma'am. And they're right fine,

too. I 'specially like the little beret. I bet it looks real cute on you."

"Isn't it adorable? It's so much nicer than the ones you can get here."

"You really had a good time, huh, Missus?"

Miss Lizbeth inhaled and clasped her hands to her chest dreamily. "The best. I brought something back for you, too."

"Now you didn't have to go and do that."

"Nonsense. The whole time I was there, I kept saying to Master Richard that I have to find something for Fanny. He'll tell you that." Miss Lizbeth looked around the room, cluttered with trunks and suitcases, and the things they were putting away. "Have you seen my . . . ? Oh, there it is." She opened a suitcase they hadn't gotten around to unpacking yet and pulled out an embroidered cotton shawl. She shook it out and held it up with a smile.

"Oh, my, Miss Lizbeth," Fanny said. "For me?"

Miss Lizbeth draped it around Fanny's shoulders, and Fanny turned so they could see it.

"How do I look?" Fanny said, holding her arms out and smiling.

"It's perfect for you," Miss Lizbeth said, clasping her hands.

"It's lovely," Susan said.

"Everyone is always saying Fanny is the best-dressed Negro around the mansion," Miss Lizbeth said.

"That's 'cause of you, ma'am. You spoil me something awful."

"Nonsense. You deserve nice things." Miss Lizbeth touched her forefinger to her lips. "Now, I need to find something for Susanne." She moved back to the suitcase. "I'm sure I must have something in all these things that I can give her."

Susan's eyes widened. "No, ma'am. You don't have to do that."

"But I insist," Miss Lizbeth said as she pulled garments out of the suitcase, one by one, and tossed them onto the bed.

"I have an idea, Missus," Fanny said. "If I may offer a suggestion."

Miss Lizbeth stopped tossing and looked up. "Yes?"

"When we went into town to do some shopping the other day, we saw the nicest handbag at Mr. Levy's. Sister Susanne fell in love with it. Right?" Fanny looked at Susan.

"Er, yes, but I . . . I—" Susan stopped. She didn't know what to say. She didn't know Miss Lizbeth well enough to be asking for gifts. She'd never known any mistress that well. But the handbag was awful nice.

"We didn't get it, 'cause I didn't want to spend money on that kind of thing without asking first," Fanny said.

"It sounds perfect," Miss Lizbeth said. "Can she use it for church?"

Fanny nodded eagerly. "Yes, Missus. It's just right for church. 'Course all the other coloreds will be talking 'bout how you spoil her when they see Sister Susanne with a pretty bag like that."

Miss Lizbeth laughed. "Oh, I love it. Let me see how much money I have." She moved to her dresser and opened a small porcelain box. "I dare not ask Master Richard for another cent at the moment. We could always have them put it on Father's account, but I promised my husband I wouldn't do that anymore. He wants to be responsible for me now." She took out a fat wad of bills. "Do you remember how much it was, Fanny?"

"No, Missus, I didn't think to look. But it was at Mr. Levy's so I don't reckon it would be all that much."

"Very well," Miss Lizbeth said. She put the money back in the box and dabbed her nose with the handkerchief. "I should have enough. Come to me tomorrow morning and you shall have the money, then you can go and pick it up." She lifted her skirt and walked to the doorway. "If it's as nice as you said, we don't want to dilly-dally and let someone else get it first, do we?" She smiled and left.

Susan turned as Fanny wrapped the shawl back around her shoulders. Fanny twirled around, then went to stand in front of Miss Lizbeth's looking glass and admired herself.

"Thanks for asking her about the bag, Sister Fanny."

Fanny waved her hand nonchalantly. "Oh, shucks. It's for me as much as you. I love getting out to shop." She draped the shawl around Susan's shoulders. Susan smiled and rubbed her hand over the intricate needlework. She could get used to this in a hurry, she thought. And the handbag, if she got that, would be the most precious thing she had ever owned. She closed her eyes and tried to visualize it. She remembered that it was round and blue, a soft blue like . . .

The smile fell from her lips. She removed the shawl and handed it back to Fanny.

"Something wrong?" Fanny asked, sounding worried.

Susan shook her head. "I'll get over it in a minute. It's just that sometimes I get to thinking of home and . . ." She paused and looked down to hide the tears she felt welling up in her eyes.

Fanny nodded. "I see."

Susan tightened her lips. She wanted so badly to share her thoughts with Fanny. But no one would understand this unless they'd lived through it. She had never understood it herself, even when slaves were sold away from their families at Montpelier. Now she understood. Just about everything brought back memories of Mama and Ellen.

"With time, it will get better," Fanny said, sniffing herself from the cold. "You'll see. Time heals everything."

Time nothing. The only thing that would heal her was home. But she needed money to get there.

"Shopping helps, too," Fanny said, smiling thinly. "First thing tomorrow, we'll get the money from Miss Lizbeth and go get that handbag for you."

Susan nodded but her mind was elsewhere as her moist eyes moved slowly up to the little porcelain box sitting on Miss Lizbeth's dresser. She almost gasped at the terrible thought that crossed her mind.

She tossed and turned. She beat the pillow with her fists. She rolled over on her back and stared into the darkness.

She had never, ever stolen anything in her life. Well, maybe a bite of forbidden food from the kitchen at Montpelier, but that didn't count since no one would really have cared. If caught, she would have been scolded and told not to do it again. Stealing money, well, that was a whole different matter. If she got caught, she could be whipped or sent to jail or sold farther away down South. Even if she didn't get caught, she'd probably feel guilty for the rest of her life.

Mama would have skinned her alive for stealing money at Montpelier. But this was different. After all, these people had taken her away from her family. Even if they did pay for her, it was wrong. She didn't care how many times they said it was legal or justified or written down in the Bible, in her heart she knew it was just plain wrong. How could something so painful to so many be right in the eyes of God?

She exhaled. She was going to do it. Jail, whip, auction block, she didn't care anymore. And as guilty as it might make her feel, she would feel a hundred times worse if she stayed here the rest of her life without ever trying to get back home. The first chance she got, she was going to sneak back into Miss Lizbeth's chambers and take that money out of that box. Pft! The way she saw it, they owed it to her anyway for all the work she did. Lots of slaves here got paid when they hired themselves out. Why should some of them get paid and not others? That's what she wanted to know.

She sighed. She knew she was scratching for excuses so she wouldn't feel so guilty. In the end, it was still stealing and still wrong. She would have to find another way.

She woke up to the sound of Fanny coughing. She opened her eyes in the early morning darkness and saw Fanny sitting on the edge of her bed, her back quaking with each cough. Susan got up and lit a lamp. "You look terrible and you sound even worse today than you did yesterday."

Fanny responded with a nod of her head and another cough.

Susan frowned. "Want me to ask somebody to get the doctor?"

Fanny shook her head. "No." Her voice sounded like a frog's. "Just fetch me some tea from the kitchen, will you?"

Fanny lay back down as Susan lifted the lamp and walked to the door. "I'll be right back."

Fanny looked up. "You can get dressed first. I'm not going to die 'fore you put your clothes on."

Susan put the candle down and dressed quickly. Then she had the cook, already hard at work on breakfast, make a cup of tea. She returned to Fanny minutes later with Aunt Martha. The old woman sat on the bed and touched Fanny's forehead and cheek.

"No fever," Aunt Martha said. "It's probably just a bad cold." She made Fanny get back under the covers, then stood up. "I'll tell Miss Lizbeth you're sick and fix you up something for it." She left the room, and Susan gave Fanny the tea.

"This is going to spoil our trip into town for that handbag," Fanny said between coughs.

"Don't even think about that," Susan said as she fussed with the bedcovers around Fanny. "We'll go after you get to feeling better."

"Bag will be gone by then," Fanny said. "You go without me. You know the way. I'll talk to Miss Lizbeth."

"You sure about that?" Susan asked.

Fanny nodded. "Go on. Put on something nice for town."

Just as Susan finished buttoning her good dress, Miss Lizbeth walked into the room, still wearing her nightclothes. Fanny made a move to get up but stayed when Miss Lizbeth put up a hand to stop her.

"Aunt Martha said you weren't feeling well?" Miss Lizbeth sat on the edge of the bed and touched Fanny's forehead.

"It's just a cold, ma'am," Fanny said. "I'll be up just as soon as I finish this here tea that Sister Susanne brought me."

"Nonsense," Miss Lizbeth said. "You'll rest today. I'll have Master Richard come and look at you."

"But what about you, Miss Lizbeth? You'll need help."

"Susanne can help me dress today."

"I thank you, Missus," Fanny said. "A day's rest is all I need. I'll be up and about first thing tomorrow. Are you feeling better this morning?"

"Much." Miss Lizbeth smiled and nodded for Susanne to follow her.

"Missus?" Fanny said. She paused to cough as Miss Lizbeth turned to face her. "If you remember from yesterday, we were supposed to go into town to get that handbag for Susanne."

Miss Lizbeth nodded. "Ah, yes."

"I'm too sick, but Sister Susanne knows the way by herself. I don't want to waste anymore time getting back there, less it will be gone."

"Very well," Miss Lizbeth said. "I'll give her the money and she can go into town right after she helps me dress this morning."

"Thank you, Missus," Susan said.

Fanny smiled. "I thank you, too, Missus. When you see it, you'll understand. It's the prettiest little thing."

"I can't wait to see it," Miss Lizbeth said. "Now you rest up, Fanny."

Susan took the empty teacup from Fanny and squeezed her hand. "I'll bring you something from the kitchen before I go to town." She followed Miss Lizbeth down the stairs and stood back in the doorway as Miss Lizbeth swept into her chamber. Mass Richard was still in bed and when he heard his wife enter he lifted his head, grunted, and then rolled over to the other side.

Miss Lizbeth chuckled. "He's tired from all the traveling," she said, yawning herself. "But as I'm up, I may as well get dressed. I'll nap later." She turned and looked at Susan standing in the doorway holding the teacup. Missus raised an eyebrow as if expecting something, but Susan didn't have the faintest idea what. She used to help Miss Rebecca, but things were different at Montpelier. She knew where to fetch water, where Miss Rebecca kept all her personal belongings, and what she expected from the help. She knew because Mama and Ellen and the others had taught her those kinds of things from the day she could walk.

"What do you want me to do, Missus?"

"Why, run my bath water, of course. Then fetch me plenty of fresh towels. I'll be along shortly."

"Yes, Missus." Susan backed out of the room. Fresh towels she could find. But she had no idea how to run the contraptions they used to pump water. She ran into the bathroom and stood over the tub. It was a big porcelain thing with little knobs on one end. She knew how to stop up the hole in the bottom under the knobs, but the tub had been full when she bathed.

She didn't want to bother Fanny. She didn't want to mess with Aunt Martha, either, but the old bag seemed the better of the two. She knew she had to hurry and do something before Miss Lizbeth strolled in looking for her bath.

She ran down the stairs and left the cup in the kitchen, then she found Aunt Martha out in the yard supervising the workers there. Aunt Martha said she was too busy to come now but she told Susan where to find clean towels and how to run water into the tub.

"Just turn both the knobs, the water will come out. Let it run almost to the top. That's how Miss Lizbeth likes it. Then turn the knobs back. Put the stopper in first."

Was it so simple as that? Susan ran back into the mansion and up the stairs. She put the stopper in the tub and turned the handles, then she went to find clean towels. By the time she returned and opened the door, the bathroom was all steamed up and Miss Lizbeth was there, turning the knobs to stop the flow of water. Susan couldn't believe that big tub had filled so fast as she thought of all the trips from the well to the fireplace and tub that it used to take to fill a much smaller one at home.

"Oh, there you are," Miss Lizbeth said. She gave Susan a sharp look. "The water nearly overflowed."

"Sorry, Miss Lizbeth. I was getting some towels for you. I didn't know it would fill up . . ."

"Never mind," Miss Lizbeth said, waving her hand wearily. "Just be careful next time. Right now, I just want to lie back and soak in a nice warm bath. I can barely remember the last time I had one." She removed her bathrobe. "Come and do my back in a quarter hour."

"Yes, Missus," Susan said. She placed the towels on a chair near the tub and turned to leave. But just as she put her hand on the doorknob, she heard a scream that made her blood curdle. She spun around to see Missus hopping around on one foot. Her flushed face looked like it had just been struck by lightning.

Susan ran up to help. She grabbed a towel to wrap around Miss Lizbeth's leg, but Missus shoved her away with such force that Susan stumbled backwards.

"You idiot! Are you trying to kill me?"

Susan squeezed the towel in her arms as Miss Lizbeth slipped into her bathrobe. What happened? She did everything just as told.

"That water is hot enough to boil a chicken," Miss Lizbeth said.

Susan blinked just as Mass Richard came running into the room, the edges of his robe flapping in the breeze. "What's going on?" he asked when he saw his wife hopping on one foot.

"This stupid girl is trying to kill me," Miss Lizbeth said, limping toward her husband. "She ran my bath water so hot, it's nearly boiling."

"Sit down and let me take a look at it." Mass Richard guided his wife to the chair and lifted her leg. Then he carefully dipped a finger into the tub. He glanced at Susan as he shook the water from his finger. "Good God, Susanne. What the devil is the matter with you? She could have been seriously burned."

"I'm sorry, Massa. I didn't know it was so hot. It's my first time."

Mass Richard looked back at his wife. "You'll be all right. Does it still hurt?"

"No, it's—"

"What happened in here?"

They turned to see Miss Nancy burst into the room, tying her bathrobe around the waist.

"Oh, Mama. It's better now."

"Susanne made the bath water too hot," Mass Richard said. "Nearly burned Elizabeth. But she'll be fine."

"Are you all right, dear?"

Miss Lizbeth nodded.

Miss Nancy glared at Susan, then she looked back at Miss Lizbeth. "Do you think she did it on purpose?"

Miss Lizbeth shook her head and frowned. "I . . . I don't know. I don't see why she would. . . ."

"No, ma'am," Susan said. "I would never do something like that on purpose. It was the first time I—"

"Shut up," Miss Nancy said. "You've done enough already. I should make you get in that bath water yourself."

Susan closed her mouth and cast her eyes toward the floor.

"Just so you can see how it feels," Miss Nancy said. "It would serve you right. Now leave. Get out of here."

Susan backed to the door.

"Mama, I don't think she did it on purpose."

"It doesn't matter, dear," Miss Nancy said. "It's inexcusable."

"She's only been here a week," Mass Richard said.

"I won't have her endangering Elizabeth. I'm going to speak to Willard as soon as he gets home from the bank. She's got to go."

"Back to Montpelier, you mean?" Mass Richard asked.

"No. The Shaws have already left there. They moved to Washington, D.C. But somewhere away from here."

"I don't think it's that serious," Mass Richard said. "She just needs more time to get used to us."

"It doesn't matter, Richard. She's—"

"She's my slave, Mama. I'll decide what happens to her."

"Think of the children, dear. She's simply not cut out to be a nursemaid to my grandchildren. She's too simple. She's got to . . ."

Susan ran into the hallway. She didn't want to hear another word. She paced up and down, wringing the towel in her hands. *Mon Dieu!* This was too much like when Miss Rebecca's skirt caught fire and the Shaws got so mad at her. Only this time she didn't have Mama to run to. Fanny. She had to get to Fanny.

She ran down the hallway past Miss Nancy's chamber, past Miss Lizbeth's chamber, and up the attic stairs. Then she paused in mid-flight. What would Fanny think? Would she try to help? After all, Fanny was Miss Lizbeth's personal maid, and it was as plain as day that Fanny adored her mistress. Fanny might even get mad at her for burning Miss Lizbeth. She didn't have a soul to turn to here. Fanny was her closest friend, yet Susan couldn't even trust her entirely with this.

She sank down on the stairs and hugged the towel. They would probably sell her down to New Orleans. Miss Nancy hadn't wanted her here from day one, now she had an excuse to get her wish. The very words "New Orleans" scared Susan. She'd rather be tied to a post and whipped for a week than sold to that dreadful city. She knew all about New Orleans, and she was never going down there, no matter what she had to do to stop it.

She threw the towel on the stairs and ran back down to the hallway. She had every intention of running out the front door and down the street until she was out of breath. But she reached the doorway to Miss Lizbeth's chambers and stopped. The door was wide open. She looked up the hallway, then down. She stepped just inside the room and looked around. No one was there. Her eyes traveled around the room until they came to rest on Miss Lizbeth's little box on the dresser.

She stepped back and glanced up the hallway. Then she ran up to the dresser and lifted the top of the box. Sitting there beneath some jewelry was the big, fat wad of paper money. She stared. Did she have the nerve to take it? She didn't need to think on that a minute longer. It was this or New Orleans. She didn't know how much she'd need, so heck, she'd just take all of it.

If she was going to sin she might as well do it thoroughly. Miss Bubbly could always get more money from her daddy.

She reached in, grabbed the wad, and stuffed it into the bosom of her dress. Then she turned and fled.

21

Susan stopped in the center hallway and snatched a bonnet from the hat rack. Her breath was coming fast and heavy as she ran out the door and raced down the stairs. She skipped down the last three steps and tripped over her skirt, hitting the ground on her hands and knees. She jumped back up, brushed off her dress, and glanced up at the mansion.

She put the bonnet on and tied it into a bow under her chin. She had no pass, no note. So she had to look like a lady, a white lady at that. And a lady never left the house without hat and gloves. This bonnet would do. She couldn't do much about gloves except keep her hands hidden in the folds of her skirt. She was thankful that she had put on her best dress. She ran down the block but quickly realized that she would most definitely have to slow down in this hot sun, or else she'd break out into a sweat. She changed her stride to a brisk pace.

She walked east on Grace for several blocks, trying to remember the route they had taken in the carriage the day she arrived. The last thing she wanted was to stumble on some slave market or auction block or an area where coloreds were forbidden. Up ahead, she could see the tall steeple and bell tower of Massa's church. That had been one of the first things she noticed on the skyline as they rode in the carriage that first day, and she knew the station wasn't far from the church. What she couldn't remember to save herself was whether the station had been east or west of the church. So she kept walking down Grace, hoping to spot something familiar.

Before she knew it, she was right upon the church. She frowned. This was all wrong. She knew because this was where Grace Street ran into Capitol Square, and now she remembered that her first time seeing the square was when she walked into town with Fanny. She also remembered Fanny telling her that coloreds weren't allowed on the grounds of the square. She could see an armed guard just up ahead patrolling the building. Fanny said they put the guards there after Gabriel Prosser led a slave rebellion in Virginia back around 1800.

Now what to do? She could walk through the square pretending to be white, but that would be plain stupid. No one had stopped her or looked at her funny so far, but she wasn't going to press her luck by crossing the square in front of an armed guard. The church was to her right, and since she hadn't come this close to it when they rode in the carriage she decided to go left.

Oh, heck, she thought, after she'd walked a ways. This didn't look right, either. At the next corner, she turned again. But within a few blocks, she knew she was hopelessly lost. She could see Main Street just ahead and things were starting to look familiar again, but for all the wrong reasons. This was near Mr. Levy's shop and the slave mart. *Mon Dieu.* This was the last place in all of Richmond where she wanted to get caught without a pass. She bit her lip, trying to calm the butterflies in her stomach.

She turned at the very next intersection and found herself in front of a grand hotel, its sidewalks littered with cigar butts and tobacco spit. She stepped gingerly through the mess, then picked up her pace until she found herself on a narrow street, not more than a few blocks long, lined with small brick buildings. Up ahead, a crowd of people lounged about. Her eyes scanned the buildings, looking for anything familiar. And then she saw it right smack in the middle of the block. A red flag hanging above a doorway. That was when it dawned on her that the group of people up ahead were all men.

Mon Dieu! The butterflies sprang to her breast. She had walked straight into hell. She started to turn and run. Get the heck out of there. But running would attract too much attention. So she clenched her fists in the folds of her skirt and turned ever so slowly. She had walked only a few feet when a door swung open steps beyond her, and a young white man with sideburns and whiskers stepped out.

"Sale is about to commence," he yelled to the crowd behind her. "This way, gentlemen, this way."

Suddenly, the very men she wanted to escape surrounded her. They were everywhere—behind her, beside her, in front of her. They ran the gamut from finely dressed gentlemen with gold-handled canes, to crackers wearing slouch hats who looked as if they could hardly afford the raggedy shirts on their backs. Most of them seemed to barely notice her, although a few turned and stared outright. Her mind flashed back to Mama's stories of a drunken Mass Todd attacking her in her sleep, and Grandma Susie helping her beat him off. Mama had said she could smell his stale breath all . . .

"Miss?" Her head jerked up. The whiskered man who had opened the door was smiling at her strangely, baring his tobacco-stained teeth. All the other men were inside the building, leaving only her on the street. Now what to do? She wished Mama was here, or Ellen. Running now was out of the question. Her legs felt like lead, not to mention all the attention that would attract. So she avoided his eyes and looked straight ahead as she walked past the door.

"Miss, you lost?"

She blinked. All right. All right now. Calm down. She was white, remember? She paused. "Um, yes. I seem to be." Instead of looking directly at him, she pretended to be searching the surroundings.

"I thought so, ma'am. This ain't no place for a lady by herself. Where you headed?"

She tried to think as a loud thump came from inside the building and another man's voice drifted out to the street.

"Gentlemen, y'all know good niggers when ya see 'em. Come here, gal. Hold up that fine, healthy baby there."

Susan swallowed hard. "The train station."

The whiskered man chuckled as the voice behind him droned on.

". . . all in good health. You-all ever see a finer lot than this here? Come on up. See fo' yo'self."

"You way off," the man in the doorway said. "Now let me see heah." He rubbed his whiskers and thought for a moment.

". . . goin' to give ya a bargain, gentlemen. All of 'em fo' eight hundred fifty dollahs."

"Eight sixty," another voice bid.

"Eight sixty. Thank ya. Now who'll say eight seventy?"

"You got to go up this way here," the whiskered man said, pointing in the direction they were facing.

She nodded.

". . . las' call. Goin', goin', gone." *Crack!* "Sold fo' nine hundred dollahs to Mr. Byrd here."

". . . and just follow the road on up to Broad Street, there. Ya can't miss it if you just do that, ma'am."

Susan nodded, thanked him, and scurried off. Just as she was about to turn the corner, she glanced back. He was still standing there, watching her. She rounded the corner, then stopped and leaned against a tree trunk in front of the hotel and post office. A white couple strolling by stared at her openly, but she didn't care. She had to catch her breath. She was thankful to be off that block.

She was standing there huffing and puffing when a gruff-looking white man dressed in black from head to toe walked out of the hotel. She stood up straight and watched as he led a group of four coloreds, two men and two women tied to a rope at their wrists, out of the building. They were all dressed in thin, filthy rags, and they were soaking wet.

The white couple that had been so interested in her stopped and stared at the coloreds. Another white man carrying a cane strolled up from the opposite direction and stopped next to the couple.

"What did they do?" the man with the cane asked the couple.

"Nothing," said the man with the woman.

"Well, why are they tied like that then?"

"Why, to keep them from running."

"Where is he taking them?" the man with the cane asked.

"To the market to be sold, I reckon. They'll be cleaned up first. Probably just come by boat or train." He looked the man with the cane up and down. "You aren't from around here, are you?"

"No. New York."

"Ah."

Susan walked away as quickly as her heels would carry her. The city was crawling with slave traders, and it made her sick to her stomach. She had to get out of here, no matter where she ended up.

By the time she found the train station she was so drained that all she wanted to do was sit. Her feet were killing her, cramping and stiff at the arch. She saw a bench and heard a whistle all at the same time, then looked up to see the train approaching the station. No time to sit. She would do that on the train.

As it rolled into the station and stopped, she remembered that she didn't have a ticket. Where did you go to get one? How much did it cost? She looked up and down the street for a place to buy a ticket as people got off and on the train. A part of her wanted to just get on and take her chances. The heck with it.

Then two colored women wearing stained kerchiefs tied around their heads appeared in the doorway at the back of the train. One was dark, the other nearly as light as Susan was. As soon as their feet touched the ground, a white man, again wearing all black, walked up to them, tied their wrists, and led them off. The light-complexioned one started to cry and pulled back on the rope. The other one cursed at her reluctant companion just as they walked past. "Aw. Quit that bawlin'."

Susan turned her head away slightly, and her mind flashed back to the day of her own arrival—the fights with the slave dealer, the long bumpy ride in back of the wagon, the hot, cramped train. It seemed that this whole city was one big slave market.

She turned back toward the train. She knew she didn't have much time. If she was going to get on, now was the time to do it. But her legs wouldn't move. She was so scared she would do the wrong thing and make someone suspect that she wasn't white. She had to buy a ticket but she didn't have the faintest idea where or how to do that. She'd have to ask someone and that would attract attention—the last thing she wanted. Then once in Orange, she would need a ride to Montpelier. She couldn't walk because she didn't know the way. And walking or riding, there was always the risk that she would run into someone in Orange County who knew who she really was.

She sighed. One slip and she could end up being

dragged through the streets and then on the auction block, paraded before a bunch of lecherous old men and sold to the highest bidder, like so many others. She could end up being carried even farther away from Mama and Ellen. Getting on this train could be akin to chopping off her foot to stop the cramping.

The wheels started to move, and she sank down on the bench and watched as the train pulled out of the station. It was perfectly all right, she told herself. She would be on the next one. She just needed a little time to think things over. She reached down under her dress and discreetly pulled off the shoe on her cramped foot, and rubbed the arch against her other leg. As soon as her weary feet felt a little better, she was going to get up and find out where to buy a ticket and where to get off for Montpelier. Then she was going to get on the train and ride to her destination and then . . . then. Somehow she was going to have to find a carriage or wagon for the rest of the journey to Montpelier. She sighed. Getting back home was going to be harder than she'd imagined.

She slipped her foot back into the shoe and stood up. But before she could take a single step, she saw Fanny walking straight toward her. She gasped. Did Fanny know about the money? Susan's first instinct was to flee in the opposite direction. She could outrun Fanny easily, especially with her being sick. But that would cause a commotion and attract attention. She would just have to stay and face Fanny. Fanny couldn't make her go back.

Susan held her head up defiantly as Fanny walked up beside her and sat on the bench.

"Thought I'd find you here, Sister Susanne," Fanny said. She coughed into a handkerchief.

Susan felt bad about Fanny dragging herself out of bed on account of her. Fanny was the last person she wanted to suffer in all this. But it wasn't her fault. She didn't make Fanny get up out of her sickbed. If anything, she would have preferred that Fanny stay at home. She stayed on her feet and stared straight ahead at the train tracks.

"Why didn't you get on that one?" Fanny asked.

"I don't have a ticket. Yet."

"I see."

"But I'm getting on the next one."

"With money you stole from my mistress?"

Susan licked her lips. So Fanny did know about the money. "Did Miss Lizbeth send you here? Or was it Miss Nancy? I'm surprised they didn't send a slave catcher."

"They don't know you're running. Yet."

Susan turned and looked down at Fanny. She was puzzled. "Then why are you here?"

"I told them you probably went to get the handbag from Mr. Levy's shop."

"Where . . . then where do they think I got the money?"

"Told 'em I lent it to you."

Susan blinked. Fanny lied to them for her? She looked back toward the track. "You didn't have to do that."

"No, but I did. They were looking for you, so I told 'em you probably got lost trying to find Mr. Levy's and I would go and find you and bring you back. You would have been in a heap of trouble if I didn't tell 'em something."

"Well . . . well, I thank you, Sister Fanny. But I'm not going back there."

Fanny let out a deep breath of air.

"I didn't mean to get you caught up in this," Susan said. "But I can't go back there. I belong at Montpelier."

"If you get back there, and that's a big if, what you going to do then?"

"I'm going to see my mama and my sister. I have to find out if Ellen is alright."

"Their new massa going to take you back?"

Susan blinked. "I . . . I'm going to ask him to. I'll beg if I have to."

"A lot of good that'll do. You'll be a runaway. These white folks don't like no runaways. You know that."

Susan was silent. If she worried about things like that, she'd never get back.

"Most likely, they'll just sell you off somewhere else, since the Montgomerys won't want you anymore, either. You thought about that?"

Susan looked down at her fingers. "I'm ready to take my chances."

"Don't be a fool. I've seen it happen before. I had a sister here." Fanny paused and coughed. "She's three years younger than me. She ran off with some free man up there to New York. Massa hired one of them agents to go and search for her. Massa wouldn't let up either till he found her. Took him almost a whole year. I thought she was safe and he would never find her." Fanny shook her head. "He had her brought back down here. They made her walk most of the way, then he sold her down to Mississippi. That happened, oh, it's been almost ten years now. I haven't seen her since."

"Mass Willard did that?"

"No, she belonged to a different family, but she was the only family I had here. I asked Mass Willard to buy her after they caught her but he said no, he wasn't going to buy no runaway. You think you got it rough now." Fanny paused and shook her head. "It'll be a hundred times worse if you run and they catch you. Mass Willard will do the same thing. He'll hire an agent and hunt you down till he finds you 'cause he got money in you. Then he'll sell you. He a banker, too? Unh-uh. The last thing you want to do is mess with his money or his property."

Fanny paused and blew her nose. Susan glanced at her out the corner of her eye, trying to tell if Fanny's nose was running from crying or from her cold. Susan could feel tears burning in the corners of her own eyes. She wished Fanny would shut up and go home. She didn't need to hear this. Not now.

"Everybody thinks I'm so devoted to Miss Lizbeth. And I am, in a way. But it's for me as much as her. The Montgomerys will do right by you, better than most, unless you cross 'em."

Susan knew much of this. All white folks were the same. But she wanted to go home so badly, she didn't want to admit it to herself. Besides, there were other reasons why she couldn't go back to Grace Street. "But I can't go back there. Miss Nancy was talking about selling me after I burned Miss Lizbeth. She doesn't like me. Never did."

"Aunt Martha told Miss Nancy and Miss Lizbeth that it wasn't your fault about the bath water being too hot. Aunt Martha said she didn't instruct you proper."

"Aunt Martha said that?"

Fanny nodded. "'Sides, it's not for Miss Nancy to decide if you stay. That's up to Mass Willard, and I suspect it will take more than that for him to sell you."

Susan glanced down. Did Fanny suspect that Mass Willard was her daddy, too? But Fanny's face wasn't giving anything away. Susan looked back at the track. She wasn't going to think about that now. She sat down on the bench. "I miss my mama. And I'm worried about Ellen."

Fanny reached out and patted her leg. "I know, Susan. But there's not a lot you can do about it. Running is going to make things worse. Mark my word."

She noticed that Fanny had called her by her real name. It felt so good hearing that again. She lowered her head and wiped her eyes. Fanny was right, of course. As much as she hated admitting it to herself, Fanny was so right. She whimpered and tears welled up in her eyes again.

"Listen, I can't make you come back," Fanny said softly. "I just wanted to tell you that if you want to, the way is clear." She stood up. "I'd best be getting on back myself. If you want, I'll tell 'em I couldn't find you."

Susan swallowed. "What about the money?"

"You need that for the train."

"I mean, if I go back there?"

"You still have it on you?"

Susan nodded.

"Give it to me, I'll put it back. I doubt she's missed it yet. If she did, I'll think of something. And we'll tell her the bag was already sold when you got there."

Susan sniffed and wiped her eyes. Then she reached into her dress and took out the wad of bills and handed it to Fanny.

"Oh, Mama," she whispered. She stood up and followed Fanny to the mansion on Grace Street.

22

It was one of those dreary early spring mornings, the kind when a woman often wanted to do nothing more after breakfast than curl up with her knitting needles in front of a toasty fire. But it would take a lot more than a few threatening clouds to keep Susanne from her daily walk to the park with the children. She went every Saturday and weekday morning after breakfast and on Sunday following church, weather permitting. It was what got her through the rest of the day. Miss Nancy and Miss Lizbeth could stay in the mansion for days on end. So could Fanny and the other servants. Susanne couldn't understand it. She dreaded cold winter days or when one of the children got sick and she had to stay cooped up in the mansion.

She especially didn't want to miss her walk today, she thought as she buttoned her dress. She didn't even want to be late. Due to a strange twist of fate, she had finally decided to accept Oliver's invitation to join him one Sunday at the African Baptist Church. She had been seeing him most mornings for months now as he walked through the park on his way to his store. He first extended an invitation a few weeks back, but she politely declined. He asked again about a week ago, and again she turned him down.

But now Miss Lizbeth had hatched some crazy plan to match her up with Alfred, of all the men in this crazy city. She liked nothing about the man. He was one of the Montgomery slaves, but he lived in a room down by the river and worked at the ironworks by day. That wasn't so bad. What she didn't like was that from everything she had heard and seen about this Alfred, he was a ladies' man through and through, a regular rascal, with his smooth copper complexion and thick, dark mustache. She wanted no part of it.

Who she did want, although not another soul knew it, was Marcus, the Andersons' butler. She first saw him when she took the children to the mansion to play with the Anderson children. When Marcus opened the door for them, he looked so dignified in his livery that Susanne nearly fell over the threshold. He was tall and fair, with jet black hair and perfectly straight teeth. He didn't say much, but he smiled a lot and seemed to find all kinds of excuses to come into the playroom, where she sat with the children and Hattie, the Andersons' nurse.

"Good day, Sister Susanne," Marcus said as he escorted her and the Montgomery children to the door. "I hope to see all of you again right soon."

She was planning their wedding in her head all the way home. Never had any man had such an effect on her.

She tried to tell Miss Lizbeth that she wasn't ready to jump the broom. The truth was that she wasn't ready to jump it with Alfred and never would be. Now Marcus was a different story. Still, Missus wouldn't hear it. Susanne was almost seventeen, Missus said, and it was time for her to think of marriage and babies. "So they can grow up with my children," she said. And no doubt wait on them, too, Susanne thought wryly. Miss Lizbeth had even gone so far as to ask her parents if Susanne and Alfred could use the small parlor where Susanne did her knitting for some Sunday afternoon courting.

"Since he lives out, it will give them a chance to get to know one another."

Miss Nancy smacked her thin lips. "That's the most ridiculous thing I ever heard. What would the neighbors think? Our friends?"

Amen, Susanne thought. For once, she sided with Miss Nancy.

"I couldn't care less what they think," Miss Lizbeth said, holding her nose in the air. "Susanne is more well-bred than half of them anyway. And I want her to find a suitable mate. Everyone else in our household is either too old or too young or not good enough for her. And Alfred needs to settle down."

Not with her, Susanne thought. Find him somebody else.

"Well, I hardly think Alfred fits the bill for a suitable mate," Miss Nancy said. "He's an iron worker."

"A puddler," Mass Willard said. "Same as Fanny's husband, Raif. They both bring me a tidy sum out of their earnings."

"And he's your property, Father," Miss Lizbeth reminded her daddy. "That's better than if she should meet someone who belongs to someone else."

"You don't need to convince me," Mass Willard said. "I'm all for it. Alfred's a smart one, too. He's strong and capable. I like the idea myself."

"He and Susanne will make such a nice couple, Mama."

They went on and on like that for goodness knows how long, right there in front of her. Deciding her fate as if she were some child.

"If you want her to leave you alone about it," Fanny told her later that evening, "you best find somebody on your own."

"But who?" Susanne had asked, frowning. She'd only seen Marcus once, so he was out of the question for now.

"All the other men here are the wrong age or already married or not suitable for one reason or another."

Fanny shrugged. "I don't know, but Miss Lizbeth's not going to let up till she sees you courtin' or married. She's stubborn that way when she thinks she's right. She's the one that got me together with Raif. 'Course Raif is altogether different from that Alfred." Fanny shook her head. "Maybe Brother Alfred would settle down for you."

"And maybe he wouldn't. 'Sides, I don't find him at all handsome."

"I didn't exactly fancy Raif at first, neither," Fanny said. "On account of him being so light-skinned. But he kind of grew on me, I reckon." She snapped her fingers. "What about Brother Oliver?"

"Oliver Armistead?"

Fanny nodded.

Susanne turned up her nose. "I don't think so."

"Listen, honey," Fanny said, chuckling. "Brother Oliver may not be the prettiest man around, but they don't come any more respectable. He's good folk. And I see how he looks at you whenever we run into him."

"He just smiles at me," Susanne said incredulously.

"Uh-huh," Fanny said. "He never smiles at me like that. Didn't you say you see him most mornings in the park?"

"Lately I have."

"That's probably no accident."

Susanne smiled. "He invited me to go to church with him one Sunday."

"Well, you see."

"I turned him down."

"Oliver Armistead? Umph-umph, child. No colored woman in her right mind would turn him down." Fanny shook her head with disbelief.

"He's . . . He looks to be a full-blooded African," Susanne said.

"And?"

"You know how they can be. So . . ." What was the right word?

"Proud?" Fanny filled in for her.

Susanne bobbed her head from side to side. "I was going to say more like stubborn. Stuck in the old ways. Some of them seem to think they're better than the rest of us 'cause their blood is purer or something."

"Uh-huh," Fanny said, as she placed her hands on her hips. "Sounds like somebody else I know."

"I'm not stuck up. I can't help it if I'm proud of who I am."

"There's nothing wrong with that. All of us got something to be proud of one way or 'nother, I reckon."

Susanne thought of Marcus, with his fine self. She wanted to ask Fanny about him, since Fanny knew everybody who worked for the old Richmond families. But what if he wasn't interested in her? She'd just make a fool of herself. She would wait until she was more certain of how Marcus felt before she asked anybody about him. "'Sides, Brother Oliver is free," Susanne said. "You and I both know white folks don't like us mixing with free issue."

"I have the feeling they'll make an exception for Brother Oliver. White folks love that man on account of him being descended from that James Armistead Lafayette. I told you about that. Anyhow, you better do something, and fast, before Miss Lizbeth gets her mind too fixed on Brother Alfred."

So now Susanne thought that maybe she would give this Oliver a second look, and she was anxious to get to the park before she missed him. Only two-year-old Miss Caroline had other ideas. A few months ago, she had decided that she was now old enough to pick out her own outfit for the day. Most of the time Susanne let her, even when the child insisted on wearing a party dress to play in the park. Susanne didn't have a whole lot of choice, since Miss Caroline had gotten into the habit of running to her mama whenever she didn't feel like obeying Susanne, knowing full well that she had her mama wrapped around her little finger. But this was different. This morning the child was clinging to a flowered cotton dress and ignoring the more sensible woolen outfit Susanne had laid out for her.

"But I want this one."

"That's for summer," Susanne said calmly. "You need to wear something that will keep the early spring chill off your bones."

The little girl eyed the dreaded dress on her bed with venom. "But I don't like that one. It's ugly."

"Then we'll pick out something else. You can't wear cotton in April, especially so early in the morning." Susanne noticed that Miss Caroline had loosened her grip on the cotton dress, and Susanne reached out and snatched it from her.

Miss Caroline stamped her little foot and puffed her pink cheeks. "I'll tell Mommy."

"You go right ahead," Susanne said as she shook the cotton dress out.

Miss Caroline did just that. She ran out the door clad only in her ruffled pantalets. Susanne rolled her eyes to the ceiling. She would never catch Oliver at this rate, all because of this spoiled little child. She sighed and glanced down at Mass Ward. The six-month-old was fast asleep in his crib. Susanne tucked the covers around him, then followed Miss Caroline to Miss Lizbeth's chamber.

The missus was sitting at her vanity, her back facing the doorway while Fanny pinned up her hair. Missus was chatting about a play that she and her husband had seen the night before.

". . . but my absolute favorite actor is J. B. Wilkes."

"J. B. Wilkes?" Fanny asked.

"My husband says that's his stage name. His real name is John Wilkes Booth."

"Oh," Fanny said, as if that cleared things up.

"I'll never forget the night we saw him at the theater a couple of years ago. You remember. It was the same night of that raid on the armory at Harper's Ferry by that madman John Brown."

"That was just awful, ma'am," Fanny said. "Just an awful time."

"Now we have this news that we've fired on Union soldiers at Fort Sumter. What's the world coming to? My father is so worried."

"Last night Raif said folks are real jumpy in town, 'specially down at the river."

"Oh, I hope this doesn't mean we're going to war. Father says—" Miss Lizbeth stopped abruptly when she saw Miss Caroline. Susanne stayed in the doorway as the child climbed up into her mama's lap.

"Is he a good actor, Missus?" Fanny asked, obviously changing the subject for the child's sake. Susanne was glad. She didn't like all this talk about war, and it seemed to be heating up the past few months.

"Who?" Missus asked.

"J. B. Wilkes."

"Oh. He's so handsome, who cares if he can act?" Missus said with a toss of her hand.

Fanny gasped in mock astonishment. "Miss Lizbeth, you're a married woman."

Miss Lizbeth blushed and giggled. "Oh, I suppose he can act. His father is a famous actor in England, I think. I wanted to get his autograph but there must have been a hundred women back there at the stage door. I would have stayed and waited but Master Richard didn't have the patience. He—" Miss Lizbeth stopped as Miss Caroline pulled on her mama's chemise to get her attention.

"Good morning, my precious," Miss Lizbeth said as she kissed Miss Caroline on the forehead.

"Mommy, I want to wear my flowered dress to the park."

"Why, that's fine, dear."

"But Susanne won't let me."

Miss Lizbeth turned and looked up at Susanne, a puzzled expression on her face.

"It's cotton, missus. It's much too chilly out."

"You'll freeze," Fanny said, tugging on one of Miss Caroline's curls. "And your nose will turn red and fall off."

The little Missus giggled.

"Susanne's right, dear," Miss Lizbeth said. "It's too cold out for cotton this time of year."

"But I don't like the dress she wants me to wear."

"I told her she could pick something else out, Missus," Susanne said.

"But I want to wear the flowered one." Miss Caroline poked out her lip and batted her eyelashes at her mother.

"Oh, all right," Miss Lizbeth said. She looked at Susanne. "Let her wear it. Just make sure she puts on extra clothing on top of it."

Susanne resisted rolling her eyes to the ceiling. She shouldn't be surprised. That was what was wrong with the child now. Her mama had no backbone. "Yes, ma'am."

Miss Caroline jumped down from her mama's lap and ran off. As soon as she was out of earshot, Susanne stepped into the room. Miss Lizbeth smiled and held her hand up, palm out, toward Susanne. "I know, I know. I spoil her."

"Ma'am," Susanne said. "I thought we were going to start being firmer with her."

Miss Lizbeth sighed. "Just this once, then I promise to back you up in the future. It's just that I find it so difficult to tell her no."

"It only gets harder every time you let her have her way, Miss Lizbeth."

"You're absolutely right, Susanne. Master Richard tells me the exact same thing."

"That stuff is cute when they're little, Missus," Fanny said. "But it won't be so cute after she's old enough to know better."

"Not to mention that she can catch cold," Susanne said. "It's only April."

Miss Lizbeth let out a deep breath of air. "You're right." She stood up. "I'll go tell her she can't wear the cotton."

"It's for the best, ma'am," Susanne said.

Miss Caroline bawled like the spoiled child she was, but Miss Lizbeth held her ground. And like a two-year-old, the little missus had all but forgotten that she didn't get to wear her flowered cotton dress by the time they got outside in the fresh air. She skipped along happily and helped Susanne push her baby brother in the carriage.

They reached the park, a short walk from the mansion, and Miss Caroline ran off to play with the other children while Susanne sat on a bench and rocked Mass Ward in his carriage. Every few minutes, Miss Caroline ran back to explain to Susanne what they were doing and to check on her baby brother as he napped. Susanne smiled as Miss Caroline ran off once again for another game of tag. She really was a delightful little girl if you could get past the willfulness. Her mama said she was just spirited, but Susanne worried that if that spirit wasn't checked the little missus would soon become a little brat. Every time Miss Lizbeth overruled one of her decisions, her job got a little harder. Susanne couldn't blame the child, her mama was the problem.

She kept looking up the block, hoping to spot Oliver's brown face. She stood up and spent some time chatting with the other nurses, gave Miss Caroline a cookie and little Mass Ward his bottle, and still no sign of Oliver. Just her luck, Susanne thought. When she wanted to see him, he was nowhere about. She sat back on the bench and rocked Mass Ward as he sucked on his bottle. This was the best part of the day. She got to talk to other nurses in the neighborhood and a few minutes to sit, relax, and think. Her mind almost always drifted back to the morning not long after she and Fanny returned from the train depot and Aunt Martha told her that Mass Willard wanted to see her in his study.

She remembered wondering what in the world Massa could want with her? She had been so scared as she walked down the hallway to his study she couldn't see straight. She bumped into a table and almost knocked the crystal flower vase over. She caught it just in time, set it back upright, then smoothed her skirt over. She had no idea what this could be about. Fanny had sneaked into Miss Lizbeth's room and replaced the money in the box as soon as they returned from the train depot, and no one had said a word about it since then. Miss Lizbeth didn't seem at all suspicious. She had even given Susanne some money the other day to go and find another handbag for church. And Susanne hadn't done anything wrong since the day she ran off, as far as she knew.

She took a deep breath and knocked. Mass Willard's voice told her to enter, and she opened the door, then stood beside it. This was her first time in his study, and it reminded her of the library at Montpelier, with its dark mahogany furniture and bookshelves filled with leather-bound volumes. It even smelled the same, except for the cigar. Massa sat in a big upholstered armchair puffing and reading the newspaper. He put the paper down in his lap when she entered and took the cigar from his mouth.

"Come here, Susanne," he said and she went and stood in front of him. "I've just come from up North, and I stopped at Montpelier on the way back."

She nearly gasped out loud.

"I know there was some confusion when you were brought here, with Ellen running and hiding. . . ." He stopped and frowned.

"Yes, Massa?" She knew better than to interrupt, even if he did pause, but she was so anxious to hear about Ellen and Mama.

"I thought you'd want to know that I saw both your mother and your sister, and they're fine. Their new owner is a good man."

But did they punish Ellen for running? What did they do to Mama? She had a hundred questions but was afraid to ask even one. Would she go to her grave without ever knowing?

"I told Clara that you were well and happy here." He paused and looked at her as if waiting for her to confirm his opinion.

Susanne lowered her head and bit her lip. She couldn't do that. She couldn't lie with a straight face. And she doubted Mama had believed it, either.

He dumped the ashes from his cigar into an ashtray. "Mmm-hmm. Is everyone treating you well?"

Susanne kept her head lowered. "Yes, Massa. Everyone is nice to me here."

"Then what seems to be the problem?"

She hesitated.

"Speak up. Don't be afraid to say what's on your mind. I won't punish you."

She knew she should lie. But he seemed so nice and she missed home so much. She had to take a chance. Maybe he would let her go home if he only knew the truth.

She looked up. "It's just that I . . . I miss Mama and Ellen. I think about them all the time."

He grunted. "Well, I suppose that's natural. You've only been here about a month."

She looked back at the floor. "I suppose, Massa." She looked back up. "But I would give anything to go back. Please, send me back home." There. She'd said it. If he was going to punish her, so be it.

He sighed. "I can't do that, Susanne. You're a part of this family now. Young girls not much older than yourself get married and leave home all the time. Not much difference."

"But they get to go back home and see their families sometimes."

He grunted again and puffed on his cigar as he stared straight ahead. "Well, I don't suppose that would hurt. I'll take you back for a visit. How would you like that?"

She smiled. It wasn't exactly what she wanted but it was more than she'd expected to get. She nodded vigorously. "Yes, Massa, I'd like that just fine."

He smiled. "Good. Then it's settled. Perhaps next spring we'll go back."

Next spring? Next spring? That was almost a whole year away. She had to wait that long to see her family again? Well, getting back there on her own was about impossible. She found that out the hard way. And going back next year was better than never seeing them again. She would have something to look forward to. "I thank you, Massa."

Mass Ward began to whimper, and Susanne snapped out of her reverie. She picked him up out of the carriage and put him in her lap. This was going on the third spring since that day in Massa's study, and she hadn't been home for a visit yet. Not once. Every spring she prayed and waited for Massa to say tomorrow was the day. And every spring she was disappointed. She sighed and patted Mass Ward's back. She'd done everything they wanted. She took care of their children as if they were her own. She smiled a lot and never gave them any trouble. She'd even accepted the name they'd forced on her and now even thought of herself as Susanne. All in hopes of someday going home for a visit.

Well, this last notion of theirs was too much to bear. She wasn't about to marry Alfred, and she didn't care how much Miss Lizbeth got her heart set on it. She looked up the block. Still no sign of Oliver. She sighed as she put Mass Ward back in his carriage and packed up. There was always next week, thank goodness. She would be sure to get here on time on Monday. If little Miss Caroline wanted to come out in her drawers, Susanne would let her just to get here early enough to see Oliver.

As soon as she stepped through the door to the mansion she heard Mass Willard's voice coming from the drawing room. "Is that you, Susanne?"

"Yes, Massa."

He stuck his head out the door and smiled. "Thank goodness you're back with the children."

"Yes, Massa, we're back."

Susanne frowned as he retreated to the parlor. She wondered what that was all about as she leaned down to unbutton Miss Caroline's coat. Mass Willard had left for a meeting in town early that morning. He was going to a lot of meetings lately since he was a member of a state convention formed by the governor earlier that year to decide whether Virginia should leave the Union. The delegates had voted against secession, but Southern-rights fire-eaters were adamant that Virginia secede. They had formed another convention and threatened to go against the governor, and Mass Willard had become increasingly agitated over the past few days.

"Dad-blame it. Those cussed fire-eaters will ruin us," Mass Willard said, his loud voice drifting out into the hallway as Susanne removed her own coat. "All this talk about secession is just plain foolishness. It would mean financial ruin for Richmond. At the very least, we should wait to see if Lincoln defends Fort Sumter."

Miss Caroline ran into the parlor as Susanne picked up Mass Ward and followed. She stood back near the doorway holding the baby and looked on anxiously as Mass Willard paced the floor and repeatedly slapped a newspaper into the palm of his hand. Miss Nancy sat with her daughters at the round marble-topped table in the center of the room. All three of them had put down their knitting and sewing needles and focused their attention on Mass Willard. Even Mass Richard had come home from his office, and he stood in his usual spot near the fireplace, resting his elbow on the mantelpiece. He was still wearing his white frock coat over his street clothes, and his black bag stood at his feet.

Miss Caroline ran up and kissed first her granddaddy, then her daddy, since she was seeing both of them for the first time that day. Then she hopped into her mama's lap.

"And the newspapers have behaved so damned irresponsibly," Mass Willard said.

Miss Nancy coughed. "Your language, dear," she said, nodding toward Miss Caroline.

"Oh. Sorry. Their editorials have encouraged secession from the beginning, especially the *Examiner*, calling convention delegates traitors when they don't like the decisions."

"One of the delegates shot at the editor of the *Examiner* over on Franklin Street after he printed a piece calling him a 'fat poodle,'" Mass Richard said.

"Yes," Mass Willard said. "That was old Marmaduke. It's a pity he missed."

Mass Richard chuckled.

"Caroline, dear," Miss Nancy said with a thin smile. "Why don't you run up to your room and play?"

"Yes, Caroline," Miss Lizbeth said. "Mama will be right up." Miss Caroline jumped down as quickly as she'd hopped up and ran out the door. Susanne started to follow until Mass Willard called her. She went to him as he put down the newspaper. He took the little massa from her and bounced him up in the air.

"There's my grandbaby."

Mass Ward gurgled with delight.

"Where is this Fort Sumter, Father?" Miss Lizbeth asked.

"South Carolina," Mass Willard said.

"Is that one of the states that have already seceded?" Miss Ellen asked.

"Yes," Mass Richard said. "All the states of the deep South have left the Union."

"Do you think Lincoln will defend the fort, dear?" Miss Nancy asked.

"I should hope not. He knows that will just inflame passions here and force Virginia to side with the Confederacy. The Confederacy is weak without Virginia's industry, and I should think Lincoln would want to keep it that way. The ironworks are here, and we've got the biggest flour mill in the world right down there on the river."

"And if we join, the other states still sitting on the fence will follow our lead," Mass Richard said. "They look up to Virginia."

"I can't believe all of this is happening," Mass Willard said as he handed his grandson back to Susanne. "Why this mad rush to destroy all that our grandfathers built for us? Especially here in Virginia. Washington, Madison, Jefferson, Monroe, all sons of Virginia. They would turn in their graves at the very notion of splitting up the Union. I knew Madison personally, spent time at Montpelier. So I know what I'm talking about. We have a tradition to uphold. And Virginia must lead the way." He banged a fist on the table. "Lincoln has already said that he would not interfere with slavery in the states where it already exists. That's good enough for me."

Susanne turned to leave. "Wait, Susanne," Mass Willard said. "I want you to hear this, too. Do you know anything about this secession business?"

Susanne nodded. "I know a bit about it, Massa."

He turned back toward his wife and daughters. "Well, this is what we came home to tell you. Things don't look safe in town just now. A huge crowd has gathered down at the river, hundreds from what I've heard. They're waving the Confederate flag, and I'm told that some of them are armed."

There were gasps all around the table.

"Oh, my," Miss Nancy said.

"I don't want any of you to leave the house without either Richard or myself accompanying you until things calm down. Is that understood?"

They all nodded as Mass Willard reached for the newspaper and Mass Richard stood up straight from his lounging position at the mantelpiece. "We're going back into town now," Mass Willard said. "See what's going on."

"You won't stay for dinner, dear?" Miss Nancy said.

"We'll grab a bite at one of the taverns. We just came home to tell you the news. Will you be all right here alone, dear?"

"We should be fine. I'm sure it will all blow over soon."

"I don't think it will come to any real fighting," Miss Lizbeth said. "And I refuse to even allow myself to think that way."

By dinnertime, Susanne had heard "Dixie" being played by the bands roaming the streets so many times that even when it wasn't, the tune blared in her head. Throngs of people had been marching up and down the streets and singing to drums and bugles all evening long. When the sun set, they lit torchlights and the festivities continued.

There was a knock at the kitchen door, and Aunt Martha got up from the table where several of the house servants were having their supper. Things had gotten so wild, they had taken to locking up the mansion at Miss Nancy's orders. As soon as Aunt Martha opened the door, the noise from the street blared into the house. A firecracker blasted in the distance. Susanne covered her ears until Aunt Martha slammed the door shut.

It was Mabel from the yard asking for more food for the children. "Them white folks is stirrin' up a ruckus out there," Mabel said, as Aunt Martha filled a pot with mush. "All that hollerin' an' singin' an' carryin' on."

"For the life of me," Aunt Martha said, "I can't understand why anybody would be singing about going to no war." She shook her head.

Mabel shrugged. "Some of 'em happy, some of 'em ain't. Brother Joseph was over earlier and he say Miss Hill over on Cary is fit 'nough to be tied. She thinks the town done gone mad."

"My mistress was upstairs crying, she's so upset," Aunt Martha said. "Mass Willard worked so hard on that convention to keep this from happening. And look what it's come to."

There was another knock at the door, and Fanny got up to answer it. This time it was her husband, Raif. He was a mulatto, and his cheeks were pink with excitement.

"Them white folks going crazy down at the docks and over at the Capitol. They lighting bonfires and shooting guns and cannons." He sat at the table and Fanny fixed him a plate. "I heard it was five thousand people out there at one time."

"They're shooting cannons?" Fanny asked, her eyes wide with horror.

"Heard they shot at the governor's place even," Raif said.

"Oh, my goodness," Susanne said.

"They wants war," Raif said, banging his fist on the table in mock anger.

"This isn't anything to be joking about, Raif," Fanny said. "War is serious business."

"Fanny's right," Susanne said. "I'm worried sick about what will happen to Mama and Ellen if we have a war."

The hardest part was that she would have no way of knowing how they were doing.

Mabel left with a basket of food, and Aunt Martha sat back at the table. "For the life of me, I just can't understand it."

"Guess what I done heard down at the docks," Raif said as Fanny put a plate of food in front of him and sat down. From the tone of his voice, they knew that what he was about to say wasn't for white folks' ears, and they all leaned forward. "One reason they want to fight the North is that Mass Lincoln don't want no more slavery."

"What does that mean?" Fanny asked. "He going to end it?"

"Don't nobody know for sure. That's what they all upset about. Some of 'em say it just means he don't want no slaves in them new states that's opening up out west."

"I heard Mass Willard say Lincoln promised not to mess with slavery in the states where it already was," Susanne said.

"So it just means in the new states?" Fanny asked.

"Praise the Lord," Aunt Martha said. "Don't want to hear anything about some freedom."

"Why the heck not?" Raif asked.

"What am I going to do with freedom? Where am I going to go? Huh?"

"You don't give yourself 'nough credit, Aunt Martha," Raif said. "We can find jobs and take care of ourselves just as good as they do. I work. Pay my own room and board, too. If it wasn't for slavery, I wouldn't have to give a third of my money to Massa. Think what I could buy then."

"Maybe y'all can do it," Aunt Martha said. "You're still young. But not me. I'm more than sixty years old and all I know how to do is take care of this house and the missus. Think she going to pay me for that?" Aunt Martha shook her head. "That'll be the day."

Freedom wasn't for her, either, Susanne thought, as she lay in bed that night listening to revelers outside still demonstrating. The idea of freedom sounded exciting, but when you really thought about it, it was downright scary. Mama had said freedom didn't mean the same thing for them as it did for whites. And she was right. Susanne had seen how some of the free coloreds lived around here. Most of them stayed in shacks that were in worse shape than any cabin at Montpelier. Some lived out in the streets, and they had to scrape and beg for their next meal. They were often treated far worse than slaves since they didn't have a massa to protect them. Imagine if all of them suddenly were set free. The white folks would be so mad they'd make life hell for them. She'd gotten a good feel for what it was like out there on your own the day she ran off. She had never been so scared in all her life.

And what about Mama and Ellen and Squire May? They had never set foot out of Orange County or worked for wages. Unh-uh. She might be a slave but at least she had a decent bed to sleep in every night, plenty of food to eat, and comfortable clothes to wear. She still missed her family, but she had learned to live with that. Wasn't much else she could do. And even though Mass Willard had yet to honor his promise to take her home for a visit, she still had hopes that someday he would, maybe even this spring if they didn't go to war.

Hopefully, she was wasting her time thinking about all this. No one had said anything about freeing the slaves living in Virginia. If anything, they were only talking about the new states. She couldn't imagine that white folks would fight each other over that. They were too busy fighting the coloreds, she thought, chuckling. They loved their way of life too much to mess it up with a war.

* * *

On Monday Lincoln declared war on the South, and ten days later, Virginia joined the Confederacy.

23

In no time at all, Richmond was dubbed the capital of the Confederacy. The city was one of the South's most prosperous, with a rich base of commerce and industry—the Tredgar Iron Works, banks and tobacco factories, and some of the largest flour mills in the world. Several railroads entered the city, and now all sorts of characters eager to take advantage of the spoils of war—wealthy businessmen, speculators, and prostitutes—alighted at the depots and fanned onto the streets heading for Richmond's hotels and boardinghouses. They also came by boat, carriage, and on foot.

Public parks and squares were turned into training grounds for the thousands of soldiers streaming in to defend the new capital of the Confederacy. But training wasn't all that the soldiers were up to. In the evenings, they landed at the city's saloons, brothels, and gambling houses; and fortified with spirits, got into all kinds of mischief. The *Examiner* and *Enquirer* were littered with news about street brawls, rape, and theft.

For weeks, Mass Willard forbade his family to step foot out of the mansion without him, Mass Richard, or another white male companion, day or night. This applied only to the white women and children in the house, naturally.

The colored women who did the shopping and ran errands for their mistresses were still allowed, even expected, to go about their chores as usual. Aunt Martha had taken to carrying a big stick with her whenever she left. Fanny, an umbrella. Luckily, none of them ever encountered anything more threatening than a few menacing hecklers on the street corners.

Susanne was spared having to travel out-of-doors, although she had mixed feelings about it. She was confined to the mansion along with the children, except for church outings with the family on Sundays. That meant safety, but any chance of running into Oliver had all but vanished. The only good to come out of all the talk and worry about war looming on the horizon, to Susanne's way of thinking, was that Miss Lizbeth forgot her little scheme to mate her with that dreadful Alfred.

Still, the more Susanne thought about Oliver, the more she wanted to "bump into him"—scheme or no scheme. It had been a while since she'd last seen Oliver, but what she remembered grew dearer over time as she sat in the nursery with the children day after day. He was on the short side, but well-groomed. And he always had a smile on his face, at least for her. But the thing that impressed her most was that he talked so proper. He was the best-talking Negro she'd ever met.

True, he was free, and freedom was no piece of cake for coloreds in the South. Most of them were poor and lived in the shabbiest parts of town. And just like slaves, they weren't allowed in parks and public squares unless whites accompanied them or they had special permission. As the children's nurse, she lived well enough and could go anywhere with them. She wouldn't trade places with a free colored for all the gold in California.

But a few free coloreds seemed able to get around many of the barriers, and Oliver was one of them. She didn't know how or where he lived, but he did own his own store. She'd love a chance to talk to somebody like that. With the war going on, she missed her chats in the park with the other nurses. She adored the children, and little Miss Caroline could talk up a storm. When they took tea in the afternoon after the children's nap, Miss Caroline would chatter on and on about her dolls and toy teacups. But Susanne needed some colored grownup company now and then, too.

It finally dawned on Miss Nancy and her daughters that the war wasn't about to end any time soon, and that they were living like prisoners in their own home. They began to protest their confinement. At first, Mass Willard turned a deaf ear. The city was flooded with people of questionable character, he said. Soldiers were getting drunk and sleeping in the streets and committing other atrocious acts that he dared not even discuss in front of them.

Then Varina Davis, wife of Confederate president Jefferson Davis, arrived in Richmond shortly after her husband and began to take her friends along on rides in an open carriage through the city. And many of the ladies were getting together in churches and each other's homes to sew Confederate banners and uniforms. Miss Nancy put her foot down and insisted that Massa relax his rules and allow them to leave with male household servants during the daytime. Mass Willard finally let up, but Mass Richard still insisted that his children stay at home until things calmed down, whenever that might be.

Susanne thought she would burst if she didn't get out more often, and she told Miss Lizbeth so. Besides, she added, the children themselves were growing antsy being confined to the house. Miss Lizbeth agreed and promised to speak to Mass Richard. Susanne overheard them talking.

". . . and you're certain that Susanne is happy here with us?"

"Why, of course she is," Miss Lizbeth said.

"You don't think she might try to run up North with the children or something, do you?"

"That's preposterous!" Miss Lizbeth said.

"She has an awful lot of freedom with the children," Mass Richard said. "And with her light coloring it would be quite easy for her to abscond with them."

"But why in heaven's name would she do that? What can they possibly offer her up there that she hasn't got here?"

"Freedom, dear."

"Oh, well. But she lives practically as well as we do here. Her life is vastly superior to that of any free Negroes. I'm sure she realizes that. No, I'm quite certain that Susanne is loyal to us. I wouldn't have her minding our children if I thought otherwise."

"Well, if you're sure."

Susanne was flabbergasted. She was offended that Mass Richard even thought she'd run off with or without his children. True, she had tried to run once, but that was so long ago and the Montgomerys knew nothing about the ill-fated attempt. She had devoted herself to the children since they were born. She loved them dearly and would never do anything to hurt them. At least Miss Lizbeth understood that, and now finally, she could go back to her morning walks with the children.

On their first trip, she was so happy to be getting out of the mansion that she put on her new dress. One afternoon when they were all stuck indoors, Miss Lizbeth had decided to go through her clothes and give the household help everything she had grown weary of. Susanne had ended up with a plaid dress with an off-the-shoulder neckline and fringe on the sleeves.

It was a beautiful summer morning, she thought, as she pushed Wade in his carriage. Perfect for a stroll to the park. She took a deep breath of air. At least this neighborhood hadn't changed much. It was a different story downtown, where they said rowdy soldiers, out-of-towners, and prostitutes ran all about. The only reminders of war out here were the Confederate flags hanging from some houses and the soldiers passing by on horses waving their rifles.

That changed when she reached the park and discovered to her surprise that most of the grounds had been set aside for Confederate troops. Almost everywhere she looked, white tents were lined up one after the next, and men and boys drilled and marched about with muskets slung over their shoulders.

A small section had been set aside for the public and this was where the nurses gathered with their charges. Susanne sat on a bench, and Miss Caroline sat down beside her instead of running off to play as she used to. The child was unusually quiet and seemed to be dazed by all the activity in her little park. Susanne noticed that the other children were also sticking close to their nurses. She put an arm around Miss Caroline's shoulders, and the little girl leaned against her. The park was no longer the quiet retreat Susanne had come to love, but she was finally out of the mansion after weeks of being cooped up. She wondered if Oliver even came this way anymore. She craned her neck and looked up the street.

And then she saw him. She couldn't believe her eyes. After all these weeks there he was, walking briskly in her direction. He was dressed in a dark suit and wore his customary bowler hat cocked rakishly to one side. He saw her and a big smile crossed his cheeks as he removed his hat with a slight bow. "Good morning, Sister Susanne. And how are you on this fine day?"

She smiled. "Good, Brother Oliver. I'm just glad to be out taking in some fresh air for a change."

He nodded understandingly. "I haven't seen you out here lately."

So, he had missed her, she thought with satisfaction.

She smoothed her skirt. "Why, I wouldn't have thought you'd even notice my absence, Brother Oliver."

He raised an eyebrow. "Shucks. How could I not miss the prettiest rose in all of Richmond?"

She smiled with embarrassment. "Oh, go on with your sweet-talking self."

"I mean every word of it. The war kept you in?"

She nodded. "Mass Richard wouldn't let his children out till things calmed down some. Can't say as I blame him, given all that's been going on of late."

Oliver shook his head. "This war is bad business." He pointed beside her at the bench. "Do you mind if I sit down?"

Susanne was impressed by his good manners. "Not at all."

He sat on the other side of Miss Caroline and placed his hat in his lap. Little Miss Caroline had dozed off but she woke up when Oliver sat down next to her.

"Good morning, ma'am," Oliver said.

Miss Caroline squinted up into the sunlight and eyed him suspiciously. Susanne patted her arm. She thought that all the war talk and activity around the city was making this normally willful child wary.

"And what's your name, Miss?" Oliver asked.

Miss Caroline looked up at Susanne as if asking for approval to tell him. Susanne smiled and nodded.

"Miss Caroline," she said.

"I'm pleased to make your acquaintance, Miss Caroline. My name is Oliver."

Miss Caroline didn't say a word. Then suddenly she jumped up from Susanne's embrace and pointed toward Oliver's lap.

"What's that?" she asked.

Oliver lifted the hat by the brim. "That there's my pride and joy." He flipped it to rest the tip of the crown on his forefinger, and twirled it like a top. Miss Caroline smiled with delight. The hat was very different from the top hats her granddaddy and daddy always wore. Without missing a beat, Oliver flipped the hat and caught it by the brim.

Miss Caroline clapped. "Show me how to do that," she said, reaching out for the hat.

"Brother Oliver doesn't have time for that," Susanne said, pulling Missus's hand back. "He has to go to work now."

"Tell you what, though," Oliver said to Miss Caroline. "Ask Sister Susanne to bring you and your brother over to my shop across the way some day. I'll have you spinning this hat in no time."

Miss Caroline nodded eagerly.

"Has all this war business been much trouble for you?" Susanne asked.

"Not really. At least not so far. They rounded up all the free Negroes last week, and some of them are being called for military work at the armory. They're stepping up production of guns and ammunition." He shook his head. "But they're not paying much. And I was reading an article in the paper the other day telling the city to brace for blockades."

Mon Dieu. Oliver could read the newspaper? Susanne was stunned. She was able to pick out a few words here and there, and she could write her name, but to be able to sit down and read a newspaper was something else altogether. And he used all those big words. She frowned. "Blockades?"

"The North might block our ports to try and stop supplies from getting down the river to us. Food, coal—notions like that."

"Will that be a problem for you?"

"It'll be a problem for all of us, if it happens," he said. "Prices will shoot to the moon. But it'll be especially hard for somebody like me. I need supplies to stock my store."

Susanne couldn't imagine the Montgomerys ever having a problem getting anything. "Do you reckon they'll do it?"

"If the war lasts long enough, it will come to that." He stood up. "Well, I'd best be on my way. It was mighty nice seeing you, Sister Susanne."

She blinked. He was leaving without inviting her out again? She tried to keep the disappointment off her face. She should have accepted his invitation the first time he asked. Or the second. Oh, well. She reckoned she'd have to come up with another plan to thwart Miss Lizbeth's scheme to hook her up with Alfred. A pity, though, since she really liked talking to Oliver. He knew so much about so many things. "It was good seeing you, too, Brother Oliver."

He looked down and fidgeted with the hat in his hands. He seemed to want to say something but was hesitant. She put on her biggest smile. Don't be shy, she wanted so badly to tell him. Third time's always a charm.

"Well, I know I already asked you this a time or two before. . . ." He paused.

"Yes?"

"I was wondering if maybe you had changed your mind about joining me at church one Sunday afternoon."

"I'd love to." Oops. That came out way too fast. She'd have to settle down or else she'd scare him off. Besides, it was only Oliver. Not Marcus.

"I know you said . . ." He looked up at her. "What?"

"Well, I . . ." Oh, to heck with it. "I said I'd love to go to church with you one Sunday."

His smile spread from ear to ear, and he pretended to wipe perspiration from his brow. "Whew. Didn't think I'd ever get to hear those words from your lips. No, siree. Truth is, there ain't . . . there's not much in this world that scares me. I've seen it all or just about. But the thought of you turning me down even one more time was more than I thought I could take."

Susanne laughed. What "all" had this man seen? she wondered as she looked into his brown eyes. They seemed to sparkle with a zest that she'd never seen in any slave.

"So," he said. "How's this Sunday?"

She chuckled. Talk about moving fast. But she didn't see how that would be a problem. She always rode to church in the carriage with Mass Richard and Miss Lizbeth and the children, but once the children sat in the family pew with their folks, Susanne stood in the gallery with the other coloreds.

"This Sunday is good."

He blinked as if having a hard time believing his good luck. "Well, this coming Sunday it is, then."

24

"Who is this Oliver, Susanne?" Miss Lizbeth asked, peering up over her needle. Like thousands of other women across the city, Miss Lizbeth was sewing uniforms for the soldiers of the Confederacy. Mass Willard and Miss Nancy were attending a dinner being given by President and Mrs. Jefferson Davis at the new "White House of the Confederacy" on Clay Street.

"A colored gentleman I met in the park, Missus."

"Is this Oliver Armistead?" Mass Richard asked, removing his pipe from his mouth.

"Yes, Massa," Susanne said.

"Do you know him, dear?" Missus asked. She looked across the table at her husband sitting in an armchair near the fireplace and reading the paper.

"I've heard of him," Massa said. "He's a descendant of that James Armistead. Isn't that right, Susanne?"

"Yes, Massa," Susanne said. "That's him."

"You've heard of him, I'm sure, Elizabeth. The Negro who spied on the British for us in the Revolutionary War. He changed his name to Lafayette after the revolution."

"Oh," Missus said, clearly having no idea what her husband was talking about. "A Negro spy? Really?"

Mass Richard puffed on his pipe and nodded. "He was

quite successful, from what they say. This Oliver owns a store near the park I believe."

Susanne nodded. "Yes, Massa."

Miss Lizbeth frowned. "You mean his master permits that?"

"He's free, ma'am," Susanne said.

"Oh. I see," Miss Lizbeth said, pursing her lips as a clear look of disapproval crossed her face. Susanne always thought Miss Lizbeth looked just like her mama when she did that. "Why on earth would you want to associate with someone like that, Susanne? I've seen some of the free Negroes about town. They're such a dreadful lot."

"Brother Oliver is very respectable, Missus." Better than that Alfred, that was for sure, Susanne thought. Oliver would do fine until she could get her hands on Marcus. "His store does right nice, ma'am."

"Yes," Mass Richard said, smiling. "I dare say you wouldn't know anything about it, Elizabeth. But this Oliver sells goods to other coloreds, and it's a fairly decent establishment as these things go."

"I see," Miss Lizbeth said. "Still, I thought you liked Alfred. I mean, it would be so much more convenient since he's from here."

Susanne cleared her throat. Convenient for who? she wanted to ask. "I really would like to go to the colored church with Brother Oliver if it's not much trouble. I've never been to one and I've heard so much about them."

"I see." Miss Lizbeth narrowed her eyes as she thought.

Mass Richard folded his paper. "I think it will be fine, Elizabeth. It's only church. The preacher is a Negro and they're allowed to run the day-to-day affairs, but it's supervised by whites. What harm can come of it?"

"All right," Miss Lizbeth said. "We can't very well control who you like, can we? You can go as soon as we get back from St. Paul's." She picked up her sewing.

"Um, Brother Oliver said something about me meeting him for an early service, so maybe . . ."

"Oh, dear," Miss Lizbeth said. "What about Miss Caroline and Master Ward?"

"I can get them up and dressed before I go. But seeing as they sit with the family at church anyhow, I thought—"

Miss Lizbeth shook her head firmly. "I'm afraid that won't do, Susanne. You know how Miss Caroline likes to sit next to you in the carriage. And Master Ward is used to sitting in your lap. And with this war going on, they're both so jumpy these days."

That was true, Susanne thought, resisting the urge to sigh, and she felt guilty about that. But she wasn't asking for much. Just Sunday afternoons. The children were perfectly safe with their parents. She was tempted to say all that and more, but then Missus might change her mind altogether about letting her go to church with Oliver.

"See if there's a late Sunday service at this other church," Mass Richard said. "It will be more convenient all around."

Susanne nodded. "Yes, Massa. I'll do that."

"I should think there must be a late service there," Massa said. "I mean, they must understand that some of you have duties on Sunday morning."

"I reckon so, Massa."

After the Sunday outing to St. Paul's with the family, Susanne helped Miss Caroline and Mass Ward change out of their church clothes. Miss Caroline was so obedient and helpful, she even put Mass Ward's slippers on his feet. And when Susanne sat them on Miss Caroline's bed and told them that she was going out for a little while that afternoon, they both smiled and nodded. Susanne patted them on the heads. "That's my little angels."

She picked up Mass Ward and sat him on her hip, then

took Miss Caroline's hand and escorted them down the stairs to the drawing room, where the family always gathered for tea after church. She entered and swept by one of the two young girls on each side of the room swinging peacock fans back and forth to cool the hot August air.

On this Sunday, so soon after the first big battle, along Bull Run at Manassas, the gathering was smaller than usual. Mass Willard had meetings in town about the war effort, and Misses Susan and Ellen had gone with their maids to help convert a part of their church into a hospital for wounded soldiers. Susanne normally sat with her knitting needles in a straight-backed chair near the doorway, just in case her little charges wanted anything, until it was time for their afternoon naps. But Miss Lizbeth had agreed to put the children down on this Sunday, with help from Fanny, so that Susanne could attend the late service with Oliver. After the children were comfortably seated—Mass Ward with his daddy in an armchair near the fireplace, and Miss Caroline on the sofa with her grandma—Susanne turned to leave the parlor. As she crossed the carpet, Miss Caroline sprang up and ran around in front of her, blocking her path.

"Where are you going?" Miss Caroline asked.

Susanne leaned down and took her chin. "I already told you, I'm going out for just a bit. Now run back and sit by your grandma."

Miss Caroline poked out her bottom lip. "I want to come with you."

Susanne took the little girl's hand and steered her back toward the sofa where Miss Lizbeth sat with Miss Nancy. "You can't come—" Before she could finish, Miss Caroline snatched her hand out of Susanne's grasp and ran back toward the doorway.

"Whatever is going on here?" Miss Nancy asked.

Miss Lizbeth stood up and held out her arms. "Caroline, dear, come sit with Mother. Susanne will be back before you know it. And it's far too hot to do all this running up and down."

The little missus folded her arms across her chest and planted her body firmly in the doorway. Susanne tightened her lips to hide a smile she felt coming on. She had a mind to take a switch to that little behind if it didn't move out of that doorway this instant. But before she could say or do anything, Miss Nancy spoke up. "Where is Susanne supposed to be going?"

"To the Negro Baptist church," Miss Lizbeth said. "She's meeting someone there for afternoon service."

"Whatever for?" Miss Nancy said. "She's just come from church."

"Well, she wants to go to the colored church now," Miss Lizbeth said.

"Who will watch the children, then?" Miss Nancy asked.

"I will, Mother," Miss Lizbeth said. She walked to her daughter and extended her hand. Miss Caroline peered up at her mama but kept her arms folded firmly.

"Do as your mother tells you," Mass Richard said from his armchair.

Miss Caroline stuck her lip out as she took her mother's hand. But when they got halfway across the floor, she bawled something awful. Susanne exhaled deeply.

"Oh, dear," Miss Lizbeth said.

"Who is Susanne meeting?" Miss Nancy asked, raising her voice over Miss Caroline's screams.

"Oliver Armistead," Mass Richard said.

Miss Nancy frowned.

"He's a free colored man," Mass Richard said. "He invited Susanne to church."

Miss Nancy's frown deepened as Miss Caroline's sobs grew more piercing. "Heavens. Should she be associating with them?"

"It's a long story, Mother. But Richard says this Oliver is quite respectable."

"Indeed he is," Mass Richard said.

"And we have to expect that Susanne is going to want to meet colored men, Mother. After all, she's seventeen now and needs to find a suitable mate. And she's one of the prettiest colored girls in Richmond."

Miss Nancy's lips tightened. "But a free colored man? And must she do her courting when the children need her?"

Since it was upsetting Miss Caroline so, Susanne was starting to feel guilty about leaving. Maybe she should have broken the child in to expect her absences more slowly, although she wasn't sure how that might have been carried out. But Oliver was waiting for her now, and Miss Caroline would be fine once she was gone. Susanne bit her bottom lip and cleared her throat. "I expect Brother Oliver's waiting for me down the block, Miss Lizbeth. Can I be excused now, please?"

Miss Lizbeth waved Susanne away as she tugged a reluctant Caroline, still screaming at the top of her lungs, down to the sofa. "Go on. But come back here as soon as that service is over."

Susanne walked to the doorway, and Miss Caroline jumped up and screamed till her cheeks turned pink. She stomped her feet. Susanne sighed and turned.

"This is too much," Miss Nancy said. "Perhaps you should wait until Miss Caroline takes her nap, Susanne. I have nothing against you going. But you see how much it's upsetting her."

Susanne looked at the little girl's sad face and nodded. "Yes, Missus. I can see that, so I'll stay. But Oliver is waiting. Can I just go and tell him . . . ?"

"We can send someone else," Mass Richard said. "I had no idea this would unsettle Caroline so."

Was it any wonder? Susanne thought. The way they spoiled the child rotten.

"Yes," Miss Lizbeth said. "That's an excellent idea. Miss

Caroline takes her nap in less than an hour. Then you can go meet Oliver."

By then the service would probably be over, Susanne thought. Did anybody think of that? "Yes, Missus." She reached up and removed her hat, and Miss Caroline ran up and hugged her around the legs. Susanne reached down and rubbed the child's back. She could feel the little missus looking up and smiling at her, and she knew she should look down. But she couldn't. Not yet. She was too disappointed.

When Susanne got out a good hour later, she had little hope that the service at the African Baptist Church would still be going on by the time she got there, especially since it was clear on the other side of town. But she was finally out of the house, so she might as well go there. Even if it was hot as blazes, the walk would soothe her frayed nerves.

It had been many weeks since she'd walked through town. She'd heard stories about how drastically things had changed since the battle at Manassas, but nothing prepared her for what she saw. Men and boys in uniform were rushing this way and that. Wagons and carts ran up and down the street stirring dust in the air, and they seemed to carry everything from cannons and barrels to dead bodies.

She was surprised to hear a chorus singing as she neared the church. She slipped inside to see the biggest gathering of Negroes that she had ever laid eyes on. Two or three whites sat on the side, but the rest were colored folks. She took a seat in a back pew and scanned the crowd looking for Oliver. They noticed each other at the same time, and Oliver got up from his front pew and slipped quietly down the aisle to join her. She mouthed the word "sorry" so as not to be heard over the preacher. Oliver smiled.

Although the preacher's voice was solemn and low, rising a pitch or two occasionally to make a point, the congregation was anything but. Screeching and moaning and shouts of joy bounced off every corner of the room. "Yes, Lord, yes! Oh, yes!" This was so different from what Susanne was used to, and at first she felt out of place. But she soon found herself clapping her hands and tapping her feet amid all the stomping and swinging. She smiled at Oliver. She felt so alive. This was just what she needed now. Up at the mansion, she almost always kept her true feelings in check. It felt good to let it all out.

"I'm really sorry I couldn't get out in time to meet you," she said to Oliver as they mingled with the others outside the church. "But Miss Caroline got to whimpering and carrying on just as I was about to leave."

Oliver chuckled. "They sent some brother named Alfred out to tell me you would be along later. The missus didn't take ill, I hope."

"Oh, no. Nothing like that. If she was sick, I would never have left her. I reckon she's just a little spoiled, is more like it."

Oliver nodded understandingly. "How do you like the Montgomerys?"

"They're a fine family, really. They treat me good and give me everything I need." She thought of Mama and Ellen back at Montpelier and how long it had been since she'd seen them. She thought of Mass Willard's broken promise to take her to see them. "Well, most everything."

Oliver nodded. "Where is your real family? Any kinfolk here in Richmond?"

She shook her head. "My mama and sister are over in Orange County, on the James Madison estate."

"That right? How long has it been since you last saw them?"

"Three years now." She didn't really want to talk about this, not when she was feeling so good. It brought back too many painful memories. "I really enjoyed the service. I had no idea it was like that. I'm surprised it was still going on."

Oliver smiled. "You obviously don't know much about us Baptists. I reckon, it's nothing like the Episcopal church. Shucks. That was kind of subdued compared to some of our services. And sometimes we go on even longer than that."

She wasn't sure what "subdued" meant, but she was too embarrassed to ask. "I thought some of the folks in there were about to pass out."

"If the spirit moves you . . ." He did a little two-step, and she laughed. "I've seen it happen on many occasions," he said. "Will you be able to join us for dinner afterwards? Some of us always get together somewhere to eat and talk. I think it's at Bertha's house this afternoon."

It sounded like fun. Besides Fanny and Aunt Martha, six other colored women worked in the mansion as ladies' maids and chambermaids, but they avoided Susanne for the most part. And while the other nurses she met in the park were friendly enough, she had never struck up a real friendship with any of them. Fanny always said it was because she was a mulatto and lots of colored folks were suspicious of her kind. Fanny suggested she bend over a bit to prove herself to them, but that just wasn't her way. If folks couldn't accept her natural ways, fine. She wasn't going to go out on a limb just because she looked different. Besides, her work with the children took up so much of her time that her only free moments were late at night, hardly the time for socializing.

As much as she wanted to go, she shook her head with regret. "I'm afraid I need to get right back. Miss Caroline will be waking up from her nap any minute now, and I'd best be there when she does."

Oliver nodded. "I'm sorry about that, but I understand. Maybe another time. May I walk back with you?"

"Oh, shoot. You don't have to do that. It's out of your way, going all the way back across town."

"Yes, it is, but nothing would please me more."

Susanne smiled. "Then I thank you."

They walked in silence for a few moments, taking in the sights and sounds of a city at war. Oliver held his bowler hat in his hand, she a little purse given to her by Miss Lizbeth. A young white man limping with crutches came out of a building as a colored woman bearing a tray of rolled bandages entered.

"It's really changed since I was last down this way," Susanne said. "I hardly even recognize the place anymore."

"We took a lot of casualties at Manassas. They had to set up makeshift hospitals anyplace they could find."

"But we won the battle at Manassas."

"Yes, but that's how war is, win or lose."

"Who are all the men I see riding in the wagons?"

"Federal prisoners. There must be hundreds, maybe even thousands, of them. They come in by the railroad, then they move them to a warehouse that's been converted into a prison."

She shook her head. "I'll sure enough be glad when it's all over and things get back to normal."

Oliver shrugged doubtfully. "If they ever do."

"Why do you say that?"

"It depends what you call normal, I reckon. No matter who wins, things are going to change. . . ."

"Why, the South is going to win, of course. Mass Willard said he doesn't think the war will last much past summer. And Mass Richard says any Rebel soldier can lick a dozen of them Yankees."

Oliver chuckled. "Yes, that's what they all say, and I sure hope they're right. Lord knows I don't want to see this thing drag on. But down at the docks, the sentiment is different. The fellows coming in on boats from up

North say the Union has got more factories and ships and ammunition. We don't even have a navy to speak of to defend our ports."

"Are you saying that you think the North will whip us, Brother Oliver?" If so, she thought, he'd best keep his thoughts to himself around here.

"Right now, they're stronger. If we can hold on long enough to shore up our defenses, maybe we'll stand a chance. But that just means it'll be a long, hard war."

Susanne blinked. She hadn't even entertained the possibility that the South would lose the war. All the white folks who visited the Montgomerys seemed so certain the South would win and would do so soon.

"Not only that," Oliver continued. "But some say if the North wins, they would end slavery. At the very least, it will mean no slavery in the states opening out west."

"Oh, *pft.* They won't ever end slavery here in Virginia. And to tell you the truth, it would scare me to death if they did."

Oliver stopped and turned. He stared at her. "You don't want to be free?"

"It might be fine for you, Brother Oliver. But most of the colored folks that live free have got it far worse than you do, or me."

"I'll give you that. But it's only because white folks do everything they can to keep it that way."

"You might be right. But no war is going to change that."

He started walking again and so did she. "Maybe, maybe not," he said. "If we had laws passed down here, well . . . There's no slavery up North. Why can't it be like that down here? I've lived as a slave and I've lived free. And I'd never go back if I can help it."

"I see."

They walked in silence for a while. He held his hat behind his back, and she shifted her purse to the other hand.

Susanne didn't know what to make of this man. He thought the North would beat the South and wasn't afraid to say so. Words like that could get a white man thrown in jail, much less a colored man. Oliver was awful proud—and stubborn. She could see that. But at least he was honest about his feelings, even if she didn't much like what he was saying.

"Do you get out much?" Oliver asked suddenly.

"I get out enough, I reckon. I go to church and such with the Montgomerys and I take the children to the park and shopping. We used to take long walks around the city on nice days before the war started."

"That's not what I meant. Don't you get time off for yourself on Saturday and Sunday?"

Susanne blinked. She knew, of course, that colored folks in town were always getting together for this and that. It was mostly free coloreds, although slaves would often slip away and join in. Even Fanny got most Sunday afternoons off, and she and Raif would sometimes get passes and go out visiting family and friends. But Susanne's life revolved around the Montgomery household, and it suited her just fine. She shook her head in answer to his question.

"That's the craziest thing I ever heard," Oliver said.

Here he goes again, she thought. "Why is that so crazy? The children need me."

"What kind of family would work somebody like that? More important, how am I going to ask you out if you can't get any free time?"

Susanne resisted the temptation to smile. She was too busy defending herself and her way of life. "It's not that I can't get it. I haven't asked. I'm sure they would give it to me if I did. They treat me almost like a member of the family."

"Uh-huh."

He sounded doubtful. "It's true. They give me plenty of clothes and all the food I could possibly eat."

"Well, you do always look right nice, if I may say so. But a real family means more than clothes and food."

She looked at him out of the corner of her eye. Was he sassing her? He obviously thought he was better than her because he lived free. But just because it was right for him, didn't mean it was right for her. "I know that, Brother Oliver. I have a family in Orange County, remember?"

"So how'd you end up so far away from them?"

"I . . . I was sold."

"To the Montgomerys?"

She pursed her lips and nodded. She knew what he was thinking. No family would buy and sell its members. But he didn't understand.

"I see," Oliver said. "Well, I'm sorry about that."

At least he was courteous enough to back off at some point. "Nothing to be sorry about. I'm doing just fine."

"I expect you are." They reached the front of the mansion, and he turned to face her. "Well, I would love to escort you to a ball being given by a group of us free colored men next month. That is, if you'd like to go with me and can get away. We're going to be raising money for the slave hospital down at the river."

She knew what this was about. He thought she wouldn't be able to get away. Well, she'd show him a thing or two. "I'd like it just fine, Brother Oliver."

"Really?"

"Yes."

He flipped his hat in the air and caught it in the other hand.

25

Susanne wasn't even sure she wanted to go to the ball with this Oliver Armistead. He was so blasted arrogant, with his uppity free self. And she was tired of folks putting her down for some reason or another. First it was the Montgomerys when she got here because she was from a plantation. Well, she had shown them. She was as refined a servant as the Montgomerys had now. Even old Aunt Martha approved of her. Miss Nancy was still standoffish much of the time, but Susanne was used to it now. She and Miss Nancy pretty much stayed out of each other's way and that suited Susanne just fine.

Most of the house servants didn't exactly stumble over their toes to be friendly, either, probably because she was a mulatto. But she had learned to live with that just fine, too, thank you. Everyone else was kind enough, especially Mass Willard. He failed to live up to his promise to take her home for a visit, but he always smiled at her. Miss Lizbeth was fine, too, as long as her mama wasn't around. She was always giving Susanne a dress or shawl or shoes from her own wardrobe. Susanne had carved a nice little place for herself in this household over the past few years, and she was proud of herself.

But she had something to prove to this Oliver

Armistead. He seemed to think he was something special just 'cause he was free. *Pft!* If there was one thing she couldn't stand, it was somebody thinking they were better than she was. She could do anything he could, more even when she was with the children. She had no doubt whatsoever that Miss Lizbeth would allow her to go to the ball. She was also sure the missus would give her regular free time. All she had to do was ask. She had never asked before simply because she hadn't wanted it. She didn't have any friends outside the household and she liked spending time with the children. With them, she could go just about anywhere in the city and no one would question her. Without them, she needed a pass, and even with a pass there were plenty of places she'd be chased away from.

The trick was to find the right time to talk to Miss Lizbeth. It had to be when Miss Nancy wasn't around. That wouldn't be much of a problem, since the older woman spent a lot of time at the church hospital these days. A steady stream of wounded soldiers was pouring in from the battlefields around Richmond, and the Montgomery women and their servants spent their days helping to nurse them, like most other ladies in Richmond. But Miss Lizbeth always returned in the afternoon to have tea in the parlor with the children after their naps. That no doubt would be the best chance to catch her alone.

Miss Lizbeth loved flowers, so while the children napped, Susanne slipped down to the garden at the back of the mansion with scissors and a basket and picked sunflowers. She arranged them in a crystal vase on the table in the upstairs parlor where they always took their afternoon tea. Then she went to get the children up and dressed from their nap.

She was sitting at the table knitting socks for the soldiers and the children were sprawled on the carpet playing games when Miss Lizbeth returned that afternoon.

Aunt Martha's husband, Uncle Jackson, followed Miss Lizbeth into the parlor bearing a tray filled with tea, milk, and sandwiches. Uncle Jackson was as old as Aunt Martha and every bit as serious about his work. A neatly trimmed gray mustache and beard lined his dark face and he stood straight as a tree trunk, despite his years. Susanne rose from her seat and smiled.

"It gets more and more depressing every day at that hospital," Miss Lizbeth said as she strode in and took a seat at the table. Miss Nancy always said it was bordering on sacrilegious for Miss Lizbeth to share tea at the table with her children's nurse. Missus did it anyhow. "What harm can come from it?" she asked her mama. Sometimes it seemed that Miss Lizbeth went out of her way to go against her mama. But with a mama like that, who could blame her?

Still, Susanne was uncomfortable about the whole notion of sitting and having tea at the same table with her mistress. She rarely took a sip from her cup and always kept her chair a couple of feet away from the table when the missus was there. She sat back down and rested her knitting in her lap as Miss Caroline ran up and kissed her mama, then climbed into her own little chair at the table. Missus picked up Mass Ward and set him in her lap.

"The flowers are lovely," Miss Lizbeth said. "From the garden?"

"Yes, ma'am. Is it really that bad at the hospital?" Susanne asked.

"Oh, dear. You would not believe how many of our soldiers are coming in with missing arms or legs," Miss Lizbeth said. "The poor souls. Since Manassas, there's been an unending flow of them, day after day. Miss Susan nearly fainted this morning at the sight of a bloody stump."

Susanne shook her head. "Is she all right?"

Missus nodded. "She got right back up and started

working again. And my Fanny, that girl has been a tremendous help to Master Richard. Nothing seems to faze her, not even those awful bloody amputations."

"This war is dreadful business, Missus. I pray every night that it won't drag on much longer and things get back to the way they were before, nice and peaceable-like."

Miss Lizbeth sighed. "You and I both, Susanne. Well, enough of that for now. I want to enjoy my children." She pinched Mass Ward's cheek, and he giggled with delight.

"Will that be all, Miss?" Uncle Jackson asked after he had placed the tea and sandwiches on the table.

"Yes, Uncle Jack," Miss Lizbeth said. Uncle Jackson signaled with a faint flick of his wrist and Prudence, a girl of about twelve wearing a simple shift and in bare feet, slipped quietly into the room. She stood a few feet behind Missus and swung a big fan up and down, as Missus picked up the silver teapot and poured cups for herself and Susanne. Susanne got up, placed her knitting on her chair, and removed the little glasses of milk from the tray. She placed one in front of Miss Caroline and another in front of Mass Ward as Uncle Jackson bowed and backed out of the room.

"So, how was your day, Caroline?" Miss Lizbeth asked.

Susanne picked up her sewing and sat back down. She listened with one ear as the little missus chatted on about the stories Susanne told her and the games they'd played that morning before their naps. In the quiet recesses of her mind, as she waited for the right moment, she thought about the best way to ask Miss Lizbeth for permission to go to the ball.

After about an hour, the children finished telling their stories and drinking their milk, and they climbed down and went back to their games on the floor. Miss Lizbeth dabbed the corners of her lips with a napkin. "I suppose I should get back to the hospital now. Although I must confess that I'm not looking forward to it, not in the least. But we must carry on." She stood up.

"So soon?" Susanne asked, standing up after her mistress. She was surprised, since Miss Lizbeth usually spent some time reading and relaxing before heading back.

"They need all the help they can get," Miss Lizbeth said. "If it weren't for the children, I'd have you come back with me to help out."

"Would you like me to, ma'am? Prudence can watch them for a while."

Miss Lizbeth raised her hand. "No, no. I want you here with them. With all of us gone so much they need a steady companion about."

"Fine, Missus." She paused and licked her lips. It was now or never. "Um, Missus?"

"Yes, Susanne?"

"Um, I was wondering, would it be all right for me to go to a ball with Brother Oliver. It's being given by some free colored men that's trying to raise money for the slave hospital."

Missus smiled brightly. "Oh? A ball? Really?"

"Yes, ma'am."

"When is it?"

"Next month."

"Fanny used to attend these things before she hooked up with Raif. Of course, that will be fine, especially since it's for a worthy cause." She clapped her hands together. "Oh! We'll have to get you something new to wear."

Susanne smiled back. Just as she thought, all she had to do was ask. "Thank you, ma'am. Um, I also wanted to ask, could I have some free time, regular-like?"

The smile fell off Miss Lizbeth's face. She frowned. "Free time?"

"Um, like some of the other servants do. I don't need much but I thought since—"

"Oh, dear," Miss Lizbeth said, shaking her head and

twisting her lips. "That may get difficult with the children. They're so attached to you, and they need you more than ever now, with me and their father being out so much on account of the war."

Susanne swallowed. "I know, Missus. But I had thought maybe just on Saturday evenings when most everybody is here, um, unless you and Mass Richard go out, of course. They go to bed at eight anyhow and—"

"Yes, but they often wake up during the night wanting milk or something. You know that."

Susanne clamped her mouth shut. It was suddenly starting to feel awful stuffy in here, even with the steady breeze coming from the fan.

"Everyone must sacrifice with the war, you know."

"Yes, ma'am." She looked at the floor. Maybe she was being selfish. "I don't want to cause any trouble."

Miss Lizbeth let out a deep breath of air. "Let me think about this. You devote yourself to the children every day of the week, and we all need some time to ourselves. I'll speak to Aunt Martha to see if she has anyone who might be able to fill in once or twice a month."

Susanne looked up. "Thank you, ma'am." It wasn't exactly what she wanted, but it was something.

"The ball sounds exciting," Missus said. "Fanny tells me the colored ladies really do it up for these affairs. Would you like some fabric to make a new dress?"

Susanne smiled. She should have given more thought to the war before asking, maybe checked around herself to find somebody to take her place when she went out. Shame on her. Why, she could imagine that a lot of mistresses would have said no flat out in these hard times. "Yes, ma'am. That would be right nice."

Miss Lizbeth was more excited about the new dress than Susanne was. She ordered up yards of green taffeta fabric and velvet ribbon from her dressmaker. She gave Susanne one of her old crinolines and a silk fan and told Susanne to pick out anything she fancied from her jewelry box. Miss Nancy, of course, objected to all the fuss over a new ball gown for a servant, especially with a war going on. But Miss Lizbeth said that since everybody was devoting so much time and energy to the cause, fussing over a fancy dress, even one for her children's nurse, was a welcome relief. They had to try to hold on to some sanity in the middle of all this madness. Amen to that, Susanne whispered under her breath after one heated exchange in the parlor between Miss Lizbeth and her mama.

Besides, it was for the Negro hospital, as Miss Lizbeth had pointed out to her mama, and everyone knew that the hospitals in Richmond needed all the help they could get. Many Negroes were coming back sick and exhausted from digging military fortifications outside Richmond in this dreadful summer heat. Susanne didn't point out to Miss Nancy that white folks still had their fancy balls, or mention the big shipment of new dresses that had just been delivered from Paris for the Montgomery women just a week earlier.

"Oliver's gonna start pattin' the flo' when he sees you in that dress," Fanny said one night just after she climbed into bed.

Susanne was sitting on her bed hemming the new dress. She smiled at the thought of Oliver dancing. "It will be some dress, won't it?"

The night of the ball was magical. After supper, Miss Lizbeth told Miss Caroline and Mass Ward that they had to leave Susanne alone for the rest of the evening. She took them with her to the parlor while Fanny helped Susanne get ready. The missus even insisted that Susanne dress in her bedchamber so she could use the full-length mirror to see herself in the new gown. It was green silk taffeta with a velvet ribbon at the waist and a low neckline. Fanny helped her slip it over her head and down over the crinoline. Then she pinned Susanne's hair up on her head and draped some of Miss Lizbeth's beads around it.

"You look beautiful," Fanny said as she stepped back and admired her handiwork.

Susanne turned and eyed herself in Miss Lizbeth's mirror and almost jumped out of her skin. She couldn't believe how elegant she looked. The little country girl was looking like a society lady. She turned this way and that, still unable to believe her eyes. Suddenly she remembered how she used to play dress-up with Miss Rebecca. All that seemed a lifetime ago, and it was, in a way. This time it was her dress, not her mistress's. If only Mama could see her now. And Ellen. They would be proud of how well she had done for herself, she was sure of it. It was at moments like this that she missed them both so much. As happy as she was now, her happiness could never be whole, for a part of her would always be back at Montpelier with her family no matter how many years rolled by. She felt like laughing and crying at the same time. But she wasn't going to let such thoughts spoil her evening out. She turned to Fanny and gave her a bear hug. "Girl, you're a miracle worker."

"Go on. You just a pretty gal, that's all, and this dress brings it out."

They heard a carriage pull up outside, and Susanne walked quickly down the stairs with Fanny following her. She had to stop by the parlor to let Miss Lizbeth and Mass Willard see her before leaving, and she didn't want to keep Oliver waiting much longer. Miss Nancy and her two other daughters were helping at the church hospital, and Mass Richard was out doctoring patients. Susanne prayed that no one would ask her to do something at the last minute and that Miss Caroline didn't get to acting up.

She rounded the corner and entered the parlor. Miss Lizbeth gasped. "Oh! You look lovely, Susanne. Doesn't she, Father?"

"Charming, just charming," Mass Willard said, smiling and puffing on his pipe. "I dare say she looks good enough for one of our charity balls."

"Thank you, Missus, Massa," Susanne said. She smiled broadly but stayed near the doorway, hoping to beat a hasty retreat. She was about to ask to be excused when Miss Caroline ran up to her, and Mass Ward, who was just starting to walk, tottered up behind his big sister.

"Why are you playing dress-up in Mama's things?" Miss Caroline asked.

Everyone chuckled, then Miss Lizbeth took Miss Caroline's hand and pulled her back into the room. "That's not Mama's dress, dear. It belongs to Susanne. She's going to a ball tonight to raise money for the slave hospital. You and Ward will stay here with Grandpa and me. Remember when I told you that at supper?"

Miss Caroline eyed Susanne suspiciously. "But I want her to tuck me in and tell me a story like she always does."

Uh-oh, Susanne thought.

"I'll do that tonight," Miss Lizbeth said, smiling brightly.

Miss Caroline frowned doubtfully. "But you don't know Bruh Rabby."

"Rabbit who?" Miss Lizbeth asked.

"Buh Wabby," Mass Ward said.

Miss Lizbeth sighed with resignation and looked at Susanne helplessly. "Well, I . . ."

Mon Dieu. Susanne felt like slapping the woman right then and there. Here she was standing in her brand-new gown with her hair all piled up on top of her head and Miss Lizbeth was about to cave in to a child's whims.

Fanny stepped into the room and held her hand out to Miss Caroline. "I know Bruh Rabby, Miss Caroline. And if you're a good girl tonight, I'll tell you a brand-new story. That is, if you want me to."

Miss Caroline's eyes lit up. She nodded and took Fanny's hand, and Fanny led her to the door, along with little Ward. God bless that Fanny, Susanne thought as she bent down and kissed both children on the forehead. They were fine if you knew how to keep them from walking all over you.

"Now you two be good and don't go giving Sister Fanny a hard time." Susanne gently pinched Miss Caroline on the nose, and the little missus giggled and hugged her around the neck. Susanne waved good-bye as Fanny led them down the hallway. What would she ever do without that woman? Susanne wondered.

Miss Lizbeth smiled and pointed her finger, mockingly. "Now you tell Oliver I said not to keep you out too late. We have your honor to think about."

Susanne smiled thinly. Right, she thought. And the chores she had to be up before dawn to take care of, like lighting candles and running bath water and laying out clothes. If only the woman was as good at bossing her children around.

"Tell me, Susanne," Mass Willard said. "Is Oliver aware that free coloreds are needed for the war effort?"

"I don't know, Massa. He hasn't said anything to me about it."

"We need them on the railroads and at the ironworks. We're dreadfully short of labor. Tell him the Confederacy will pay him for his services. I think it's ten or eleven dollars a month."

"I will, Massa. May I be excused now? I believe Brother Oliver is waiting for me."

"Yes, of course. Have a lovely time."

She walked out the side door and around the mansion, stepping gingerly so as not to muddy her new slippers in the soil and grass. She reached the front lawn and looked down the hill, then stopped dead in her tracks. The carriage at the bottom was one of the grandest she'd ever seen. Oliver told her he was hiring a carriage and to get a note from her mistress allowing her to ride in one this evening. But the carriage sitting there was too fancy to be his, and she had just turned to look up the street when the door opened and Oliver stepped out, looking as fine as the carriage behind him, in a suit, top hat, and white gloves. "*Mon Dieu*," she mumbled under her breath.

"All this for me?" she asked as he took her hand and helped her up with one ungloved hand. His fingers were rough, a laborer's hand, but his touch was gentle.

He smiled as he climbed inside. He sat beside her and placed his hat in his lap. "Nothing but the best for you, my dear lady. And may I say that you look stunning this evening? My heart is already dancing, and we aren't even in the ballroom yet." He patted his chest.

Susanne smiled and felt her cheeks go hot. The way he piled on the compliments was embarrassing. No man had ever talked to her this way before. "Thank you, Brother Oliver. You're looking right fine yourself, tonight."

"Thank you."

He signaled for the driver to leave as Susanne smoothed her dress. The carriage lurched forward, and she took in a deep breath of air. It was all she could do to keep from giggling like a little girl. Here she was riding in a carriage with a colored man, a free colored man at that. The road was more pockmarked than usual from all the drays and wagons running up and down carrying soldiers and equipment, and it was muddy from recent rains. They bobbed up and down, jerked this way and that, but she didn't mind one bit. She was having such a grand time that she all but forgot she had only accepted the invitation from Oliver to show him a thing or two.

As they pulled farther away from the mansion, she could feel her body go limp with ease, and she realized how tense she was there, always on guard, always expecting prying eyes watching from around a corner or a command to do something else. Even when in her room with Fanny, at the back of her head she knew she could be summoned at any moment, day or night. But out here on this lumpy, muddy road, no massa or missus would disturb her. She felt a smile teasing the corners of her lips, and she turned her head to hide her face. She didn't want Oliver to think she was some kind of fool. She decided to bring up something serious to get this silly smile off her face.

"Mass Willard asked me if you know that the Confederates need free coloreds to help with the war."

Oliver's jaw clenched. "What did he say?"

"Not much. Just asked if you knew and that they pay you to work."

"Humph. I know all about it. Only we weren't exactly asked. Some soldiers rounded us up a few weeks ago and then Mayor Mayo made us register. We can't fight, but they're putting us to work down at the docks and out there digging trenches."

"Well, that's not so surprising. Everybody is being asked to help out."

"That's all well and good for some folks. But they don't want to pay enough money. I wouldn't be able to keep up my rent or my taxes on the store, and I'd probably have to give it up." He shook his head. "No, siree. That's not for me, and I intend to avoid it long as I can."

Susanne didn't understand how anybody could be unwilling to help out. It would be a shame for Oliver to lose his store, yes. But other men were dying for the cause. The South had been good to Oliver, and, to her way of thinking, he should be willing to sacrifice in this hour of need. "Mass Willard says if the South loses, we all lose."

Oliver smiled. "I thought you were convinced the

South would prevail in no time at all."

Prevail? Goodness, she thought. The words that came out of this man's mouth. "I do think we'll win, if that's what you mean, but Massa says it's beginning to look like it will take some time."

"And what do you think, Sister Susanne?"

"What?"

"You keep saying what Master Willard thinks. What are your thoughts on it?"

"Well, I . . ." She blinked. She was stumped. She realized that she sounded like a parrot—Massa said this, Massa said that. Man must think she didn't have a single thought of her own. And the awful thing was that she was afraid she didn't. She glanced away. Darn this man for making her feel like an idiot.

Oliver cleared his throat. "I didn't mean to make you uncomfortable."

She had to say something or he would think she was a fool. And this was the last man she wanted to think that. She looked at him. "You didn't, Brother Oliver. As best I can tell, I reckon Massa's right."

"Uh-huh," Oliver said.

She looked away, and they rode in silence. He was so blasted arrogant. He just didn't understand anything about her. Around the Montgomery household, everybody thought what the massa thought. And if they didn't, they kept it to themselves. So what was the point of bothering to think? Maybe she should never have agreed to go out with this man.

"Well," Oliver said, clearing his throat. "They just signed us up for now, but soon they'll be calling us up, one by one."

"What will you do then?"

"I'm hoping that if I can keep my store stocked with things folks need around here, then they'll leave me alone. And that this war will be over soon. And Master Stuart—

that was my master before I bought my freedom—says he'll help me however he can."

"I see."

"Fact is, I been saving long and hard to buy me some land, and getting called would ruin that."

She looked at him. "Buy land? What on earth for?"

"What for? What for?" He chuckled. "What does anybody want land for? Shucks. To put up a house and farm the land. I have plenty of plans for it, believe me."

Here she didn't even own herself and this man was talking about buying land. "Where would you buy it?"

"Not around here. Too expensive. I have family over in West Point, or maybe I'll even go up North. I'm a long ways from doing anything just now. I figure maybe three, four years, I'll be ready to make my move. Or at least I will be if they don't take it all from me on account of this war."

She nodded. Now she understood a little better. If he was going to avoid helping out to save his store, at least he planned to do something respectable with his money. This man was so different from any colored person she'd ever known that she wasn't sure what to make of him. He clearly had a mind of his own. And he had a dream. She admired that, but it also scared her. Many a Negro had been punished for less than the thoughts and ideas running through this man's head.

The ball was held in a big room in the Exchange Hotel with huge chandeliers hanging from the ceiling. A policeman stood guard at the entrance, and several white men lounged along the walls. Oliver said they were probably police and there was no escaping them. He suggested she simply ignore them and have a good time. She looked around and thought that would be easy enough. This was her first ball, and just watching the folks in the room was thrilling. She had never seen so many colored men and women in one place looking so splendid. Why, there must be hundreds, and they were dressed in silk and satin and adorned with flowers and jewelry, gloves and patent leather shoes, and silk hats and elegant walking sticks. Everyone danced and talked, ate cake and drank punch.

Oliver introduced Susanne to several friends and caught her up with the latest gossip. They were enslaved and free. They were bricklayers, shoemakers, barbers, and blacksmiths. One of the most fascinating to Susanne's mind was a woman named Lucy James. Oliver said she ran a boardinghouse for free blacks and slaves who lived out.

Then there was Richard Taylor, a mustached mulatto, who ran a hotel nearby bearing his name. Oliver said it was nothing more than a fancy cookshop or saloon, where men drank mint juleps and wine and played cards and dice on marble-topped tables. Running cookshops and selling liquor to coloreds was illegal, yet Susanne knew such activities took place all over the city. Most of the shops were owned by whites, and they operated quietly in back alleys and other out-of-the-way spots. Now and then, city authorities would shut them down, but they simply packed and set up shop elsewhere. Oliver said that for Mr. Taylor to get away with running one so openly must mean he had friends in high places, probably an influential white benefactor who was getting a handful of the profits. Some colored folks didn't approve of Taylor's Hotel, but Mr. Taylor always made generous donations, so he was tolerated.

Susanne was sipping punch and chatting with one of the nurses from the park and Oliver was laughing with some of his buddies when she spotted a familiar figure moving through the crowd. She followed with her eyes until he suddenly turned his face in her direction. She nearly dropped the glass of punch in her hands. Marcus.

"Sister Susanne?" Eliza said. "Are you all right? You look like you just saw a ghost."

"Oh, sorry, Sister Eliza," Susanne said. "I saw somebody I know. You were saying?"

"That my mistress is . . ."

Susanne smiled and tried to pay attention to Eliza, but she barely heard a word. She was too busy wondering who Marcus was here with. Was it another woman? The next time she glimpsed him, he was talking to Oliver and she quickly made her way across the room. Oliver started to introduce them, until Marcus pointed out that they were acquainted.

"Brother Oliver here is getting on me about the error of my ways," Marcus said, smiling at Susanne.

Susanne smiled. She barely heard a word of what he was saying, or Oliver. She was too busy admiring Marcus's face and that beautiful black hair. It slowly dawned on her from the way they talked and kidded around that Marcus and Oliver knew each other from way back, and she stopped staring and tuned in to the conversation.

It seemed that Oliver and Marcus had once toiled for the same massa, and both had worked out and paid that massa a part of their earnings. Their footprints had eventually taken dramatically different paths, though: Oliver went on to buy his freedom, and Marcus was sold to his current massa in Richmond. It seemed that what had Oliver riled at his buddy was that just the week before, Marcus had gone to his massa and given away all his savings, every last penny. He told his massa that he wanted to help the South lick the Yankees.

"You're a fool if I ever saw one, man," Oliver said. "Giving away your hard-earned money like that." He was smiling but his tone was stern.

"I reckon you would think that way," Marcus said. "But I got no use for it. Massa takes good enough care of me and I want him to be able to go on doing it."

Oliver shook his head with disbelief. "You could have taken that money and bought your freedom with it, you know?"

"I have everything I need. 'Sides, what do I know about living free? Been a slave all my life."

"There are people to help you, brother. We've got churches and societies. That's what we're here for. And you have skills. Every time one of us gets our freedom, the whole slave system gets a little weaker."

"Lordy," Marcus said, winking at Susanne. "There he goes again. Preaching that system stuff. Brother, why would I want it to get weaker when I'm a part of it?"

Susanne smiled, and Oliver shook his head and chuckled good-naturedly. Susanne understood what Marcus meant. He was of her world. Just the other day, she'd overheard Mass Willard in his library talking to Mayor Mayo about the banks. She didn't understand much of what they were saying but caught enough to know that Massa was worried about his bank and all the others throughout the South. Something about them failing if this war kept up much longer. All she knew was that if something bad happened to the Montgomerys, she would suffer, too. Still, she would never have given her money away. On that point, she stood with Oliver and she said as much.

On the ride home, Oliver took her hand quietly. She glanced down as his ebony-colored fingers laced her ivory ones. The move touched her in a way she wouldn't have expected. She tried to shake off the giddy feeling. It would do no good to start liking this man too much. As much as she admired his spirit, they were like night and day. Surely, he must realize that, too.

"I used to wish I was white when I was little." As soon as the words tumbled past her lips, she regretted them. Why had she said that? It sounded dumb to her, so it must really sound dumb to someone like Oliver.

He looked at her. "You could wish that a thousand years and it will never come true."

"I mean, I think what I really wanted was to be free."

He nodded. "You don't have to be white to be free. You do have to have a plan and a strong stomach, especially to stay in the South." He chuckled.

"Why do you stay down here, Oliver? Why not go up North where all the coloreds are free?"

"I've been up there plenty of times. Slavery might be illegal, but it's still rough going up there for us. All those people back there that I introduced you to? Up North, whites hold those jobs, and we have to compete against them. Down here, they consider that nigger work, and most of the whites wouldn't touch it even if they were starving to death. And the slave owners like it that way, 'cause they have a stake in seeing to it that slave labor has a place down here. That's what keeps their property values up."

In a way, all that just proved her point. "My mama used to say you don't have to be white to be free, but you have to be white to enjoy your freedom, even up North I guess. I've heard of slaves being set free and going up there, then they come back down here and beg their massas to take them back 'cause they're so miserable."

"Yes, and I've heard of white men finding a fortune out there in California and turning around and giving it all away 'cause the money makes them miserable. Read about some dirt farmer around here doing that. Said he didn't know what to do with so much money. He had been a dirt farmer all his life, see, and didn't know much else. But you can bet your bottom dollar that a hundred other dirt farmers would have been more than happy to hold onto that money. This poor old shopkeeper sure would have." Oliver pointed to himself and chuckled.

Susanne laughed.

"Plus down here I have family, and the whites know me and pretty much respect me." He paused. "When I asked before, you said you didn't want to be free. Do you still feel that way?"

She took a deep breath. She wasn't sure how to answer that question anymore.

"I asked 'cause some colored folks say they don't want to live free no matter what," Oliver continued. "Especially the ones that have it kind of good like you do. They think they can never live as well as they do now, so why give it up."

"That's how I thought," Susanne said. She still did if it meant living in an alley somewhere. But meeting Oliver was getting her to rethink a lot of things. "I'm not so sure anymore."

"You ever thought about buying your freedom?"

Susanne shook her head. "Women don't do that. If they become free it's 'cause somebody freed them."

"A few have, but you're right, it's not all that common."

"Where would I get the money, anyhow?"

"You cook? Sew?"

"I sew and knit."

"That's all you need is a skill. And a different way of thinking about it. Take sewing in at night when the children are asleep."

"I don't know how my mistress would take to that. She expects me to devote all my time to the children."

"Ask her, you might be surprised. And if she says no, do it anyway."

Susanne laughed nervously. "I could never get away with that. They would find out about it sooner or later, sure enough."

"Probably. But so what?" He smiled at her. "I've seen the way Miss Caroline dotes on you. With you being nurse to those children, you got a lot more power than you think. Some mammies run their households."

Power? She'd never thought of herself as having power. The very thought was ridiculous. She knew some mammies had a lot of say around the house, but they were the ones who had been with their families all their lives. "I'm not one of them. I came to this family late."

Oliver shook his head. "Doesn't matter. You just have to claim it. My master didn't like the idea of me hiring myself out at first. But he saw that I worked harder than ever once I got the idea in my head that I might be able to buy my freedom. And he liked the money I was bringing him. So we agreed on a price. It took me seven, eight years, but I did it. Now I give him a small part of my profit from the store, and he's my biggest protector. A free Negro in the South just about has to have one."

She tried to think how Mass Willard and Miss Lizbeth would react if she told them she wanted to take sewing in to earn the money to buy her freedom. She shook her head. She couldn't begin to imagine. "Brother Oliver, are you trying to get me sold down South?"

He laughed and squeezed her hand gently as the driver slowed down in front of the mansion. "That's the last thing I want. We'll have to talk more, maybe come up with a plan for you. But first you're going to have to start calling me Oliver."

Fanny was still up, waiting for her return. Even though the rest of the house was dark, Fanny was sitting on the edge of her bed in a nightdress mending one of her cotton dresses under the glow of a lamp as if it were still early evening.

"I want to hear every last detail," Fanny said before Susanne could step into the room.

Susanne laughed. "*Mon dieu,* Fanny! It's after midnight." Still, she was all too happy to tell Fanny about her evening out with Oliver as she dressed for bed—especially about their first dance and holding hands in the carriage.

"He popped the question yet?" was the first thing out of Fanny's mouth when Susanne finished.

"Huh?"

"Don't go acting dumb with me. You know what I'm talking about."

"Goodness, Fanny. I've only been to one ball with him and to church a few times."

"Fiddlesticks! You see him in the park most days, don't you?"

"Yes, but only for a few minutes."

"And you took Miss Caroline and Mass Ward over to his store the other day, didn't you?"

"Yes, but—"

"Honey, I've seen it happen on way less than that."

Susanne sat on her bed in her nightdress. "Not with me, you won't. And at the rate I'm getting out of this house to spend time with him, it never will. I'm beginning to think it's a wonder Oliver wants to be bothered with somebody like me."

"Uh-huh. Doesn't hurt to have him wanting more of you. And I notice you call him Oliver now."

Susanne picked up a spool of thread and threw it at Fanny. "Oh, you. I'm not even listening to you."

Fanny ducked and chuckled.

"Anyhow, what makes you so sure I'd want to marry him?" Susanne continued. "To tell you the truth, I am starting to like Oliver, even if he is arrogant and stubborn as a mule." She paused and smiled. "He's smart and has got so much confidence that it's contagious, but I don't see how it would work for us." She shook her head. "You know, with him being free and all. Our lives are too different." She didn't add that her dreams were filled with another man. Or at least they had been until tonight.

"Others have done it, and it really wouldn't be all that different from me and Raif since he lives out."

"Yes, it would, Fanny. Raif is still a slave and Mass Willard's property. But Oliver can go whenever and wherever he pleases without having to ask a soul. He can up and leave the state tomorrow if he wants to. He traveled up North to Boston when he worked on a steamer before he opened his store. I would just hold him back."

Being around Oliver had an uncanny way of reminding her that she was a slave. She'd always known that, of course. But the Montgomerys were good to her and it was easy to put it at the back of her head. She was luckier than most other colored folks, slave or free. She worked for quality whites. She lived in a mansion right alongside them. She wore pretty dresses and slept in a decent bed. But she was still a slave. When Miss Lizbeth told her she couldn't go to the African Baptist church regular-like, it sank in like an anchor in the sand. She had always known there were things she couldn't do, but for the first time she was starting to think that she *should* be able to do them. If other colored folks could, why not her?

"Do you ever think about freedom, Fanny?" Susanne asked as she lay down on the bed.

"Not much. And when I do, I come to my senses real quick."

"But with Raif hiring himself out and earning his own money, you could save to buy your freedom."

"Fiddlesticks! He pays most of it to Massa. By the time he pays for the room he rents, he doesn't have much left over for anything else. 'Sides, if you saw the room that Raif rents . . ." Fanny shook her head. "I don't want to live in that dump. I hardly like going over there to see him as it is."

"He gets to come and go more than we do."

"Unfortunately," Fanny said, bitterly. "He's probably down there in some cookshop right this minute throwing his money away on a card game. Which is another reason why we can't save no money. Sometimes I think whites look the other way when it comes to us gambling even though it's supposed to be illegal just so we can have somewhere to throw our money away."

"You're probably right about that."

Fanny blew out the light. “Brother Oliver been putting them ideas into your head.”

“What ideas?”

“'Bout freedom.”

“It's not like Oliver is the first person to ever talk about it, you know.”

“No, but it's the first time I ever heard you talk about it. You sure he didn't ask you to jump the broom yet?”

“Is that all you think about? No, he didn't. Besides, I kind of think like you do. I mean, I like the idea of being free, but I don't want to live in some shack down in the bottom.”

“Brother Oliver doesn't live in the bottom, and from what I heard he has a right fine house, too. Rents it from his old massa.”

Hmm, Susanne thought. She should have figured Oliver wouldn't live in some dinky old place. Still, living free was hard work for colored folks. She had it good here and wasn't about to give it up easily. “'Course, that probably depends on what you consider fine. I mean, it ain't like this.”

Fanny chuckled. “True.” She let out a big yawn.

“Not that I would need something anywhere near like this,” Susanne continued. “Just something clean and decent.”

“Uh-huh,” Fanny said, sounding half asleep.

“Still, that's a rough life, you know? That freedom.”

Susanne waited for Fanny's response. None came, so she figured Fanny must have drifted off to sleep. She shut her eyes and tried to get to sleep herself. It was already late and she had a big day tomorrow. She had to get the children up and off to their own church, then meet Oliver at his.

“Oh, Susanne,” Fanny said.

“Hmm?”

“Miss Lizbeth said to tell you that after church tomorrow, they're all going to a picnic in the park to celebrate the victory at Manassas. So she wants you to dress the children a little more casually."

Susanne's eyes popped open. "Did she say that I had to go to the picnic with them?"

"I'm sure she expects it. You know how Miss Caroline is when you go off without her."

Susanne sat up. "But I'm supposed to go to church with Oliver tomorrow. He's expecting me."

Fanny paused. "That's what Missus told me to tell you."

Susanne flopped back down on the bed and punched her pillow. At times like this, she felt like the slave she was.

26

Try as she might to change Miss Caroline's ways, the little missus put up a fight that Sunday and every other day Susanne tried to leave the family to meet Oliver. The child bit, kicked, and screamed, and finally got her way. Worse, Mass Ward began to imitate his big sister. Miss Lizbeth said she simply couldn't take it anymore and asked Susanne to cancel her church gatherings with Oliver until Miss Caroline was older or to start taking the girl to church with them.

That was out of the question, Susanne thought. She was almost eighteen now and had so little private time with Oliver or any other adults as it was. So she and Oliver hatched a plan to get Miss Caroline to stop her little tantrums. Once a week, she took Miss Caroline and Mass Ward with her to visit Oliver at his store. The two of them would climb up on the shelves, run around playing tag, and eat the peanuts that Oliver always brought back from his trips. The children liked to call them by their African name, goobers.

After a few weeks of this, Susanne sat Miss Caroline and Mass Ward down with a handful of goobers and explained that on Sunday afternoons, she needed a little bit of time for herself and that she was going to attend church with Oliver. Miss Caroline's only objection was that she couldn't go with them. She liked Oliver and his goobers.

Susanne noticed that Oliver had that effect on a lot of folks. They liked him. Black, white, children, adults. She tried to think why. No doubt it had something to do with his being an Armistead. Some colored folks even called him Mr. Armistead when they came into his store, something done rarely among coloreds and never in front of whites. But it was more than that. Oliver reminded Susanne of Mama's husband, Squire May, in a way. Neither one was particularly suave or handsome, but their looks kind of grew on you, and they were solid and dependable, always ready to lend a helping hand. On his trips out of Richmond, usually to the Virginia countryside, sometimes up North, Oliver always returned with a wagon full of much-needed supplies for the soldiers—bandages, tools, and lots of goobers. Before the war, well-to-do folks wouldn't touch this food brought over with the slaves from Africa. They fed them to their pigs and used them to make oil. But these were hard times, and peanuts were a good source of nutrients. They had become a staple in the soldiers' diets. Susanne had once thought that Marcus had so much dignity because of the proud way he carried himself. Now she knew that Oliver was the dignified one because of the way he lived his life.

When she finally got out to church with him again, he invited her to join him and a few friends for dinner at his house, and this time she accepted. She didn't ask Miss Lizbeth's permission, she just went. There was never any telling when she would get out alone again, and an extra hour or two should be all right. She was going to start claiming some of that liberty that white folks always talked about.

Oliver's home was in an area of small brick and wood houses. The neighbors were people of all races and occupations, slave and free. On one side of Oliver lived a white grocer and a white stable-keeper, and on the other a colored barber and a mulatto woman who rented rooms to slaves who lived out. Oliver's place was on the lower level of a two-family house. It had a front parlor, a kitchen, and two tiny bedrooms. It was sparsely furnished and looked barely lived in. She supposed that should be expected since he shared it with another free colored man named Solomon who hired out as a steward on steamers and was almost always at sea. And with Oliver often at the store or off looking for goods to stock it with, the place was usually empty. It was nothing like what Susanne was used to on Grace Street, nor did it live up to what she'd imagined from Fanny's description. But it wasn't the slums, either, and a woman's touch would do wonders for the place—a few pillows here, flowers there . . . Not that it mattered as far as she went. She didn't even know why the thought crossed her mind.

Some of the folks she had met at the ball were at Oliver's that Sunday afternoon, and they crammed into the small parlor and kitchen and talked, ate cake, and drank tea. Their dress was toned down from what it had been at the ball, but they still looked respectable, with the ladies in hats and gloves and the men in suits and patent leather shoes. Like everywhere else in Richmond and the South these days, the talk was about war. Some of the men thought Negroes ought to be allowed to join up and fight in exchange for their freedom. A few had even tried, but the Confederate army turned them down.

"They turned us outta there 'fore you could say lickety-split," Solomon said.

"I told you they would never go for it," Oliver said. "White Southerners will send their husbands and fathers and sons off to fight and die, but never their slaves."

"But not all of us are slaves," Solomon said.

"Tell them that," Oliver said.

After about an hour, Susanne excused herself reluctantly. She slipped her shawl over her shoulders, and Oliver walked her home.

"Did you have a nice time?" he asked.

"Yes, a real nice time."

Oliver nodded and smiled. "Good. You know, they're tightening the noose, calling up more of us to go build fortifications outside the city. Solomon is thinking of going up North to avoid it. With the war going on, there's more work up there and they pay better." He smiled. "I guess you don't approve of that, do you?"

That was hardly what she was thinking about. She wanted to know if that meant that Oliver was planning on leaving Richmond, too. "I reckon I might feel different if I was free like you," she said. "What will you do? Are you fixing to leave, too?"

Oliver tossed his hat in the air and caught it. "Shucks, no. I'll take my chances here."

It was only when her heart settled down that she realized it had been racing. She was so relieved to hear that.

"If Solomon does go," Oliver continued, "I plan to rent that extra room from Master Stuart, then I'd have the place all to myself."

"That sounds nice."

"It's a decent place to raise a family, at least to start one."

She tried to sneak a peek at his face without looking directly at him. Why was he telling her all this?

"I was thinking, would you want to get married someday?"

Susanne's tongue went dry. "I . . . I." Well, she did in a general manner of speaking. And he wasn't asking if she would marry him. "Yes, I reckon I would."

"Would you want to get married to me someday?"

Now that was a proposal. No two ways about it. Susanne thought her heart would burst out of her bodice. She didn't think he would really ask, and she had certainly never expected it so soon.

"Oh, I'd like that."

He stopped in his tracks and turned to face her. "You mean, yes, you'll marry me?"

He sounded stunned by her response. Well, no more than she was at his question. "I mean, I would be honored to be your wife, Oliver. But . . ." She paused as a white couple approached. They stared openly and suspiciously, and Oliver gestured for her to move on. He never touched her in public or walked close, and she knew why without asking. No doubt folks assumed she was white and that he was her servant.

"But what?" he asked as they continued walking.

"We're so different. You're free and I'm—"

"There are ways around that. We wouldn't be the first slave and free couple. We're good together, Susanne. We get along and I can take good care of you. Besides that . . ." He paused.

"Go on."

"I'm crazy about you. I have been since the first time you came into my shop with Fanny. And I hate that I can't touch you in public or even look at you without hiding what I really feel. But as man and wife . . ."

She cast her head down, and he paused. He was getting too personal, even if he was proposing, and it made her heart fly. It was downright embarrassing.

"I'm sorry," he said. "I'm moving too fast, I reckon."

"It's quite all right," she whispered.

"Excuse me?"

"Nothing."

They approached the mansion and stopped.

"Drat," Oliver said. "We're here already?"

She smiled. They both knew that they couldn't linger and talk in front of the mansion. Before the war, it would have been all right to chat here for a few minutes, since all the neighbors knew who she was. But these days, so many strangers were always about.

"If you need time to think on it, take all the time you

need," Oliver said. "But you'll have to come up with a better excuse than that to get rid of me."

He looked at her with such intensity that she suddenly felt shy. She stared at the ground. "Thank you, Oliver. I'll think on it for a bit."

"Can you look up at me?"

She shook her head shyly. "The neighbors will be looking."

"Shucks. I don't care about them now. I want to see that pretty face again before I go."

What was wrong with her? She was behaving like a silly child. She looked halfway up, and he stooped down to her level and lifted her chin. She couldn't believe he had touched her out here. And he was much too close. But she wished the moment would never end. She laughed softly and looked up. "*Mon Dieu.* It's just that . . . Have you really thought about this?"

"Every blessed day for a year now just about."

"How would we live? With me at the mansion and you at the house. And what if you wanted to leave Richmond someday. You've talked about moving and I—"

"Whoa. Say yes, first. Then we can deal with all those things. I'll buy you from them, if they'll allow me to."

"That takes a lot of money."

"For you, yes. At least a thousand, so it will take me some time. But I have some saved already and—"

"No. You were planning to use that to buy land."

"Why are you fighting this every step of—"

He stopped abruptly as a wagon full of soldiers passed by slowly. Susanne felt their eyes watching without even looking in their direction. Oliver took a step away from her and they stood there silently until the wagon was a good distance down the road.

"We can't stay out here much longer," Susanne said.

"Come by the store one day next week and we'll talk."

Susanne nodded.

* * *

She entered the mansion through a side door, then went quietly down the hallway and up the stairs. She hoped to make it up to the attic without being seen, change out of her Sunday dress and hat, then find the children. Hopefully, they were alone in their room playing, and she could sit and think for a minute about all that Oliver had said. The man had her brain spinning like mad. But that was not to be.

"Is that you, Susanne?" Miss Lizbeth said as soon as she walked past the missus's chamber.

Susanne stopped in the doorway. Miss Lizbeth was sitting in an armchair as Fanny kneeled on the carpet below, lacing the missus's boot. "Yes, ma'am?" Susanne said.

Miss Lizbeth yanked her foot from Fanny's grasp and stood up. Fanny jumped back and her eyes popped open but she stayed on her knees.

"Where were you?" Missus asked. "You should have been back from church more than an hour ago."

"I stayed over just a bit to talk to the minister." That was the first time she had ever told a whopping lie outright to Missus since the day she'd run away and she and Fanny told everybody that she had gone to Mr. Levy's store to get the handbag.

"For more than an hour? The children have been asking for you, and I had to put off my visit to Miss Helen's afternoon tea. Mother thinks I've been far too easy on you, and I'm beginning to think she's right."

Fanny now appeared to be studying the pattern on the Persian rug.

"I'm sorry, Missus," Susanne said. "It won't happen again."

"See that it doesn't, or I'll have to take away your church privileges altogether."

Susanne sighed as she trudged up the stairs. This was the kind of thing Oliver never had to put up with. In the bedroom, she removed her hat and unbuttoned her Sunday dress. He might not live in a mansion but he could come and go as he pleased.

Whenever Susanne took the children to Oliver's store, he gave them each a bag of peanuts. Then Susanne would take them to the park, spread a blanket, and let them crack the nuts open and eat to their hearts' content. She loved being around Oliver so much that she'd all but forgotten about Marcus now, with his money-giving-away self. Oliver was so sure of himself and what he wanted. He told her to take her time thinking about his proposal. Said he was confident that the more she got to know him the more irresistible he would become. She smiled to herself every time she remembered those words because she knew it was probably true. That, in a way, was the agony and the ecstasy of being with Oliver. It was getting so she didn't think she could live with or without him.

One morning just as they reached the park, Mass Ward started to cry. He had left his bag of goobers back at the store. Susanne knew he wouldn't be happy until he had his bag of peanuts, so she called Miss Caroline, who was skipping up ahead, and the three of them held hands and walked back toward Oliver's store. They had gone but a few steps when she saw Oliver coming toward them. He waved the bag of peanuts in the air, but before he could take another step, a soldier carrying a bayonet stepped smack in Oliver's path. Another soldier approached him from the other side. Susanne froze.

She had become so used to the presence of soldiers in the park that she hardly ever thought about them anymore. With the children, she was safe from hassle even if they suspected she was their slave. But coloreds weren't allowed in the park unless they were accompanying whites or had a pass expressly permitting entry to conduct business. Oliver had secured a pass from his former master giving him permission to cross the park walking to and from his store. Susanne was too far away to hear what was being said, but judging from the annoyed expression on Oliver's face as he held out the bag and gestured toward them, he didn't have his pass now.

Suddenly Oliver turned his back, and the two soldiers, one on each side, bayonets resting on their shoulders, followed Oliver as he retraced his steps toward the park exit. Susanne could hardly catch her breath. The penalty for being caught in the park without the proper papers, slave or free, was jail and lashes. She didn't know how many, but one was way too many.

"Where are they taking Oliver?" Miss Caroline asked, looking up at Susanne.

Susanne tightened her lips. "I don't know." She squeezed the children's hands. "Come on, let's go catch him." The three of them ran up, and the soldiers turned on their heels to face them.

"Halt," the first soldier shouted. He stuck his hand out in their direction, palm up.

"What's going on, Oliver?" Susanne asked.

The second soldier took a step toward Susanne. "Do you know this man, Miss?"

"Yes, this is Oliver Armistead. He was coming to the park to meet us."

"And who are you?" the first soldier asked.

"My goobers!" Mass Ward shouted. He let go of Susanne's hand and toddled toward Oliver, but the soldier grabbed his shoulder and held him back.

"Take your hands off that child," Susanne said, struggling to keep her voice calm. She reached out and pulled Mass Ward back. Secretly, she was glad for the distraction. It gave her an extra moment to think.

"Who are you?" the soldier repeated.

Susanne cleared her throat. "Their aunt."

Oliver blinked and Miss Caroline glanced up at her, mouth hanging slightly ajar. Shut that trap, Susanne thought, and keep it shut for once. It might be more true than any of them realized anyhow, if Mass Willard was her daddy.

"And he was coming to meet you and the children?" the other soldier asked.

"Yes," Susanne said.

"I tried to tell you that," Oliver said. He stepped forward and handed the bag to Mass Ward.

"Ma'am, you should know that slaves can't travel about in the park without a pass," the first soldier said.

"I told you, I'm not a slave," Oliver said. "I'm free."

"That's the truth," Susanne said.

The soldier exhaled impatiently. "He still needs his free papers and a pass from his employer to be in this park, ma'am."

"I don't have an employer. I work for myself."

Mon Dieu, Oliver, Susanne thought. Please, hold that pride in check for once.

"He was bringing my little brother his goobers," Miss Caroline said.

"I tried to explain that," Oliver said. "But—"

"You're an ornery one, aren't you," the first soldier said, sneering at Oliver. "You're still a nigger, so you need papers."

Oliver inhaled and clamped his lips shut.

"Yes, Oliver," Susanne said, her voice firm. "Next time you must be more careful to remember your papers."

Oliver exhaled. "Yes, ma'am," he said softly.

"Very well," the second soldier said. He bowed his head in Susanne's direction, then turned toward Oliver. "You're free to go. But don't let us catch you around here again without the right papers or it's off to jail."

Susanne exhaled with relief. She could tell that Oliver's pride had been wounded badly. But at least he wouldn't suffer the humiliation of jail. As she watched him head back to his store, she thought that the two of them weren't so different after all. Oliver was just a slave with no master.

27

Late that spring the tide turned, and it seemed to Susanne that Richmond was falling through an abyss. The victory at Manassas had been followed by a chain of defeats and soon much of Virginia was "in enemy hands," said the *Enquirer*, as Oliver read to Susanne. Anyone suspected of being a spy was rounded up and hauled off to jail. Some were even hanged.

Richmond had avoided combat on its soil, at least so far, but the city had other battles to fight. It was bombarded with refugees—speculators, drunks, thieves, prostitutes. Some said the population of the city had tripled since the beginning of the war. President Davis had declared martial law and tried to shut down all the saloons. He didn't have much luck. Then came word that Yankee gunboats were headed up the James River. Businesses closed down, homes were boarded up, and wagons filled with families and luggage headed in every direction out of the city. Coloreds were plucked from the streets and sent to work on the fortifications being dug outside the city. Those who tried to escape were shot.

Mass Willard ordered his wife and daughters to pack their things, and Miss Nancy instructed the servants to pack the valuables. They weren't going to run yet, but they needed to be ready to flee at a moment's notice. Battles raged as close as the river, and the sounds of cannon fire filled the air. Some continued to flee as others ran to the rooftops of the capitol and the surrounding hills to get a glimpse of the fighting.

Thousands more soldiers, dead and wounded, poured in from the battlefields on carts, wagons, ambulances, foot, and train. Richmond was ill-prepared for still more casualties. Every available space was set up to treat the wounded—churches, hotels, warehouses, deserted homes and stores, even the streets.

Susanne tried to steer the children clear of these depressing sights when they went out for their afternoon walk to the park. But there was no way to avoid it completely, even on the outskirts of the city. Everywhere she turned, she was greeted with reminders of the deadliness and destruction of war. Right in front of the mansion, open wagons filled with wounded soldiers moaning in pain and covered with bloody bandages rumbled down the street heading for one of the hospitals, or worse, carts filled with dead bodies wobbled past their door heading for Hollywood Cemetery. Ambulances zipped by day and night, and everywhere you looked women, black and white, ferried baskets and trays of bandages from one bloody scene to the next. And it was far worse in the middle of town, where folks said soldiers hobbled by on amputated limbs and the stench of open wounds filled the air.

General Robert E. Lee took command, and together with men like Stonewall Jackson and Jeb Stuart, held the Yankees back from Richmond and declared victory. But the boom of guns and cannon fire and the sight of Yankee observation balloons hovering on the outskirts of the city never ceased.

Susanne had Oliver read reports about the war to her almost every time she visited his store. The minute she passed through the door, if he wasn't helping a customer, she would ask if there was any more news on the war. Oliver didn't seem to mind. And he was always telling her something sweet, like she was a spring breeze in the midst of all this carnage.

But the article she would remember most, for more than one reason, was the one he read the winter afternoon she slipped out of the house while the children napped. The Montgomerys were out helping with the war effort as usual, so she told Prudence to keep an eye on the children, then she went looking for Aunt Martha for a pass. Aunt Martha couldn't write, but with the Montgomerys being away so much, they had given her several passes. All she had to do was find a slave who could write enough to fill in the blank left for a name. Susanne found Aunt Martha in the kitchen and asked for a pass to run an errand.

Aunt Martha narrowed her eyes. "Did you get permission from Miss Lizbeth to go running off?"

"Mass Wade left his toy soldier in the park this morning. I want to get it before he wakes up." She was getting awfully good at this lying, she thought, not without some shame. The soldier was in her handbag.

"Uh-huh. Seems to me that you been running 'round a lot these days."

"It's with the children, mostly," Susanne said. "They need to get out of the house now and then."

"Uh-huh." Aunt Martha reached in her pocket and pulled out one of the passes that she guarded like a hawk. "Here," she said, and handed it to Susanne.

"Thanks." Susanne turned toward the doorway.

"And tell Brother Oliver I said hello," Aunt Martha said.

Susanne turned back, but Aunt Martha was already going out the back door. Susanne smiled.

According to what Oliver read to her that afternoon, as of January 1, 1863, the federal government would consider all slaves in the rebelling states to be free. The paper bitterly denounced Lincoln's proclamation as a devious plot to incite the slaves to rebel, and it mentioned Nat Turner. Susanne hung on every word and when Oliver finished, they stared at each other over the counter. "What does that mean?" Susanne finally asked. It wasn't that she didn't understand what he'd read, but that she couldn't believe what she was hearing.

Oliver shook his head with disbelief. "The Yankees aren't ten miles out of Richmond. If you can get that far, and this paper is right, you're free." He shook his head again.

"That doesn't sound right, Oliver. You sure you read that right?"

"That's what this here paper says."

"So you say, but I don't believe it."

"Whoever wrote this piece in the paper sounds pretty steamed about it, so maybe there's something to it."

She made him read it aloud again. After he finished, they both stared at each other for a few minutes, then smiles spread slowly across their faces. Soon they were laughing with glee. Oliver ran around the counter to the door and hung up the CLOSED sign. Then he swept her off her feet and twirled her around.

"Oliver Armistead, that's the best thing you ever read to me," she said as he put her down. She felt a little dizzy and blinked her eyes.

"You know, if you would consent to marry me, I could read to you every day."

Whoa. Now she was feeling more than a little dizzy and not from spinning. This was the first time Oliver had brought marriage up since that day the soldiers stopped him in the park months ago.

"Drat, Susanne," he said. "I'm tired of holding it in. You said you couldn't marry me because I'm free and you aren't. If the North wins the war, and you're set free, what will be your excuse then?"

She smiled. "Reckon I wouldn't have much of one, then."

He took her hands. "Then why wait for the war to end if that's what's stopping you? I said I'd buy your freedom, didn't I?"

She looked down at his fingers. "Oh, Oliver. It's not that easy. I mean, you do nicely on your own, but with a family to take care of, especially in the middle of this war . . . People are starving and dying out there and—"

"Woman, you need to have more confidence in your man. It's not like I'm some bum off the streets. I take good care of myself, always have, and I'll take good care of you, too, if you'll let me."

"If anyone can, it's you. I know that. Give me just a little more time to think."

"What more is there to think about? We've been courting for a year. We're close now, aren't we?"

She nodded. She felt closer to Oliver than anyone else. That always amazed her since they were so different.

"And I know you care about me, I can see it in your face. So what's stopping you?"

She smiled. Being free scared the bejesus out of her, especially when she had it so good now. But it was also exciting. And it wasn't like she'd be going into it blind. She'd have Oliver and he knew what it was all about. He was so brave and confident about it. "Nothing, I guess."

"Then is that a yes, now?"

"You can be so pushy."

"I can be when I really want something."

It took him a few more days, but he finally persuaded her to say yes. He wanted to go straight to Miss Lizbeth and offer to start making payments on her. But Susanne thought there was a chance the missus would free her and that they should try that before Oliver spent his money. Besides, although slaves sometimes bragged about how much money they sold for, the biggest source of pride came from being set free because you were priceless. It was the highest honor an owner could bestow on a slave and it didn't come easily. "They're always saying as how I'm like family, even though we know better. You don't sell family, right? But they like you. Especially Mass Richard. He knows all about you."

"Susanne," Oliver said with strained patience. "How did they get you?"

"They bought me. You know that."

"That's what I'm getting at. If they bought you, they'll sell you."

"Pft. That was different. That was before. I've been with them more than four years now."

Oliver shook his head doubtfully. "I expect they paid good money for you and with the war on and everybody facing hard times, they're not going to want to give you away. They'll have to buy someone to replace you."

"The Montgomerys are fine with money. They have plenty of everything."

"Even if they free you, you know you have to get permission to stay here in Virginia?"

She had heard about that. Any slave freed in Virginia had to leave the state within a year unless they got special permission to stay. "How do I do that?"

"They can do it for you. If they're willing to free you, they should be willing to do that."

Susanne planned to tell Miss Lizbeth that she wanted to marry Oliver and to ask for her freedom that afternoon when Missus came home for tea with the children. But when Susanne returned to the mansion, she heard Mass Willard's voice coming from the front parlor. It was unusual for him to be home at this hour during the week. He was normally at the bank or in town at meetings about the war. She couldn't make out all of Mass Willard's words from the hallway as she removed her coat, but she understood enough. It was something about Lincoln and the

Emancipation Proclamation starting slave uprisings throughout the South. She ran upstairs and got the children up from their naps, then brought them down. They were her ticket into the parlor.

She stood in the doorway as the children ran into the drawing room. The mayor was with Massa and they both were smoking pipes. "We're going to have to do the same thing if we expect to have any chance of winning this war," the mayor said. "At this point, we may have no choice but to arm the Negroes if we're serious about defeating Grant."

"Balderdash! That goes against everything the South stands for," Mass Willard said. "They're slaves. How can we expect them to earnestly defend the South?" He paused as Mass Ward ran up to him and Miss Caroline stood at his side.

"Ah," he said as they both kissed him on the cheek. "Now run along with Susanne. I have business to discuss with the mayor."

That evening, the family gathered in the parlor and the discussion of Lincoln's proclamation continued. Susanne thought it best to wait until things cooled down to ask Miss Lizbeth about marriage and freedom.

The Emancipation Proclamation didn't incite insurrection as many white Southerners feared, but it did shift the general sentiment of blacks throughout the South as word drifted out. Suddenly, it was no longer "the white folks' war"; it was about them, and thousands of slaves fled across enemy lines offering to fight for their freedom. Virginia's booming slave market all but dried up since many of those left behind were conscripted for the war effort. Alongside free blacks, slaves were pressed into service digging trenches outside the city, working as nurses and cooks in the hospitals and as laborers in the factories. With inflation due to the war and the numbers of slaves available for sale dwindling, prices skyrocketed along with everything else.

Oliver avoided conscription because his store stocked so many needed supplies. He ran the Union blockade to get the supplies, traveling by a friend's rowboat across the Potomac River to Maryland. From there more friends would take him by wagon to the railroad. He would bring back pipes, needles, cloth, and other items in scarce supply, which was just about everything. But with the war heating up, the trip was getting too dangerous. The last time, the rowboat came within yards of a Yankee gunboat, and now he only left at night. Susanne wanted him to stop going altogether, but he worried that if his supplies ran low, he'd be sent out to dig trenches and lose his store.

As the blockade tightened and routes into Richmond became battlegrounds, food became especially scarce and prices outrageous. In the spring, a mob of hundreds of angry women carrying knives and guns marched down Main Street to Capitol Square and demanded food from the governor. Men and children joined in, and when they didn't get what they wanted, they smashed windows and grabbed everything they could get their hands on—food, clothes, jewelry. President Davis brought soldiers and after repeated warnings to stop the looting, he ordered the soldiers to fire if the crowd didn't break up immediately. They soon dispersed.

About a month later, Stonewall Jackson died of wounds received in battle, and Richmond went into mourning. Businesses and shops closed, church bells rang, and all the Montgomery women wept into their lace handkerchiefs.

"When are you going to talk to them?" Oliver asked as they sat close to each other on the sofa at a friend's gathering.

"I'm trying to wait for things to calm down. They have so much on their minds with the war going on."

"I think you're using the war as an excuse not to marry me."

She shook her head. "No, I . . . Oh, what if they say no, Oliver? That scares me."

"You mean about us getting married or them freeing you?"

"Them freeing me."

Oliver smiled wryly. "Are you afraid of them saying yes or no? Tell me the truth."

"Well, I admit I'll miss the Montgomerys, especially the children. It will break Miss Caroline's heart. But I want to be free and live with you after we're married."

Oliver nodded.

"You think I'm being silly about the children, don't you."

"I think that after you marry me and get your freedom, one way or another, you'll look back and wonder why you ever felt this way. Especially after you have a child of your own."

She smiled. "You're probably right, as usual, Oliver. I'll ask tomorrow."

"Oh, Susanne. That's just wonderful," Miss Lizbeth exclaimed when Susanne told her that Oliver had proposed and she accepted.

"So, the old boy finally got around to popping the question, huh," Mass Richard said, smiling from behind a puff of pipe smoke. "About time."

"We'll hold the ceremony right here," Miss Lizbeth said. "Of course, we'll have to keep it simple, with all the fighting and dying going on, but it will still be nice. We'll fix up the drawing room for you."

"Thank you, Missus," Susanne said. "That's right nice of you." Now for the hard part. She cleared her throat. "Um, ma'am, you know that Oliver is free."

"Of course we do."

"And, well, he has a place of his own."

"Oh? Have you seen it?"

"Yes, I have, Missus. It's very nice. And—"

"Oh! Yes, of course. You'll be wanting to spend some nights there." She looked at her husband.

"That will be a bit difficult with the children," Mass Richard said. "Especially now that we have another child on the way. But we'll work something out. One or two nights a week."

Miss Lizbeth clapped her hands. "Oh, I can't wait for the babies."

"I appreciate that, ma'am, but—"

"Perhaps we could set aside a room for them here," Mass Richard said, looking at his wife. "That way Oliver can come and stay, and she won't have to be out so much."

"That's a wonderful idea, dear. She's going to need more room anyway, once the children start coming." Miss Lizbeth turned to Susanne with a big, satisfied smile on her face. "How would you like that?"

"Missus, it sounds nice, but it's not exactly what we had in mind."

"Oh?" The smile fell from Miss Lizbeth's face.

"What then?" Massa asked.

"I'm thinking . . . me and Oliver thought . . ." She swallowed. "I'd like to be free."

Miss Lizbeth batted her eyes. "Free?"

Mass Richard removed his pipe and cleared his throat. "You aren't serious?"

"Well, yes, sir, I am."

"I . . . I'm speechless," Miss Lizbeth said, her face growing more ashen by the minute.

That would be the day, Susanne thought bitterly.

Miss Lizbeth jumped up. "I thought you liked being with Miss Caroline and Master Ward. I thought you were loyal to us—"

"Oh, I am, Missus, I assure you. I've always put them first, but now . . ."

"Then how can you talk of leaving them?"

Susanne watched silently as Missus paced up and down the carpet.

"I'm afraid that's impossible, Susanne," Mass Richard said. "We would have to replace you and that would be prohibitively difficult now, not to mention the expense."

Was that what this was all about? Money never seemed to be a problem around here before. "Suppose I still work for you?"

"You mean we'd pay you wages?" Mass Richard choked on the smoke from his pipe.

"I could work for free until the war is over. But I'd have my free papers."

"That's unheard of," Mass Richard said.

But not impossible, she thought. "I wouldn't mind. I would—"

"No, Susanne. It's out of the question."

"But why, Massa?"

Mass Richard shot out of his seat, clearly surprised at Susanne's boldness in questioning him.

"What the devil has gotten into you? It's just not done."

Or you just won't do it, she wanted to shout. But she kept her thoughts to herself. She had stepped far enough out of her proper place as it was.

"Really, Susanne," Missus said. "After all we've done for you. Why, we've treated you almost like a member of this family from the day you walked in here."

Those words again. "Ma'am, haven't I devoted myself to you ever since I came here? It's going on—"

"That's your duty as a slave," Mass Richard said.

"I thought I was like family."

"That's enough," Massa said. "This discussion is over."

* * *

"Go ahead. Say it," Susanne said as she paced up and down in front of Oliver sitting on his couch. "I can see the words just ready to hop off your tongue."

Oliver just smiled from behind his pipe.

"Don't say it then. I'll say it for you. 'I told you so.'"

Oliver smiled wryly.

"I deserve it, whether you'll say it or not. Talk about acting a fool. I thought they would agree to free me. It's not like it's never been done before."

"Yes, but it doesn't happen much, especially now that they're fighting tooth and nail to hold onto their way of life."

She continued pacing. "For four whole years, I did nothing but look over those children. Day in and day out. Sunup to sundown. Mama used to call it dayclean to daylean. You get up with the sun, before even, and work until you're leaning over at night. Do I mean so little to them? I would have sworn they'd at least think about it."

"Why? 'Cause they never took a lash to your back?"

Susanne stopped and stared at him. "It's more than that. I sleep under the same roof with them, we eat the same food, and I wear her clothes. And yes, that, too. They don't beat us."

"Don't be so quick to say they never beat their slaves. Just 'cause you never see it, doesn't mean it doesn't happen."

Susanne started pacing again. "The Montgomerys aren't like that. I'm sure of it."

Oliver shrugged doubtfully. "Most of them want to do right by their slaves, or at least what they call right. The really mean ones that beat their slaves all the time, they are few and far between. But don't let that fool you. Every last one of them will do what they have to, to keep this way of life. They believe it's their God-given right to own us. And if it means beating us or refusing to let us go under any circumstances, that's what they'll do. My master was a perfectly decent man in every normal sense of the word, but when it comes to slavery he would defend it with his last breath."

"At least he let you buy your freedom."

"He also put lashes on my back."

Susanne stopped. "Mass Stuart?"

"The overseer did. Same thing."

Susanne's mouth went dry. She didn't realize Oliver had ever been beaten. In all these months, he'd never said so much as a word about this.

"I was going to show you after we were married. But if it doesn't offend you—"

"Show me."

He stood up and removed his jacket and handed it to her. He loosened his shirttail and lifted it. What she saw brought tears to her eyes. Oliver's back was covered with old scars. She had seen marks like this when she was a little girl, on Papa Squire and one or two others at Montpelier. But this was the first time she'd seen any on someone she'd come to love so dearly. She raised her hand and touched it. He jumped.

"It still hurts?"

"Nah. I just wasn't expecting you to touch me."

"Sorry."

"Touch all you want," he said, chuckling.

"How could he do this to you?"

Oliver lowered his shirt and turned to face her. He rubbed her arms. "Honey, I don't know hardly any man that's never been whipped and not too many sisters, either."

She exhaled, trying to hold back the tears welling in her eyes, and Oliver put his arms around her to comfort her.

"Shucks. I'm all right now. This happened years ago."

"Why did he do it?"

"I tried to run. Wasn't but about fifteen, but like I told you, I was a ornery fella till Massa started letting me hire myself out. Only reason he didn't sell my tail was 'cause he was hurting bad money-wise at the time and he figured he could make more money by hiring me out."

"But he . . . you rent this house from him. He's your protector now."

"It's all about money. He gets a lot of what I earn by renting me this house. I pay a little more than he could get from somebody else, but I'm also buying protection. 'Sides, I'm a nice fellow now that I'm free." He grinned broadly, and she chuckled. But she still felt bad. She would never forget what she'd just seen on Oliver's back.

He lifted her head. "Let me see a smile on your face."

"I don't see anything to smile about."

"There's plenty. We're going to get married. At least they'll allow that. And then we'll see about your freedom. Maybe they'll let me buy you."

"You don't want to ask them first? What if they won't? Then you're stuck with a slave."

"In that case, we'll do like most of these other folks do. See each other as much as we can."

"You still want to marry me, even if I'm never freed?"

"You dern tootin' right I do."

She kissed him.

28

The wedding was on a December afternoon in 1863, the time of year usually chosen for slave weddings since they were off for the holidays anyway. It was small, and simple, yet elegant and festive. Susanne wore white from head to toe—a simple satin dress with lace veil and slippers. Oliver wore a suit, white gloves, and top hat.

Miss Lizbeth decorated the drawing room with flowers, and all the Montgomerys and their servants gathered there, along with Oliver's parents and siblings and a few of his close friends. Fanny served as Susanne's attendant and she had invited two of the nurses from the park. One of Oliver's brothers served as his attendant. The Montgomerys stood off to the side with Mass Stuart and a few of the neighbors.

A Negro preacher from Oliver's church performed the ceremony. Susanne and Oliver exchanged vows, although the preacher didn't utter the customary words: "Till death do you part," and no one expected him to. Everyone knew that this wasn't legal or binding and that a lot of events besides death could part them—like a slave sale. The preacher simply told Oliver and Susanne that they were now married and that it was a sacred bond in the eyes of the Lord.

Mass Willard had somehow managed to get some good brandy through the blockade, and he raised his glass and toasted the bride and groom. Then he and his family and friends left for other parts of the mansion while the colored folks celebrated. The cook had baked a big wedding cake and prepared a ham for a feast. Raif played the fiddle and they clapped and danced.

It would have been a perfect day, Susanne thought, as she lay awake in Oliver's bed that night, if only Mama and Ellen could have been there. It had been so long since she'd seen them, it was getting hard to remember what they looked like, except of course for Ellen's fiery red hair. Mama might not have approved of her marrying a free man at first, but she would have come to like Oliver, of that Susanne was certain. But she wasn't going to let thoughts of Mama and Ellen ruin this special day. The truth was that she was so happy at this moment, even without her family around, that she felt a little ashamed.

She looked at Oliver and smiled. He was lying on his back fast asleep. It was impossible for her to sleep even though every muscle in her body was drained from all the excitement. A few hours earlier, after a whirlwind day of dressing, greeting guests, taking their vows, eating good food, and dancing till dark, Oliver brought her here and gave her the best wedding gift she could have wished for.

"Now I want you to stand right there," he'd said after leading her by hand to the fireplace in his parlor.

"What are you up to, Oliver?" she asked. He looked as if he was about to jump out of his skin with excitement.

"Just stand there," he said. "Close your eyes and don't move. I got something for you. And no peeking."

She closed her eyes as he dashed out of the room. Whatever was he up to? she wondered. She heard his feet race down the hallway and she opened her eyes and ran to the doorway and peeked around the corner. Fanny had told her in detailed terms what to expect when it came to lovemaking on her wedding night and it didn't include standing by the fireplace with her eyes closed. The hallway was empty, but she heard his footsteps coming and she scooted back to her spot near the fireplace just as he appeared in the doorway with his hands behind his back. He was obviously holding something. "Didn't I tell you to shut your eyes?" he asked, scolding her playfully.

She did as she was told and then felt him standing beside her. "All righty now. No. Wait. Turn this way." He turned her slightly to face him. "No, wait." He turned her a bit more.

"Oliver!"

"No peeking. You peeking?"

She laughed. "No, but I will be if you don't hurry up."

"All right. You can open your eyes now."

She opened her eyes to see Oliver holding a crisp sheet of paper under her nose.

"What is this?" she asked, staring as he opened her hand and placed it on her palm. She could tell that it was a receipt of some kind by the dollar signs and numbers. Then she noticed her name and goose bumps popped out all over her arms.

"That there is a receipt for the first payment I made to buy you from Mass Richard."

She looked up at him. She wanted to ask a thousand questions but her jaw suddenly felt like lead. Maybe she had misunderstood him, but she was scared to ask because he might tell her that she had indeed misunderstood him. Yet she was holding the receipt right here in her hands. And he was grinning from ear to ear.

She burst out crying.

Oliver looked stunned. "I . . . thought you wanted this."

Susanne nodded.

"You do want it? Then why are you crying?"

"Because . . . 'cause." She sniffed. Why was she crying?

"I don't know." She laughed nervously, then threw her arms around Oliver.

He lifted her and swirled her around, then set her down. "Make up your mind, woman. You're driving me crazy. You're happy about this?"

"Yes! Oh, my Lord, yes."

He looked up to the heavens. "Whew! You had me worried for a minute there."

"It's just . . . I couldn't believe it. I still can't believe it. How did you get them to say yes?"

Oliver smiled. "I went to Mass Richard and offered to buy you about a fortnight after you asked for your freedom. He said he'd think on it and to come back in a week's time. I figured he might be more open to it after we lost at Gettysburg and Vicksburg. A lot of white folks are starting to really believe the cause is lost. Some are even wondering if Richmond will survive, much less slavery. And they're right to be worried. Even if the South does win independence from the North, which I seriously doubt now, slavery won't last. Too many colored folks have gotten a whiff of that freedom blowing down from the North. 'Sides, he's charging me an arm and a leg for you, precious." He chuckled. "Almost twice what you would have cost before the war."

"Oliver! That's too much money. Why not wait and see how the war goes?"

He shook his head firmly. "It's already gone on three years, with no end in sight. This way, I can have you bought and paid for in a set amount of time, a few years at most. And there won't be any question about whether you'll ever be free in either of our minds."

Now, she pulled the bedcovers high over Oliver's back and her own shoulders and tried counting sheep to get to sleep. The light told her that it was near time to get up, but still she couldn't sleep. This was the first time she had ever slept off her owner's property, and no one was anywhere nearby to come calling her in the middle of the night wanting this or that. When she got up tomorrow, no lingering eyes would watch every move she made. Why, she could sleep past daybreak and not worry beans what anybody would think.

And Oliver was buying her from the Montgomerys. Her eyes stung with tears every time she thought about it, although she knew it would be a good long while before he finished paying for her. And she wouldn't exactly be free, even then. Legally, she'd be Oliver's slave. He couldn't free her because she would have to leave Virginia within a year's time. These white folks didn't make things easy. But it was coming, sure as the day, and she would be able to live like a free woman. She might not be able to go into some of these white folks' precious parks and public squares anymore, but heck, she could go to see Mama and Ellen. Those white folks could have their rotten old parks.

She threw the covers back. Shucks! Who could sleep on a night like this? It was hopeless. She put on one of Oliver's shirts over her nightdress, found some soap and rags in the cabinets, and got down on her hands and knees and started scrubbing the floor. And she hummed.

29

Her life as Oliver's new wife started off nicely enough. The Montgomerys allowed her to spend Saturday evening through early Monday morning with Oliver unless one of the children took ill. There was talk about finding a room in the mansion so that Oliver could spend time there when Susanne couldn't get away, but with the war heating up and everybody being so busy they still hadn't gotten around to it by early spring. Pretty soon, it was all but forgotten.

Once in a while, Fanny stayed overnight with Raif, and Oliver would stay with Susanne in the attic. But he was never all that keen about it. He just couldn't get comfortable at the mansion. He hated the way she had to jump up in the middle of the night if one of the children called for a glass of water or simply couldn't sleep. Oliver said it reminded him too much of his days as a slave—a time he'd rather forget.

Life rolled along as ordinarily as could be expected in times such as these. Then in March, even Mass Richard, who had avoided being sent to the front because his skills as a physician were needed so desperately in the city, took up arms to defend Richmond against a direct attack. Thousands of soldiers had been lost at Gettysburg, and now nearly every able-bodied man was out at the front. When the Yankees broke through some of the city's outer defenses, the home guard was all that was left to defend the suburbs. They were mostly boys and old men but they managed to drive the enemy back. Residents cheered and carried on as before, although they felt ever more vulnerable.

Then Miss Lizbeth delivered a baby boy late that spring, and Susanne and Oliver's comfortable routine was tossed topsy-turvy. When Miss Caroline and Mass Ward were born, Susanne had slept on a pallet in the hallway outside the newborn's room until the child was about a year old. That's when Mass Richard felt they were out of danger of all the ailments that preyed on newborns. And she always slept outside the room if one of the children was sick. None of it had ever bothered her before. It got cramped, no doubt about it, especially to one who was used to the comfort of a bed, but she wanted to be close to the babies. And it was her job, after all. But this time it was different. She was expecting a child of her own that winter, and Oliver detested the idea of her sleeping on the floor throughout her pregnancy "like some animal" he said. Not only that, Joshua, Miss Lizbeth's new baby, was colicky and if he got to fussing on a Saturday evening, Susanne might not get away to see Oliver until Sunday or not at all.

"This isn't right," Oliver said irritably one Sunday evening shortly after she arrived at his house a day late. "Even field hands get more free time than you do."

She shrugged as she unwrapped the patterned scarf tied around her head and let her hair down. She usually wore a head wrap when taking care of the baby to keep her hair out of the way. "Humph. Everybody thinks we have it so easy," she said dryly. "They just don't know."

"Listen to you," Oliver said. "You even sound beat. How are you holding up?"

She sighed. "Tolerable, I reckon. Just a little tired is all."

"Shucks, Susanne. I wish you would let me talk to Mass Richard. He's a doctor. He should understand with this being your first baby and all that . . ."

Susanne shook her head firmly. "I know you mean well, Oliver, but this is my job and as long as I can stand the floor, I will stand the floor."

"What harm can come from asking?"

"Plenty. They agreed to let you buy me, but if we get to asking for too much, they're liable to change their minds. I don't want to take any chances."

"I'd rather take a chance with that than with our baby."

She exhaled. "Oliver, please. I'm fine. I just get a little tired a little faster. That's to be expected." The truth was that she got very tired a lot faster. Some of it came natural with being pregnant, she was sure. But this blasted war also had something to do with it. It seemed like it would never end. Just the other day, Miss Susan dropped one of her mama's most cherished porcelain bowls at the sound of a cannon booming in the distance, and it splintered into a dozen tiny pieces. Susanne was thankful it was Susan who dropped it. Everybody's nerves were on edge these days. The white folks prayed that Lee would keep the Yankees off Richmond's doorsteps, while the coloreds prayed that they would see the blue of the Union army sweeping through the streets of Richmond to liberate them one day real soon.

Oliver came up from behind and rubbed Susanne's arms. "The last thing I want to do is get you all upset. You know that. But you have to promise me something."

She leaned her head back against his shoulder and closed her weary eyelids. He wrapped his arms around her and held her tightly. She was thankful for these moments away with Oliver. It was the only time she could relax. And he always did something special for her, like rubbing her aching feet or fixing breakfast on Sunday morning so she could sleep a little late.

"If you get to feeling bad other than being a little tired, you tell me and let me talk to them."

She nodded. "I promise."

Before Susanne knew what was happening, the precious little time she had with Oliver was snatched away. Along with every able-bodied free colored male in Virginia, Oliver was ordered to the outskirts of the city to help shore up the trenches. With only a few days' notice, he raced around the city trying to find somebody to manage the store. But all the free black men were working for the war effort or on their way, and Oliver was finally forced to accept that he would have to shut down the store. Susanne thought she had never seen him look more crestfallen.

And if that wasn't enough, Mass Stuart insisted that he had to find another boarder since Oliver couldn't keep up the rent while he was away. Oliver spent an entire day moving all his things in with aunts and cousins scattered about the city. He was a changed man those last few days before he left. He seemed to find it harder to look her in the eye each day and he rarely smiled.

It broke her heart to see how painful all this was for him. He had to give up everything he'd worked so hard for and support a cause he didn't believe in, while slaves were allowed to stay at home on the pretext that their massas needed them. Oliver and many other colored folks were convinced that victory for the North meant emancipation. Some of the free men pressed into service digging fortifications thought it ridiculous to support bondage and ran instead, even at the risk of being shot for doing so. What was to stop Oliver from doing just that? Susanne wondered. She had already lost her mama and sister, and now she worried she might lose her husband.

She couldn't stop crying. She cried while she rocked

the babies. She cried when she dressed them in the morning. She cried herself to sleep at night. For three days she cried and she didn't care who saw her. In fact, she wanted the Montgomerys to see how miserable she was. It was the middle of the week, a time when she got to see Oliver only if he stopped by in the evening on his way home from work. If she had time to spare, she would feed him dinner from their leftovers and sit with him while he ate. More often, their weekday meetings lasted only a few minutes. But now her husband was being taken away from her under the most despicable circumstances, and she wanted more time with him before his departure.

The day before he was to leave, after a morning spent sobbing uncontrollably, she waited until Miss Lizbeth came back to the house alone for afternoon tea. "Ma'am, Oliver leaves tomorrow. If I could just have this last night with him, please." She blew her nose in a handkerchief. The Montgomerys were concerned about her welfare these days, up to a point, since she was carrying another piece of their property. So maybe all the crying and pleading would work.

Miss Lizbeth blinked. "Yes, I can see that you've been miserable, not good at all for the baby." She smiled. "I don't know that it's much help to you, but Oliver's being called to help save the South, a worthy cause if ever there was one, isn't it? That's what I told myself when Master Richard went to fight with the home guard."

Susanne bit her tongue. "Yes, ma'am." They were the hardest two words she'd ever had to utter.

"Very well, go to him tonight. Just come back before the children wake up in the morning."

There was a time when Susanne would have been most grateful to her mistress for this "privilege," but she had since come to believe that she got no privileges. Still, she thanked Miss Lizbeth profusely. It was habit, she reckoned. And survival. But it was starting to leave an awful nasty taste in her mouth.

She woke up in the middle of that night to find that Oliver wasn't in bed. She found him sitting in the parlor in the dark. She walked up behind him and put a hand on his shoulder. He jumped at the unexpected touch, then reached up and patted her hand.

"They got me this time, baby," he said.

"Don't say that." She hated hearing him sound so utterly defeated and wanted so badly to cheer him up. But she had never seen Oliver like this and wasn't sure how to go about it. She walked around the chair and sat in his lap. She reached for his hand and placed it on her stomach. The baby kicked just then, as if to tell his daddy that everything would be all right. Oliver smiled for the first time in days.

"I don't want to hear you talking like that, Oliver Armistead. We got to get through all this for this here child of ours. We have to come up with a plan."

He chuckled, then grew quiet again.

"What is it, Oliver?"

He shook his head. "Nothing you haven't heard before. All my life, I thought if I planned things and worked hard, if I just put one foot firmly in front of the next, that I'd be all right. And I was for the longest time." He paused and shook his head again.

"It's a setback, Oliver, but—"

"It's a lot more than that. I've had plenty of setbacks. But this . . . They've taken everything from me. Everything. And now I have to go help them try to win their damn stupid war." He twisted his mouth with disgust.

She took his head in her hands. "They didn't take everything, Oliver. You still have me and the baby. We're not going anywhere."

"I sure hope not. Don't know what I'd do if I lost you, too."

"You're a smart man and you're brave. They can't take that from you unless you let them."

"No, but they sure can hurt me." He sighed and squeezed her leg. "You're right, baby. And I'll be just fine."

He didn't sound convinced and she tried to lighten the moment by talking about the baby. Oliver asked her to name the baby George if it was a boy, after his father, if he wasn't back by the time it was born.

"If you promise me you'll come back to us soon as you can," she said.

"Nothing would keep me away."

"Good. We'll be waiting." She never let on just how worried she was that he might never return. She was reminded of her grandfather's hasty departure from Montpelier when he learned he was about to be sold away. Mama never talked about it much, but this must be what it had felt like—the same kind of numbing, yet gut-wrenching, pain now tearing at her insides. Oliver was right. These white folks could hurt you bad. But she couldn't let on about that now. Oliver needed her to be strong.

The following morning he walked her back to the mansion.

"I'm not going to turn back once I walk away. This is hard enough as it is and if I turn around and see you again . . ." He paused and shook his head. "I'll never get going."

She sniffed and nodded. They had said all they needed to say the night before. Besides, this was still the South, and a public display of affection between a colored man and white-looking woman would cause a ruckus. All they could do now was pray this war would hurry up and end. God, at times like this she thought she didn't care who won, as long as it ended. Oliver gave her a thin smile, then swung his knapsack over his shoulder and turned away.

He hadn't gone more than a few steps when something came over her. She yelled his name and ran up to him. She threw her arms around him and gave him a big kiss on the lips. A white woman approaching with two little girls gasped and yanked the children away. A man galloping by on a horse slowed to a trot and stared openly with displeasure as he passed. But no one seemed more startled than Oliver did. He stared at her with this delightful grin on his face. She didn't care what these farty old white people thought. It was worth the risk to see the smile on Oliver's face before he left.

"You come back to me, hear?" she said. "I love you and I'll be right here waiting when you get back." She patted her stomach. "Me and Junior, here."

"That sounds like a plan to me," he said.

She watched until he disappeared from sight, thinking that it was strange how some of life's most shattering moments sneaked up on you so quietly.

Oliver left just as the city, and indeed the whole South, seemed to sink into despair. Soldiers struggled on the battlefields without shoes, while their women and children went without food. Even the wealthy started to feel the pinch. Some of those who could afford the outrageous prices still lived extravagantly, dining shamelessly on multicourse meals and entertaining lavishly in their parlors. Their excuse was that these were the last days of luxury and they were going to enjoy them while they could.

But most began to cut back. Mass Willard walked around the mansion pointing out things he thought were too extravagant and places where they needed to sacrifice. He told his daughters to cut back on the new dresses and shoes. Last year's gowns would have to do. Champagne and lavish meals would be had only at Christmas and New

Year's. Leftovers were to be donated to the needy. The whole household was told to cut back on soap and firewood. Susanne saw her own portions of food grow smaller just at a time when she needed the most, but she told herself that these were minuscule sacrifices compared to the people who were living in damp basements and begging in the streets.

For all practical purposes, many thought the war was over, that the South as they knew it was doomed. So many women wore black in honor of lost loved ones that the whole city seemed to be in mourning. Mass Willard huddled in his study almost daily with the city's dignitaries. Susanne once overheard him arguing with the mayor and some others about enlisting slaves as combat troops, with freedom promised after the war in exchange for fighting. At this point, Richmond's very survival, and especially its banks, was in question. From that time on, whenever Massa talked with others in his study, Susanne would try to find an excuse to linger in the hallway, her ears glued to their voices. There was a time when she would have chided a servant for sneaking about like that. But times had changed.

Early one October morning, she woke up gritting her teeth against labor pains. Fanny ran to get Aunt Martha and they took turns all morning and afternoon holding her hand as she squeezed and cooling her face with a wet towel. That night, just when Susanne started to feel that she couldn't stand the pain one minute longer, Aunt Martha said it was almost time but that she didn't like the way things looked. So Miss Lizbeth sent for Mass Richard, and he broke away from his work at the hospital and came rushing home at the last minute to deliver a baby boy.

As they agreed before Oliver left, Susanne named the child George. The Montgomerys lightened her load but that didn't last long. Within a week, she was back at her job full-time, from dayclean to daylean. She spent most of her time in the upstairs parlor with Miss Caroline, Mass Ward, and the babies. Little George was often sick and needed extra time and attention, but Susanne was hard pressed to give it to him now that she was in charge of four children, two of them just out of the womb. Between Mass Joshua and the older Montgomery children, somebody always needed something—a change of diapers or clothing, a bottle or afternoon meal, or for her to settle a dispute or soothe a teary-eyed face.

There were times when George cried persistently, and all Susanne could do was glance at him to make sure he wasn't in some kind of danger. Or ask someone else to look in on him. Mass Richard examined him and said it was probably something he would grow out of. Many evenings she went to bed without taking the time to eat all day long, but she always ended her day holding George in her arms, no matter how late or how tired or hungry. She was filled with guilt throughout the day, and needed this moment with him.

It wasn't that she didn't love her son, she reminded herself as she rocked him and told him all about his daddy. But she'd heard horrid tales of nurses who neglected their white charges being sold away, or worse, their babies. Miss Lizbeth was already making plans for George to become Mass Joshua's valet when they got older, and more than a few times the missus had gone to George herself when she heard him cry in his crib in the nursery and Susanne's hands were full. She would pick him up and cuddle him just as she would her own. But Susanne knew that Miss Lizbeth and all the rest of them would be generous only as long as their own were being well cared for. Barring that, they'd be ready to ship her down the creek on the first boat leaving.

30

The weeks dragged on. Susanne heard grisly tales of even white folks dropping in the streets from starvation, of prostitutes taking over whole sections of the city, and profiteers swindling decent folks out of their last penny. Now they were getting reports that the Yankees, led by General Sherman, had taken Atlanta and were marching through Georgia burning and pillaging everything in their path—homes, farm animals, food.

Susanne had reached a point where she didn't care how they got here, as long as they did. And the sooner the better. Not so much for her. She had done all right for herself under slavery. But if the South should somehow prevail, what would it mean for Oliver to come home to nothing and have to deal with angry white folks still in power? Some free coloreds were saying there was no way they'd stick around with a bunch of resentful whites if the South won. She wasn't sure what the end of slavery would mean, but she thought things would be a lot better for her husband if the North won.

Talk of enlisting coloreds grew louder, and it seemed to Susanne that whenever she overheard Mass Willard arguing with someone in his library these days it was about that. General Lee's army had dwindled to the bare bones and he was begging for men. The only white men left in Richmond, indeed in the South, were over fifty or wounded or needed desperately at home to keep things going. Thousands of field hands had already fled across the lines and donned the blue uniforms of the Union army because they wanted freedom. Why not offer slaves the same to fight for the Confederacy? So the argument went.

But it was too little, too late. Yankee troops cut across central Virginia, and Sherman advanced through North Carolina planning to meet Grant in Virginia. Although they had given up on winning the war, Richmonders were confident that General Robert E. Lee would defend their borders, just as he had done countless times before. The beggars continued to beg, the thieves kept right on stealing, and the church-goers prayed as cannon blasted in the distance.

Reverend Minnigerode led the kneeling worshippers at St. Paul's in prayer for Richmond and President Davis. Susanne loved the soothing sound of his voice, but as she kneeled in the west gallery with the other slaves her silent prayers were for the Yankees to get there as fast as they could and for Oliver to return safely. With every passing day, she worried that he would be more tempted to take off for the North. Was a new wife and child enough to bring him home, given all that he had lost? Lord, let it be so.

Suddenly a messenger entered the church and the congregation grew quiet as he approached President Davis in his pew and handed him a telegram. The president's face went gray as he read it, then he stood and strode out of the church. Whatever that had been about, it didn't look good, Susanne thought. Other officials were summoned, including Mass Willard, and a soft murmur floated through the pews. The reverend raised his hand and began to pray.

When the Montgomery household reached home,

Uncle Jackson told them that Mass Willard was waiting for the family in the drawing room and had something important to say. Massa wanted Susanne to leave the children with Prudence and join them. Susanne entered the room and took her usual seat in a hard-backed chair near the door. It had been many months since the entire family had gathered together in this room for tea after Sunday services. Everyone always had other business to attend to.

This was vastly different from those earlier meetings, judging by the glum faces all around. Mass Willard's hand trembled as he lifted a dainty china cup to his lips. Susanne looked into his face and was startled by what she saw. He had really aged over the past few years. His hair had gone white, his color was parched. He looked utterly crushed. Mass Richard stood at the fireplace as before, but he stared solemnly ahead, seemingly at nothing. Miss Nancy sat in her usual spot on the sofa looking prim and proper and stared at her fingers. Misses Lizbeth, Ellen, and Susan sat around the table.

Mass Willard cleared his throat. Susanne had been so transfixed by his face that the sound startled her, and she jumped.

"This is a most trying time for us," Massa said, his voice cracking. "And I'm afraid I have more bad news." He blinked and looked down at the floor. Then he inhaled deeply and looked up. "General Lee has been defeated."

Not a sound was uttered. Not a move was made. Susanne supposed that, like herself, they were dumbfounded, but for different reasons. Those were words she'd longed to hear. But now that Massa was saying them, she felt numb. Did this mean that Oliver was finally on his way home? And that she was free?

"I understand, too," Massa continued, "that the government and the army will be evacuating the city today and tomorrow. The Yankees are expected here any moment."

Miss Nancy gasped and her cheeks went blood-red. She covered her mouth with her hands.

Miss Lizbeth jumped up. "Oh, my God, Father."

Susanne looked down at her fingers. She was torn, as if she could laugh and cry at the same time. The old South was really gone, and good riddance. But not knowing what lay ahead stirred up its own kettle of fear. She wanted to sneak looks at Uncle Jackson and Fanny, who were also in the room. But she dared not.

"But, Father," Miss Susan said, her voice rising to a wail. "We've heard that so often."

"Yes," Miss Ellen said. "And it was a rumor every time."

Mass Willard shook his head. "This time I fear it is true. That telegram delivered to Mr. Davis in church this morning was from General Lee. Grant's troops are fast approaching Petersburg, and Lee is urging that Richmond be evacuated immediately."

Miss Lizbeth flopped back down into her chair and all the young misses clutched hands and began to sob loudly. Miss Lizbeth extended a limp hand toward Fanny, expecting a handkerchief. When none appeared, Missus looked up with red eyes to see Fanny standing there with her mouth hanging open. Fanny finally noticed her mistress and jumped, then fumbled in her apron pocket for a handkerchief. "Sorry, ma'am," Fanny said as she shook it out and gave it to her mistress.

"Are the Yankees really on their way here?" Miss Nancy asked as her maid gave her a handkerchief, too.

Mass Willard grimaced. The answer was obvious.

"My God," Miss Nancy said, barely above a whisper. "What's to become of us?"

"I need a brandy," Mass Richard said. He turned toward Uncle Jackson, standing discreetly in the doorway. The butler bowed slightly and turned to leave the room.

"Make that two," Miss Lizbeth shouted as she jumped up again and paced the floor.

It suddenly dawned on Susanne how utterly dependent these folks were on their slaves. They used them for everything, even the slightest want or need. As much as she worried about her own welfare with the end of slavery, these folks also had a lot to worry about.

"Then it's over, Father?" Miss Susan asked between sobs into her handkerchief.

"I'm afraid so."

"What do we do now?" Miss Ellen asked.

"We'll stay put for the time being," Mass Willard said. "But there's no telling what the Yankees will do when they get here, so we should be ready to leave at a moment's notice. Pack some personal things, the valuables . . ."

Pack? Leave? *Mon Dieu!* She couldn't leave now, Susanne thought. She had to wait until Oliver got back. If she left now, he might never find her. Oh, Oliver, she thought. Please hurry back.

Susanne and Fanny sat up all night talking and listening to the sounds of a defeated army in retreat. In all the confusion, the servants slipped in and out of the side doors easily and brought back bits of news. The Confederates had torched the tobacco and cotton warehouses, set fire to the arsenals, and blown up their own boats, all to keep them out of enemy hands. Then they headed over Mayo's bridge and torched that, too. The explosions rocked the city for miles around, shattered windows, and blew off doors. The area near the river was an inferno, with fires spreading everywhere.

Thousands poured into the streets looking for the Yankees. Blacks with glee, whites with dread. Thousands more, overcome with fear, fled as fast as they could. They packed a few personal belongings and jumped onto canal boats, hopped into carriages and onto wagons, rode on horseback, or walked. They went south and west—anywhere but north.

At about midnight, Raif came tearing into the room, his eyes wide with excitement. "The Yankees coming tomorrow!"

"Shh," Fanny said, pointing to little George sleeping on Susanne's bed.

Susanne laughed. She wanted George close by in all this excitement and had him lying between pillows. "I reckon if all that noise outside hasn't woke him up yet, nothing will."

"They saying they'll be here by morning," Raif said softly, his voice dancing with excitement. "And guess what?"

"What?" Fanny asked.

"They say colored troops will be the first ones here, 'cause they's in front."

"You lying," Fanny said incredulously. "Colored troops?"

Raif grinned and shook his head. "That's what they saying, I swear."

"I'll believe that when I see it," Fanny said.

"I expect you just might real soon now," Raif said, raising a fist with glee. "Only problem is that the Confederates burning everything in sight. Even the railroad and the bridges. I just hope them Yankees can get here."

"And quick," Susanne added. "'Cause the Montgomerys already talking about leaving and—"

Just then there was a big explosion, and the three of them nearly jumped out of their skins.

"Glory be," Susanne said. She looked over at George, still as a stone.

"If one more of those blasted things go off, I swear I'm liable to have a heart attack," Fanny said.

"Don't y'all go to sleep, now," Raif said, heading for the door. "Fires spreading like crazy and you need to be on guard."

"I don't think anybody in this town is sleeping tonight," Susanne said. "Other than babies."

"I thought that the fires were just down at the river," Fanny said.

"The wind done shifted and it's heading toward town now and up this way. A couple of houses done caught fire not more than a few blocks down from here."

"Oh, Lord," Susanne said, standing up. "Maybe I need to go get my babies from their rooms and bring them in here with me."

"I seen them downstairs when I came up."

"Who?" Susanne asked.

"All of 'em. Mass Willard and Miss Nancy, Miss Lizbeth. The children were down there, too." He chuckled. "Never seen a sadder looking bunch of white faces."

"You stop that funning, Raif," Fanny said. "I feel kind of sorry for 'em."

"Me too," Susanne said.

"Not me," Raif said. "Not much, anyhow. I just want them Yankees to hurry up and get here." He turned toward the door.

"You not going back out there?" Fanny asked. "It's crazy out there."

"Can't sit here, that's for sure," Raif said.

Fanny jumped up. "Then hold up. I'm coming with you."

Susanne giggled. If it wasn't for George, she'd probably go out, too. It was frightening and exhilarating all at the same time. But Raif shook his head firmly. "It ain't safe out there for a woman tonight. Stay put and keep your eyes and ears open till morning."

"Raif, I just want to know one thing," Susanne asked. "Are we free yet? 'Cause nobody around here has said a word."

"Don't expect they will just yet. They still in shock, I reckon." Raif paused and blinked as his eyes got moist. "But I reckon so, Susanne."

Things got quiet for a moment as Fanny and Raif hugged. Susanne blinked back her own tears.

"Didn't think I wanted it," Fanny said. "But it sure does feel good being free, doesn't it?"

Susanne nodded. "I wish Oliver would get back here safe and sound where I can see him. What if the Montgomerys decide to leave before he gets here? What am I going to do then?"

"I 'spect Oliver will be here soon," Raif said. "I seen some of the other fellas coming back from the trenches tonight. It's rough going, though."

Fanny put an arm around Susanne. "Now don't you worry none. Oliver can take care of himself. And now that he knows you're free, won't nothing stop him from coming back here. I'd be surprised if he isn't back by morning."

"I hope you're right, Fanny. Lord knows I do."

The Union army marched into town the next morning, and just as Raif had said, the first soldiers to enter were colored. Richmond's colored folks poured onto the streets to greet them. Many of them had been up and about all night. Word had gone around that Lincoln was coming and they talked about the Messiah, sang, and danced alongside the troops. They threw flowers at them and shouted hallelujah.

Susanne watched the jubilee from the window in the upstairs parlor as she rocked Mass Joshua in her arms. In contrast to the celebration outside, the mansion was as quiet as a graveyard. Miss Caroline and Mass Ward were playing on the floor, and George was asleep in his crib. While most of the household help was in the streets whooping it up, the Montgomerys moped about looking as if they were at a funeral. Uncle Jackson was still there along with Aunt Martha, both tiptoeing around quietly and as faithful as ever. But even Fanny had gone out early that morning with Raif. Susanne didn't know whether to sit and wait for Oliver or to go out and search for him.

Around noon, Miss Nancy strode into the parlor,

wringing her handkerchief in her fingers. "Susanne, have you packed the children's things?" she whispered so the children wouldn't hear.

Susanne sprang up out of her seat. Jesus, Joseph, and Mary. Were they about to leave now? "Yes, ma'am. We're not fixing to go yet, though, are we?"

"I fear we may have to leave tomorrow. It's not safe here, and I don't want the children to have to see this sad turn of affairs. My husband will decide tonight. But be ready in any event." Miss Nancy turned toward the door.

"But, ma'am . . ."

Missus paused without turning back around.

"I . . . I." Why waste her breath? Susanne thought. This woman wouldn't understand, or care. "Nothing, ma'am."

Miss Nancy turned and gave Susanne a funny look, then smacked her lips with impatience and walked out. Susanne sank back down in her seat. *Mon Dieu!* If they left tomorrow and Oliver wasn't back, he might never find her. Then again, it was taking him awfully long to get back. Maybe he didn't want to find her. She sniffed but refused to cry. She wasn't going to start thinking that way yet. Oliver loved her. Of course he was coming back.

She stood up. She could stand it no longer. Even if she couldn't find Oliver, maybe someone had seen him or knew his whereabouts and could get word to him that she might have to leave Richmond. She paced the floor until Prudence came back shortly after the midday meal. Susanne asked her to watch over George, then called for Miss Caroline and Mass Ward and marched them down the stairs. She found Miss Lizbeth in the parlor with Miss Nancy and Misses Susan and Ellen. The drapes were drawn, and all four huddled quietly near the fireplace. Mass Willard had been out at the bank all morning to help salvage what he could. Mass Richard was at the hospital. Susanne walked right in and planted Mass Joshua in Miss Lizbeth's arms.

"Not you, too," Miss Lizbeth said, her eyes wide with shock. "It's not safe out there with the Yankees, Susanne."

Maybe not for you, Susanne thought. "I'll be fine, ma'am. I want to see what I can find out about Oliver."

"Oliver?" Miss Nancy asked. "Where is he?"

Susanne felt like shaking the old woman. "He was sent out to the trenches, Missus."

"Oh."

"You mean he hasn't returned?" Miss Lizbeth asked.

"No, ma'am."

"I see," Miss Lizbeth said. "Well, don't be long. We need you here now. All the others have run off."

Susanne sighed. If four grown women couldn't figure out what to do with their own babies, well, no wonder the South lost the war. She lifted her skirt and turned on her heels. "I'll be back before you know it."

"Oh, and Susanne," Miss Nancy called after her. "Be sure to pack some of the children's toys if you haven't already."

Toys? Toys? Of all the . . . She clenched her fists. "Yes, ma'am."

The smoke smacked her in the face as soon as she opened the door. She coughed and unwrapped the scarf around her head and used it to cover her mouth. Less than a block away, she saw a house that had burned to the ground. Its ruins were still smoldering. Glass littered the streets, and people of all colors moved about in every direction. A wagon full of colored folks rumbled past, its occupants whooping and hollering and waving their hats with delight. "We's free, we's free. Glory hallelujah, we's free." Moving in the opposite direction was a wagon full of whites packed with furniture and boxes, the unsealed tops bouncing in the breeze. What stunned Susanne most were the dozens of black and white folks hurrying by with their arms full of goods looted from the shops in town. She recognized many of the faces.

She soon reached the Stanard mansion on Franklin Street, or at least what was left of it. At first Susanne thought her eyes were playing tricks on her. Miss Stanard's mansion had been one of Richmond's finest homes, and now it was a bare shell. Miss Stanard was a widow and a good friend of Miss Nancy's. She entertained often and lavishly. This couldn't be her house, Susanne thought. But then she saw Miss Stanard sitting on a trunk in front of the ruins of her mansion and Susanne knew her eyes weren't deceiving her. The woman was dressed in one of her ball gowns and peering through her lorgnette toward all the activity in town.

Susanne slowed her brisk pace when she reached the trunk. Miss Stanard had always been friendly toward her, and Susanne wanted to ask if she could be of help. As her footsteps neared the trunk, Miss Stanard peered over her lorgnette. When she saw Susanne she scowled, turned up her nose, and quickly looked away. Now what was that all about? Susanne wondered. They had always behaved civilly toward each other before. And then it hit her. They had always behaved civilly when she was a slave. That had now apparently gone down the drain. Susanne picked up her pace and walked right past the old woman. Fine, she thought, if that's how the hag wanted to be. She had more important things to do now anyhow than worry about these silly white folks.

"Morning, Miss Stanard," she said without looking back when she was several feet past. "Exciting day, isn't it?" Susanne didn't expect an answer and didn't get one.

As she neared town, the air grew heavier with smoke. Scattered fires still burned here and there, and more of the buildings looked like Miss Stanard's mansion. It seemed that most of the houses closer to town had burned down, along with shops, saloons, and banks. Every store left standing had been looted. Susanne found herself zigging and zagging to step through the debris in the streets—

brick, glass, wood from the buildings, goods from the shops. White folks lounged about as if in a daze. Some cried openly.

It all looked so strange, Susanne could hardly tell where she was. It felt as if she'd gone to bed in one place and woken up in another, as her eyes scanned the blocks for Oliver. If she had time, she would walk to one of the slave markets to see how many of *them* had burned to the ground.

And then she saw him, a lone figure dressed in gray among a sea of blue. Several colored soldiers dressed in the uniform of the Union army had formed a bucket brigade to put out a fire in a colored church and Oliver was helping them. Susanne was so glad to see him safe that she just stood with the scarf over her nose and watched for a few moments. Of course, that was so like Oliver to stop and help where he might be needed. He looked a bit tired and thin, but otherwise he seemed as fit and spry as before.

Four rowdy-looking white men rounded a corner. Susanne thought they looked as though they hadn't bathed in a month of Sundays. "Look at them nigger soldiers trying to put out a fire," one of them shouted as he doubled over with laughter. Another one cupped his dirty hands over his mouth and hollered, "All y'all niggers ought to go on back up North. We don't want y'all down here." Suddenly one of the roughnecks lit a wooden torch and threw it into the smoldering ruins. Then they all took off. Just like the cowards they were, Susanne thought. A couple of the soldiers broke away from the brigade and chased them.

Just then, a group of colored boys ran out of a shop behind Susanne, their arms stuffed with looted food and clothing. It seemed they had been waiting for the soldiers to be distracted to make their getaway. They brushed by, almost knocking Susanne off her feet. Oliver heard the commotion and turned just as one of the boys passed within a few feet of him. He reached out and grabbed the boy by the arm and all of his booty fell into the street. "Don't you know stealing is wrong," Oliver scolded.

"I's hungry," the skinny little boy said defiantly. "Starving ain't right, neither."

Oliver tightened his lips. Then he bent over and picked up the bread and potatoes dropped in the street. He shoved them in the boy's arms and waved him away. "Go on. But don't let me catch you out here again."

The boy took off and Oliver chuckled. Then he saw Susanne. He smiled and handed his bucket to someone else, then ran up and lifted her into the air. She laughed as he set her down and kissed her smack on the lips. Not so long ago, such behavior could have landed them both in jail or onto the whipping block, she thought. What a difference a war makes.

"What are you doing out here?" he said as he let her go.

"Come to find you, and it's a good thing I did, too."

"You shouldn't be out here by yourself. But I'll tell you, you sure are a sight for these tired eyes."

"Tired my foot," she said. "You look about excited enough to burst."

"Me? What about you? You're a free woman now." He picked her up again, then set her down. "And the baby?"

"He's fine. You have a son."

Oliver blinked. "Man. Is this what it feels like in heaven?"

"Oh, I don't know about no heaven," she said, shaking her head. "Your store is gone, and where will you stay? It's only—"

He touched her lips with his finger. "Hush, baby. I'm not worried about that. Too damn happy to worry about anything just now."

"How can you say that? You need a place to stay, you need

to earn money so you can eat. And the Montgomerys are talking about leaving."

He looked worried for the first time. "Leaving? When?"

"Maybe tomorrow. I already have our things packed."

"That's fine. But you're coming with me, not them."

"Where to?"

"We're going to start over," he said, lips set firmly.

Susanne frowned. "Start over?"

"I'm taking you away from here, first chance we get. You, me, and my son."

"What on earth are you talking about, Oliver? Where?"

"West Point. That's what took me so long to get back here. I was down there for a couple of days looking things over. A lot of folks talking about heading out that way and starting a town. We'll have schools for the children, churches, and—"

She frowned. "You mean, leave Richmond? And the Montgomerys."

"That's exactly what I'm saying. You belong with me now. I mean, I wasn't planning on it happening tomorrow, but we'll find you someplace around here until we're ready to make our move."

"Slow down, Oliver. You just got back. We—"

"Slow down? Look around you. There's no time to slow down. You said the Montgomerys are about to leave."

She shook her head to clear it. "I think we need to take this slow. People are starving all over the South now. And I know you don't want to hear this, but at least the Montgomerys give me food and clothes, and maybe they can pay me now that the war is over. They'll come back to Richmond sooner or later. This is their home."

"Pay you? With what? Southern money is worth less than the rubble you see lying in the streets around here. I buried a sack full of bills behind the store just before I left, and it's not worth the dirt it's covered with now."

"But they're still white folks and this is still the South. We need . . ."

He exhaled, then lifted her and sat her down on a stump. "Listen here. You and your mama survived on that plantation back there in Orange County, right? Even with all those different masters coming and going? Some good, some not so good?"

Where was this leading? She nodded.

"And you made it when they came and took you away from your mama and sister and brought you all the way down here?"

"Yes, but I—"

He put his hand firmly over her mouth, then let go when she quieted down. "You weren't but a girl then. And you made a place with a new family here in Richmond?"

She nodded. Now she saw where he was heading. "Yes, I reckon I did but—"

"Baby, anybody that can survive all that can make it living free. That's what I liked about you in the first place, that can-do spirit. You talked about me being brave before I left. You're pretty brave yourself, you know? We can do this together, baby."

She blinked as she thought back. Her, brave? They were some tough times back there for sure, especially when they stole her from Mama. There were days when she thought she'd never make it after that, but she'd done all right for herself. She'd done damn good for herself. But that was just it. It had taken a lot of sweat to get where she was, and it was scary to give it all up and start over, again.

"And another thing," Oliver said, as if sensing her lingering doubt. He smiled broadly. "You hooked one of Richmond's finest bachelors, didn't you?"

She laughed and hit him playfully on the arm. "Oh, you."

Oliver feigned a look of alarm. "Well, shucks. You

mean I wasn't one of Richmond's most desirable bachelors?"

"Of course you were."

He chuckled. "Well, then."

She smiled. "Tell me more about this West Point."

31

In the months after the surrender, the South was in a state of despair. Ex-Confederate soldiers trudged back into Richmond, looking the perfect picture of gloom and doom. Refugees from the countryside followed, scrounging for food and shelter. But all that could be found were burned ruins and some measly potatoes and scrawny chickens, even in the markets. Thieves and pickpockets lingered in every dark corner ready to pounce and snatch anything of value. They broke into homes, stores, even churches.

Colored folks' euphoria at being set free was short-lived. Lincoln was shot and killed barely two weeks after the South surrendered. The soldiers in the Union army who were sent to Richmond to keep the peace harassed colored folks on street corners. Fights broke out between blacks and whites, and many blacks were arrested for the most minor offense, some even shot. Coloreds were still forbidden in many public areas and segregated in others, like in the theater and on railroad cars. Some began to organize and fight back with the help of the Freedman's Bureau, but it was slow going.

As anxious as Susanne and Oliver were to run off and start a new life together in freedom, they knew it didn't make much sense under these conditions. They had no money, and no place to stay in West Point. So Oliver took whatever work he could find to earn the federal greenbacks that would get them out of the city. A lot of white folks complained that there were no jobs to be found, but Oliver had no trouble finding work. He helped clean up the burned rubble in town, worked down at the docks loading ships and served as a cook on boats going from Richmond to Baltimore, Norfolk, and West Point. And when he stayed in town, he boarded in a cheap rooming house with other colored men.

"All these white folks complaining about how they can't find work," Oliver scoffed as he pulled a wad of bills from his pocket and handed it to Susanne. They figured it was safer for her to put the money under her mattress at the Montgomerys' than for him to keep it at the boardinghouse, where all kinds of shifty characters came and went. "There's plenty of work out there," Oliver said. "These fancy white folks just don't want to do it 'cause they think it's 'nigger work.' "

"That's all right," Susanne said as she licked her fingers and counted the bills. "Let them go right on thinking that way."

Susanne and George stayed on with the Montgomerys. They couldn't pay her, but at least she had a roof over her head. And lately that was all she thought of it as—a place to park until they were ready to make the move to West Point. The only thing Susanne asked of the Montgomerys in return for staying was to be given two evenings a week to attend one of the reading classes being set up all over the city by schoolteachers from the North. Miss Nancy would look at her as though she was plain crazy whenever she left the house on her way to class wearing one of her best dresses and her hat pinned tidily on top of her head. But Miss Nancy giving her nasty looks was nothing new. And at night, whenever Oliver was away at sea, Susanne would pull out her lesson books and read by candlelight.

Then in August of 1866, George died suddenly in his sleep. He was just two months shy of his second birthday. No one was sure what had taken her baby away. Oliver blamed the lack of food and rest during Susanne's pregnancy. None of them had eaten right since the war started, especially the former slaves, whose diets had suffered the most. But Susanne blamed herself. She was convinced that if she had spent more time with George, this wouldn't have happened.

"There was nothing you could have done," Oliver said as they walked slowly away from the burial plot. He put his arm around her shoulders as she cried softly. Up ahead, Miss Lizbeth, dressed in all black, was being helped into her carriage. Fanny and Raif had left the Montgomery household soon after the war, but they were there for George's funeral. They and a few servants from the household walked solemnly, a short distance behind Susanne and Oliver.

"I could have done a lot different," Susanne said defiantly, her head bowed to the ground. "All those times when he was crying and I didn't go to him 'cause I was holding one of them Montgomery children, I should have gone to my baby anyhow, but . . ."

Oliver twisted his lip. "That's easy to say, hard to do," he said softly. "You know that."

". . . but I couldn't see it." Susanne shook her head and continued as if she hadn't even heard Oliver. "I thought I was doing the right thing by seeing to it that the Montgomerys were happy with the way I took care of theirs. I was so hell bent on making them think they needed me, so they wouldn't—"

"Hush," Oliver said. He stopped walking and turned and hugged her. "It's not your fault, and you have to stop blaming yourself. You did the best you could at the time."

She buried her head in Oliver's shoulder and shut her

eyes tightly, trying to stop the tears from flowing. In a way, Oliver was right. If the Montgomerys had ever been unhappy with the way she treated their children, it could have been a disaster for her and George. Miss Nancy couldn't stand her as it was. But Susanne would never be able to believe that she wasn't at least partly to blame for her son's death. George needed extra time and attention and she didn't give it to him, no matter what the reason. And that was wrong. She would never, ever allow that to happen again.

They started walking, and Oliver put his arm around her shoulder. "I think it's about time to slip on out of here."

She wiped her eyes with a cotton handkerchief and looked at him.

"Boats are running straight from West Point to Baltimore and Norfolk every day now, shipping just about everything you can imagine—iron ore, salt, tobacco, fish. Things are really picking up down there."

"Do you mean it, Oliver? Are we really ready to go now?"

"I was going to wait a few more months, but heck. After this, and the way I see it's troubling you, let's go ahead and go now."

Susanne exhaled loudly. "Lord knows I don't want to raise any more children here."

He squeezed her shoulder. "They even have a colored school now, started by a colored man named Beverly Allen. I met him the last time I was there. That's where I want our children to go to school. And at night, they teach adults to read, so you could still study. We'll have to walk probably, oh, about two days. I was trying to save enough to buy us a horse and—"

She touched his arm. "Say no more. You don't need to say another word to convince me. I'm ready even if we have to crawl every inch of the way."

* * *

"What in heaven's name are you doing?"

Susanne jumped at the sound of Miss Lizbeth's voice coming from the doorway behind her. She had been leaning over a tattered leather satchel that Oliver found for her, throwing a few extra things in with what she'd packed quietly the night before. As soon as she was done, she was going to tell the Montgomerys that she was leaving in the morning. She'd had a feeling that she'd better be ready to go right quick after she gave them the news. She straightened, turned to face Miss Lizbeth, and clasped her hands together in front of her. "I'm packing, ma'am."

Miss Lizbeth frowned. "Packing? What on earth for?"

Susanne licked her lips. "Me and Oliver are moving to West Point."

"West Point? I've never heard of it. Is that down near the docks, where the colored folks live?"

"No, ma'am. West Point is down in the Tidewater area. Oliver says it's a couple days' walk."

Miss Lizbeth blinked as a look of confusion crossed her face, then understanding. "You . . . you mean you're leaving Richmond? Leaving us?" She laughed nervously. "Oh, dear. And I suppose Oliver has a job down there and he'll be able to take care of you in the manner you're used to?"

Susanne resisted rolling her eyes to the ceiling. You mean as a slave? she was tempted to ask. "No, ma'am, he doesn't have a job yet. But it's a shipping town, and he's pretty sure he can get work at the docks. And they have a colored school down there and . . ."

Miss Lizbeth let out an exasperated breath of air. "Goodness, Susanne. I can't believe you're doing this. Do you know what you're getting yourself into? This West Point, it sounds like one of those frontier towns popping up nowadays since the war. You'll probably be living in some kind of shack and . . ."

Susanne bit her bottom lip.

". . . and you know how attached the children are to you." Miss Lizbeth removed a silk handkerchief from her bosom and dabbed her brow.

Now the missus was getting around to the real reason she didn't want her to go, Susanne thought. The woman didn't care a fig about her welfare. But it would do no good for Susanne to say these things now. Let Missus go on thinking her little nursemaid still believed the lies. "Yes, ma'am, and you all have been right good to me. But Oliver and me, we want to make a home together, and he thinks we'll have better luck down there."

Miss Lizbeth fanned herself with the handkerchief. "I can't believe this is happening. First Fanny, now you. And so soon after the war." She tightened her lips. "When . . . when are you planning to go?"

"Tomorrow morning."

Miss Lizbeth's eyes widened. "Tomorrow? Why, that's impossible. You can't leave tomorrow. The children will need more time to get used to the idea. How can you be so selfish to even try a thing like this, Susanne?"

Susanne tightened her lips and looked at the floor. Selfish? She had already given them a lifetime practically. From the day they stole her and took her name away to this very moment.

"Father's not here but maybe Mother can talk some sense into you." Miss Lizbeth wheeled around and ran from the room. "Mother!"

Susanne took a deep breath. That woman seemed to be getting more like her mama every day. It was all Susanne could do to keep from grabbing the bag and running out the door that very minute. She knew that a hasty departure would be hard on the children, but Oliver had said it would be best to make a clean break rather than drag it out. She sighed. As much as Miss Nancy and Miss Lizbeth could get on her nerves, she didn't want to hurt the children more than necessary. Maybe she could work something out with the Montgomerys for a short period of time, a week or two at most. Oliver wouldn't be happy about it but he would come around. She followed Miss Lizbeth down the stairs, and as she approached the parlor, she heard Miss Nancy's voice.

"It's probably best to just let her go, dear."

Susanne stopped in her tracks, just out of view of those in the parlor.

"How can you say that, Mama? You know how attached the children are to her, especially Caroline. Why, just the other day, she asked me if she could have Susanne as her personal maid when she gets a little older. I want Susanne to stay for a few more months and break it to the children slowly."

"Well, I never thought Susanne was experienced enough for them anyway. We'll find someone better. It shouldn't be that difficult with so many people looking for work now."

Susanne could hear Miss Lizbeth's skirt and petticoat swish as she paced the floor. "How? Father says we haven't much money and won't for a while. How can we get someone without paying them? You're not making much sense, Mother."

"Calm down, Elizabeth, and don't you talk to me that way. We'll use someone else around here until your father gets those things worked out. Then we'll get someone really good, someone with experience. The children are young, they'll get over Susanne in no time. You'll see."

"Mother! How can you be so cold? They are your grandchildren. Susanne has been like a member of this family, almost. Why, I sometimes think of her as a cousin or even a sister."

Susanne caught her breath. There was a long moment of silence, and she wished she could see the look on Miss Nancy's face at that last comment. At any rate, this was obviously not the time to make her presence known. She was about to retreat back up the stairs as the front door opened and Mass Willard stepped in. Susanne nearly jumped out of her skin at being caught eavesdropping. She clasped her hands together in front of her and bowed her head.

"What's going on here?" Mass Willard said, a smile playing around his lips.

Before Susanne could respond, Miss Lizbeth sprang out of the parlor. "Oh! Father! I'm so glad you're home." She ran up and clutched her father's jacket. "Susanne wants to leave. Right now. Tomorrow morning. Can you believe it, Father? You must make her stay a bit longer. Think of what it will do to the children if she leaves tomorrow, especially Caroline."

Make her stay? The words pounded Susanne's head like a hammer. Make her stay? They could ask, but they couldn't make her stay. Not anymore. Would Missus ever get that through her thick head? Probably not. Neither would the others for that matter. Despite all the talk about family this and family that, they would always think of her as their personal piece of property. Even Miss Caroline was learning to think that way.

Mass Willard frowned as Miss Nancy came and stood in the doorway. Susanne thought he looked older and wearier each day. "Is this true?" he asked Susanne. "You're leaving tomorrow?"

"Yes," she said softly.

"Father, do something."

Mass Willard held his hand up in front of his daughter's face impatiently. "With Oliver?" he asked Susanne.

"Yes, sir. Going to West Point."

"Goodness. You know how things are out there?" he asked, his brow wrinkling. "Richmond is in a state of chaos now. It's like that all over the South."

"I know," Susanne said. "But Oliver wants us to start over down there."

Mass Willard sighed and looked at Miss Lizbeth. "I'm afraid there's nothing I can do, dear. We lost the war. She has every right to go whenever and wherever she pleases."

"But can't you pay her, Father? Just for a few months? The children need more time."

"I can pay her a small wage for a month or two. But I'm afraid that's all I can manage."

Miss Lizbeth smiled brightly. "Oh, thank you, Father."

Mass Willard looked at Susanne. "Come to my study in about an hour, and I'll let you know how much . . ."

Susanne shook her head. "No."

". . . I'll be able." Mass Willard paused. "Pardon me?"

"No," Susanne said softly. Her eyes were cast toward the floor but her voice was firm. She realized that this was the first time she had ever uttered that word to white folks, and her stomach tingled with excitement. For some reason, telling them no made her feel freer than she ever had before, even in the moments after the war ended. "No. I'm not staying, even if you figure you can pay me now."

"But why?" Miss Lizbeth protested.

"Because I don't want to."

Miss Lizbeth gasped. "Are you getting insolent with me?"

Susanne exhaled loudly. "No, ma'am. All I'm saying is that Oliver's my family, my only family here. He wants to leave now, and I belong with him."

"It's fine, dear," Miss Nancy said to her daughter. "If Susanne wants to go, we can—"

"Fine, nothing." Miss Lizbeth glared at Susanne. "Very well. If Oliver's your *only* family, then let him take care of you. Don't take one single thread or piece of jewelry you got from me with you. Not one. And I want to see your bag before you go. Do I make myself clear?"

Susanne clenched her jaw. What a nasty blow, she thought. Miss Lizbeth knew perfectly well that every last thread she had was from her.

"Don't forget about the dress she's wearing now, dear," Miss Nancy said. "Why don't you have Nelly get something from the attic for her to wear when she leaves?"

Miss Lizbeth ignored her mother. "Do I make myself clear, Susanne?" she said impatiently.

Fine, Susanne thought. Let the old hags take their things. She would demand something back that was far more important.

"The name is *Susan*," she said. Susan, Susan, Susan.

Miss Lizbeth jerked her head back. "You ungrateful little bastard wench." She lifted her skirt and stormed off down the hall.

"Oh, my," Miss Nancy said, clasping her hand to her breast. She glared at her husband. "I told you the day that . . . that girl arrived that she had no business in this house. Now look what it's come to." She ran after her daughter.

Mass Willard sighed and rubbed his forehead. "A pity."

Yes, Susanne thought. It really is. She turned toward the stairs.

"So you're leaving first thing in the morning?" Mass Willard said.

She paused on the stairs. "Yes."

"Then let me give you this." She turned to see him reach into his pocket and pull out a small velvet sack. "What's in here is everything that I've got for the foreseeable future. All our banks have failed." He paused and cleared his throat. His voice was cracking. "I haven't even let them know the full extent of our financial troubles, you see. But here. I want you to have this." He pulled a few coins from the sack, reached for her hand and placed them in her palm, then closed her fingers. She opened them and looked down at the brightly shining coins. Her first instinct was to shove them quickly into her pocket before Miss Nancy saw them and persuaded him to change his mind. Lord knew she was entitled to it, considering all the years she'd worked for them with not a penny of pay.

"Go ahead, Susanne," he said, as if sensing her hesitation. "It's not much, but it should help for a short while, until you and Oliver get on your feet."

In a flash, she remembered the old white man coming to her room every night at Montpelier. He had stood there smiling as he placed a shiny new penny in her hand and in Ellen's. She looked up and stared directly into Mass Willard's face for the first time ever. He was even older now—his brow was lined with creases, his hair was thinner and whiter. But just like back then, he wasn't prepared to give her what he'd denied her all these years, what she wanted most. An identity. A real family. So she wanted nothing else from him.

She took his hand and gently placed the coins in his palm, much to his obvious astonishment. She wasn't sure whether he was more surprised that she'd returned the coins or that she'd touched him in that way. And she really didn't care. He smiled with embarrassment, and she turned toward the stairs.

Miss Nancy forbade her to see the children again before she left, claiming that it would be less upsetting for them. So she stayed in her room most of that morning, and a few of the servants came to say good-bye. In the afternoon, she walked to visit with Fanny. They said a tearful good-bye, and then she went back to the house on Grace Street and spent her last night there alone.

She came downstairs before the sun was up the next morning. The hallway was dark and empty, and when she walked out the door, all she had was an old calico dress on her back, and Oliver waiting for her.

They reached the bridge crossing the York River into West Point the following evening, just as the sun was setting. They had walked and hitched rides on the backs of wagons for two days to get to this point. Oliver removed his dusty bowler hat and beat it against his leg. Over his shoulder was an ax that he had used to cut firewood when they camped out on the edge of the woods the night before.

"Doesn't look like much from here, does it?" he said as they looked across the bridge at a rickety skyline of wooden warehouses and storefronts sitting near a railroad track. Fishing boats, big and small, sat in the harbor. Oliver smoothed the hat and put it back on his head, then he draped his arm around Susan's shoulders.

Susan rubbed her fingers through the fur of the kitten she had befriended along the way. She had felt sorry for the little lost creature when it came to their campsite the night before and made the mistake of tossing it a few morsels of food. It had followed her all that morning, weaving in and out of her skirt so closely she could hardly walk without stumbling. By late afternoon, she was carrying it in her arms.

Oliver was right. The town wasn't much to look at. There was a time when she would have turned and run at such a sight. Living in a dusty, half-built town, staying God knows where, was going to be a whole lot different from living in a mansion in Richmond. And she was looking forward to every minute of it.

32

Susan knelt, poked a bean seed into the soil, then stretched her arm and planted another. She was going on seven months pregnant and had to be careful with all the crawling and reaching, especially in this Southern summer sun. Oliver had dug up the soil for her the evening before, but now he had his own work to tend to, and the garden was up to her. She had three children, from ages eight to two, another on the way, and a husband. And they all had to eat.

She didn't really mind doing this, though. Of all her chores—cooking, cleaning, washing, and feeding and bathing the children—this was the one she enjoyed most. She found it relaxing to dig her own soil in her own garden and grow food for her family. When she first started the garden, Oliver used to tease her about not wanting to get her hands dirty. She had been a house slave, and she couldn't help it if she knew next to nothing about planting and harvesting. But he didn't laugh at her anymore, not with the fat potatoes and juicy tomatoes now coming up out of the soil.

She struggled up to her feet—no small task these days—and wiped the sweat off her brow. She knew from the way the sun was right overhead that it was time to get back in the house and make dinner, then get the children up from their naps and feed them. After that, she would start on supper. Then she would bathe the children and put them to bed. But first, she bowed her head to thank the Lord for all he had blessed upon them since they'd left Richmond nine years ago.

And she always prayed that she would find Mama and Ellen someday. Although as the years dragged on by, that was starting to seem less likely. The government agency that was helping them look closed down a couple of years back, and it had been real slow going since then. Oliver would write a letter and they'd wait weeks, sometimes months, to get a response. Then he'd write another. The agency had said thousands and thousands of former slaves were looking for lost relatives, most with no known last names or addresses, and it would take some time to find them.

Susan sighed. They should have started looking right after they left Richmond, but they were so busy just trying to survive. She could hardly count the number of times Oliver had changed jobs or was without work or they had moved. Then there were babies, one after the next.

She brushed her hands on her skirt and headed toward the house, stopping at the well to retrieve a bucket of water. She placed the bucket down in front of the line of laundry she had hung out to dry that morning and removed the clothing and draped it over one arm. Then she picked up the bucket and walked toward the back steps, shooing the chickens along the way.

If it was meant to be, the good Lord would see to it that she found Mama and Ellen somehow.

Susan shifted two-year-old Minnie from one hip to the other and cocked her head to the side as she stood over the stove. She thought she'd heard Oliver's horse and wagon, but that didn't make sense. It was only noon, and he should still be on his rounds delivering the mail. In the afternoons he ran his cab service, shuttling the town's white folks about, and he almost never came home until supper. Lately, he hadn't even been coming home in time to have that meal with the family. He was making plans to open a store down by the river and the railroad tracks, and there was always somebody to see about something.

Their oldest child, Robert Oliver, was at the Beverly Allen school. His four-year-old brother Ocran Kelly, was throwing toys around on the kitchen floor and making enough noise for both boys. Susan looked down at him and put her finger to her lips. "Shh," she said. "I'm trying to hear."

"Get up there, Bell Boy!"

Susan smiled. That was definitely Oliver, talking to his horse, Bell Boy. She walked into the parlor, with Ocran following on her heels, just as the door opened and Oliver stepped in wearing a smile as wide as the York River. He waved an envelope over his head. "Guess what? It's a letter from Ellen."

"My sister, Ellen?"

Oliver nodded.

"How can you be so sure?" They had gotten their hopes up twice before by an Ellen in Orange County, only to learn that it wasn't really her Ellen.

Oliver removed his hat. "It's her. I feel it this time."

Susan frowned. She was still afraid to be too hopeful. "But I thought you said they had closed down the Freedman's Bureau."

"They did. Two years ago."

"Then how did you find this woman?"

"I'll explain that in a minute. Go on, open the letter."

Susan placed Minnie down on the floor next to her brother and wiped her hands on her apron. She wasn't wiping away much, but it seemed the proper thing to do before taking such an important letter.

"A few months ago, a preacher from up that way came by the church," Oliver said. "I asked him, same as I ask anybody I think might know something, if he knew of any Ellens in Orange County. He said that I should write this other preacher by the name of Johnson. It sounded like a long shot, so I didn't get around to writing the letter till last month. But go ahead, look at the return name."

Susan swallowed hard as she stared at the envelope in her hand. "Susan Madison Armistead, West Point, Virginia." She turned it over. The back flap read, "Ellen Madison Johnson, Orange, Virginia." Ellen Madison. This was the first Ellen she'd heard from who called herself Madison. Her heart thumped like a beating drum. She looked at Oliver and smiled, as much from jittery nerves as excitement. Thank goodness she could read it on her own, she thought, as she loosened the flap. She tried to be careful, to preserve as much as possible, but her hands were shaking badly. Her voice was hoarse as she read aloud to Oliver.

"Dear Susan,

I'm so glad you found me. I've been searching for you for years, but mostly around Richmond and I didn't know your last name, so I guess that's why I didn't have much luck. I am well but I have some bad news. Mama died a few years after the war."

Susan swayed and Oliver helped her down to the sofa. Mama was dead? Susan closed her eyes, and, probably for the hundredth time, saw Mama running behind the wagon with those blue beads in her hands. It felt as though it had happened yesterday.

"Rest, Mama. You don't have to run no more."

She opened her eyes and read on. Papa Squire was still living, Ellen said. He had remarried, to a woman named

Rose. Ellen had married a preacher, Reverend Philip Johnson, the man Oliver wrote to. Susan paused and looked at Oliver. He shook his head. "The Lord works his magic in strange ways."

"Amen to that," Susan said.

Ellen and Philip had two children, a son named William and a daughter named Georgia. Everybody was healthy. Mama and Papa Squire May had three more children after Susan left. So Susan had a bunch of new relatives to meet. Was there any chance that Susan would be able to come back home to Orange County to visit?

Susan folded the letter and put it in the envelope. She couldn't hold back the tears stinging the corner of her eyes any longer. She just tried not to cry too loudly for the sake of the children. Both of them were now staring at her strangely.

Oliver sat beside her and draped an arm over her shoulder. "Sorry to hear about your mama, but that's a nice letter, isn't it?"

"It sure enough is." Susan exhaled and looked at the back of the envelope. She laughed. "I still can't believe it's really her. After all these years. I'm going to write her back as soon as I get a free minute."

Minnie stood and walked to the couch, her face the picture of concern for her teary-eyed mama. Susan picked her up and smoothed her curly red hair. "You can't read this yet, Minnie. But this here is a letter from your Aunt Ellen." Minnie looked at her mama with a puzzled smile, and Susan chuckled. "I'll tell you all about her someday. And about Mama."

Oliver put his hat on and moved toward the front door. "I best be getting on back to finish my deliveries now."

"Will you be home for supper?"

"Reckon not. I want to talk to somebody about buying that store down on Seventh Street."

Susan nodded and looked back at Minnie. Her daughter had bright red hair just like Ellen. Susan let out a long, deep breath. What a moment. Here she was holding her daughter in her arms and a letter from her sister in her hand. And to think, she could read it herself. It was as if all the evening classes and prodding from Oliver to help with her reading lessons were leading to this very moment. Bless that man.

Oliver. She looked up at the front door, but he was gone. She sat Minnie on the floor next to her brother, then struggled up off the couch. She hurried out and saw Oliver just about to climb onto the wagon. She called him and he stopped and turned to her. As she walked down the path leading to the road, the chickens in the yard clucked and scurried out of her way. She reached up and gave Oliver a big hug. "I forgot to thank you. I reckon I was so surprised to hear from Ellen."

Oliver smiled. "I told you we'd find your family someday."

Susan lifted the hat off his head playfully, then put it back on. "You mean a part of my family. The most important part is right here. But, Oliver, I want to go back there and see her after the baby is born. I know we don't have much money with you wanting to set up a store down at the river, so I can go by myself and then later maybe you and the children can—"

Oliver kissed her forehead. "We'll find a way."

33

Some things never change, Susan thought, as she watched the Virginia countryside roll by. It had been eighteen years since her first train ride, but the accommodations were almost as bad as they were then. Negroes still rode in dirty, raggedy cars, whites in fine ones. If anything, they were more segregated than before the war, since slaves no longer rode up front with masters.

She removed a white cotton handkerchief from her purse and covered her nose. It was still warm, with fall taking its sweet time journeying to Virginia's borders. Every window in the car was open, supposedly to let in fresh air, but what they really got back here was thick black smoke and cinders from the burning coal. Still, there was a world of difference between then and now. She was a free woman and could get off this train when and where she pleased. And she was riding to her family, not being ripped apart from it. No amount of soot could tarnish that.

She wondered what Ellen would look like after all these years. Was her hair still fiery red? And what would Ellen think of her? Would they even be able to recognize each other? She thought about Mama and Ellen and those last days at Montpelier until the train pulled into the station in the town of Orange several hours later. Her stomach tingled as she tried to brush the soot off her dress. It was pretty much hopeless, but she was too excited to care. She reached up and patted the bun at the back of her head into place, then put on her bonnet.

She stepped onto the platform, satchel in hand, and looked up and down. Folks were darting this way and that. It was a far cry from the last time she was here, when the only others on the platform were a white man and his slaves. She shook her head to clear it of those old thoughts. She was here to make new memories. So, where was Ellen? Susan saw no one who resembled her sister and was starting to worry. Had they gotten the dates crossed? She noticed a woman in an old gray work dress, simple black shoes, and a man's wide-brim hat looking her way. The woman looked a bit outlandish but she was the only one on the platform not hurrying away, and Susan had just decided to ask her if she knew Ellen Johnson when the woman suddenly took off her hat. Her hair was the color of the rosiest leaves on the trees surrounding the station.

"Ellen?"

"Susan?"

They both broke out into wide smiles. Susan put her bag on the platform and they embraced, holding each other for a long, tender moment.

"You're beautiful," Ellen said, holding Susan out at arm's length.

"So are you." Susan reached out and touched her sister's hair. It was in a style similar to her own—with a part down the middle and tied into a big bun at the back. The difference was that Ellen had short bangs—that, and the color. "Your hair is still so red."

"And you're still such a tiny little thing," Ellen said. "Not much bigger than you were when you left here." She put her hat back on, then picked up Susan's bag. "Come on. I've got a wagon for us right up the way."

"You're driving it?" Susan asked, as they walked arm-in-arm across the platform.

"I sure enough am. With Philip being a preacher, he's out a lot and I can't always depend on him to get me where I want to go. So I made him show me how back when we first got married."

"I should have done that," Susan said, smiling. "Now I couldn't get Oliver to sit still long enough to teach me."

Ellen laughed. "It's so good to see you," she said as she tossed Susan's bag into the back of the wagon. They climbed up, and Ellen shook the reins. "Giddyup!" The old horse broke into a slow walk and turned up a dirt road.

"We live out in the sticks, so it's a long ride, but it'll give us some time alone." She patted Susan's knee. "We can catch up."

They had so much to talk about. After Susan left, they got a new master at Montpelier, an Irishman from Baltimore named Thomas Carson. And believe it or not, Ellen said, Confederate troops camped on the estate during the war. After it was over, some of the slaves began to leave. Susan talked about her time with the Montgomerys and how she suspected that Mass Montgomery was their daddy. This was news to Ellen, since Mama took that bit of information with her to the grave.

They had been talking and riding nearly an hour when Susan finally got around to asking the question most on her mind.

"Ellen, what happened to you and Papa Squire after I left?"

"We came back after a few days, but you had already gone by then. When Mama told me they took you instead of me, I couldn't believe it. I cried for days, sure enough. Kept thinking what you must be going through."

"That was a crazy old time. Just awful. What did they do to Papa Squire?"

Ellen was silent for a moment. "His master had him whipped, and I was whipped, too."

Susan was stunned. Her sister had been whipped? Suddenly, the clop, clop of the horse's hooves became the sound of the lash bearing down on Ellen's back. It was all Susan could do to keep from clasping her hands over her ears to block the sound. She wanted to say something, but her mouth felt as dry as the dirt road they traveled on.

"Mass Shaw had already left by the time we came back," Ellen said quietly. "But the overseer, John, you remember him? He saw to it that I got my due."

Susan swallowed hard. "You . . . you have marks on your back?"

Ellen nodded. "They'll go with me to my grave, sure enough. But it was nothing compared to what happened to you."

"Still . . . I can't believe it. What about Mama? Did they—"

"No, thank heavens. But she was so upset about us, they might as well have. Mama lived about four years after the war and there were some good times for her, but she never got over that. You taken away, me beaten. She blamed herself, even though I always told her there was nothing she could have done to stop it. Nothing." Ellen paused and shook her head as if Mama was still there and needed persuading.

That sounded exactly like what Oliver had told her when little George died, Susan thought. They had done the best they could at the time. "What about those old blue beads? Mama got them from Grandma Susie and tried to give them to me when they took me. What happened to them?"

"Oh, yes. Mama buried them at Montpelier down where she last saw you. Then after the war, she dug them up and buried them in the yard at the house where she and Papa Squire lived. Said if she buried them near where you left, that you'd come back one day. The last thing she said to me before she died was that when I found you, we had to look out for each other." Ellen looked at Susan and smiled. "Sure enough, here you are. You found me first, but heck, that's just as good."

"Yes. Only it's too late to see her. Do you know where she buried the beads?"

"No. Besides, that land is gone now. Papa Squire sold it and bought some other land after he got married again."

Susan blinked back a tear. "Too bad. I would have liked to have them to give to Minnie someday."

"Hey, no long faces, now. Mama's spirit is resting and watching over us. We're together, and I got a house full of relatives just dying to meet you and hear all about what happened to you. Then they'll get to telling you about their crazy old selves. Papa Squire will be the first one in line." Ellen chuckled. "Heck, you'll take home enough stories for Minnie and the boys to last a lifetime."

Susan smiled, until Ellen suddenly pulled back on the reins. "Whoa."

"Why are you stopping?" Susan asked as she grabbed the sides of the wagon to steady herself.

Ellen looked at Susan. "You want to give it a try?"

Susan blinked. "What?"

"You said you wanted to learn to drive a wagon," Ellen said as she hopped down. "Now's your chance. We don't have that much farther to go, and there's nothing to run into out here."

"You can't be serious, Ellen. I've never even—"

"No, buts," Ellen said. She removed her gloves and put them on the seat for Susan, then got out and walked around the back of the wagon. "You said you needed to learn and Oliver doesn't have enough time to show you."

Susan looked at the gloves on the seat, then slid over and put them on as Ellen hopped up. "All right, but don't get mad at me if I ruin your wagon."

Ellen gave her some instructions and Susan shook the reins. As they got closer to Ellen's place, the hazy outline of the Blue Ridge mountains came into view. It had been a long time since Susan had seen them, and they brought back fleeting memories of Montpelier. But she had to focus on guiding the horse and wagon, so she put those thoughts out of her mind. This was more fun than thinking about those old days anyhow, she thought. "Wait till Minnie and the boys hear about this," she said, giving the reins a hearty shake. "Me driving a wagon. Oliver will be tickled to death."

"You're doing fine," Ellen said. "Is he good to you?"

Susan nodded enthusiastically without taking her eyes off the road. "I couldn't have asked for a better man. We have a nice home and four beautiful children."

"The new baby is healthy?"

"Henry Meads is fit as a fiddle."

"You look real happy, you know."

"I am. The last few years have been really good for us. Oliver's established himself in the community. I have my babies and the house. What about you? Is Philip good to you?"

"Oh, yes. He's a good man, respected around these parts."

"We did all right for ourselves, didn't we, sister?"

Ellen nodded. "Sure enough. Mama would be so happy to know that and to know you finally came back."

Susan smiled. "Oh, I reckon she does know."

Author's Note

The sisters riding off into the evening were my great-great-grandmother Susan and her sister Ellen. Susan's daughter Minnie had a daughter named Corine, Corine had Alyce, and Alyce had me. I was introduced to Susan and Ellen when I was about eight or nine years old. I had noticed two portraits perched on my grandmother's bureau, and the women in them were very light-complexioned. So I asked: "Grandma Corine, why do you have pictures of those white ladies on your bureau?"—or something like that.

She chuckled and said: "They aren't white. That's your Grandma Susan and her sister Ellen. They were slaves on President James Madison's plantation." Needless to say, that bit of information was quite tantalizing for a curious black child, not to mention confusing. These women were my great-great-grandmother and a grand aunt, yet they looked nothing like me. How did they get like that? What were their lives like? Were they happy? I had a million questions, and over the years, I talked to relatives; collected old letters, photos, and Bibles; and visited libraries and archives. I uncovered a lot of anecdotes, information, and long-forgotten tales. Unfortunately, given the nature of slavery, the fact that the Madisons had all of their personal records destroyed, and that many records were lost in the Civil War, there were some things that I couldn't uncover. What I did learn is here, but much of it is also my imagination—what I think life must have been like for Susie, Clara, Susan, and the thousands of women like them.